because

JACK A. LANGEDIJK

Library and Archives Canada Cataloguing in Publication

Langedijk, Jack A., author
    Because / Jack A. Langedijk.

Issued in print and electronic formats.
ISBN 978-0-9937586-1-4 (paperback).--ISBN 978-0-9937586-0-7 (ebook)

    I. Title.

PS8623.A63B43 2015   C813'.6   C2015-908315-X
                                                 C2015-908316-8

DEDICATION

To all those who may feel alone in their struggles.
And to each and every person who takes the time
to show them that they are not alone.

BECAUSE - CONTENTS

Asking questions is what makes us who we are.

1. 16 WEEKS AGO – SEEMA'S OFFICE

"I'm not supposed to be here!" Robert Sanchez spoke the moment Seema Pourshadi walked into the room.

"Seriously, this is wrong! I'm not supposed to be here. Really, I don't know why I'm here. I never requested this."

Without a word, Seema went and sat behind the desk facing Robert.

"No offence to you and what you do, but I'm not supposed to be here."

Seema simply smiled and nodded. Her reaction surprised him.

"Oh—Okay then. So me being here—this *is* a mistake?"

Seema kept smiling as Robert rambled on. "You see, when Benny said I had an appointment with you after my session, I thought you were a new specialist I had to see—you know, going to talk about the new—Argh! Anyway, it doesn't matter, it's pretty obvious you are a...a...you know— Anyway, I'm sorry. Benny must have made the mistake. I'm not supposed to be here, right?"

"Okay. But Mr. Sanchez, do you know where it is you're supposed to be?"

The question stopped Robert cold. He knew it was not meant to be anything more than just asking him what room he was supposed to be in but the innocent question forced a dawning realization that other than the multitude of doctors' appointments and physio sessions, he really didn't have any other place that he was supposed to be. The purpose of his days had changed. He had now become the one seeking help from other people.

Seema waited for Robert to answer her question. It soon became obvious that he was lost for words, so she spoke. "Benny didn't make a mistake, Mr. Sanchez. He was the one who told me I needed to see you."

"No, Benny would *not* have done that! He knows! I told him. We talked about it. He knows."

"Knows what, Mr. Sanchez?"

"Can you please stop with the 'Mr. Sanchez'? I'm not here for a job interview!"

"All right, 'Roberto,' is it?"

"Just call me Robert."

"Oh, Robert, that's such a great name! All right, Robert, you were saying Benny knows something. So what does he know?"

Robert squeezed his eyes shut and took a deep breath, trying to calm himself down. Other than his parents, very few people ever called him Roberto. The name had suited him more when he was in his twenties when his dark brown hair was all slicked back and he sported a very stylish Clarke Gable moustache. But now at forty-eight, a clean-shaven Robert with a receding hairline was a much closer match to Alan Alda during his last days in *MASH*.

"Look, he just knows, okay?" Robert held his hand up as if to signal he wanted this conversation to be over.

Seema just nodded in agreement.

"Don't do that, okay?" Robert looked at Seema who just stared back at him.

"Okay—look, please just don't do that!"

"I'm sorry, do what?"

"That...that...nodding your head all the time, like you know something I don't. I've worked with a lot of people, you know, and I know what *this* is. And I'm sorry if Benny asked you. That just makes him another...Damn him! Great! Another person I can't trust around here!"

"I don't think he meant you any harm, Robert. Please don't think Benny was being untrustworthy. I wouldn't want to—"

"—But he knew! I told him. We talked about it so many times."

"About what, Robert?" Pourshadi asked calmly in her pleasant Middle Eastern accent.

"About this! About seeing any kind of shrink, therapist, mind doctor. I don't know, whatever the hell you call yourself. 'Cause he knew! He damn well knew that *I don't want to be here!*"

"Well, if he knew that you didn't want to be here, do you think Benny knows where you want to be, Robert?"

"No! No! And what the hell kind of question is that? Just stop it, all right?"

"I'm sorry, Robert, stop what?"

"All these damn questions! Look, I don't think anybody knows

2

where I want to be, all right? For God's sake, I don't even know where I want to be anymore!"

Seema watched Robert squeeze his eyes closed again, lower his head, and then rock slightly in his chair. After a few moments, he lifted his head and scanned the room, purposely avoiding her eyes.

The room was a small office space with one window that overlooked a schoolyard. Seema sat in a red cushioned chair behind a plain dark brown desk. On the wall hung a single, framed picture of a majestic black horse flying through the clouds. Among some obvious therapy-titled books, the few bookshelves behind the desk contained a strikingly diverse selection of novels. It looked as if the complete *Twilight* series, *Hardy Boys* and *James Bond* were there. *Miss Marple*, *Jane Eyre* and many of John Grisham's books were scattered over three different shelves. Another shelf seemed completely dedicated to the works of Dr. Seuss. The desk was virtually empty except for two unopened white envelopes and a cup filled with pens and pencils. Dr. Seuss's book entitled *Happy Birthday to You!* laid open and face up.

Robert looked up at Seema. Her short dark hair reflected a red glow from the scarf that was loosely draped over her head and around her neck.

"I'm sorry, all right?" Robert spoke unapologetically. "I'm sorry I got upset, but please understand, that ever since this happened, it seems that I have no choice anymore...about anything. Everyone always tells me to be here or there, see this doctor or that specialist. And I made it very clear to everyone—no offence to you, Doctor, but I've made it *very* clear that I don't want to be in any, you know—this! Therapy! That's why I said I'm not supposed to be here. Is that clear?"

Seema's face was hard to read. She possessed vaguely masculine features, and although the deep-set eyes and square jaw did not make her outwardly attractive, her blue eyes seemed to soften all the features of her face when she smiled.

"Well, Robert, first let me tell you that my name is Seema. I am the rehabilitation centre's assessment consultant. If I don't give your insurance provider an assessment they will stop paying for your treatment. And second, concerning choices, I am also here to consult with you and help you with all the choices you have now and after you leave this rehab—"

"—Choices? What the *hell* does that mean?"

Seema's smile disappeared from her face. "Well, Robert. Even right now, you have a choice. When you came into this room you had the choice of whether to say, 'hello,' or to just keep rudely interrupting me."

Rudely interrupting her? Robert's jaw dropped and his eyes widened. He was no longer accustomed to anyone being so blunt towards him. Ever since that day, no one had ever spoken to him like this no matter how irritable or nasty he became. Regardless of his behaviour, everyone always seemed to become more understanding and show more kindness towards him, whether he deserved it or not.

"And maybe to help with your choice making," Seema continued, without any hint of playfulness, "I should also tell you that today is my birthday."

Lately, hearing the word "birthday" or even the slightest mention of anything to do with celebration would cause Robert to react with extreme irritability verging on anger. He had developed some kind of resentment to all things celebratory. But he definitely didn't want Seema diagnosing anything more about him so he masked his reaction with a forced smile and gestured to the opened Dr. Seuss book on her desk.

"Oh. So that's why you have that book on your desk?"

"Before I answer your question, Robert, I would like to know what choice you have made."

Robert gave her a puzzling look. "What the—"

"—The choice to say, 'hello,' or interrupt." She smiled.

Robert rolled his eyes as he responded, "Oh God, you're kidding me! Really? Choice? Yeah, okay then, sure..." He forced another smile. "Hello."

Seema waited for a moment for his greeting to register, nodded her head and smiled, "Hello, Robert." She then picked up the book. "And *yes*, to answer your question, that is why this book is on my desk; it's a gift from my son and daughter. Mr. Seuss was quite a profound writer, don't you think?"

"Dr. Seuss." He corrected her.

She simply smiled again and flipped to a page. "Listen to this: 'Today you are You, that is truer than true. There is no one alive who is Youer than You.'"

Seema turned the book around for Robert to see the picture inside. It was a bright orange furry creature happily blowing out the rainbow of candles on his colourful cake.

"I've gotta get the hell out of here," Robert said as he abruptly turned towards the door.

2. PRESENT DAY – DRIVING TO THE HOTEL

I took my love...
Climbed a mountain...
Turned around...

The song played. Not a sad song. Not really a happy song either. But it was *their* song. Monique turned up the volume and smiled a hopeful smile while looking at her husband, Robert, in the rear-view mirror. They always played this song while driving to the airport to drop off Robert for one of his mountain climbing adventures.

Robert had always half-joked that the song was bad luck because of its title, but Monique would always say, "No, it has nothing to do with luck; the song's title is just a metaphor. You know, Bobby...to me the song is about some kind of cleansing."

"Oh, of course," Robert once joked. How did I not see it? It's a song to inspire janitors!" Yet, his funny responses only encouraged Monique to dig even deeper.

"It's like...really touching honesty or maybe finally realizing what one's true love is."

"Ah! So, in the end it's just another silly love song?" Robert always tried to get his wife to finally commit to one meaning, but Monique loved the challenge of coming up with different meanings throughout the years.

"Okay, maybe it's finally facing the truth of one's self—No, wait. Wait, I have it! You know how a snake sheds its skin?" She would get so excited. "Oh wait, I know...maybe a mountain has to shed things too and maybe it's saying that we are mountains...and, just like mountains, we all have to shed our masks at some point in our lives as well."

Although Robert's mind was often preoccupied on those drives to the airport, this song never failed to connect them. It didn't matter what was said; it was more about what was felt and these conversations always left Monique with the closeness she so desperately needed before seeing him off. A protection against the fear that this might be the last moment they would ever share together.

Monique and Robert had a pact to never speak about this fear. The two of them avoided any conversation mentioning the dangers of those climbs and the reality of death on those mountains. Yet, the thought that something terrible might happen was always alive inside her the whole time he was gone. She never really got used to it. So, no matter how tired or sleepy they both might be, she always made sure to somehow make this drive to the airport count.

The conversation today sadly ended up becoming a monologue as Robert sat in a stony silence in the back seat. His empty eyes just stared straight ahead, not once catching any of Monique's smiles or her playful winks in the mirror. So she tried the only other way she knew to connect with him. She started to sing along with the song and with each verse, sang a little bit louder. This had always provoked Robert to sing along, mostly to keep her in key or to get her to sing the right words.

Monique had a unique gift for rhyming and changing the lyrics to any song. It was her way of communicating a message. There was the time when her daughter needed to clean her room, and she used the song "When You Wish Upon a Star" but changed the lyrics to *"If you do not clean your room, you'll be waking to your doom..."* And after her rhyming couplet, like a performer in a Vaudeville show, Monique would stop and hold her hand out, to encourage her audience to finish her thought and sing back to her. So that day her daughter completed the song by singing, *"Yes I know, that dirty socks just...do...not...bloom..."*

Monique leaned forward in anticipation, turned up the volume and looked in the mirror. But just as she did, she caught Robert impatiently sighing and rolling his eyes. *Wham!* Another door slammed shut and the hope of any clever rhymes quickly escaped her.

"Oh sorry, Robert, I guess that was too loud. Sorry!"

She tried to hide her hurt as she turned the sound down and for the next minute she just sang quietly along with Stevie Nicks.

When it came to the part where Stevie stopped singing and spoke, "I don't know" to the question about "being able to handle the seasons of one's life," Monique also stopped and made another attempt to reach out. "I love those lines. It's so true, isn't it, Bobby, that the older we get, the more it seems we don't know?"

Robert finally broke his silence. "Really, Monique? Of all the songs, you have to pick this one? *This* one? Do you even know what that song is called?"

"Yes, it's called..." Monique's face went pale instantly. *Oh my God! Landslide...The song is called...*"Landslide," she whispered slowly to herself.

"I'm sorry, Bobby...I'm so sorry, I wasn't thinking—It's just that I thought since you are talking today about—Oh, I'm sorry, Bobby—you're right, I *wasn't* thinking!" She turned off the CD player and looked in the mirror, smiling apologetically, but Robert just looked straight through her with the same emotionless stare that had masked his face for the past six months.

During those months, as Robert was drifting farther and farther away from her, Monique had desperately tried everything she could to reach out to her husband and pull him back to her. Now it seemed that even their song, the old failsafe—the trusty emergency lifeline that had rescued them many times before—had failed to conjure up even the tiniest bit of a connection between them.

Keep smiling, she said to herself. *I know today will help him. I know it will! I know it will!*

She gave Robert one last look in the mirror, trying to hold on to her smiling disguise despite the stabbing pain of losing one more thing that they had always shared.

Monique drove on as the silence deepened, listening only to the rhythm of the windshield wipers beating against the snowy wet rain and, from the rear-view mirror, she watched her husband drift even farther away.

3. 15 WEEKS AGO – SEEMA'S OFFICE

"Look, I came to see you because my wife got a call from our insurance company and they said they hadn't received an assessment from you yet."

Seema stood up from behind her desk to greet Robert. "Hello, Robert."

Robert ignored her. "So, it seems that I have to do this."

"Hello, Robert!"

"So, let's do it. What do you need to assess?"

Seema raised her hand like a young girl in classroom wanting to ask a question. Robert's hands opened up.

"*What?*"

"Robert? Hello!"

Robert snorted impatiently, "Oh, God! Yeah, whatever—Hello! Is that what you are assessing...if I say hello or not?"

"Well, not really, Robert. It's just...No, actually—I'm sorry about that. I changed my mind. Yes, it *is* part of the assessment."

"So the insurance will stop paying if I don't say hello?"

"Let me ask you a question, Robert. It's a fairly straightforward question. Before you came here, before this happened, did you usually say 'hello,' to people when you met them?"

Robert rubbed his face and exhaled with a low, exasperated sound. "Yeah, probably—I always said 'hello.' So?"

"And now you choose not to say, 'hello'?"

"Look, lady! Do you have any idea what I've been through, or what it's like for me now?"

"No, Robert, I don't. I absolutely have no idea. And that's why you're here, so I can find out. So I can assess how much time, resources and care you will need."

Robert arched his head back and ran his hands through his hair. He looked up at the ceiling and muttered, "Okay, okay, okay! Please! Can we just get this done so I can get out of here?"

Robert stared at the ceiling, his hands supporting his head and waited for her questions, but Seema stayed silent. Then he heard her open a drawer, pull out a piece of paper and start to write. He lowered his hands and looked at Seema, who was now intently focused on what she was writing.

Robert waited for her to stop, thinking that she was going to ask him the assessment questions, but Seema just kept on writing. Robert lifted his head slightly to look, but he was too far away to make out what she was writing. Seema stopped for a second, put the pen to her lips, thought for a moment, then went back to her paper and wrote something more.

Robert started to feel a little anxious about what she could be putting down about him, so he finally blurted out, "All right already! What are you writing?"

Without looking up, Seema gave him a wait-a-second signal with her hand and kept on writing. He waited a couple of beats, watching her pen furiously scratch down word after word. Robert couldn't take it any longer and he slammed his hands down on the arms of his chair.

"What the hell are you saying about me there? What...just 'cause I didn't say hello?"

Seema wrote for a few seconds more, then stopped. She looked up at Robert and smiled slightly. "I'm so sorry Robert. I didn't mean for you to get upset. It's just...well, I had to write that down before I forgot it. Otherwise it would bother me all day."

"*What?* That I didn't say, 'hello'? Look, I'm sorry. I didn't mean to hurt or bother you."

"Oh no, Robert. No, you didn't hurt me, not at all! But I must confess that it did bother me, you *choosing* not to say hello...but we'll speak of that later. No, I was writing about something I heard last night. I saw that film *Les Miserables*. Have you seen it?"

Robert shook his head.

"It is just this one line that got me wondering. It's near the end and all the characters are singing together and they sing—"

Seema stopped and raised her hand. "Oh, please don't worry, I won't sing it. But it goes something like 'to love another person is to see the face of God.' It's a curious line, isn't it? I mean, at face value, its literal meaning seems obvious, but is it?"

Robert looked annoyed and said nothing as Seema continued, "Anyway, I just needed to jot down some ideas I had about that line because, in one way, I'm wondering, is it when we love someone that we...that we can see the face of God? So, if we love many different ways and many different people, does that mean God's face also changes? Or is it saying that only when we love do we get closer to actually facing God and then realize all that God means to us?"

Seema saw Robert look away. "Oh, don't worry, Robert, I'm not expecting you to answer, it's just that it really made me think. Because it could even be this: when we stop loving someone, does God's face then suddenly vanish from us? It's quite interesting, don't you think? One simple line and *so* many questions! Don't worry; I'm not a religious fanatic, but don't you just find it incredible when one thing can have so many meanings? Anyway, forgive me, but if I didn't write that thought down, I just know my focus would have been off. So, thank you for giving me time, Mr. Sanchez."

Robert squinted and felt a bit uneasy. "That's good—Ah, whatever. Good, you got that down. So, um...can we just start this assessment you have to do?"

Seema's blue eyes smiled. "Thanks for being so understanding, Robert."

She opened the drawer, pulled out a file and put it on the desk. "Well, Robert, I already have quite a bit of an assessment from Benny and your doctors. But one of the things I need is your assessment of yourself."

"Well, that's not too hard. Look at me!" Robert held his hands up to display himself. "There's my assessment. I can't do anything I used to do."

Seema looked at Robert and smiled. Today she was wearing a blue patterned scarf that somehow made her look much younger than her forty years. "Yes, Robert, let's talk about that: what you used to do."

Robert started to nervously tug at his eyebrows and shift in his chair as Seema spoke. "So I see here that you are self-employed. What is it you do?"

"Used to do," Robert quickly corrected her.

Seema waited for Robert to continue, but it seemed he had said all he was going to say on the matter. He found it difficult to look at her, so he turned his head to look out the window. Robert could see kids running and playing in the schoolyard behind the centre. Seema turned and looked out the window.

"I can't tell you how refreshing it is to have that school outside my office," she said.

"Yeah, well, if you want to know...that's one of the things I used to do. I worked in schools." Robert turned away from the window and looked at the floor.

10

Seema looked back in the file and read aloud, "Leadership and safe school programs?"

"Yeah."

"It says here you are—I mean, *were* a speaker as well?"

"Yeah."

"And you spoke about what, Robert?"

"Different things."

"And it says you led leadership adventure treks."

Still staring at the floor and playing with his eyebrows, Robert nodded.

"And where did you do these leadership adventure treks, Robert?"

Robert sighed. "Mountains."

Seema tried not to comment on anything he said in hopes of encouraging him to continue speaking.

"And you would lead students on these treks?"

Robert whispered, "Yeah."

"And it says here—it was on one of these student treks that the accident happened?"

Robert's head jumped up. "Accident? Is that what you call it?"

"No, Robert, I'm just reading what is written here."

Robert raised his voice. "Well, an accident is usually something you can avoid or you caused. This wasn't any goddamn accident. No, wait, I take that back...it was exactly that! It's exactly like that...that thing you were talking about..."

Seema's whole body perked up as she felt him opening up. In a soothing voice to encourage more, she asked, "What thing was I talking about, Robert?"

"Seeing the face of God. What happened to us *wasn't* an accident...it was God showing His face to us that day and believe me, when we saw the face of God it sure as hell didn't have anything to do with love."

Robert looked directly at Seema now. Though she could feel the violence of his stare, she didn't look away for fear it might defuse the energy he now displayed.

"Okay, so what did it have to do with then, Robert?"

"Those kids...Those poor kids, they had already gone through so much in their lives. Why the hell did I take them there?"

"And this was on Mount Ever—"

"Don't! Don't dare say it. Okay? Just...look...Just don't say it!" Robert then remained quiet.

Seema silently cursed herself. She knew not to say anything. *Just let the volcano erupt! Just let it explode if you want to see what's inside.*

She watched him stare out at the kids in the schoolyard. She stood

11

up and took a step towards the window.

"Would you like me to open the window so you can hear them?"

Robert ignored her question but then it came—the very volcano Seema had anticipated slowly erupted with a forceful quiet intensity. "The school board had organized this whole trek. I was taking three, what they called 'at risk kids'...teenagers—the ones most think are beyond saving. We weren't going to climb all the way up, just getting to base camp is quite a feat in itself. Every day, we filmed our journey and we put it on this...this website for all these kids in schools back home to watch—kids around the same age as those kids outside there...'The Living School Project' they called it. It was supposed to be...it was supposed to be..."

Robert paused.

"It was our last day. We were supposed to leave late that morning. Yeah...right after um, we visited the Khumbu Icefall we were supposed to pack up and go home. The four of us went with three Sherpas. Phi..."

He paused again and started rubbing his knuckles as he continued, "Every day they were filming to show all the kids back home so they could, you know...follow our story. But that day was different 'cause—That day we were...what they call a 'live feed.' You know—It was amazing...we were up there in the middle of nowhere, eighteen thousand feet up in the air and we had all these little kids in gyms and classrooms actually all watching us live that day."

Like a switch inside him had suddenly turned off, Robert stopped. His whole body just froze and he stared off into space. Seema waited for a few moments, walked back and sat down, but Robert still didn't move. She picked up a pen and opened the file and just as she put the pen to paper, Robert spoke again.

"How many floors are there in this building?" he asked.

Seema cocked her head in reaction to the unusual question. "Five, I think. No—wait. There are six if you count the basement."

Robert looked at the only framed picture Seema had on her wall. He pointed at the horse that was flying through the clouds. "Imagine this building—and this whole building is up there—up on one of those clouds," Robert then looked towards the schoolyard, "and that cloud is right above that schoolyard out there. And then out of nowhere, suddenly that building—this six-storey building—just fell off that cloud and came crashing down on top of that schoolyard."

Seema's eyes opened wide in fearful wonder, unsure of what Robert was getting at. He then looked directly at her as he pointed out the window. "And imagine all those kids out there—every single one of them—they are all watching it. They're all watching this huge, white, six-storey building fall off that cloud. It's coming so fast...it's crashing down on them so fast that they don't have a chance to move."

"What do you mean by saying all those kids are watching a building coming down off a cloud, Robert?" Seema asked.

Robert looked at her and shook his head. "Did you not listen? We were filming it and all these students back home—hundreds and hundreds of kids were watching us. For six weeks they had been following us online. They were getting to know who we were. My three leader students spoke to them daily. It was almost like we were talking to our families back home...and these kids who were really getting to know us, care for us, and then in one second—in one split second, they saw that goddamn avalanche come crashing down on us."

Seema waited for him to continue, but Robert was silent.

"Oh, I'm sorry. I...I guess I didn't understand." Seema paused, hoping Robert might add something more, but he just looked back out the window. A school bell could be heard faintly in the distance and the kids were now forming lines to go back into the school.

"So all those young kids watching the live feed saw this happen to you?" she asked. Robert barely nodded his head.

"That must have been quite devastating for them." She looked at Robert, but he was still staring out the window, watching the children file into the school.

"And your three leadership stud—"

Robert quickly cut her off. "—Can we please get this damn assessment over with?"

4. PRESENT DAY – JENNY'S RESIDENCE

Three hundred kilometres away, Robert and Monique's daughter, Jenny, was in her kitchen, warming up her voice for an audition she had that afternoon. A cover band called Simply Yours was looking for a lead singer.

Dressed in a comfy purple housecoat, Jenny had just finished pouring her coffee and, after blowing the steam away, she took a sip. With her head bouncing from side to side, she loudly belted out a song about exploding like fireworks and showing off what you're worth.

Jenny loved to sing. Her dad said it was her passion, the same way mountain climbing was his. Jenny, although two inches taller than her mother's five-foot-two, was a carbon copy of her mother. She had a full, dark wavy mane of hair and beautiful round pouting lips that could blossom into a crazy happy smile that her father simply adored. He always told her that it was that same crazy happy smile that made him fall in love with her mother.

Jenny left home at twenty-one. A couple of years earlier, she sung in a band called Out on a Ledge. Two months after the band was formed, they had landed on one of those TV talent shows that were searching for the country's newest talent. Although Out on a Ledge came in second, they quickly became an overnight sensation. Being on a national television program had helped them line up gigs for the entire upcoming year, but it all came to a sudden end two weeks after the TV show finished.

Jade Sinclair, lead guitarist and the composer of all of the band's songs, along with Bud Light, the band's drummer, had driven their car off the road after a drunken celebration at a friend's house. The car went through a fence and both men fell two hundred meters to their death. The media was cruelly creative in using "Out on a Ledge" and its members' deaths in their headlines.

The band was formed during Jenny's last year of high school and most of the band members had grown up and gone to school together. Bud Light, whose real name was Brian Light, lived two doors from the Sanchez family. Although Bud's late night drumming had caused much neighbourhood grief and frequent calls to the local police station, he had also endeared himself to the community by raising twenty-three thousand dollars playing his drums for nineteen hours straight on a makeshift stage in the front of his house. It was difficult this time for Bud's neighbours to have the heart to stop him or call the police, since everyone knew that Bud was trying to raise money to help his sixteen year-old little brother, Gary, who had just been diagnosed with leukemia. Jenny and some of Bud's friends used their home phones as a call centre. It was never mentioned in the papers, nor spoken about in the neighbourhood, that the majority of the money was raised between two a.m. and three a.m. but among friends, they joked that Bud's neighbours had paid him to stop. In reality, the whole street was quite proud of what Bud did and some believed the massive media coverage of Bud's efforts probably raised the real estate value of houses on Ellington Court. After all, who wouldn't want to live on that famous street where the drummer kid played to save his little brother, Gary?

Jenny was supposed to have been in the car the night of the accident, but had decided to leave early and walk home. Though her life was spared, she was devastated by her friends' deaths. She stopped singing completely and abandoned the idea of pursuing a singing career. Instead, she got a job as a store clerk at a game and puzzle store.

In many ways, Monique was secretly happy to have her daughter home, out of the limelight and not a part of the 'dark' world of bars and bands anymore. She made sure not to tempt Jenny back into the song world—no longer singing any of those song rhymes in the house and always found reasons not to have any music playing at home. Robert and Monique quietly fought about this.

"Mon, you can't hide her passion from her. Jen was born to sing."

Monique would respond with a protective instinct, saying, "And sometimes people change, and their passions change."

Robert knew his wife's hidden message was more pointed towards him, for as much as she loved him and tried to show her support of his mountain climbing passion, she hated wondering if he would come home alive. So, secretly, she wished his passion would change as well.

"Don't you miss her singing, Mon?"

"Of course, I do, Bobby, but at what cost?"

"Cost? Look at her...she's hiding from the world. We need to do something to help her get back out there."

"Give her time. Don't you like having your daughter home?"

"Truthfully? Not like this, Monique."

"Like what then, Bobby? You want her running around in those dark smoky bars, singing to all those drunk—" Monique stopped herself from saying what she always said about the accident: "If those kids weren't around all that alcohol...all the time, those boys would still be alive."

"Monique, you think this is Jen's big ambition, selling puzzles?"

"Well, she seems happy doing that."

"Happy? Happy, Mon?" Robert voice almost cracked as he questioned his wife.

"For God's sake, Robert, it's safer than where she was headed. You know...you know, Robert, she was supposed to be in that car that night."

"But she *wasn't*. Monique, she wasn't! Come on, love, we can never know what unexpected accidents await us when we walk out that door each day."

"But it's a lot safer going to that store everyday than having her coming home in the middle of the night from some bar."

"Safer for who? Jenny or you?"

Monique's eyes opened wide in shock. "Is that what you want, to have your daughter drunk and driving off some cliff?"

"Mon, come here, love...Please come here." Robert opened his arms and Monique hesitantly moved to her husband. "We didn't raise her to do something stupid like that." Robert cupped his hands around his wife's face. "Love, if Jenny had known how much her friends were drinking that night, do you really think she would have let them drive?"

Monique's eyes looked down and she whispered. "No, I know she wouldn't. She would have thrown those keys in some sewer before she'd let that happen, but Bobby..."

"Shhh...shhh..." Robert smiled and gently kissed his wife's forehead. "She has to start living again."

"I know, I know but...Oh, Bobby, it scares me."

"I know, love, it scares me too, but it scares me more to think she might never do what she truly loves."

Monique hugged her husband tight. "Please...Bobby, just give her time, she'll find her way. She'll find it, Bobby. She will."

Yet after eight months living in the quiet Sanchez household, Jenny seemed to wander deeper into depression. She came home right after work, sat in front of the TV and always found excuses not to return calls from friends. Robert knew he had to do something to help tear his daughter from this silent cocoon of grieving she seemed lost in. So, one Thursday night, Robert announced that it was time to have a father and daughter night at the gym like they had often had during Jenny's teenage years.

Throughout the years, Robert would take his daughter out to rock climbing gyms, but after a couple of months, Monique told Robert she didn't think it was a good idea. Jenny was always coming back with some minor scrapes or bruises and her mother said that maybe it was too dangerous. Monique asked Robert if he could find something else for them to do on these nights. Robert knew it wasn't the minor aches or bruises Monique was worried about. In truth, she feared these climbing adventures might lead Jenny to follow her father onto one of his mountains.

Jenny cried and begged her father not to stop when Robert told his daughter they needed to do something else. So together, they came up with a little deceptive plan to ease Monique's worry by telling her they were going to a movie. They always planned their alibi by reading a review of the film on the way to the gym so that they could tell Monique the plotline when she asked them about the film. Some nights they had more fun creating the stories they thought could be in the film than they did climbing. They would laugh and sometimes almost tear up as they told imaginary tales about some funny or touching moment that could have been in the film.

So, that night at the supper table, Robert tried to ignite the memory of their past glories and asked Jenny if she wanted to see a film with him.

"Come on, a father and daughter night again!"

"No," Jenny replied instantly.

"Jenny, it will be good," her mom pleaded. "Jen, remember all those movies you and your dad saw together. Oh, the two of you would come banging through that door all excited and full of life, telling me in so much detail I thought I'd seen the movie!"

Robert winked at Jenny. "Yeah, come on, Little Rock, let's find a good one to tell your mom tonight!"

Jenny shook her head.

"Come on, there's that new Tom-Cruise-saves-the-world-on-a-motorcycle movie. You know your mom won't see it because of all the fighting. Please, Little Rock, it'll be fun to tell mom all about it."

Robert winked again. "Please!"

Jenny paused, looked at her father and then realized what he was up to. She gave in to him with a little smile. "Okay, but I'm picking the movie."

Jenny giggled when she got in the car, opening her bag and showing her father the climbing shoes hidden inside. But just as they had fooled Monique for all those nights, this time Robert was planning to fool his daughter. He was about to try something that he prayed would pull his daughter out of her self-imposed, depressed silence. They drove for about ten minutes and entered a familiar parking lot where he had dropped her off and picked her up countless times before.

Jenny was just about to step out the car when she suddenly realized where they were.

"Daddy, what are we doing here?"

"I thought we'd—"

Jenny cut him off, "—No, Dad. I'm not going in there—And I thought you wanted to go climbi—Argh!" she screamed, startled by the sound of two hands hitting the passenger side window.

"Jenny? Jenny Sanchez?"

Jenny looked out the window. She could not make out the face as the lights from the lampposts cast a dark shadow over the hooded figure. The figure quickly pulled down his hoodie, revealing a young teenage boy.

"It's great that you came!"

Jenny, still startled by the sudden slam of the hands on the window, looked to her dad. Like a dog that freezes and jerks its head the moment it hears a noise in the distance, Jenny did a double take to look at the dark figure outside the car.

"Gary? Oh my God! Dad, it's Gary Light!"

Jenny opened the door, jumped out and spread her arms wide.

"Gary...Gary, it's so great to see you!"

Gary moved towards Jenny and hugged her in an awkward teenage embrace.

"What are you doing here?" Jenny asked.

"You kiddin', Jen?" Gary smiled. "I've been waiting for you."

Jenny looked at her dad with a puzzled, almost angry stare. And at that moment she noticed the illuminated sign of Maggie's Pub directly behind him: *Playing tonight—Precipice.*

A loud sound came from the pub. Screams, yelps and a crazy cheer filled the air.

"Damn—I gotta get in there. Hurry up, Jen, everyone's waiting!" Gary said as he sprinted across the lot parking to the door.

"You get in there, Gary. We'll be in soon," Robert called out.

"Sure thing, Mr. S. See you, Jen." Robert and Jenny watched Gary as he flung the door opened and yelled, "Hey Jen, you gotta sing a tune with us tonight, okay?" then quickly disappeared into Maggie's.

Jenny was familiar with Precipice because two members from her old band were playing in it. What she didn't know was that Gary took over as a drummer for his deceased brother, Bud Light.

Robert looked at his daughter and extended his hand towards her. "It's time, Jenny; you have to get back to your life."

Jenny didn't budge. She just stared at the billboard.

"Baby, you have to get back to living your passion, Little Rock."

Jenny turned around and opened the car door. "No, Dad, no! I don't want—and if mom knew I was here..."

"Mom just wants to keep you safe, Jen. Look, she means well. She just doesn't want you to get hurt again. She's always trying to do the same to me. Do you know how many articles and things on YouTube she shows me to warn me before I go up a mountain? I look at them and I thank her for caring about me, but she never stops trying to warn me how dangerous it is. I guess, in that way, I know she never stops caring. And Jen, can you imagine what she's showing me before I go to Everest next month? Every dead body she can find a picture of and let me tell you, there's a lot of them!"

"But Daddy, I'm scared too. I don't really want you to go up there either!" Jenny climbed back into the car.

"Hey, wait, this isn't about me. You know I take every precaution, Jen. I know I have to do it. Don't ask me why; it's one of my reasons for living, *just* like singing is yours. We have to follow those reasons, Jen, or we just end up living with this question—a question that will just gnaw at you forever. Constantly asking you why you never tried."

Jenny closed the car door and put her head down. Robert walked to her side window and pressed his face against the glass, distorting his face in a funny way, and said in a humorous voice, "You *can't* hide in there forever!"

Robert had done this many times throughout their lives whenever Jenny was nervous about something she was about to do. The first time was on Jenny's first day in kindergarten. She absolutely refused to come out of the car to join her class and Robert had tried everything to coax her out. At last, he got out of the car and closed his door, leaving her alone in the car. He then crawled around on his knees to her side of the window and popped up. "You *can't* hide in there forever!" Even though she knew it was her father, it scared Jenny so much that she screamed for her daddy to help her.

Robert yelled to her, "But you have to open the door, Jenny!" Little Jenny struggled to open the door and jumped into her daddy's arms. And as Robert held his young daughter and carried her into what he called the 'safety of the school', Jenny triumphantly cheered, "We did it! We did it, Daddy! We showed him, Daddy, didn't we? We're not scared of that crazy guy in the window!"

And later that day when he picked her up from school, she asked her father to repeat the episode and victorious triumph over the weird goblin-faced guy in the window. And so, throughout their lives, father and daughter played the fear-facing game together at Jenny's piano exams, swimming tests and even on her graduation night when Jenny had to deliver her valedictorian speech about facing the fears of life after high school, but had refused to get out of the car because she had spilled ketchup all over the front of her beautiful white gown.

"You *can't* hide in there forever!" her father cried out in a silly cartoon voice.

But tonight the crazy-faced goblin was ignored and Jenny kept her head down.

"Come on, Little Rock, please? Come on, let's go in. Just watch your friends play and listen to them sing again and then, even after just a couple of songs, if you tell me that you don't want to ever sing...*ever* sing again, I promise you, Jen, I'll never say another word. Promise!" Robert pleaded softly.

Jenny looked upward, closed her eyes and whispered something. Robert looked up as well, right up into the street lamp that was shining a circle of light around the car. Into the night, he whispered a hopeful prayer that his daughter would come back, back into the wonderful passionate adventure of life she had been living before the accident. Robert smiled as he looked back into the car at his daughter. He held his smile so that, when Jenny opened her eyes, a smile would be the first thing she would see.

Jenny's lips stopped moving. She opened her eyes and saw her father staring at her, smiling. She grimaced and shook her head as if she knew this was a mistake, but opened the car door anyway.

"Okay, you go, Daddy. I'll follow you."

"Are you sure?" Robert held his smile.

"Yes, but please you go first."

She watched her father walk towards the building and then she called out to him, "And Daddy, stop smiling like that—you'll freak everybody out."

Robert let out a laugh and walked about twenty steps. Just when he was about to open the door, he turned around and saw Jenny still hadn't moved. And then, this father who had taken his daughter on many rock-climbing trips, swung his hands over his head as if he had an imaginary rope and threw it over to his daughter. "Catch and tie on. I won't let you fall." Jenny kind of laughed, caught the imaginary rope and made a gesture as if she was securing it around her.

Jenny followed her father step for step, staying a good eight feet behind him. But with each step, the sounds of "Ordinary Day" grew louder. Robert stopped at door and turned around. It was as if he was watching his daughter take her first steps. He held his arms open and she walked into them.

"I'm going to open the door now okay?" he said and Jenny nodded.

Jenny placed her hand on the bar door, feeling the beat of the drums vibrating through the thick wooden door. Robert slowly opened the door to the pub. "Ready?"

She nodded with the beat, "Lead on."

Jenny stood behind her father and closed her eyes. Robert could feel her hand on his back so he stopped and slowly looked over his shoulder. It was like she was meditating. Robert reached for her hand and started to turn around, when suddenly Jenny burst into joyful tears and wrapped her arms around her father, holding him as tight as she had as a little girl before her first day at school, and said, "Thank you, Daddy, thank you!"

Jenny let go of her father. And there she was, where she had been so many times before, belting out in full voice with everyone else in the room and with the guy who sounded so like Alan Doyle of the Great Big Sea. Jenny sang with every fibre of her being, *"It's all right, it's all right, it's all right..."*

When they got home that night, Monique was sure Robert had taken Jenny rock climbing and accused him of it but Jenny sprang to his defence and said, "No, you're wrong, Mom. It was better! He took me singing!" And just before her mother could say anything, Jenny sang to her mom, *"It's all right, it's all right, it's all right..."* and she suddenly stopped, kissed her mom and said, "I am sorry, I know I've been—"

"—Don't, honey. You don't need to say anything. I've missed that sound so much...so much." With Jenny tucked tightly in her mother's arms, Monique looked at her husband and mouthed, "Thank you. Thank you. I love you."

Four weeks later, Jenny still worked at the games and puzzle store but was also working four nights a week as a backup singer for two bands. And in only half a year, Jenny moved three hundred kilometres away when she found work teaching at an arts school that her high school music instructor had started. Jenny was teaching her joy and her passion full time and still sang whenever she could find work, always in search of another band.

This morning, while Jenny was warming up, singing Katy Perry's "Firework," she thought of her father and remembered when he first heard the song. He had actually pulled his car off the road to call her. "Hey, Little Rock, I found a song written just for you!"

What Jenny and her father had was unique. They had the closest thing to a friendship a daughter could ever have with her father. She was the only one he ever confided in about his concerns and even fears about climbing and it was on this day, in the middle of her warm up, that she found out just how much her father needed to talk.

As Jenny sang, the doorbell rang. It rang a few times before she heard it. She opened the door. There stood a UPS driver with a small brown package. Right away she saw her parents' return address. She was sure that it was a book from her mom. Monique loved sending her daughter a book she had read, "so that we always have something in common, something to talk about."

Jenny opened it right away. There was an envelope and a worn hardcover red book. Jenny recognized it immediately. Her mouth fell open and she couldn't move. Suddenly, she almost felt like she would faint. *What?* she thought. This was her dad's mountain journal. *Why did he send it?* Her father had always told her that this journal would be her inheritance after he died.

As she sat there, the song she was singing to played on, echoing the words: reasons...doors...searching...open one...

5. PRESENT DAY – ARRIVING AT THE HOTEL

Monique looked back at Robert, who had his eyes closed. She had not let his loud sigh discourage her. She couldn't, not today. In the last fifteen silent minutes of the drive, Monique kept trying to convince herself that this was what Robert had to do. For the last six months, she had tried so many things to shake her husband back into the world of the living. She clung to the hope of what this day might bring, despite her close friends' comments, saying things like "she was now living with a corpse" and there was probably no way she could "save her marriage." Even some specialists had warned her of how even some of the strongest and healthiest relationships couldn't withstand the changes they were about to face in their lives. Yet Monique kept telling herself, "*I don't care and I'm willing to lose the marriage...If I can just...If I can at least bring my best friend back to life...*"

Lost in that thought, Monique suddenly realized she was about to pass the hotel entrance so she slammed on the brakes. The abrupt motion jolted them both from their shared silence.

"What the hell are you doing, Mo?" Robert shouted.

"Sorry, Bobby," she apologized. "I almost missed the hotel."

Monique backed up the minivan twenty feet or so until she was in front of the hotel's main entrance. She looked at her watch—nine fifteen. This gave her forty-five minutes to set up. The hotel doorman, a very tall young man with a deep African accent came to the side window and asked if she needed help.

She pressed a button on the door and pointed to the back of the van. "Yes, please help my husband."

The back door of the vehicle opened upwards. Distinctive sounds of mechanical movements filled the air as a platform raised up, protruded out and finally lowered down. The doorman waited at the side of the car. He smiled at Robert who was sitting in a sturdy, non-mechanical wheelchair.

"Hello sir, welcome to the—"

Robert cut the doorman off. "—Thanks, but I can see where we are."

The doorman laughed. "Of course, sir. Sorry, but it is my job to greet everyone like that. It does seem quite silly though, since the sign is so large and you are standing right in front of it."

"I'm not standing in front of anything," Robert said gruffly.

"Of course, sir. I'm sorry."

Monique interrupted the two of them with a nervous laugh. "Yes, the sign is right in front. Oh, it is truly crazy, isn't it? The redundant things our employers have us do. Anyway, thank you for helping him."

The doorman smiled. "Yes, and I am sorry, sir. I should have said the sign is standing in front of you. It was not a very good choice of words. I am sorry."

Monique quickly interjected as she handed the keys to the doorman. "Here are the keys to the car. Where do I pick it up later?"

"I will show you, but please wait here for a moment. In order for you to get your car back, I need to get you a ticket first." The doorman took the keys and walked away.

As the doorman passed in front of them, Monique saw Robert look up and then close his eyes as the cold wet flakes hit his face.

"Why are we doing this, Monique?"

6. PRESENT DAY – JENNY'S RESIDENCE

The old beat up red journal lay on the table in front of Jenny. She dared not touch it for fear of what it meant. She held her hands motionless, inches from the journal, as if an invisible force field was preventing her from touching it. As she stared at the journal, so many questions and thoughts exploded in her head. *Daddy would never let me have this unless he was...*She shut her eyes tight before she could complete the thought.

When she opened her eyes, she saw a white envelope neatly tucked under the elastic that bound the journal. Jenny slowly slid it out from under the elastic with great trepidation, as if she was defusing a ticking time bomb. Once released from the elastic, she slowly brought the envelope to her face and sniffed it as if she could smell whether it contained heartbreaking news or not. With a steady intake of breath, she detected nothing, but then suddenly tossed it upon the table as if the envelope had given her an electric shock. She was not ready to read it.

Jenny then became aware of the song that was playing. A ballad she was to sing today at the audition—"The Look of Love." It was right at the point when Diana Krall was about to go on her jazzy piano solo riff and repeat, *"Don't ever go, I love you so."* Just as the trumpets came in, Jenny whispered a defiant little "no!" and then snatched up the envelope and ripped it open. Immediately, she recognized her father's very poor handwriting.

> *Hi Little Rock,*
> *I hope this day finds you with reasons to sing out loud! I'm sorry we haven't talked in a while....Sorry...Ever since this all happened, I haven't really felt like talking to*

25

anybody....Anyway, here is my journal...doesn't seem to be any reason for hanging on to it any longer. Sorry about some of the pages being taped up...I got upset...Sorry...Your mom saved it and taped it up...and she told me that I had always promised you, that someday it was going to be yours....So sorry for the shape...but here it is!

Open arms of all that is...

Daddy

All Jenny could focus on was how many times her dad wrote the word "sorry". *Five times!* Before the accident, her father had a way of always spinning a positive out of every situation. Words like, "I'm sorry," and "I don't know," were foreign to her father. He had always taught Jenny that repeating such words was just another way of saying you won't or can't do something. People mainly used these terms to disguise the fact that they refused to do something or were unable to change something, or maybe had given up, he always said.

Over the last six months, her father had become a different man. And after his last surgery, her father avoided almost anything that remotely resembled a conversation. Whenever she called home with any news, he would always say, "Tell your mother, she'll tell me later." Now, with all these apologizing words, she wondered if he had maybe simply given up.

Suddenly, she jumped. "Oh my God!" she said aloud. She had just remembered her mother calling her late the previous week, complaining that her father had bought a gun. "Why a gun?" she had asked her mom, almost laughing as she thought it was just her mom's way of making a point.

"No, Jenny, a gun, he bought a *real* gun!" her mom said as serious as she had ever heard her. "Daddy says we need it because he can't protect us now."

"Really, Mom? I can't believe it! A gun?"

"Yeah, I asked him if he was so worried about protecting us, why did he leave us alone so many times to climb those...those mountains?"

For the past ten years, Jenny had heard her mother complain numerous times of how her father left them alone for almost two months out of every year. And as Jenny grew older, she witnessed a great tension between her parents each time her father came home from a climb. It took her mother weeks before she could connect and feel warm and loving to her father again.

"Mom, you shouldn't have said that."

"I know Jen, but it's almost like he's—oh, I don't know, honey...I just don't know anymore with Daddy. Look, Jenny, please come home for a visit soon. We need to see you. He needs to see you. Please, baby?"

Jenny hadn't been home for months; it was so busy at school and she was singing five nights a week. Also, she had just started a relationship with a fellow piano teacher named Kyle Le, a young man whose parents had emigrated from Vietnam in the late seventies. Jenny had always shared everything with her parents but now, because of her father's depressive behaviour, she tended to downplay all her good news. She hadn't even told her mother about Kyle and how happy and deeply in love she was with him.

"Yes, Mom, as soon as I can, but I'd—"

Her mother, who had called from work, had to take another call and so they said a quick goodbye. "Sorry, honey, we'll talk later. I have to go. Love you. Bye!"

Jenny sat there trying to piece together if there was any more to that conversation with her mom that she might have missed. She soon started feeling a little short of breath. *Why did Dad send this journal today—the day of his big talk? Why give me this journal: he wouldn't even let me read it, always saying that this journal would be my inheritance?* Each time they spoke, her mom would tell Jenny how much he was changing. But now it seemed he wasn't changing anymore—he had changed! And, today, the words "sorry" in the letter, the gun he bought...Her breathing was getting quicker with each thought. Jenny put her hands on her chest and tried to take in a big breath. She dropped the letter to the floor and picked up her phone.

7. 14 WEEKS AGO – SEEMA'S OFFICE

"My wife and my daughter came to Katmandu two days after it happened."

Seema looked at Robert waiting for him to continue.

"Well, isn't that what you wanted to know? That's when they first saw what happened to me."

Seema waited a moment and looked back into the file. She searched for some information then looked up at Robert. "I was actually asking about the surgery. The surgery was not done in Katmandu, was it?"

Robert shook his head in annoyance. "No, and it was '*surgeries*'. Eight, I think it was. And I thought you wanted to know when they first saw me after it happened."

Seema looked back into the file. "Mr. Sanchez, I have only five surgeries and—"

Robert snapped, "—Eight, five, does it matter? They had enough tries at it, didn't they? And look what happened?" Robert pointed at his legs. His right leg was amputated above the knee and the left leg was in a large white cast with metal bars protruding from it. Seema looked at Robert's legs and nodded her head sympathetically.

"And how did that make you feel?"

"Make me feel?" Robert stared at Seema with an intense, burning anger.

"I'm so sorry. I didn't mean the question to sound trite or uncaring, Robert. I was just wondering how it made you feel facing so many medical decisions. Did you trust that these decisions were still yours to make?"

"Mine to make? Do you know how many doctors have—No. Stop it! Why are we talking about this anyway? Who cares who decides?"

"Well, it is important that you feel your still in control of—"

Robert jumped in. "—Control? What control? I've never had any decisions to make at all. I was just given what they call 'options.' And even then, each option they said I had—well, it didn't matter, because as soon as I was given these options...they just all started to disappear. Then some doctor is sitting like you behind some desk and telling me, 'I'm sorry, Mr. Sanchez, but you have no options left and this is what we *must do.*' So no, Miss Pourshadi, I don't think I ever had a decision that was actually mine to make!"

Seema pursed her lips and jotted something down. Robert sighed and shook his head in disgust.

Seema looked up, "Okay, well, tell me about when your wife and daughter first saw you in Katmandu."

"What do you want to know about it?" Robert sighed.

"Well, Mr. Sanchez, how did you feel seeing them?"

Robert turned his head and looked out the window. It was a Saturday afternoon and the schoolyard was quiet. He could see a father and son flying a big yellow kite. Robert spoke as he watched the yellow kite gliding through the air.

"I was so..."

Robert paused. Seema looked at him intently and smiled slightly, hoping that Robert would let out his feelings.

"I don't know how I felt. I mean, my wife and daughter, they thought I was already dead for almost a full day. They had already called my parents and well, everyone thought I was dead. So I guess it didn't matter how bad I looked when they saw me. They didn't even notice...I guess they were happy just seeing me...seeing me lying there alive. Even though I probably smelled like a piece of rotting meat because of the gangrene. But they said they didn't smell anything—I don't know, I guess they were just so happy to see me alive."

Robert was still staring at the yellow kite twirling in the air. Seema looked out the window and saw the kite Robert was watching. "Everyone thought you were dead for a whole day? That must have been—"

Robert cut her off. "—You see that kite, Miss Pourshadi?"

"Yes?" she answered.

"The way that wind is blowing, do you know what would happen to that kite if someone just cut the string?"

"It would blow away?" she answered him with a question, hoping whatever she said he would continue on.

"Yeah, it would blow away. And I bet it would go pretty far. And then that kid would be feeling all upset and start to cry, probably one of those big huge cries. So then the father, feeling how upset his kid is, he does everything he can to find the kite. But even if he did find it—with all those trees and wires—I'll bet that kite would probably be completely bent and busted up. More than likely, completely wrecked, right? But the father, he'll still try to fix it. Do you know why? It's completely destroyed. So why does he try to fix it?"

Robert stopped and looked at Seema with a harsh vacant stare. He could see in her face that she was searching for the right words to say. Robert snorted. "Don't you get it? All that time that's spent crying over a wrecked kite that's beyond repair and all the effort that dad spends trying to make it better...it's just a waste of time. It's the same as you asking me how I feel—because when something is too broken up to ever fix, it doesn't matter how anyone feels. I don't know why we can't face it. That some things can never be fixed."

Seema watched the yellow kite swirling in the open blue sky. She smiled sadly as Robert's words echoed loudly inside her: *Some things can never be fixed!*

She turned to Robert and asked him, "So, you think that if that kite fell and was completely broken—the father shouldn't even try to fix it?"

Robert was staring at the floor as if he had not even heard the question, but he answered her firmly. "Yes."

Seema waited, thinking Robert had more to say, but nothing came. So she asked him another question.

"Do you believe some things are just not meant to fixed?" He didn't answer, so she asked again. "You think once something's broken we should just go out and replace it?"

Robert spoke without raising his head. "It doesn't matter what I think or believe. But sometimes, we just have to face the fact that *some things just cannot be fixed.*"

"Okay, Robert, then who makes the decision of whether something can be fixed or not?"

Robert rubbed his face roughly and let out a tiny pained breath. "It's not anyone's decision, it just is. If it can't be fixed then it can't be fixed. It's a fact."

"What's a fact, Robert?"

"That it's broken!" Robert said, looking up at Seema.

"Yes, I understand that, Robert, but who decides when something is too broken to be fixed?"

Robert said nothing and looked back at the floor.

"Who makes the decision, Robert, about whether something is too broken and not worthy of being fixed?"

"That's the problem." Robert raised his voice but kept looking down. "That's the problem! Too many bloody people think it's their decision to make when it's not. It's not their decision to decide."

"So then, Robert, who is the one that makes the decision about the kite?"

Robert looked up with a confused looked and mumbled, "What?"

"The *kite*, Robert, remember we were talking about the kite? Who makes that decision? Is it the son or the father? Who makes the decision about whether the kite is too broken to be fixed?"

Robert let out another sound of annoyance and then spoke insolently. "Look, Miss Pourshadi, all I'm saying is they see the kite—they can see it, right? They look at it, see it's smashed, right? They see it's all fucked up...so walk away. Just walk away! Don't let the kid feel...you know, get all worked up about it. Why get him crying? And why get that kid all hopeful...hoping to fix something that is just plain unfixable?"

Robert sharply turned his chair to face the window. The yellow kite was still happily flying. Seema looked at it as well and now couldn't help wondering about the fate of that little yellow kite. She knew she had to ask Robert the obvious question. But she almost winced before it came out of her, fearing his reaction would be loud and angry.

"Is that how you feel, Robert? That you are unfixable?"

Robert's reaction surprised Seema. He didn't get angry, raise his voice or get defensive.

"Is that how you feel, Miss Pourshadi, that all people are fixable?"

Seema's eyes opened wide. She was surprised how the question unnerved her completely. She wished her answer to be an immediate "yes, of course, everyone is fixable". But after spending three years working in one of the country's largest maximum security prisons, she discovered something she would never readily admit. In there, she assisted a doctor who was responsible for the psychological assessments on some of the most depraved prisoners—child rapists, abusers, wife beaters and even a serial killer who tortured his victims over prolonged periods and then would release them into a forest only so he could hunt them down and murder them.

She had seen firsthand that every single one of these prisoners had been broken in some way or other. And it became obvious to her that it was the broken part of them that led them to their sinister and cruel behaviours. She knew some of these broken inmates could be rehabilitated and she even saw that some were. They could be fixed. But some, she came to realize, were broken, beyond the chance of living a normal life—the broken part of them could never be fixed.

Seema's education was based on psychological causes and effects: *Find the cause and you can help alter and change the effect.* The thought that a person could actually be unfixable terrified her. That was the sole reason she came to work at the rehabilitation centre. Here, she felt, was a place where she could provide true hope for the people who had been broken. Here, she felt confident she could help fix them.

Robert looked up. Her pained face didn't stop him from asking again, "So, Miss Pourshadi, do you think all people are fixable?"

Seema quickly turned her head towards the window. Her hands played with her scarf. Roberto Sanchez was not a heinous criminal, nor had he done anything more than find himself in the wrong place at the wrong time. *Is Roberto Sanchez fixable? Are all people fixable?* Seema honestly didn't know.

A knock at the door saved her.

"Sorry to interrupt," Robert's physiotherapist, Benny Tucci said.

"Your wife is here, Mr. Sanchez. She says you have a doctor's appointment today?"

Robert turned his chair around to face Benny and said dully, "Yeah."

He then turned back to Seema. "You know what they are going to decide for me today, Miss Pourshadi?"

Seema nodded her head grimly.

"Yep, they're going to help *fix* me!" Robert said sarcastically. "Let's go, Benny. Don't want to miss a minute of someone telling me how they may have to cut my other leg off, do we?"

8. PRESENT DAY – AT THE HOTEL

Monique avoided Robert's question of, "Why are we doing this." The aching pain in her heart just wanted to scream out, "We? When was the last time you and I were a 'we' Robert?"

Yet, as soon as she thought that screaming question, she was struck by the happy fact that Robert did say "we", not "I" or "you". She couldn't remember the last time he had referred to her or Jenny as an "us" or even a family. Although Monique Sanchez was a very practical, matter of fact woman, she also had the uncanny ability to find hope in the most hopeless of situations.

And lately, hope would be difficult for anyone to find at the Sanchez residence. Every day since the accident, Robert had sunken deeper into depression. He refused to go back to work and had almost completely retreated from the world. What hurt Monique most was how he found new ways to hide from his own family. The distance between them grew every day. In many ways, Monique wished Robert was off on one of his climbing expeditions, for at least then he wrote letters, called or sent faxes. Now it was hard to connect with him in even the simplest of ways; even merely asking him what he would like to eat for dinner had become daunting and emotionally taxing.

Robert and the doorman watched as Monique reached into the passenger door and pulled out a fairly large green duffel bag. She handed it to the doorman. "No, leave that there. I don't need it," Robert snapped.

"But Robert, don't you think—"

He threw his arms in the air. "—Okay. I don't care! Take it, leave it—This is your crazy idea, Neek, not mine!"

Neek! He called me Neek. So there has to be some hope, she thought.

Robert had called Monique many pet names over the years—Little M, Moanie, Mo—but Neek was a name Robert rarely used. And although she was embarrassed by Robert's behaviour in front of the doorman, she managed to turn her head away from Robert and smile a hope-filled smile.

"Sorry," she said to the doorman. "Could you put that green bag back in the car, please? Thanks." She then reached for a small backpack on the front seat.

Feeling the awkwardness of the moment, the doorman quickly offered to carry the backpack, but Monique just flung it over her shoulders and said, "It's okay. I got it!" She then reached back in to grab a black computer bag, which she slung over her other shoulder.

"I can take that for you." The doorman extended both his arms. Monique was just about to hand it to him, but quickly changed her mind when she saw his hand. "No, no, that's fine. I'm used to it."

Robert jumped in, "Just close the door and let's get this over with."

Monique gave the doorman an embarrassed smile as he closed the car door. "I'm sorry," she whispered to him.

The doorman smiled back. "You don't have to say that. I truly understand. I do. Come. Please, let's go inside."

They entered the hotel lobby. It was alive and buzzing with people gathering, coming and going. Monique walked beside Robert as he tightly gripped the wheels of his wheelchair and pushed it forward. The wheelchair's shiny silver leg and foot holders glistened as they reflected the light from the impressive lobby chandeliers.

Robert was dressed in a black T-shirt and dark navy pants that were folded and pinned closed at the knees. Earlier, Monique had tried to get him to dress up, but Robert defiantly refused. "You say they want me, then they will have me the way I am!" he had said.

In contrast, Monique was radiant. She was dressed in a deep red V-neck sweater, an attractive tailored navy jacket and a knee-high flowing black skirt. With her long dark hair pulled back loosely with a large, beautiful African-designed silver clip, she looked ten years younger than her forty-four years.

"Monique, Monique!" A short, sturdy, and impeccably groomed Chinese man in his thirties came to greet them. "You look great in that backpack, Monique!" He spoke with absolutely no detectible accent whatsoever.

"Ah, Robert, wonderful to see you again!"

"Yeah," replied Robert sourly.

Monique quickly jumped in. "Robert, you remember Greg Wong, the president of Elevation?"

Greg held his hand out to Robert, who lifted his right hand from the push ring of his wheelchair and said, "I don't think you want to shake this grubby paw."

Oh my God! Monique thought. Robert had opened his mouth only twice and still could not muster a single pleasantry.

Yet, Greg surprised her when he took Robert's hand and said with a laughing voice, "Well, we'll be even then, because you don't know where my hand has been either. Great to see you again, Robert!"

Greg's comeback stunned Robert too. He let Greg quickly shake his hand while Monique laughed an ah-he-got-you kind of laugh. Monique was used to Robert always being the one who could find ways to ease any tense situation. She smiled at her husband, hoping he would appreciate what Greg had just done, but Robert just lowered his head and put his hands quickly back onto the wheels of his chair.

"Sorry, Monique, but I must get back in there. And, Robert, we all are looking forward to hearing you." Greg looked at his watch. "I'm meeting with the team for fifteen minutes, but you can go into the room and set up. There is a technician in the room although, Monique, I'm sure you won't be needing one. So please, do what you need to do, and oh, we are in the Leaning Tower of *Pizza* room."

As Greg walked off, a pleasant yet distinct smell of cologne trailed after him. Robert waved his hand as if to clear the air.

"If they all smell as much as him, I may die of asphyxiation in that room."

Monique ignored Robert and turned to the doorman. "Leaning Tower of *Pizza?*"

The doorman laughed. "Pisa not Pizza! The rooms are all named after and themed around the Wonders of the World. The tower is a great room, but the Taj Mahal is my personal favourite. Really, do try to take a peek at it if you can before you leave. I'm sure they put you in the Leaning Tower of Pisa because it has the best acoustics for presentations. Come on, follow me."

The hotel was a large circular building and the lobby hallway circled around all the conference and meeting rooms. The Leaning Tower of Pisa was halfway around. They passed the rooms called Stonehenge, Great Wall of China, Colosseum, and Niagara Falls and as just they passed the Taj Mahal, the doorman stopped.

"I wish you could see it now." He pointed to the door. "Please make sure you see it before you leave today. You won't be disappointed!"

They stopped at the Leaning Tower of Pisa room. As the doorman opened the door, they were hit with the rousing sound of Steppenwolf's "Born to be Wild."

"Oh, looks like they are checking the sound." The doorman raised his voice over the loud music. He then took the computer bag from Monique and placed it on a table near the door and, just before he exited, he turned around and bowed slightly, saying, "I pray your day is successful and may you have a wonderful experience today!"

"Thank you so much!" Monique touched the doorman's shoulder as he was leaving.

"Great! The Leaning Tower of Pisa," said Robert as the doorman left the room. "They put your company in a room that's named after something that looks like it's about to fall down."

Standing by the door, Monique tried to muster a smile as she watched Robert push that mysterious brown leather bag deeper between his left leg and the chair. The same leather bag that he forbade her to touch and yanked from her when she was about to put it in the backpack earlier. The music seemed harsh for the early morning. She couldn't make out the exact lyrics, only the hurting words of: making something happen...firing a gun...and exploding into oblivion...

It hurt her even more as Robert stopped his chair and chirped with a swagger, "Yep, Steppenwolf's got the right idea."

9. PRESENT DAY – JENNY'S RESIDENCE

"Hey, Mom...Just calling to say hi...wondering...Oh my God, of course you're probably gone already...but—Hey, Daddy, if you're still there, pick up...Mom? Dad, you there? Pick up! Okay, I'll try Mom at her work number...Bye, love ya!"

Jenny called her parents' house and left a rambling message. She felt a sudden panic come over her and started bouncing from side to side, saying out loud, "Daddy, where the hell are you?" Then, in a lightening second, she took her hand and hit herself a little too hard on the head. "Oh my God, you idiot—You *freaking* idiot! Today's Friday. Dad's talk—they are at the hotel by now—" She then tried to take a deep breath to calm herself. "Stop panicking! Daddy's not going to kill himself!"

Jenny quickly covered her mouth in a gasp. She couldn't believe those words actually fell out of her. *Kill himself!* She couldn't believe she had that thought about her father. "Daddy would never do that!"

But the image of her father from her last visit home told a different story. When she hugged her mother goodbye at the door, her father was sitting in his wheelchair with his back to her and he didn't even turn around when she said, "Bye, Daddy, love ya!" He just waved his hand.

Her father was always big on "hellos" and "goodbyes." He had always taught her, "Eye contact, Little Rock. Please don't just walk into the house and go straight into your room without us seeing each other and saying 'hi'." He was constantly reminding her that when someone came home, you drop everything to welcome them and when someone leaves, you go to the door to say goodbye and wave until you can no longer see them.

Why? Why didn't I just go back into the living room, look in his eyes and hug

37

him or maybe even chastise him like he would have done to me if I didn't come to the door to say goodbye?

Jenny's eyes spied the letter on the floor. She picked it up and looked at her father's last line. "Open arms of all that is..." *What did he mean 'all that is'? Is what?* she wondered. Seeing the red journal on the table, a panic seized her again. It was the echo of the last conversation they had at suppertime together, when her mother spoke about her father's talk for her company's event.

Jenny had looked to her father and saw his blank expression, so she smiled and said, "That's great, Daddy!" Robert just nodded his head and replied with a sarcastic sigh, "Yeah, it's great!" and then wheeled himself from the dinner table to the living room.

Jenny leaned over and whispered to her mother, "Really, Mom? I mean, do you think he's ready?"

Monique quickly put her hand to her lips. "Shhh!" She then quickly changed the subject by directing her daughter into the back bedroom with the intention of showing her a new dress she had just bought for the company's big event.

The moment they walked into the bedroom, her mother closed the door and leaned her back against it.

"Jen, I don't want to scare you but I'm starting to get worried about Daddy. He told me not to tell you tonight, but he just found out that he may lose his left leg too if it doesn't show any signs of improvement in the next two weeks."

"Oh, my God, Mom, I didn't know! Oh, what an idiot I am! There I was asking Daddy when will he get the cast off and get that new leg so we could start running again."

"It's okay, honey, you couldn't have known."

"Mom, do you think Daddy is ready to do this thing—this talk about...you know?"

"Honey, your father needs something...something else to focus on, other than—Look, he needs something, Jen. Every day he seems to—I don't know, become more and more...lost."

"But Mom, does he want to do it?"

"I don't know, Jen, he doesn't really talk to me. But this presentation for my company was planned months before the accident. And your father has cancelled everything—all his workshops, any meetings. He never returns anyone's calls...But this...this talk, even though he acts as if he doesn't want to do it, he hasn't said no. He stills sees me planning and talking about it and he never really stops me."

Monique rubbed her eyes hard and then sat down on the bed beside her daughter.

"He has so much to share. Your father is an amazing man, Jen. He needs to know that and feel that again. And maybe if he could talk about his climbing, maybe that will instil some new passion in him. Lots of people make their living speaking about that mountain stuff, you know..."

Jenny stared at her mom with curious wonder and shook her head ever so slightly.

"Jenny, why are you looking at me like that?"

"You know, Mom, I've never heard you use that word 'passion' before. It was what Daddy always called his climbing."

"Just because I don't use it, doesn't mean I don't understand it."

Monique leaned over and touched her daughter's leg, "Oh baby...I...I really regret the way I acted with your father whenever he came back from his climbs. I was happy he was back, but I was kind of resentful he had left."

"I know, Mom. It wasn't hard to see."

"I was wrong in so many ways, Jen. I feel so ashamed of myself now. Don't get me wrong, it was really hard when your father was gone on those mountains...and I know I was difficult to be around when he came back. It always took me weeks before I could forgive him for leaving us...But now, Jen, I think those mountains might be the only thing that will help him."

"It's okay, Mom." Jenny patted her mother's hand.

"But now I need your help," Monique said as she put a hand on her daughter's cheek and gently pushed a lock of Jenny's hair behind her ear. "Look, Jenny, I need you to go back in there and try to encourage your father about doing this. He listens to you. He needs to hear it from you."

Jenny stood up and then smiled a huge I've-got-an-idea smile. Jenny had lots of experience of getting through to her father and convincing him to agree with something she wanted him to do. Like that time when she was fourteen and had to ask her dad to help convince her mother to let her go for a week with her best friend's family to Disney World.

"I'll try, Mom."

Monique reached out and held her daughter as tight as her arms had strength to.

"Daddy's so lucky to have you, Mom."

Monique needed to hear those words from her daughter. For the last few months, she had been the absolute pillar of hope. From that very first moment of seeing her husband lying in a bed in a Katmandu clinic, she never wavered. Even the first time the sheets were removed and she saw the sickly sight of her husband's completely shattered-beyond-recognition legs, she stayed positive. And even today, living and sharing a home with the hurtful monster that possessed the caring loving husband she had once known, Monique still had never spoken a hopeless word or let herself feel defeated.

But in her daughter's arms, Monique's hopeful armour finally cracked and the warrior wife and mother cried for the first time.

Jenny held her mom and kept repeating, "I love you, Mom. I love you."

After a few minutes, Monique sat back down on the bed, completely spent from the emotions she had just released. Jenny faced her mother with a smile—that crazy happy smile that could win over anyone.

"Don't worry, Mom," she said. "Daddy's going be all right."

Her mom's whole body smiled back at her daughter. "Okay, baby." Pointing at Jenny's smile, she said, "Now, you go give some of that to your daddy."

Jenny left the bedroom and gave her mom a little wave as she closed the door. She could see her dad from the hallway. She took a long, deep breath and then walked with a focused purpose into the living room. She tried to look as playful as possible, swaying her arms and, with a carefree bounce, she threw herself onto the couch.

She leaned over to the iPod dock on the side table, picked up her purse from the floor and pulled out her iPod. Scrolling through her playlists, she stopped when she found one labelled 'Daddy's Garden.' She had this for the many car trips they shared over the years. 'Daddy's Garden' was a list of songs Robert had found and sent to Jenny. Every time he found a song he thought his daughter would like he would say, "That is definitely one for the garden, Little Rock. Let it bloom!"

Her father had once explained that, "Anytime you hear a song that makes you feel something, it will then create a memory inside of you. The more you feel, the longer it stays inside of you. The feeling of some songs can last your whole life...It's just like something saved to the hard drive on your computer, Jen. You may not see it on your desktop, you may have forgotten you downloaded it, but it is always there, ready to be accessed— this emotional recording. And I call it a garden because once a song makes you feel something, that song is now planted inside you and like anything that is planted, well, it starts to grow inside of you...To me, Jen, every great song I love is like some beautiful flower, and every time I hear the song again, it's like this little flower inside of me starts to bloom and opens up the memory of that feeling again. And so, the more songs I have, the bigger my garden of feelings is."

Oh man, she thought, *which song?* Her little fingers spun the long list up and down and wow, there it was "Lost" by Michael Bublé. *It's perfect!* That was a song from the CD her dad sent her when she had lost her two band mates a couple years ago.

As she put the iPod in the dock, she glanced back at her father. It was strange to see him sit there in his wheelchair under the lamp where his big comfy La-Z-Boy chair once was. They used to call that chair 'The Head Quarters.' It was her father's mission control centre whenever he was planning his mountain climbs. He always had books, maps, letters and sometimes a crampon or rope he was fixing. 'The Head Quarters' had been moved into the garage as Robert felt there was no use for it anymore.

Her plan was set.

Jenny started the song softly, barely audible, as if to show she was not about to disturb her dad's reading. She was secretly hoping her father would ask for her to play it louder so he could hear, but he had not even looked up when she came into the room. So, she lay down on her stomach with her legs kicking up on the big green sofa and pretended to read a magazine about health products.

She felt her father look up towards her, but she acted as if she was engrossed in her reading, making sounds like "Oh," "Wow" and "Hmmm, didn't know that." Jenny always knew how to get her dad's attention.

She then slowly turned the music louder and started singing along. She also knew how to get into her dad's heart. Halfway through the song, Jenny felt the moment was right and she turned up the volume and Mr. Bublé and Jenny sang together words about life just tearing you down, and yet something stays the same...

And as the music built, Jenny got up from the couch and started moving directly toward her father, who had not budged from his book. Jenny reached down and took her father's hand. Oh, how many times since Jenny was a little girl had they held hands just like this? It would always lead to the magical moment of a daddy and his little girl twirling together. Sometimes, Monique would jokingly pout and jest, "I'm jealous, Jenny, you always get the man."

Jenny swayed and took her father's hands in hers. She started to pull his wheelchair into the centre of the living room. "Come on, Dad, let's get lost together."

"Jenny." Her father broke the mood. "*Please.* I have a headache. Can you turn that music off?"

It was like a dagger piercing her heart! Her father was always the one to ask her to sing louder and after Jenny moved out, he would almost beg her to sing just one more song before she left to go home.

Jenny froze for a moment but regrouped quickly. "Sorry, Daddy, but I'm just so excited that you're going to tell your stories at mom's company event. I wish I could be there! Those people are so lucky. It will be like you're taking them climbing with—"

Robert snapped and cut his daughter off. "—*And* what? And talk about the last goddamn time I ever climbed? Talk about something I can never do again?"

Yes, Jenny remembered that night: of hiding her own tears after experiencing her father's reaction, his harsh words, "the last goddamn time I ever climbed." She painfully recalled feeling her mom cry in her arms and then she realized there was yet another thing she had lost: she would never stand in his arms again and feel that father's hug—the place Jenny had always felt was the safest place on the planet! As she looked down at the red journal, she had to rub her eyes to keep them from bursting into tears.

Why had she not listened better when her dad said, "talk about something I can never do again?" *He sounded so final! "Talk about something I can never do again?" Why didn't I talk to him about it? Why didn't I listen? I just ran out the door and now this...sending me his journal?*

Jenny rushed to the phone, started to press some numbers, but stopped then said out loud, "Why can't I ever remember mom's cell number?" as she grabbed her purse.

10. PRESENT DAY – AT THE HOTEL

The Leaning Tower of Pisa had lived through many exciting corporate events and had happily celebrated hundreds of Italian weddings. The floor was covered in a tasteful, stone-patterned carpet. There was a hardwood stage on one end with a huge mural of the Leaning Tower of Pisa as its backdrop. Walking into the room felt like walking into the Pisa's grand cathedral square. The walls were colourfully decorated with Italian street scenes. The ceiling was a deep sky blue, sparkling with clusters of gold coloured stars. Yes, there was the feeling that this room had celebrated many times before!

Without saying a word, Monique picked up the computer bag and walked towards the technician who was working on the soundboard up on the stage. She left Robert on the ground level, hoping to avoid hearing whatever negative comment he might share with the next person he met. This was brand new territory for Monique. She was not an outgoing person; in fact, she was quite shy. Robert was the one who always took the initiative to ensure his wife felt comfortable whenever they found themselves in a new situation or adventure. But in a strange way, Robert's physical and personality changes had created a new and welcome independence in Monique, giving her the confidence to take control of certain situations that she never would have in the past.

Robert wheeled his chair to sit facing the stage. Directly above the stage was a big banner hanging from the ceiling displaying the company's name and logo. *Do they really need it that big? It must be as big as a movie screen*, he thought.

It was a tasteful banner with a bright aqua-coloured background. The company's name, ELEVATION, was printed in dark purple lettering and above that were jagged lines, much like the lines on a stock market chart. The three lines formed into three separate peaks. At the bottom of the banner was the slogan, "Always Elevating Software above and beyond SEE Level."

Robert smirked to himself at the lame word play of "SEA" to "SEE."

Greg came in behind Robert and asked, "Do you like our banner?"

"What are those lines?" Robert asked.

Robert waved his hand noticeably in front of his face, anticipating the strong odour of cologne that surrounded Greg, but Greg didn't see him. The startling sound of drums boomed throughout the room. Greg and Robert both looked up at the stage at the same time.

"Sorry about that!" Monique called down.

She went back to connecting her computer to a projector as the technician continued playing with the sound levels. The startling drums soon transitioned into a quiet mournful song; the singer's voice had a definite sounding ache. It was the unmistakeable voice of Bruce Springsteen, who was singing something about being bruised and battered, and seeing a reflection and didn't know his own face…

"Do you like it Robert? Although it wasn't intentional, those lines actually represent mountains," answered Greg. "You see, when we came up with the company name 'Elevation,' we wanted to find a logo that depicted something on the rise. So we hoped the logo would stand for the stock fluctuations, and indicate that our stocks are always going up. Do you know what they were before the mountains?" he asked with a laugh.

Robert barely heard what Greg said. His brain only had room for the song and its words. Robert knew the feeling of this song—the memory of this song—it was in his 'garden of songs' but it was now flowering like a thorny weed, piercing him with shame. It was as if the song was exposing him: look at the cripple about to speak about climbing Mt. Everest, something he can never do now. *Yes*, he thought, *I am truly unrecognizable to myself!*

Lost in his depressed thoughts, he hadn't noticed that Greg was waiting for a response. Despite not hearing what Greg said, Robert quickly composed himself and blurted, "Oh, good…it works!"

"I'm sorry…" Greg said. "What works?"

Robert was flustered. Why didn't he just ask Greg to repeat what he had said? But at the same time, he just wanted to end this conversation, so he said, "It all does—Good work—Looks good."

"Well, thanks to your wife. You see, with our recent merger, we needed to strengthen and firm up our image but we wanted to do it without really changing our logo, and it was Monique's idea to change those wavy graph lines into mountains. The three peaks represent the three companies we are now composed of. Yes, you have a very intelligent and creative wife, Robert!"

A drop of sweat trickled down Robert's forehead, visible enough that Greg quickly snatched up a napkin off a nearby table and offered it to him.

"Yeah, thanks." Robert took the napkin and wiped his forehead. He felt uneasy and almost short of breath.

"Yes, of course. Go prepare. Sorry to take up your time. Oh...but, Robert, please know how grateful I am that you are here, because we really need a talk like yours today. You see, Elevation has always prided itself on teamwork, but now with three separate companies trying to forge into one—well, it's not an easy task. Ever since the announcement of the merger, I have been fearing we might become fractured or split. Like that Chinese saying: 'we are like a bucket of sand.'"

"Sand?" Robert stammered.

"It's like we are all in the bucket together, but, like sand, nothing sticks together—and I fear the changes going on within the company might prove to too much for us to handle and we won't be able to stick together. We really need this event and someone to inspire and help bring us together, make us feel we all are on the same team. So thank you, Robert, for helping us today." Greg put his hands together and repeated, "Thank you," with a reverent bow.

Robert just nodded and then swiftly turned the wheelchair with a strong-handed jerk down on one wheel in the opposite direction of Greg. *Inspire? Help you? Well, you've got yourself the wrong man, Mister Wong!*

With his sudden move, the napkin flew off his lap and landed on the floor and just as Robert was about to turn back, Greg smiled. "No, no, don't worry. I have it."

"Great—Yeah, you have it," Robert said, trying his best to muster a smile. And as he pushed himself towards the stage, still holding that forced fake smile, he thought, *Yeah, everyone's always super helpful to the cripple!*

Monique had been keeping an eye on Robert and fearing the worst as she saw him talking to Greg. So, she was happy to see them part at least with what looked like smiles. She greeted her husband at the bottom of the stairs to the stage.

"Oh, no!" *There were six steps and no ramp!* she thought.

The technician working on the stage noticed this right away. Amir Satchu was a scrawny little man from Guyana. His weathered face made him look much older than his forty years.

"Ah, Miss Monique," Amir said, his wide-open smile sparkling with three gold-plated teeth. "Does your friend here need assistance?"

"Well, what is the best way to do this?" Monique asked.

"Ah, there is always a way—and I know the perfect one!"

Amir arrived at the top of the stairs and then called out to Robert. "Okay, sir. Jump and I'll catch you!"

Oh my God! Monique closed her eyes preparing for Robert's worst response.

"How high?" was Robert's reply. "Think you can catch all this weight?"

Monique was relieved and shocked that Robert didn't get insulted and chew poor Amir's head off.

"Stop! Wait!" Amir playfully yelled. "I just remembered, I forgot to eat my Wheaties this morning. Jumping and catching might be bad for your health, sir. We must think of something else."

"What's your name, strong man?" asked Robert.

"Amir, sir. And, as I'm sure you can see by my towering physique, many call me 'Amir the Giant Satchu'. At your service, sir."

Monique let out a small laugh, thinking she could probably catch and carry the small-sized Amir herself. *What a relief it was to laugh out loud!* Monique thought. *What was it about Amir that had Robert displaying glimpses of his former self?* she wondered.

"I'll tell you what, Amir the Giant. Come behind me," Robert instructed. Amir quickly hopped down to the floor level. "Now, let's go backwards up the stairs."

Amir, who could not have been much taller than Monique, latched onto the handles at the back of Robert's chair.

"Okay, lean me back. Just balance me, don't take all the weight, I'll turn the wheels and we'll go up one step at a time. Remember, I'm the motor, right? Okay, you ready, Giant?"

Robert, co-operating with someone he just met...and calling him endearing names? It seemed like a miracle to Monique!

Step by step, Robert encouraged Amir and after each step Robert asked, "How's the Giant doing? Ready for the next?"

Could it be it's because he was climbing? Monique mused.

Amir then stopped on the fourth step and joked, "Okay, sir, it looks like time to switch places. It's my turn to sit in the chair."

Monique held her breath, shrinking back from what might come out of Robert's mouth, but he just laughed and said, "There's only one Giant Amir and that's not me!"

Finally at the top and just as Amir was setting the wheelchair level, it almost tipped forward, threatening to throw Robert to the floor. Monique leaped up the stairs just in time to put her hands on Robert's chest to steady him while Amir quickly put his arms around Robert's shoulders to keep him in the chair. Just as Robert was upright, the mysterious brown leather bag that Robert had been holding fell out. *Wham!* The weighted impact sounded as if it would surely make a good-sized dent on the hardwood stage.

Monique went to pick it up.

"No!" Robert yelled a little too loud. "Don't anybody touch it!" He swirled the wheelchair to its side and reached down to pick the bag up.

Right at that moment, Monique's cell phone went off. She reached into her purse for the phone and said, in a joking way to lighten the moment, "Good thing that went off now and not in the middle of your talk, Robert." Without checking the incoming number, she switched it off and put it back into her bag.

Robert totally ignored her, turned to Amir and snapped, "All right, what do you want me do?"

Monique's heart sank hearing the return of Robert's harsh tone. The climb was over and they had summited the stage, only to find *the little giant miracle* had not made it to the top with them.

11. 12 WEEKS AGO – SEEMA'S OFFICE

"Hi Robert!" Seema spoke gently as Benny pushed him into her office. It had been a few days since Robert had been told the bones in his leg were just too splintered to fix. The doctor said that they had tried everything possible and nothing had worked. His left leg must also be amputated as soon as it could be scheduled.

"It's okay if you don't want to talk today. I truly understand. I do, Robert. I truly do."

Seeing that Robert didn't respond, she turned to Benny. "So, it's all right, Benny, you can take Mr. Sanchez back."

Benny turned Robert around and moved him towards the door. Robert opened his arms and grabbed onto both sides of the doorway to stop the chair from rolling through it.

"No wait, Benny." Robert then turned the wheelchair around to face Seema.

"Why do you say truly? That you *truly* understand?" he asked her.

She looked at him with a quizzical look. "I'm sorry, what do you mean?"

"You said you truly understand. So does that mean you weren't being true when you said you understood all the other times?"

Seema pulled at her dark purple scarf. "Well, it's just an expression, Robert. I think I say 'truly' because this time I want to...to show you...well, to show you compassion."

"So the other times you were not showing compassion?"

Seema stammered because she knew she wasn't going to find the answer Robert might be looking for.

"No, no, Robert, it's just...I realize with the news you received a few days ago, you might not want to speak today and I guess my saying 'truly' was a way of telling you I understand and that I know the news you received the other day was not...well, good."

"So you don't want to talk about how I'm getting all fixed up? Don't wanna speak about how my other leg is being hacked off tomorrow?"

"Of course, we'll talk if you want to...I'm here to talk to you—I just thought..."

"Do you *truly* want to talk about it, Miss Pourshadi? Really? It's pretty gory. Did you know they actually use an electric saw? Did you know that? An *electric saw!* Oh, so I'm sorry, I guess it's not really hacking it off; it's more of a quick buzz." Robert mimed an electric saw and its sound as he passed it over the cast on his leg.

"Benny, it's okay to leave Mr. Sanchez here. I'll call you when we are finished."

"Sure thing, Seema." Benny put a hand on Robert's shoulder. "See you later, Roberto." Benny went out of the office and closed the door.

Seema looked at Robert. He looked right back at her as if he was about to say something, but then stopped himself and wheeled his chair right up to the window.

"No kids today. No kites, not even a dog walker," he said.

Seema moved to the front of her desk and leaned against it. "You missed a little soccer match some girls were playing this morning."

Robert reached out and scratched at some faint drops of white paint that had probably been on that window for years. He surprised her as he spoke with sincere tenderness. "So you do know what's going to happen tomorrow?"

"Yes, Robert. I'm truly sorry."

Robert turned around and looked at Seema with a sad grin.

"Oh my God," she said. "Truly, I did it again, didn't I? I guess it's a habit. I'm so sorry, Robert."

Robert put his hand up to stop her. "It's okay. Frankly it doesn't matter how sorry anyone is. Apparently the best way of fixing me is to cut this damn thing off. Yep, tomorrow night I'll be *truly* one hundred percent without legs."

"And uh..." Seema stopped and put her hand in front of her mouth, and feigned clearing her throat, realizing she didn't know what to say to him next.

Robert took a deep breath and wheeled his chair towards the front of the desk and stopped directly in front of Seema.

"Look, today I did want to talk...so I could...well, ask you if you could do something for me."

"Of course, Robert, what is it you would like me to do for you?"

"Would you drive me to the hospital tomorrow?"

Seema was startled by Robert's request. Not only had he always been what seemed intentionally distant to her, but also bringing someone to the hospital for an operation was something usually left to family or friends. Seema was neither of these to Roberto Sanchez.

"Robert, I can do that for you, but why don't you want your wife—"

Robert cut her off. "We don't have time to discuss it. My wife and daughter are coming to pick me up in about ten minutes. I'd really like it if you could talk to them first."

"About what exactly, Robert?"

"Please tell them you are taking me to the hospital. Tell them something about you think it's best...or it's the centre's request."

"Do your wife and daughter not feel comfortable going to the hospital, Robert?"

"Please, can you just tell them? Tell them it's Benny's idea or something—I don't know, but please. Just please, do this for me?"

"I can't lie to your family, Robert. I really can't—"

Robert cut her off again. "—Please, please—for God's sake, just make something up, please!"

"Mr. Sanchez, I really cannot—"

"—Tell them the truth then!" Robert almost screamed. "Tell them I can't see their faces! I can't! I can't have them seeing *this* again, watching me have another piece of my body ripped off. Tell them I just can't see them looking...looking that way again."

Seema put her hand out to touch Robert's shoulder. But he pushed it aside. "I don't need your hand...or your—Look, *please*, just do this for me. I'll come here every day and tell you whatever you need to know. Just please, can you do this for me?"

12. PRESENT DAY – JENNY'S RESIDENCE

Jenny called her mother's cell phone, but kept getting her voicemail. On the fourth try, Jenny finally released all the dark thoughts that were invading her heart's mind into that receiver.

"Mom, Daddy's journal...he sent it to me...It's here, I have it. Right here, Mom...in my hand...right here! The thing he said he would never show me and only give to me after he died...Why did he do this, Mom?...Daddy's changed, Mom...We need to...and...and...and okay—Why does Daddy have a gun? What the hell does he need a gun for, Mom? Mom, I think it's a bad idea today—You should see the letter he sent with the journal...Mom, please call me...Daddy doesn't want to talk to people! I *don't* think you should let him talk today..."

Then came the sound of a beep.

Every ounce of Jenny was spent. With tears filling her eyes, she held the phone limply at her side and repeated softly to herself, "I think Daddy wants to die...I think he just wants to die...I think...Oh, Daddy..."

A knock at the door interrupted Jenny. She wiped her face with the long soft sleeve of her housecoat as she opened the door.

"Surprise...I thought you maybe could use a—"

Jenny grabbed Kyle with all her might and wept loudly.

"—an accompanist...to help...you...warm up?" Kyle said sheepishly, but instantly knew something had happened and so he returned his newfound love's embrace and held her as tight as he could.

"What's wrong, Jenny? What's wrong?"

13. PRESENT DAY – AT THE HOTEL

"Just say something, Mr. Robert," Amir said, smiling. Robert was now sitting in the centre of the stage. Amir had just hooked up a microphone that came alongside Robert's right cheek. The skin-coloured microphone was attached and secured on Robert's ears, sitting just like a pair of glasses would but with the wire going behind the head instead of over the nose.

Robert vacantly looked out into the room. It seemed larger now from the stage. There had to be about fifty tables with at least eight chairs around each. All the tables were covered in white tablecloths and decorated with floral centrepieces. Each table had two clear glass water jugs and tall drinking glasses. A pen and a pad of paper had been provided in front of every chair. A dozen hotel staff members were running about setting up while Greg was animatedly speaking to the hotel's head guy and giving him instructions.

"Mr. Robert, sir, please, I need to check your level," Amir said patiently.

"Yes," Robert said robotically. "I am sitting on the stage with the Leaning Tower of Pisa behind me and..." Robert glanced at the huge clock hung over the door, "it is nine-thirty."

"Mr. Robert, sir, can you just pull your mic away from your face a little?" Amir gestured to Robert, showing him how to do it. Amir was sitting to the side of the stage behind a table with a soundboard, four iPods and the computer Monique had set up.

Robert tugged a little at the microphone, bending the flexible metal attachment a little farther from his cheek. "Okay, how's that?"

"Yes, perfect. Thank you with all kindness, Mr. Robert," said Amir.

"Thanks, Bobby," Monique said, coming to stand beside Amir at the sound table.

Robert said nothing to either one of them. He just sat there, staring blankly out into the room, listening to the clinking and clanging noise the staff made as they set up the hall.

"How does the screen come down, Amir, for all our projections?" Monique asked. She had done a set up like this numerous times and was pretty sure she knew how it worked. But after Robert's little outburst at the stairs earlier, she found concentrating on the set-up was helping to calm her nerves a little.

"Ah, watch this, my dear!" Amir stood up, walked to the wall and pressed a button. A huge white screen came down about twenty feet behind Robert and stopped about three feet above the floor.

"Great, can we check out some of our visuals?" Monique asked as she went to the computer and opened up a program.

"Just press play." Amir smiled.

"Okay, this is Robert's intro," Monique said.

The screen went dark blue and, as the sound of trumpets filled the air, the screen came to life: first with the name "ROBERT SANCHEZ", which dissolved slowly into a photo showing the magnificence of Mount Everest. As the drums started building, it seemed as if the mountain was coming closer and closer to the audience and then, just as the oboes sounded, the mountain turned into a picture of Robert, who was standing on the edge of a frightening and jagged glacier and smiling the smile of a conquering hero. His dark sun goggles were flipped onto his forehead, his hair tossed by the wind. Robert was dressed in a red winter jacket and pants with bright yellow boots that came almost to his knees. Just as the piano, clarinets, flutes and a harp joined in, a colourful collage of photos danced across the screen in time with the music. Robert clinging to the side of a frightening ice fall with his ice pick dug in, Robert scaling a precarious 90-degree ledge of ice, a dramatic shot of Robert walking across a ladder that bridged a deep hollow pit of what looked to be a snowy grand canyon.

As each picture filled the screen, it would then crack like ice and fracture into many other smaller, more dangerous looking photos of Robert's mountain adventures. Then, as the cornets, trombones, bassoon and what sounded like a huge timpani drum played, the screen started to fill with multiple pictures of Robert in other parts of his life: some of Jenny appearing with the words "the Father" and Monique with "the Husband and Partner" followed by photos of Robert with huge groups of teenagers and younger students in what looked like school gymnasiums.

The last picture was one of Robert with a small group of children of different ages and diverse nationalities. Slowly the camera closed in on Robert, focusing on his colourful orange T-shirt, which read "QUEST-I'm-

ON". Soon the screen was left with only the word QUEST, which then faded into a stunning mountaintop high amongst the clouds.

And just as the unmistakeable music of John Williams came to its majestic end, Robert wheeled around and faced the screen. It was at that precise moment that the irony hit him with a sickening thud.

This music, he thought, *the music Monique picked for this intro was from the sound track of Superman.* His head sank to his chest when his mind captured the image—not of Christopher Reeve playing Superman and flying mightily in the sky to save the day, but rather of the Christopher Reeve sitting tied into a wheelchair with an oxygen tube coming out of his neck—the Superman who had become a quadriplegic after a horseback riding exhibition.

Amir stood up and clapped. "Wow, that is great! Just amazing, Mr. Robert!"

Robert didn't move. Monique looked at her husband, sitting in that wheelchair, facing the screen with his head down on his chest. *Maybe he can't do this today?* she thought.

Never before had this question been asked! Although Robert had withdrawn from the world and became distant, Monique still never questioned if Robert actually had the strength to do something.

Even after seeing her husband in the hospital, grimacing in excruciating pain after the accident, even before the first surgery to amputate his right leg and even that night when he came home broken and sobbing because one of his students had committed suicide, she had never questioned Robert's unique will and fortitude. No matter what happened, Monique had always seen Robert resiliently and passionately push forward.

She had believed so strongly in her husband's strength to battle any adversity that even when Doctor Alman had thought maybe one leg could be saved, despite the devastating condition of both of his legs, Monique was adamant that the doctor to be frank with Robert and not give him false hope.

But this morning, seeing Robert sitting in his wheelchair—a dark silhouette sitting in front of the mountain on the screen, the same mountain that took his legs—she thought he looked so small. His slumping shoulders only revealed a man who was defeated and hopeless.

She now needed to cling to Doctor Alman's response to her when she told him not to give Robert false hope. The doctor had quietly pulled her aside as the nurse took some blood from Robert.

"Mrs. Sanchez, forgive me for saying this. I know you want me to be truthful. And of course I will, but I believe that no matter what, it's important to always encourage, to always give the hope of good news, regardless of how bad it might turn out. Because, Mrs. Sanchez, it's been said that human beings can live for a month without food, a whole week without water, but we will most likely only survive a minute without hope."

And today, seeing the only man she had ever loved look so beaten, Monique closed her eyes and prayed that that minute had not yet passed. But lately, she felt hope was hiding in some other room and quickly sealing the door shut. And so, she thought she had better do something soon, before that door was locked up completely.

14. 10 WEEKS AGO – SEEMA'S OFFICE

Seema opened her laptop, typed something and within a couple of seconds, her office was filled with the sound of Claude Debussy's *Clair de Lune*. She always played this music when she needed to calm herself and now she definitely felt the need to quiet her nerves. Today was going to be the first day she would see Roberto Sanchez after his operation.

She stood up and leaned her head against the window. She let out a sigh, which fogged the glass. As she wiped it clear with the end of her scarf, she could see that a young girls' soccer match was happening outside. *Such a force of might and will! Such abandonment of joy expressed! No one was thinking, just doing, just being—being part of a game.* It was all so beautifully simple.

A knock at the door startled her momentarily. She quickly muted the sound on her computer and wrapped the dark green scarf from her shoulders over her head.

"Yes, come in," she called out.

The door opened. It was Benny. He was alone.

"I just came up to warn you about Mr. Sanchez."

"Warn me, Benny? Why would you need to do that?"

Benny anxiously swayed back and forth as he spoke. "Well, Seema, maybe 'warn' is not the word, exactly. It's just, Robert...I've seen him three times since the operation, and—Well...well, he just doesn't talk. He doesn't say a word. As a matter of fact, it's like he's a zombie or something. He just doesn't respond to anything...and I mean anything. Can't explain it. Just stares like he is looking through the walls."

"I'm sure we have seen this behaviour before, Benny."

"I don't know, Seema, I'm not sure. I have been working here at the centre for a long time now, and I don't think I've ever seen someone

56

look like this."

"What do mean, Benny? Look like what?"

"I don't know. I can't explain it exactly, but it's weird. I'm sorry, I just wanted to tell you before I bring him up to you. I guess you can see for yourself."

Seema gave Benny a concerned smile. "Thank you, Benny. You can go get him now."

Benny shrugged his shoulders and exited the office. "Okay, just thought I should tell you."

Seema sank into her chair. She was just about to un-mute the sound on her computer, but quickly stopped herself. It wasn't Debussy or calming she needed now. It was *ideas*. She knew she had seen this behaviour Benny was speaking about before. Benny had too. Then Robert's silent ways must be more profound than either of them had ever seen. She leaned back in her chair, looking at the ceiling, stretched out her arms and let out a long mournful sigh.

She sat up as Benny rolled Robert into the room.

"Okay, here you are, Robert. I'll be back for you in half an hour. Thirty minutes, is that okay?"

Robert didn't respond. His eyes stared without blinking. Seema couldn't help but notice how much Robert resembled one of those homeless war veterans she often saw on her way to work. He looked as if he had not slept in months. His greasy hair was uncombed and it looked like he had not shaved for days. *Benny was right*, she thought. It wasn't like he was depressed and didn't want to communicate. He just *wasn't* there! It was as if he wasn't even in the same room, much less the same planet as her.

"It's okay, Benny, we will see you in thirty minutes," she said. Benny sadly lifted his arms as if to say "good luck because I didn't have any" and left the room.

Seema stood up, walked to the door and closed it. As she stood at the door, wondering what to do, Robert's move surprised her. His hands clutched the wheels of his chair and then he rolled himself to the window.

She cautiously walked towards Robert, who was just staring out the window. She noticed the soccer game was finished and the schoolyard was now empty except for a woman walking her two dogs. The woman had unleashed her pets and threw a couple of tennis balls, which the dogs furiously ran after and then returned to their master, dropping the balls at her feet. The dogs then sat there—anxiously waiting, trembling inside their skin with such a pent up excitement to chase after the ball again. Seema couldn't help but notice that it looked like they were going to explode if the woman didn't throw the ball immediately.

Seema moved to the edge of her desk, sat down behind Robert and watched the dogs repeat the task over and over again.

"It's incredible, isn't it, the way those dogs sit there? They seem to have that same intensity every time, don't they? They act as if it will be the first time they ever chase that ball."

Robert did not respond to her comment.

The couple of times Seema looked at him, the same thought of Robert's smallness annoyed her. *Of course*, she thought. *That huge white cast protruding out is no longer there. Or is it that he now has a larger wheelchair? He just looks so much smaller.*

Contrary to what Benny had said earlier about Robert never saying a word, it was Robert who broke the silence.

"Look at them—those dogs. Must feel good to them. They chase that ball as if they've finally found their true purpose in life."

Seema waited to see if he would add to his comment before responding.

But Robert never spoke again.

A few minutes later, the dogs' owner leashed her dogs and walked away. And for the rest of the session, the two of them sat staring out the window, not breathing a word.

The dead quiet of the room was interrupted by Benny's knock at the door.

"Well, Roberto, time to get ready, your wife will be here soon."

Robert turned the wheelchair around to face Seema, but never lifted his head to catch her eyes. Benny manoeuvred himself behind Robert to push him out of the office, but Robert grabbed the wheels of his chair firmly and pushed himself forward and out the door before Benny could touch him. Benny followed him out, but then popped his head back in.

"How did it go, Seema?" he whispered. "He didn't say anything, did he?"

Seema didn't turn to Benny right away. But when she did, her face was filled with a questioning glance.

"Not a word, eh?" Benny sadly shook his head.

"No, he spoke," Seema said, still deep in thought.

"No! Really?" Benny took a step inside the office. "I knew it! I knew if anyone could get him talking, you could. I know you can't tell me what you talked about but—"

"It's all right, Benny, he only said one thing. We were watching a woman in the schoolyard play fetch with her dogs and then he said something about the dogs, like...it was as if they had finally found their only purpose in life."

"That's it? Nothing else?"

Seema shook her head.

"What d'ya think he meant by that? Does it mean anything?" Benny asked, scratching his head.

"I'm really not sure, Benny. I really don't know, but Robert was studying those dogs go after that ball as if it was the first time in his life he had ever seen that happen."

"Yeah, that's it! Yeah, Seema, that's what I was trying to tell you before. He seems to look at everything like he's never seen it before. Kinda strange...like..." Benny turned his head in thought. "Yeah, that's it! It's like he's some kind of alien who's come to earth and—Ah, I'm not sure, but something like that."

"Like he has never been here before, Benny?" Seema asked.

15. PRESENT DAY – JENNY'S RESIDENCE

Jenny sat directly in front of Kyle at the kitchen table, clenching her hands as she spewed out every dreadful thought and concern she had for her father.

"And, Jenny, you believe because of—well, this talk, you think he...he might..." Kyle's words stumbled out and he couldn't finish the sentence, but they both knew the next words were "kill himself."

In that silence, Jenny just sadly nodded and nodded.

"But, Jenny—I mean...everything you have told me about your dad, I think, well, I mean of course he's going to be depressed—and...nobody knows him better than your mum, and if she thinks him doing this talk is going to help him, well—"

"—He *sent me his journal*, Kyle! *Today!* Why today of all days? You know, I never thought about it. When my Mum spoke about it, it sounded like it was the right thing but now—I mean, think about it; him having to be on that stage, talking about climbing mountains and now he's sitting in a wheelchair. He'll be so—Oh, he's giving up. I know it, I just have this horrible feeling, Kyle, that...that he's giving up!"

Kyle reached over and pulled Jenny closer to him. "Jen, Jen, you don't know that for sure. When my dad found out he had cancer, he went into some kind of depression for over a year until he actually started to deal with it. I mean, your dad—It's only been six months and look what he had to deal with."

"But Kyle, I just don't know anymore! And it's not like he's even my dad now, it's like he's somebody else...like somebody else took over his—Oh God!"

Jenny dropped her head on the table and started to cry. Kyle delicately stroked her hair, "Okay—So you called your mom and she didn't answer. Is there anyone else you can call to help?"

Jenny kept her head down, shook it back and forth. Kyle gently lifted her up and kissed her forehead.

"What time is the presentation Jenny?" asked Kyle.

"Twelve-thirty," Jenny replied in a small, tearful voice.

"Come on, get dressed. Let's go!" Kyle said in a positive, take-charge kind of way as he stood up. "It's nine-thirty; we have less than three hours to get to your father."

"How, Kyle? How?" Jenny's sniffing voice pleaded with Kyle, hoping that he could maybe instil the situation with some hope.

"My uncle, Daniel, works at the small city airport for Fastjet Airline. They have planes that leave every hour on the half hour to where your parents live. If we can get that ten-thirty flight, it's a forty-five-minute trip so we'll be there in plenty of time to get to the hotel and—"

Jenny wiped her eyes and shook her head in bewilderment at Kyle's knowledge of flights and times. "—Do you have another job I don't know about? Because that sounded like an advertisement."

"Do you think it will work?" Kyle asked.

"Oh yes, yes, Kyle!" Jenny joyously jumped up. "Wait!" She landed, frozen on the spot, but still swaying slightly from side to side like a sprinter waiting for the starting pistol to go off.

"What's wrong, Jen?" asked Kyle gently.

Jenny didn't answer him. Her eyes were darting back and forth in a pensive, calculating way.

And then as if the starting pistol had gone off, Jenny burst from the starting line and blasted off to her bedroom. But, almost in a millisecond, she ran back out into the kitchen and directly towards Kyle. He smiled and held his arms open, ready for Jenny to dive into.

Yet, she stopped a few feet in front of him. Then, in the clearest and the most cohesive voice Jenny had had all morning, she said, "I knew, I just knew the moment you walked into that studio to accompany my singing class and sat at that piano in that funny blue and yellow striped shirt and played 'Here Comes The Sun', I knew...I just knew I'd fall in love with you, Mr. Kyle Le," and with that, she ran back into her room, leaving Kyle standing there with his arms opened wide.

"Are you sure your father wants to be stopped from talking?" Kyle shouted through the closed bedroom door.

But there was no answer to his question. He looked down and realised he was wearing the same shirt he had worn that first day he met Jenny, a few months ago in her classroom.

Kyle turned to Jenny's bedroom door and added, "Hey, and what's so funny about this shirt?"

16. PRESENT DAY – AT THE HOTEL

"Six more?" Greg Wong almost shouted into his cell phone. "Who told you this?" He looked up to make sure no one saw his loud reaction and then lowered his voice. "They just quit? But that's what today's for: to show them...to show them they don't have to worry. It's a partnership...a partnership. Did you tell them? Okay...okay...I know...How many is that so far?"

Greg shut his eyes as he listened. His body sagged against the wall. "All right. Don't worry, just get here. We're going to make this work, starting today—Okay. See you soon."

"Partnering" was the term Greg always used in discussing the transition of the three companies becoming one. But on paper it wasn't a partnership or a merger; the simple fact was Elevation was buying Linkup and Metronome. And as much as Greg Wong tried to reassure all the employees that there would be no downsizing or jobs lost, there were still lots of grumbling and resentment brewing within the three companies.

The acquisition had been in negotiations for over a year and had only been finalized two months ago. Today's event brought all the employees of the three companies together for the first time. Greg had spent a small fortune arranging this day because he was aware that the main failure of most acquisitions was due to employee turnover. It was not uncommon for many employees to quit when their company was bought by a bigger one because people tended to lose their desire and drive to work for an organization that would willingly sell its own vision and direction to another.

Since the news of the partnership had been released, some key personnel at Linkup and Metronome had already given their notices and now he just heard six more had quit. So Greg Wong was on a mission today: he was not going to lose one more employee. He wanted everyone to understand exactly what was happening and to view this big change not as an acquisition, or even a merger, but as a partnership, and stress that each company would maintain its own focus, direction and independence. That was why he loved Monique's idea of redesigning Elevation's logo from graph lines to three distinct mountains, all standing independently, but forming a beautiful landscape together.

The plans for Robert to speak at Monique's company's event had been negotiated a few months before Robert's last climb. Even after the news of Robert's accident, Greg had never considered finding someone else to speak at the event. Monique agreed and had planned everything about this day meticulously. She had not left much to chance. As much as she believed doing this talk could be very therapeutic for Robert, she also wanted to make it as easy for him as possible. She designed Robert's talk around the most stunning visuals of his climbs and his life's work. She had put the presentation in such an order that all Robert really had to do was to go from photo to photo and talk a little about each one. She had inserted music to underscore certain dramatic and even comedic moments. She interspersed certain quotes that would hopefully inspire and move the audience throughout the presentation.

Monique had left only one thing to chance and that was the hope that, by today, Robert would be excited to be here and maybe even feel a little passionate about talking and sharing his life and accomplishments. But that hope was becoming more and more remote as she looked across the stage and saw her husband sitting there with his head hung low, looking completely disinterested.

The entrance doors to the hall crashed open with a huge spontaneous cheerful sound. All at once, the room was filled with a dozen of Monique's laughing co-workers. Lou Zheng, a tall overweight Chinese man probably not older than thirty-three, was the only man in the group. Lou was Elevation's top salesman and number one clown slash magician of the office. It seemed that everyday Lou had a new magic trick that he used to accentuate some hilarious story. What made Lou such a successful salesman was how he used his magic in sales pitches and how he was not beneath divulging some of his secrets in order to close a deal. Lou once made a three-million-dollar sale in a single afternoon and did it without even showing the client how Elevation's software worked. He made those cool millions by showing ten managers in a small boardroom how the incredible illusion of making a coin pass through a glass table worked.

And this morning, Lou had his captive audience in tears of laughter. Holding a huge pair of men's briefs in his hand, Lou was making it look as if he had just pulled his own underwear off without removing his pants. What made it funnier was that the briefs could have fit an elephant. And now Lou was asking for a volunteer so he could magically pull their underwear out. All the women were pointing at each other laughing until someone looked up the stage and said, "Try it with Monique."

That made the happy group turn to Monique and Robert.

"Well, Mrs. Sanchez," Lou asked Monique, still holding the humongous underwear in his hand. "Shall we see what you're wearing?"

The explosive force of energy that came from her co-workers, who were so buoyantly full of that giddy out-of-the-office joy, instantly flung Monique out of her deep, desperate thoughts.

Seeing the enormous underwear, she smiled and then completely surprised herself by replying to Lou's comment, "Sorry, you might be disappointed. I don't wear anything that small."

Monique's response brought down the house. The women squealed and roared with laughter and some clapped at Monique's witty comeback. Monique's eye caught Robert, who still hadn't moved. His back still faced the gang of workers at the front of the stage.

"Hey, Mr. Sanchez," Lou said, "is that really true?" as he held up the huge briefs. "Monique's undies are bigger than these?" That stirred up a bit more laughter, but it quickly quieted down as Robert did not turn around or respond to Lou at all.

Robert had met Lou and most of the women over the years at different company events: Christmas parties, company picnics and some work friends' visits to their home. Yet no one, not one person from Monique's office, had seen Robert since his accident. Today would be the first time they would to see him as he was now: legless and in a wheelchair.

The awkward quiet was quickly filled by the gang of merry workers, who said things like:

"Oh, hi, Robert!"

"Great to see you!"

"You look wonderful!"

"Looking forward to listening to you."

"Long time no see..."

Robert still did not turn around.

Monique tried to cover her husband's non-responsiveness. "He's focusing," then whispered, "He's pretty nervous."

"Oh, sure, of course...For sure...Okay...Good luck, Robert!" everyone said in low hushed tones and then the group started to quickly drift away into the hall and mingle with the other employees who were coming into the Leaning Tower of Pisa.

"Knock 'em dead, Robert. I know you will," Lou said cheerfully.

"Thanks, guys," Monique said with a forced smile and watched the laughing group turn and dissolve into the stream of people now entering the room.

Amir tapped Monique on the shoulder. "Is there anything else, because I need to put some ambiance music on now. People are coming in."

"No, that's great, Amir. Thank you so much."

Amir disappeared behind his sound table and switched on some music. The volume was quite low, but still present enough that the lyrics of the song spoke to Monique.

A soft, *"One, two..."* sounded and then came the words. They spoke of time and wanting to be let in. A fast paced guitar strummed as the tempo kept building.

She walked back towards Robert, who just sat there in his now familiar, sad and pathetic pose.

The song begged for someone to unlock a door because—because they are waiting. Chris Martin sang with a whispered ache. At that moment, Monique knelt in front of Robert. The room was filling with the sound of chatter and laughter, almost drowning out Coldplay's lyrics, but Monique lifted her head and strained to listen. The words were so...so familiar to her.

She knew waiting all too well. Waiting for the months to pass as Robert summited his mountaintops. Waiting for Robert to come home. To come together. To have him pour his thoughts and feelings into her and her into him. To connect once more. And now, since the return from his fateful accident, she had been waiting once more. Waiting for her lover to come back to their bed. Waiting—just waiting for some part of her husband that she could just hold onto again. To touch...touch...touch anything again. Just a word, a sign, anything. She waited so patiently for him to come back—not just back to his life, but back to an 'us'—a life together.

Kneeling before him, Monique boldly took a chance and put her hand gently on Robert's leg. Robert had given her so many excuses about why he didn't want her to touch his legs: he wasn't ready, his legs were in too much pain, they still needed more time to heal...but the plain fact was Monique had yet to see her husband's naked legs since they had been amputated.

The pleading romantic ache of Coldplay flowed into the room: A story of waiting for that someone—a tale about that someone they would wait for.

"Roberto," Monique called out as tenderly as she could. Seldom had she ever called him by that name. Robert told her he simply didn't like being called Roberto, that it made him feel too ethnic and like he was still a kid because that was the only name his parents ever called him. But since the man wouldn't answer, today Monique tried to reach the little boy and so she repeated, "Roberto, I need you today...I really need your help."

But Robert didn't look up. He just said, "Can we please get off this stage now?" But then he looked at the staircase. He thought about the difficulty that it would present in the Leaning Tower of Pisa, which was almost half filled with employees of all three companies now. He couldn't stand the sickening thought of having all those people watch him being carried down.

"No, let's go behind that curtain there," he said.

"But Bobby, you don't speak for two hours," Monique's voice filled with the sound of pleading.

"Well, I don't see any ramp and I'm not—Look, you go and do what you want. I'm just going to stay up here!"

Robert turned his chair and swiftly moved towards the side of the stage behind the red velvet curtains, leaving Monique alone, kneeling in the centre of the stage.

As she watched him wheel away, Monique put her hands on the floor to help lift herself to her feet. Despite feeling the sting of Robert's harsh reaction, she still smiled ever so slightly herself. *Thank God!* she thought. *If he's staying on the stage then it means he's not leaving. At least, not yet. Maybe, just maybe, he did hear the words "I need you...I need your help."*

A burst of laughter once again shot out from the middle of the room. It seemed as if Lou had now pulled Greg's underwear out from behind him and handed it to Linkup's president. "See, here at Elevation, we have nothing to hide!" Seeing Linkup's president's hearty laugh, Greg's trepidation about the day left him momentarily. He walked behind Lou and slapped him on his back.

"Thanks, Lou. You have no idea how much I needed to see that. Don't know how you do it, but you have a way of always making it seem like everything will be all right. Don't know what I'd do without you!"

Monique pulled a chair and moved it beside her husband's wheelchair. Robert didn't look at her. From the other side of the stage, Amir watched her sit down and when they caught each other's eyes, Amir gave her an is-there-anything-I-can-do-for-you look. Monique returned with a calm shake of the head and a hopeful wink.

17. PRESENT DAY – AT THE AIRPORT

Kyle paid the cab driver and ran after Jenny into the airport. It was a small building that served only two airlines that ran domestic commuter and cargo flights. One complaint many people had was that the airport had only two check-in counters to serve customers and this often meant long line-ups and waiting that sometimes resulted in missed flights. This morning was no exception. As Jenny and Kyle bounced up the flight of escalator stairs and turned the corner, they were met with two lines with about twenty to thirty people in each.

Jenny was panting and a bit winded when she reached the line-ups. "Oh my God, Kyle! We'll *never* get on that ten-thirty flight. It's ten o'clock already! By the time we reach the counter there won't be enough time to even board the plane!"

"Wait here, Jen, I'll see if I can find my uncle. I hope he got my message—"

Kyle ran to the front of the two lines. His uncle Daniel was nowhere in sight. Then he looked through the small glass windows on the doors that led to the security and boarding area. Still no luck! He tried to get the attention of one of the check-in servers, but she looked harried and was dealing with a difficult customer. Kyle pulled out his cell phone, pushed some keys and waited for an answer. Nothing!

"Get to the back of the line, buddy!" said a man in an impeccably tailored suit.

"I'm not—"

Another passenger anxiously waiting in line cut off Kyle. "—Yeah, we all have to wait!"

"I've been here for forty minutes," said a businessman who was

68

about sixth in the line-up.

Kyle walked to the back of the unfriendly line-up and was greeted with Jenny's sad and worried face.

"Jen," he said, "if we can't get on the one at ten thirty, do you still want to go?"

"Of course, Kyle. I have to—"

"—Sorry...Shhh...Jen," Kyle gently interrupted Jenny. "Listen..." They both looked up as if they could listen better that way to the announcement system.

"Kyle Le and party, please report to check-in counter one. Kyle Le and party, please report to check-in counter one."

Smiles sprang onto Jenny and Kyle's faces.

"That must be my uncle. Quick!" Kyle took Jenny's hand and they ran to the front of the line.

Standing next to the woman serving at the check-in counter was Daniel Le, Kyle's uncle. He was dressed in a suit that was the same colours as the airline's bluish grey. Daniel was not smiling and he was looking very stern as Kyle and Jenny approached the side of the line. Daniel took a step towards the wall, as far from the line up as he could and motioned for Jenny and Kyle to meet him there.

Just as Kyle was about to say, "Uncle," Daniel cut him off with a very matter-of-fact question. "You are Kyle Le?"

Jenny looked at Kyle with a concerned oh-no-what's-wrong look.

"Yes," Kyle said, looking at his uncle with the most incredulous what-the-hell's-wrong-with-you look.

"Good," Daniel said in a very official voice. "You will find everything here." He handed Kyle an envelope. Then, in a louder, more projected voice than Kyle thought necessary, Daniel said, "We are so sorry for your delay. We hope this can make up for everything."

Kyle was perplexed. His uncle was acting like he was a stranger. He was just about to ask his uncle what was wrong when Jenny looked back to see the worn, tired faces of the waiting travellers, and caught on.

"Yes, thank you. It has been a very difficult twenty-four hours."

Kyle was now totally flummoxed but Jenny put her hand on Kyle's arm and said, "It's okay, honey. It's okay."

Daniel walked Jenny and Kyle to the counter. A mother and her young daughter were just about to be served at the counter, but after overhearing the conversation between Daniel, Jenny and Kyle, the mother turned to her child and said, "Come here, Claire. These two have waited longer than us." They both took a step back and the mother waved to Kyle and Jenny, indicating they should go before them.

"That is most kind, madam. And you too, little princess," said

Kyle.

"My name's Claire," the little girl said proudly.

"Well, Claire, we will always remember your kindness. Oh, and your mum's too!" Jenny said, bowing her head slightly to the young girl and her mother.

Daniel went behind the counter and said to the woman, "These are the two I was telling you about."

"Of course, Mr. Le. Sir, your tickets please?" the woman asked Kyle.

Kyle looked at his uncle with a questioning smile and his uncle gestured at the envelope in Kyle's hand. Kyle opened it up and there he pulled out four vouchers for Fastjet Airline. Kyle took them out and handed them to the woman.

"Just two, sir. The other two are for the return flight."

As the woman was processing the check-in information for Jenny and Kyle, the man with the impeccably tailored suit was at the other counter. He turned to Kyle and said, "Sorry, buddy...about what I said. I didn't know...you looked like you were trying to...*uh*...cut in."

"No problem, sir. We are all on a bit of an edge when travelling," Kyle said.

"Anyway, have a good flight, buddy."

"You too, sir," replied Kyle.

"And here are your boarding passes," the woman at the counter said. "Your flight is boarding now."

"That's fine, thank you, Barbara," Daniel said to the checkout woman. "I'll escort them."

As they passed through security, Kyle tried to talk to his uncle, but Daniel raised his fingers to his lips and said, "Later."

Quietly, the two of them went through security. Jenny smiled and whispered, "Your uncle Danny seems to be a wonderful person." Kyle looked over to his uncle, who was waiting for them on the other side of the security gate and smiled at him, but he was still acting like Kyle was just another passenger he was helping.

As soon as they passed through the gate, Daniel joined them and said, "Follow me this way."

They passed through a large waiting room with many business-type passengers. They were all reading a newspaper or staring at some electronic device. Daniel took their boarding passes and handed them to the person collecting them at the gate. The security agent scanned them and handed them back to Jenny, who put them in her purse.

Then they followed Daniel down a long winding hallway. As they passed the first turn, Daniel opened the door and waved Jenny and Kyle

70

into a small room that was empty except for a couple of chairs.

As the door closed behind them, Daniel raised his arms for a hug and exclaimed, "Special K, so happy to see you!"

Kyle opened his arms and hugged his uncle. But then Daniel pulled Kyle from his embrace. "And *really*, is this the only way we get to see you now?"

"Thank you, Uncle Danny, thank you!" rejoiced Kyle, relieved to finally be greeting the playful uncle he had always known.

Daniel's eyes then turned to Jenny. "Ah, is this her, Kyle? The reason we haven't seen you in months? The incredible song bird you told me about?"

"Hi, Uncle Danny," Jenny said. Daniel turned to his nephew with an approving smile.

"Sorry about the official business back there, but we must respect the people waiting. Don't want to provoke an angry mob. "

"Thank you so much. I will repay whatever the cost is," Jenny said.

"What! After your incredibly long twenty-four-hour wait?" Uncle Danny said with a hearty laugh. "Oh, you my dear, were superb! Twenty-four hours...haha! And the tickets are free. Please don't worry; I do get some perks with this job you know! Oh my gosh, look at the time. You have only ten minutes! Please you must go!"

Daniel opened the door and Jenny and Kyle walked out into the hall. Daniel pointed the way. "It's just around that corner and, Kyle, come and visit soon. My children need their Special K! And Jenny, of course, you are most welcome anytime."

Just as Kyle was about to go and hug his uncle goodbye, the mother and her daughter Claire passed them by. So to keep up the charade, Kyle reached out his hand and shook his uncle's hand and said, "Mr. Le, Fastjet Airline has no idea how lucky they are to have someone like you."

"Safe travels, you two." Daniel waved as Kyle and Jenny followed the mother and daughter to the entrance.

Jenny turned to Kyle and asked, "Special K?"

"Don't ask," Kyle said.

Jenny wrapped her arm around Kyle. "I like it...I think I'm going to call you that too."

Kyle laughingly rolled his eyes as they made their way to the small line waiting to board the plane. There were about six people waiting. The last three were the man in the impeccably tailored suit, the little girl Claire, and her mother.

As Jenny and Kyle approached the line, Jenny nervously started humming *"Leaving on a Jet Plane."* The line moved quickly and just as the stewardess asked for Kyle and Jenny's boarding passes, the little girl Claire looked up at Jenny and said, "Hey, that's my daddy's song!"

"Really, it's your daddy's song?" Jenny asked.

"Yes, my daddy sings it to me every time he has to go on a plane."

Jenny and Kyle laughed but Jenny's smile vanished as she opened her purse to reach for the boarding passes and saw the red journal.

"But this time we are on the plane! I'm going to see Daddy. We're going to surprise him, aren't we, Mommy?"

The mother turned around to her daughter. "Yes, honey. Now come on, we have to let everyone on the plane so they can sit down."

"Bye," Claire waved to Jenny. "We have to hurry to surprise Daddy."

Yeah, we have to hurry to surprise Daddy, too, Jenny thought as she and Kyle entered the plane. *I just hope we're not too late!*

18. PRESENT DAY – AT THE HOTEL

The Leaning Tower of Pisa was quickly filled with all the employees of Elevation, Linkup and Metronome.

Robert had manoeuvred himself behind the huge red curtain at the side of the stage, just far enough to be hidden from anyone's view. And for the last ten minutes, he and Monique had silently sat beside each other, not taking much notice of any of the lively room's occupants.

She closed her eyes and drifted. *If only, if only we could go back in time. Just six months. Oh, remember how we both so looked forward to this day, happily anticipating how special it was going to be! We would have been busy setting the stage and Bobby would be teasing me and constantly reminding me not to worry. It would be so much fun; we would mingle, and he would joyfully tell everyone little stories and anecdotes about how hard I worked on the event. He and Lou would probably be competing on who had the funnier story about the last company Christmas party. And all the questions people would ask: "What's it like on top of the world?" and, "How cold is it? Were you scared? Where do you go to pee up there?" Oh, and how we would move—dancing with anticipation throughout the room...everyone we pass telling Bobby, "Can't wait to hear your talk, Mr. Sanchez!"* Yes, Monique couldn't wait for this day to come.

But there was no magical time machine that could transport them to that wonderful future she had happily anticipated. *Feeling anticipation can be so cruel now.* She sighed deeply. Happy and anticipation were words that no longer came together. Because she knew when she opened her eyes, they would both be in the same position they had found themselves so many times in the last six months: sitting beside one another, waiting, anticipating an unknown future that lay ahead of them. Anticipating the test results. A doctor's words. Waking in a recovery room. And with each waiting anticipation, fewer words would be shared. One anticipation after another, enormous conversations were left unspoken. And now, the only thing they had in common was the new silence they were hatching together.

Monique let out a long sigh, wishing to exhale every depressing thought that sat inside her. *I need to focus. I need to think. Okay, think of how the day will play out. Soon, Greg will come up on the stage and talk for ten minutes...then the other two presidents from Metronome and Linkup will speak for another ten minutes...There was about an hour's worth of information on how this partnership was going to work...that's an hour and twenty minutes...and then it will be time for the keynote speaker, Robert.* Monique glanced at her watch: *Ten past ten. But we'll probably start late, by ten or fifteen minutes. So it will probably be close to twelve when Robert's talk starts...but they wanted lunch to start at twelve thirty....so that's pretty tight.*

Calculating the timetable was helping distract Monique from her grief, but was also starting to make her quite anxious.

Monique brought her hands to her face and rubbed the sides of her head in a circular fashion. Nothing, it seemed, was going to ease the nervousness welling up inside her. Then she tried taking some slow, deep breaths. Nothing was helping. She remembered this anxious state, had felt it before. *How many times have I felt this kind of nervousness before Jenny was about to sing?* All those numerous singing recitals and contests where she and Robert sat anxiously, waiting for Jenny to come out on an empty stage to sing.

The two of them would always hold hands. Their hands would grip tighter together as their only child's voice soared and then even tighter, when little Jenny reached for notes that she unfortunately sometimes missed.

Yet, her memory wasn't about Jenny's singing or whether or not she'd been successful in the various recitals and contests they'd attended over the years. What Monique remembered most about those moments was that feeling of 'together'. It was in those moments that the two of them, as one, would direct every ounce of their being, their attention, their love, to the little one who was usually alone on the stage, baring her soul for all to see.

Silently in the dark, they would sit watching Jenny. And even if something miraculous, or disastrous, occurred with Jenny's performance and Monique felt as if her heart was about to beat out her chest, Robert would always gently lift their entwined hands and put them to his lips. Not kissing them, just breathing soft and slow as if to warm them and ease her heart back into her chest. It was his way of saying, "Don't worry, she's not alone, you're not alone, I'm here with you both."

There was that one night in their favourite restaurant after one of Jenny's recitals that Monique had declared, "When you are up there, Jenny, and your father and I are watching you—It's so...so—It's hard to describe, but I have to tell you that's when I feel the most alive!"

"*Whoa*, what?! Wait a minute!" Robert raised his hand in mock anger. "I thought that was my special thing!"

"What, Dad, what's your special thing?" Jenny laughed.

"'Feeling most alive!' is what she said about me, when I first met your mother!"

"Yeah, we know, Dad, we know. It was in a bookstore."

"Okay, Little Miss Smarty Pants, what was the book she stole out of my hands?"

"The Alchemist, *and* it was the last copy in the store! *And* you had it in your hands and mom grabbed it!" Jenny had heard this story many times before.

"Okay, wait a second," Monique interrupted her daughter. "First, I didn't steal or grab anything. I asked your father, very nicely, if he wanted to be a gentleman and let me have the last copy!"

"Oh, no you didn't," Robert said, turning to Jenny and re-enacting the scene. "Your mother's exact words to me were, 'Do you know the premise of the book?'" He smiled at Monique, eyes twinkling with the memory, and continued, "I told her it was about a shepherd boy and about him finding his purpose in life, right? And then your mom says to me, like she's the author herself, 'It's called Personal Legend, not purpose; and it's about finding true love and it says, 'when you really desire something, the universe comes together to help you achieve it' and I really want that book, so thank you for helping me achieve that!' And then she just took the book right out of my hands and walked away."

Jenny turned to her mother, "Really, Mom did that? I can't believe it! Really! Mom, you did that?"

"Well, kind of." Monique smiled. "But your father came running after me and said, 'Well, I want that book too, so how is the universe going to help me achieve that if there's only one book?' So I told him 'Okay, then let's read it together!'"

"Read it together? Mom, you picked Dad up? You picked up a total stranger in a bookstore? You never told me this part."

"That's because, Little Rock, you were too young for that part then—" Robert chimed in. "So, it's about three weeks later, your mom and I were sitting in a subway station waiting for the next train. And sitting there on that bench, we finished the book. And the moment after I read the last line of the book, the next train came and stopped. So I got up, but she grabbed my coat and pulled me back down onto the bench and said, 'Let's wait for the next train,' and she took the book, opened it up and asked me to re-read the last line, which I did. And then, well, your mother, she took the book and put it in her bag and didn't say anything. I said, 'So we missed that train because you wanted to hear the last line again?' She said to me,

'No, it wasn't finished because after you read the last line I needed to tell you something.' Then she turned to me and said, 'I love you.' And it had only been three weeks since we'd met, so I asked her how she knew she was sure. And that's when, Jenny, your mother put her hand right here on my chest and said to me, 'I know because when I'm with you, Roberto Sanchez, that's when I feel most alive!'"

"Monique, Monique!"

Suddenly she was thrust from her poignant memories back into the Leaning Tower of Pisa. "Excuse me, Monique. I need to talk to you for a moment."

Monique automatically bounced up and walked to the front of the stage to meet Greg.

"Monique, sorry to interrupt you and your husband's preparations but I can't find Shelley. She was supposed to make sure all the employees of each company were spread out amongst one another. And there are no place cards on the tables and it looks like we got three separate parties going on out there."

Monique looked out into the hall. Greg was right. It seemed like all the Elevation people were gathered to the right, and even though she didn't know any of the other company's employees, it was evident there were two other distinct groups that had formed on the left of the room and at the rear.

"When are we starting?" asked Monique as she crouched down to be at eye level with Greg, who was standing on the floor in front of the stage.

"We have to start in five minutes," replied a nervous sounding Greg. In all her eight years of working with Greg, Monique had never seen him so fidgety and worried looking.

"You know," Monique started tentatively, wanting to calm her worried boss, "maybe it's better this way, Greg, maybe it's better to have people in their comfort zone first instead of forcing them to sit with strangers and be somewhere they don't want to."

"Yes, yes, of course. Good idea, Monique! Okay, then let's just..." Greg was now terribly distracted and kept nodding his head up and down as he spoke. "Well, I guess that's why we hired your husband right? Let's just hope Robert can...uh, well, make us feel like a..." Greg was looking for the right words. "Yes, you know...help us to feel we are all climbing the same mountain...all going in the same direction...Thanks, Monique. Sorry I'm so jumpy. Really, thank you. Okay then, five minutes...Oh, can you get the soundman to raise the volume of the music? Maybe that will help! Thanks..."

She watched Greg walk away and noticed even his walk appeared restless. Monique moved to the sound table, towards Amir, who had his headphones on. She had to tap him on the shoulder to get his attention.

"Hi, Amir, we're starting in five minutes. Could you please make the music louder?" Amir smiled, nodded, put his finger on a lever and started to push it up.

"Mama Mia...Mama Mia..." got a little louder.

"Miss Monique, Abba's a good choice. Don't you think?"

Monique looked out into the hall. Amir was right. As the music got a little louder, people in groups started bouncing their heads and swaying, and of course it gave Lou another chance to pull out and swing the oversized underwear from side to side like a giant cheerleader's pompom.

She stopped and listened to the exuberant lyrics. The words 'just how much I've missed you,' seemed to catch her attention. For the first time that day, Monique felt as if the Leaning Tower of Pisa was showing a little, tiny, spark of life. It was just a small flickering ember, of course, but as she remembered the story of the little shepherd boy and his Personal Legend, "When you really desire something, the universe comes together to help you achieve it," she looked at her husband, who was still sitting there staring and clutching that mysterious brown leather bag, and she prayed the universe was still listening.

19. 8 WEEKS AGO – SEEMA'S OFFICE

"As promised, one Sanchez a la carte," Benny joked as he entered Seema's office with Robert in front of him.

As they entered the office, Robert immediately pulled away from Benny and wheeled himself directly to the window without even acknowledging Seema. They both watched Robert without saying a word. Seema waited for about ten seconds and then gestured to Benny that he could go. Benny pointed to his own mouth and made some sign language hinting to Seema that Robert still wasn't talking. He then waved and left the office.

Seema walked over and stood directly behind Robert. "You can really see that the change is just starting to happen, can't you?" she said.

Robert didn't reply.

"Last fall was beautiful. I think it was because of all the rain we had. The colours were just spectacular." Robert still didn't reply.

Seema picked up a book she had on her desk. "I have been reading this, Robert...*The Adventures of Sherlock Holmes*. Ever read it?"

Even though it was clear Robert wasn't going to answer, she still waited for a response each time she asked a question.

"It's a collection of short stories about Sherlock Holmes. And in the fourth story called *'The Boscombe Valley Mystery,'* I read this one line that just...well, it made me think of you, Robert. Seriously, I read it and immediately thought of you. Would you like to hear that line?"

Robert sat motionless as Seema thumbed through the book, found the page she was looking for and then read it out loud.

"Okay, all right, here it is: *There is nothing more deceptive than an obvious fact.*' And would you like to know why that made me think of you, Robert?"

Still Robert held his statue-like pose.

"I thought of you and the obvious fact of your silence. I mean, everyone here does everything they can think of to get you to talk. They sometimes go way beyond the call of duty to get you to respond, to just say one word. And yet, you don't say a thing. Nothing. You stay silent. But you see, Robert, I think the obvious fact of your silence is very deceptive."

Robert's head jerked to the side. He couldn't see Seema, who was standing directly behind him, but his movement showed her that he had heard what she said.

"You see, Robert, first, I'm thinking the obvious fact surrounding your silence is pretty straightforward. See, ever since that last operation, I think you are telling us that losing your other leg has affected you very, very much, right? And you are telling us that fact with your silence. And so, every time someone tries to get you to talk, you just end up prolonging your silence and repeating the same fact, which is that you are hurting! But that's not enough for you. You want to show everyone that they still don't get it; they still don't understand how much losing your legs has affected you. That seems to be the obvious fact, right? I mean, the fact is, you only stopped talking after the operation, correct? Now, the part I think is the deception is..."

Seema paused. Her prolonged pause caused Robert to turn his chair so he was now directly in front of her. Although his face was completely expressionless, he looked up, straight into Seema's eyes.

"I think the deceiving part is this..." she repeated. "That it doesn't matter how long you prolong your silence, because your silence just keeps repeating the same thing to us; that we don't know how much you hurt, right? And I think that's deceptive because if you know something that we don't know, well then, *talk, tell us what it is*! It's kind of deceiving to keep silent about something you want us to know. And then, no matter what we do to get you to talk, you never tell us. That's not fair, is it...that you just keep being silent?"

"Ahhh..." Robert let out an irritable gasping breath and angrily charged his way to the door to leave.

Seema called out to him, "Robert, are you a man of your word?"

Robert stopped the wheelchair and, without turning around, he said, "Another obvious fact you forgot, Miss Holmes, is that I didn't come here to have you hurt me more than I am already hurting."

"And how would I know that fact, Robert, unless you tell me?"

"Well there, I told you!" Robert started back out the door.

"No, I didn't ask you how much you hurt, I only asked if you are a man of your word?"

Robert turned around and raised his head in exasperation. "You just don't get it, do you? What the real fact is? The obvious fact is: *I. Don't. Want. To. Talk!*"

"But I need you to, Robert. *I need you to!* Look, Robert, I don't want to blackmail you or 'guilt you' into speaking with me, but I must remind you of your promise. You gave me your word that if I brought you to the hospital, you would speak to me and talk about anything I needed to know. Well, I filled my part of the bargain: I spoke to your wife and daughter. I took you to the hospital. And now I need to talk to you because, Robert, *this is my job!*"

"Well, it's not mine!" Robert wrapped his hands around the wheels of his chair and was out the door in three swift turns of the wheels. Seema lowered the yellow scarf from her head as she moved to her chair and sat down. She lowered her head upon the desk and rubbed her neck hard. As she raised her head, she saw Robert, sitting in the doorway of her office.

They looked at each other like two weary boxers who had just gone fifteen long grinding rounds. Robert spoke in an emotionless whisper, "Look, I've been losing a lot of things...and not just my goddamn legs. Frankly, you know what? I don't have any idea of what I still have." He paused, the defeat in his eyes evident. "But I've still got my word and that has to stand for...Look, I made a promise. Okay? So I'm here."

Seema pulled her yellow scarf back up onto her head. "Okay, Robert, and so am I."

20. PRESENT DAY – JENNY'S FLIGHT

"No, Kyle, please let me sit on the aisle." Jenny already felt a little claustrophobic and she knew sitting by the window would make her even more restless.

"Hey, we're neighbours." A happy little voice surprised Jenny as she sat down. It was Claire and her mother, who were sitting across the aisle from them. "We're fourteen C and D."

"Excuse me," Claire's mother spoke out. "Could you please do me a big favour and take down that orange bag above our seat? I forgot to get out a book for Claire. If I don't, she might talk your heads off."

"That's fine. Maybe my head needs to come off today."

Claire started giggling. "It won't really come off, will it?"

As Jenny smiled at the girl, she longingly wished she too could feel what that little girl felt: the excitement of going to surprise her father. She reached for the orange bag and handed it to Claire's mother.

"Thank you so much." The mother pulled out some books and asked her daughter which one she wanted.

"Dora! Dora!" Claire said, taking the book and hugging it before she laid it on her lap to read.

Dora the Explorer, Jenny said to herself, shaking her head with the wonder of the memory. She remembered the day her father came home with five or six *Dora the Explorer* books for her to read.

Jenny's father was fourth generation Argentinean; his parents never spoke Spanish and neither did he. But he had wanted his daughter to learn a little Spanish, so he got the Dora books because he'd been told they were helpful in introducing kids to Spanish.

Jenny was ten and had already started reading small novels so when she opened Dora's *Eggs for Everyone*, she'd complained to her father.

"Daddy, these are picture books...for little babies," she moaned.

"Oh my gosh!" Robert said, "but the bookseller insisted that these could definitely help us learn some Spanish."

Jenny's mother leaned over and looked at the book and laughed out loud. "Oh well, maybe you can return them?"

"Well, not really," Robert said sheepishly. "The 'bookseller' is actually a mother at my work who said her son didn't read them anymore so, I paid her twenty bucks for them."

"Who was this?" asked Monique.

"You know, Lisa," said Robert.

"Lisa Mildenburger?"

Robert nodded his head. "Yeah."

Monique laughed even louder now. "Robert, we just bought a birthday card for her son last week. You picked it out yourself, remember? *'Seven is heaven,' it* said. So if he is seven and doesn't read them anymore, why would you think..."

"Oh my gosh, yeah...right." Robert slightly slapped his forehead. "Just really never put two and two together, sorry Jen."

But as soon as Jenny heard this, she playfully leaped on the couch beside her father as she always did when she was younger and he read to her. She put the book on his lap, put her thumb in her mouth and in the cutest little baby voice said, "Daddy, read me...please now."

He played along and started reading but stopped after a few pages.

"Daddy, read a little more."

"It's okay, Little Rock, I know it's a little baby book...so let's go and..."

"No, Daddy, really, can you? I kind of want to find out who Boots gives his eggs too!"

And so in the following weeks, Dora became the after-supper ritual. Each night, the three of them took turns reading Dora out loud and learning all the Spanish words Dora could teach them.

Suddenly, Jenny was catapulted out of her memory as the plane's departure announcements of the safety rules came over the speakers. The flight attendant followed the taped announcement with precision, showing how to pull down the oxygen mask and how to click the seat belt.

Kyle put his hand gently on Jenny's knee. "You okay?"

"Did you ever read any of those books?" Jenny asked, pointing to the book Claire had opened up and was reading.

Kyle leaned down to look across the aisle and read the title of Claire's book—*Dora Climbs Star Mountain.*

"No, I never have. Say, Claire," Kyle leaned towards Claire, "do you mind if I read that book when you're finished?"

Claire didn't hear Kyle over the noise of the motors, as the plane started its take-off. Jenny smiled at Kyle's attempt to cheer her up. He had a gift of making Jenny always feel safe. Kyle sat up and pulled her close. Feeling the comfort of his arms, she dared to reach into her purse and pull out her father's red worn journal. She laid it down on her lap.

"So that's your dad's book...his journal?" Kyle asked.

"Well," Jenny said. "It was mine first. My dad bought this book in a gift shop at the hospital where I was born."

Kyle was treated to the story of how this book started its life within the Sanchez's family. Her mother was holding Jenny, who had been tucked away in her mother's womb only three hours prior. When her mother had drifted off to sleep, her father stopped off at the hospital's gift shop.

Upon returning, her father had placed Jenny in her mother's arms, held one hand behind his back, took his wee daughter's fingers with the other and said, "Well, my daughter, you are no longer a blank page because today, little Jennifer Alida Sanchez, today your story begins!" Just then, he pulled out the red book from behind his back as if it was the sweetest cuddly teddy bear and held it in front of his tiny precious daughter. Monique, who was still showing all the exhaustion of having survived twelve hours of labour, started to laugh.

"The story changes here," Jenny told Kyle. Sometimes her mother laughed until she cried with tears of joy. And sometimes, her mother told her dad, "You get back to that shop right now and get this child something furry that she can hug..." but usually the story had her mom frozen in disbelief, just staring at her dad incredulously while he explained to her how they would write all about her in this red book. "We'll call it '*The Book of Jenny*.'"

But her mother had already bought a couple of those time capsule books for recording all your child's major moments in life and so the red book sat unblemished on a shelf in Jenny's room until she was five. That was the first time Jenny used the book. It became a handy tray to serve tea at her teddy bear's tea party where it got marked with a dark yellow Kool-Aid stain. Apparently the blame fell on Winnie the Pooh, Jenny had said he was fooling around and ended up spilling his tea all over the cover and it left a strange R-shaped blot. But it was the odd shape of that stain that gave the red book its real purpose.

Everyone forgot about the book until it resurfaced again as a Christmas present Jenny gave her father.

"Look, Daddy, it even has your initial on it. Winnie put it there for you! You can write me and Mommy when you go climbing!"

So Robert did take it and started writing in his red book by journaling his climb up Mount McKinley in Alaska, in 1995. When Monique and Jenny picked up Robert from the airport after that trip, the first thing Jenny asked was, "What did you write us, Daddy? What did you write us?"

Robert realized that the journal was filled with many thoughts and things that were inappropriate to share with a five-year-old, so he told Jenny that he had lost the book. She cried and made such a fuss at the airport that he quickly bought her another red book on the way home and told her she would be a better keeper of the book and she could use it to write him the next time he was gone.

When Jenny was twelve and was helping her father get ready to climb Mt. Denali, she spotted her father tucking the red book in his knapsack. She recognized it immediately and started jumping up and down in celebration. "Daddy, you found it! You found it! You found *The Book of Jenny!*"

And so, her father came clean about the red book.

"Little Rock," he had said, "I think it's time to tell you that Daddy never lost this book. I mean, really, did you think I would ever lose *The Book of Jenny*? But you see, Daddy has written lots of stuff that you are not really old enough to read or understand."

"Oh, Daddy," she begged with those big, open, huggable eyes. "I am old enough now...I read the Secret Garden, Charlotte's Web and the whole Little House series already and they are way bigger than that red book!"

"Oh, Jenny, there is nothing more I would want to do but share this with you. But you'll have to wait. First, it's not finished yet; there are still so many empty pages to fill and more mountains to climb. And if I give it to you now, I won't have anything left to give you for your inheritance."

"What's an inheritance?" Jenny asked.

"It's something someone gets after someone dies," Robert explained.

"*What?*" Jenny said with her face all scrunched up, disliking the sound of what her father was saying.

"Well, some people leave money for their kids..." Robert stopped himself. Even he didn't like the sound of this.

But Jenny got it right away. "You are only going to give this to me to read after you're *dead?*" she said, each word a little louder than the one preceding it until the last word, 'dead,' came out almost in a scream.

"Well, then I'm never reading it!" And with that, little Jenny got up, left her parents' bedroom and closed the door as loudly as she could, for effect.

Jenny and her father never really spoke about the red book again, but Jenny asked her mother why her dad wouldn't let her read his journal. Her mom always gave the same answer:

"Ask your father."

"Yeah, but he wants to be dead when I read it though—"

Jenny stopped talking and she put the journal on Kyle's lap.

"Are you okay?" Kyle asked softly.

Jenny was pale and a little short of breath as she responded, "Yes, I think so...Yeah, I am. I haven't thought about that book for years. I don't even know if he still brought it to the mountains with him."

She and Kyle looked down at the book on her lap and then at each other at the same time.

"Do you want to look inside?" Kyle asked.

"I do, Kyle, I do. But it's like, I'm too afraid to know..."

"So then I'll read it to you. I mean, if you want me to," said Kyle in a gentle, caring voice.

Jenny pouted her lips and softly agreed.

Kyle lifted the red ribbon that kept the book bound. He slowly turned the hard book cover to reveal the first page. There it was, the same horrible handwriting that she had teased her father about so many times. But in the overwhelming emotion of the moment, Jenny found the words were just a blur. She picked up the book and handed it to Kyle and said, "Please read...thank you, Kyle."

Kyle held the open book in one hand and pressed the pages down with the other as if he was a blind man preparing to read Braille.

"Hey, Jen, look! There's a quote here on the cover. It says, '*There never was a time when you or I did not exist. Nor will there be any future when we shall cease to be—Bhagavad Gita.*' What's that, Jen?"

"I'm not sure, Kyle...What's the first date my dad started writing?"

"May 23rd 1995, Mt. McKinley. Are you sure you want me to read?"

Jenny sighed and leaned into Kyle. "Yes, yes please."

Dearest heart,
*   Well, here are the first words in the 'Book of Jenny'. ONE whole world of a story that you and I*

created! Do you remember when I first got this book? Little Rock was only a couple of hours old. I'm smiling now thinking of what you said then. Do you remember? Well, you were pretty mad and...well, you ordered me out of the room and said, "You go and get your little girl a teddy bear, something she can actually hug!!!" and I guess you were right because she still has that bear!

You know, I've never kept a diary in my life so I'm feeling a bit...not sure what...maybe awkward? What should I write? Am I writing to me? Who's going to read this anyway? You know, I always thought people that kept diaries or journals (grown-up diaries!) were mostly people who were alone and didn't have anyone to tell all their deep dark thoughts to, so they wrote it down...Hmmm...hey, I guess that's me at the moment, isn't it!

Okay, so I'm sitting completely alone in this tent and, without any wind tonight, the only thing making any sounds of life is the scratching of this pencil.. But you know, love, when I'm alone like this...and this kind of alone on the side of some mountain is so special because this aloneness seems to bring me closer to everything that makes up my life...Sometimes I see things clearer up here—all the whys of me seem to be living out their answers...

A lot of climbers say they feel the presence of God when they are so close to the top and some feel they can talk to God up here...And you know I believe in a god...yet, who do I talk to sitting on these ledges? Even writing this diary, which is supposed to be all my own private thoughts...Who do I talk to? Who do I reach out to...you!

Remember that poster Little Rock had on her bedroom door—"Don't forget to be awesome!" That's another thing I find up here...it's that amazing sense of awe....And do you recall when Jenny first saw that poster, she didn't even know what that word meant but she had to have it because she loved the colours and then after we hung it, she asked us what "awesome" was? Do you remember what you told her?

I don't remember it word for word but it was something like this: you said Awe is something we find...or something we can create...and...if we live being awe-some then somehow it touches who we really are—because then we find all these little bits of ourselves—for each time you feel, touch or see anything that actually awes you, you will then feel a reason to exist!....And then you said to her that feeling awe is just like...feeling real love. Well, Monique, then you should know...you are all awe to me!

It's the last night before we summit...Don't worry, the weather is perfect and 14 climbers have already returned from successful summits...I know we have argued about why I have to climb mountains and I know I will never be able to give you an answer that satisfies you about why I feel I have to do this...yet. Yesterday at supper, one of the climbers told us he was writing a book on why people climb. He has done lots of interviews and found that no one really has the same answer...He said some do it for the challenge, some to find themselves, kind of like they hope they are going to find some deep answer that is buried inside them...Some do it for the adrenaline rush and some...to get away from the world or their own lives...

But I think I'm here because most of us exist in the world which is mostly human made—in a world of TVs and computers, we tend to forget that there are places on this planet which do not respond to the flick of a switch...that these mountains exist without us...and I guess I'm one of those that feel a need to sometimes exist with them.

"Who's your dad writing to?" Kyle asked Jenny.

"That's my mom. My dad has given me a lot of names over the years but 'dearest heart,' well, that's only Mom."

"Wow! So his journals are...like love letters to your mom?"

21. PRESENT DAY – AT THE HOTEL

"So I guess the real question is, how will each of us face the challenge of this change? But, I also acknowledge that this change will, of course, take time. If we want the three companies to feel as if we are one team, then we must move forward with patience," Greg said, trying to end his speech with energy and flourish.

Greg was not prepared to begin the day this way. He had hoped to have both Metronome and Linkup's presidents on stage with him for this speech. But ten minutes ago, he was informed that Mario Romano from Linkup was delayed and would be close to an hour late. Greg knew he could not wait an hour, so was attempting to energize the room, then do the one-hour work session, and follow it by Robert's talk. After lunch, he would bring the other two presidents on stage with him and present the bigger message.

Yet, it had been rough going so far. Right from the moment he opened his mouth to welcome everyone, he felt a very obvious lack of excitement in the room. So Greg pulled out his famous "I'm-the-Boss" joke, which always proved to be very effective with new employees, showing them that he didn't take being the boss too seriously. Greg smiled as he spoke.

"Do you know what happened to me yesterday?" He asked the question like an old vaudevillian comedian would, hoping the audience would all ask, "What?"

But the room was still unfocused, people at some tables were whispering to each other and not all faces were even facing the stage. So he spoke a little louder, in a more pronounced way, to get everyone's attention.

"Do you know what happened to me yesterday?"

No one answered him, but at least the room was now quiet.

"Yesterday, I was complaining in our staff meeting that I wasn't getting any respect. So later that morning, I went to a local sign shop and bought a small sign that read 'I'm the Boss!' and just before lunch, I taped that sign to the middle of my office door. I wanted to give people a chance to read it while I was out of the office and then see if anything would change. Well, anyway, later when I returned from lunch, I found that someone had taped one of those post-it-notes on my 'I'm The Boss' sign. And do you know what it said?"

Greg could see all eyes were now on him. So he paused a moment before hitting the punch line. And with a dead-pan voice he said, "The post-it-note said, 'Mr. Wong, your wife called, she wants her sign back!'"

Greg had told this joke a handful of times at work and it always got a hearty laugh and he thought since the room was two-thirds full with people that didn't know him, the joke would go over well.

Yet other than a few polite haha's and Lou's overly forced laugh, the room was awkwardly quiet.

Greg felt the blow of this silence and so he went off course and started spouting generic ramblings about how happy he was that the day had finally come for him to meet all the people that he and the Elevation team were going to climb to higher heights with. The more he spoke, the more he felt he was losing the room.

Greg was used to public speaking and had even taken a three-month Dale Carnegie course two years ago, when Elevation had gone on the stock exchange. As he was rambling, the other side of his brain was madly recalling what he had learned in that course about what to do when your speech was on a quick nosedive and crashing.

Just as he got to the point of saying that he and the Elevation team were going to climb to higher heights, *it hit him!* Make it personal. Make it real!

"Sorry everyone, I guess I'm rambling. You see, I'm quite nervous today. This new adventure excites me, but scares the hell out of me as well. Reminds me of when I was a little boy growing up in Hong Kong and, well, I was the tallest kid in my class."

Laughter! Ahhh, relief! This was probably due to the fact that Greg was barely five foot six. And the thought that everyone was shorter than him would seem funny to anyone listening.

Greg smiled and acknowledged the murmuring giggles. "Yeah, can you believe how small we all are back home if I'm the tall guy?" Again, *laughter*, he felt as if the room was warming up to him.

"Anyway, being the tallest kid in class, I was chosen to be on the basketball team. Now I've never played basketball in my life but I was *chosen.* Chosen for something...me! And boy, was I excited about that! So, I shot out of school that day, and just flew home. The moment the door opened I shouted out to my mom, my dad, my little sister and a couple of her friends, 'Guess what? I was chosen...Me, Gregory Wong, is going to be a basketball extraordinaire!' I don't even think my dad knew what basketball was but, man, he was just ecstatic...his *son* was chosen. I'm sure my father didn't really care what it was. Just hearing his son was chosen for something was like fulfilling his prophecy that his son would come to great things someday."

Greg then played the part of his father shaking his hand.

"My dad came to me grinning and shaking my hand up and down so fast, like he was trying to get that last drop out of a stubborn ketchup bottle. And my sister and her little friends were squealing with delight saying things about how I was going to be famous. And then my mother, who actually did know what basketball was, put her hand on my shoulder and said, 'Greggy, you don't play basketball, do you? Greggy, be realistic: you don't even play sports, do you?' Suddenly, the vision of me riding in that championship parade disappeared. My father stopped shaking my hand, my sister and her friends ceased the glorification of my celebrity status. Everyone froze and stared at me, wondering if their adoration of me was a little bit premature. But, I wasn't about to let the reality of my life interfere with the fame that awaited me. After all, I was the chosen one! I turned to my mom and said, 'Don't worry, Ma, I'm going learn,' and then I shouted out with glee that I was going to be the first kid from Hong Kong to play in the NBA! The parade was back on. My dad started shaking my hands again and I think I was asked to sign a couple autographs for one of my six-year-old sister's friends.

"Now my mom was right. Reality was going to show its ugly face sooner or later. She was dead on: I'd never played sports. My exercise consisted of having to constantly fix that nagging cable behind the monitor of our family computer that was always falling out while I was playing one of my computer games. Yet, being a chosen one was something new to me. That title...Well, it kind of thrust me into action. So, being the nerdy kid I was, if I was going to play basketball, I had to know everything about basketball: how it was played, its rules, how it evolved. I needed to know the complete history, the whole existence and evolution of basketball. So I went to the library, I studied and looked up everything I could get my hands on about basketball. I knew all the stats of every famous player, what a double dribble, a three pointer and a technical violation was. And then, one week before my very first basketball practise, my parents asked me how my road to the NBA was going. I told them everything I learned...Oh, my dad was so proud. He was absolutely blown away to learn that the last two months since being called 'the chosen one,' I had not wasted my time. He just kept repeating, 'my son...this is *my* son!' as I spouted off some unknown stats that would have made any NBA sports analyst proud. But my mom, even after hearing me shout out some of the most incredible intricate stats of the game itself, was...well, let's say, a little...no, actually, a lot...she was...ah, well, quite shocked to find out I had yet to even touch a basketball!"

The room roared with laughter and Greg was on a roll.

"That's when my mom, who always had a Chinese saying for everything, said," Greg said something in Chinese then continued, "which means, how can you get the tiger's cubs if you don't go into the tiger's cave? Which, translated is 'you may see what you want but that doesn't make it easy to achieve it. But in a less complex version, she was trying to tell me, 'get a ball, you idiot, and learn how to use it!'"

Greg laughed at himself and had fun imitating his mother's high-pitched voice.

"So, my mom walked me directly to the school. We got a ball and I started practising. And I started to understand what my mom meant: it is not easy getting close to those tiger cubs with the mother around because, despite the fact I knew who held the Guinness world record for everything related to basketball, I was completely unable to dribble the ball and run at the same time. And after three days and maybe six hours of trying to run and dribble the ball in the back alley of our building, I gave up and kicked the ball in frustration so high that it landed with a splash inside one of those garbage dumpsters in the alleyway. It made a big splash because that dumpster was filled with the garbage from the meat plant behind us. And, well, that was it. Chosen one or not, basketball was over and there was no way I was even going to go near that smelly dumpster. So, I cursed my way into the house in total impatience and pronounced, '*I quit!*'

"My mother, who had apparently been watching me from our apartment window, stopped me right at the door and, of course, had another Chinese saying: 'Be not afraid of going slowly, be afraid of standing still.'

"'Come on Mom, I can't play!' And then my mom kind of hit me with a sucker punch: 'I know, I have been watching you...' and said something that shocked me...she actually quoted something that *wasn't* Chinese! She said, 'Rome wasn't built in a day. Now you get back out there, pull that ball out of all those chicken guts and don't ask your little sister to do it for you! Now go Greggy, you get that ball and start learning how to play something you have been chosen for.'

"And I did and I played basketball for the next six years."

The room cheered and applauded. Greg raised a hand to quiet

them. The story was not finished.

"Now, unfortunately more reality came to show its face in one short year. Me, I, the tallest chosen one! Well, that changed! Everyone else grew, except me. Yep, I became the shortest guy on the team and I was usually the last player on the bench to ever get to play. I got on if we were losing badly, real bad...BUT they kept me on the team for the next five years. Do you know why? *Because*...the chosen one had still found his passion! Well, let me tell you...I was the best damn statistician that team ever had!"

The audience laughed and gave an applause, which made Greg blush.

"And my mom's saying is quite apropos for all of us today. Here in this room, three teams coming together to form one. We must all remember that Rome wasn't built in a day and neither will this team be. We need to be patient, design the city, the team that we all want to build, then slowly form a strong foundation, and raise it up to be somewhere that we all want to live."

As the applause filled the room, Greg thought maybe, just maybe, his desire to start building the team was happening because, for the first time, everyone in the room was doing something together. *Yes*, Greg thought, as he looked out into the room, *yes, it does seem as if everyone is clapping.*

Greg looked at Amir, who played a rousing upbeat song. Chanting voices filled the room along with celebratory and exciting drumbeats: *"...getting stronger...like a waving flag..."*

Robert raised his head in recognition. This was the song that played during the entire tournament when he and Jenny watched the 2010 FIFA World Cup of Soccer. Robert and Jenny had watched soccer together ever since she was a little girl. He had even coached her team for a couple of years. The two of them sang that song at the top of their lungs in the final ten minutes of their favourite Spanish team's victory over the Netherlands. And how sweet it was that day when Monique came home and father and daughter squeezed her tight the second she stepped into the house. They told her to keep her shoes on because they were going out for Spanish food and dancing. *Dancing*, Robert thought as he shook his head. He hadn't even thought about dancing! Another thing to add to the list of things he'd never do again.

Monique, standing beside Amir, was not listening to the music. She had one hand over her ear and the other was listening to her cell phone to Jenny's voicemail. She heard her daughter's crying voice: *"Mom, Daddy's journal...he sent it to me...It's here, I have it. Right here, Mom...in my hand...right here! The thing he said he would never show me and only give to me after he died...Why did he*

92

do this, Mom?...Daddy's changed, Mom...We need to...and...and...and okay—Why does Daddy have a gun? What the hell does he need a gun for, Mom? Mom, I think it's a bad idea today—You should see the letter he sent with the journal...Mom, please call me...Daddy doesn't want to talk to people! I don't think you should let him talk today..."

22. 6 WEEKS AGO – SEEMA'S OFFICE

"And at home, what are some of the changes you find most difficult?" Robert looked at Seema as if she was speaking another language. "Like, getting into the house or..."

Robert cut her off. "She *built* a ramp! I don't know how the hell it got there so fast. Like she had it stored in the garage all winter and just pulled it out...like we do with the patio chairs each summer. I mean, did she *already* have that ramp knowing I'd be needing it someday?"

"You mean, Monique, your wife?"

"Yeah, who else?"

"You mean the ramp for the..."

"*Wheelchair*, yes!"

"So, seeing the ramp upset you?"

"Is *this* how you want to talk?"

"I'm sorry, what do you mean?"

"Did seeing the ramp *upset* me? What the *hell* do you think? Of course that thing upset me—I never needed a goddamn ramp before, did I? How do you think I'd feel seeing my house set up for an...an invalid! And knowing *I'm* the goddamn cripple?"

"I'm sorry, Robert. I'm not trying to be insensitive. I need to ask you these questions to assess if you have any other needs that are not being taken of."

"How long have you been doing this, Miss Pourshadi?"

"You mean here at the centre?"

"I mean how long have you been asking questions like 'how does that make you feel?'"

"Well, Robert, I'm not really sure what you are asking me."

94

"Does it really matter how I feel? Really? 'Cause so far nobody asked me if I wanted that damn ramp or that handle on the toilet...the bench in the bathtub...You see, asking me how I feel is pointless 'cause, it doesn't matter how I feel, does it? All you people...everyone...you all are...are going to do what *you think* I need anyway, right?!"

Robert then looked at Seema with a smiled snarl. "Oh, and I bet you're just dying to ask me 'how I feel' about all that, aren't you?"

Seema leaned her head on one hand and rubbed the back of her neck with the other. She tried not to show any emotion and definitely did not want to give Robert any indication that he had already answered her question quite acutely. He was telling her exactly how he felt and she wanted to keep him talking so she asked him, "Is that what you think, Robert? That we all take care of your needs?"

Seema's question stopped Robert's tirade for a moment. He paused and jerked his head back with a look like he just bit into a sour lemon.

"My needs," Robert huffed, "*my needs?* You know, Miss Pourshadi, there's a big difference between what you or anyone assessing my needs determines my needs to be and what I actually need...No, *no*, I'm sorry, I'm wrong. The thing is *not* giving me what I need but giving me what I don't need!"

"And what is that, Robert? What are some of things you don't need?"

Robert sadly lowered his head and spoke quietly. "Look, I had been climbing for over thirty years. *Thirty years!* And months before every climb, my wife would find anything she could get her hands on about that mountain. Any story of someone that got killed up on that mountain or maybe a picture of some hazardous cliff or crevasse. It got to the point where she would read more about that mountain than I did...and she always felt the need to point out every possible danger that might exist..."

"And you didn't need that?" Seema gently asked.

Robert looked up. "Of course I didn't need that! I prepared extensively for every climb. I went over and over every detail...She knew that, she saw me doing that! You know, it's hard enough doing all that preparation and then doing the actual climb...I didn't need her...all her doomsday warnings....always sitting in the back of my mind."

"Did she ever ask you not to go?"

Robert paused and thought about the question.

"Well, no...No. Not at all, really. Actually she was like a best friend about it all. It's just...it's just...what she'd always say...she'd always..." Robert stopped.

"What did she say, Robert?"

Robert rubbed his face as if he was washing it clean. Seema asked the question again. "What did she always say?"

"That she didn't know what she would do if something ever happened to me!" Robert roared.

Seema allowed the echo of Robert's words to drift off before she spoke again. "Do you mean like this? If something like *this* happened to you?"

"What the *hell* do you think? Of course like *this!* She didn't want me coming back like this...like some mangled, half-man, cripple!"

Seema wanted to keep Robert talking so she went back to his question about needs. "And so, Robert, I still don't understand. What is it that you don't need?"

"Not knowing what she'd do!" Robert's voice started to sound exhausted, like he had been talking for hours. "I can't have *her not knowing* what she would do *now*, now that I'm like...like this!"

"And why do you need her to know what she would do, Robert?"

"Because! Because...I need her to—Oh, just forget it!"

"But Robert, your wife is as new to all this as you ar—"

"—No! I gotta go. Sorry, Miss Pourshadi...I told you all about people doing things I don't need and I damn well don't need *this* either!"

Robert wheeled his chair around and started for the door. Seema stood up behind her desk and called out, "Please, Robert, please just tell me why do you need Monique to know what she would do if something like this happened?"

Robert stopped cold. His back straightened, he waited for a brief moment and then he was gone. But as he wheeled out the door, like a wounded animal trying to pull its leg from a snare, he painfully panted, "Because I don't! I don't. Okay...Okay?"

23. PRESENT DAY – JENNY'S FLIGHT

"Can't she read?" Claire asked Kyle.

Kyle smiled at Claire across the aisle. "Yes, but the writing is so bad and it looks like my handwriting so I can read it better than she does."

"Oh, let's see...Can I see?"

Kyle tilted the journal towards the little girl. "Oh, my gosh, that's like Callum's."

"And who is Callum?" Kyle asked.

"He's the annoying boy who sits beside me in class. Always talking and getting *me* in trouble."

"Claire, that's not a nice thing to say." Her mother quickly jumped in.

"That's okay. I'm sure I was pretty annoying to all the girls when I was your age," Kyle laughed.

"I can read this whole book by myself." Claire held up her book. "*Dora climbs Star Mountain*," Claire proudly read out. "...and so what's your book about?"

"My dad, Claire, my dad." Jenny tried to smile, hoping the little girl was finished with her questions. She then put her hand on the journal. "Kyle, can you find any entries starting April 2012?"

"Was that when it happened?" Kyle asked

"What happened? What happened?" Claire cheerfully pleaded.

"I don't think she wants to talk about it, Claire." Kyle quickly jumped in, sensing Jenny's mood.

"No, it's okay, Kyle," Jenny said as she leaned over the armrest and got as close to Claire as she could. "My father used to climb mountains, Claire."

"Did he climb Star Mountain?" The little girl pointed at the book on her lap.

"No, Claire, I don't think he climbed that one but he did go to the top of some the highest mountains on the earth."

Claire's mother looked at Jenny and listened in.

"And this red book is filled with all his stories about those mountains."

"*Everest*? Did he ever go to Mount Everest?" Claire's mother asked in admiration.

"Two times," Jenny nodded.

"*Two* times! Your father climbed Mount Everest two times?" Claire's mother sounded as if she knew something about mountain climbing. "Claire," she put her arms around her daughter, "Claire, that's the same mountain your Uncle Sean went to last year. Remember the picture of all those triangle flags you liked so much?"

Claire excitedly turned to Jenny. "Maybe Uncle Sean knows your daddy then?"

"Oh, I don't think so, Claire." Her mother kissed the top of her head. "There are a lot of people up there and besides, your uncle didn't climb to the top. Remember what he told you?"

"Oh yeah." Claire looked sadly at Jenny. "My uncle couldn't go to the top because he lost all his money up there." She turned to her mother. "Right, Mom?"

Claire's mother chuckled. "Not exactly, Claire. What she means is her uncle, my brother Sean, couldn't climb to the top because apparently they had some kind of avalanche up there last year. It cost him a small fortune to go up there and because of that avalanche he couldn't get to the top, so he felt he lost all his money because he couldn't climb to the top. But thank God he wasn't climbing that day!"

Jenny glanced at Kyle, who was still searching for the entry in the journal. Kyle had heard what Claire's mother said and gave Jenny a supportive smile.

"And did your father get up there last year?" Claire's mom asked. Kyle put his hand on Jenny's shoulder and rubbed it slightly. "Or did he have to turn back like my brother Sean did?"

"Oh, he...he turned back too," Jenny replied with a limp smile.

"Well, thank God he did. Apparently, they say it was the biggest avalanche anyone has ever seen there. I'm not sure how many died or..." Claire's mother tilted her head in thought. "Well, I'm not sure, but Sean was close enough to see it. And he told us it was one of the most frightening moments of his life. I'm just hoping it scared him enough to not go back there!"

Jenny was in a bit of daze at hearing about someone who was there that same day her father was. Not knowing how to respond, she just simply nodded and said, "Yeah, let's hope."

"Does your father still climb?"

Jenny quickly responded, "No, no, he doesn't."

Claire's mother hugged her daughter. "Well, good. It's such a worry for all of us back home, isn't it? Always wondering if they made it safely. You must know the feeling? The day when they leave to finally summit? And you are like millions of miles away waiting for that call—did they make it—did something happen to them? And they always call hours after they say they will call right? And when you're talking to them on the phone, they act...like it was nothing. They just sound all excited and triumphant, like they knew it would be fine...but you have been, like, holding your breath for twenty-four straight hours or worse, trying to get your heart to start beating again. How did you and your mother ever stand it? Sean isn't married yet and I'm his only family so we are his main contacts—anyway, I'm always begging him to stop. Thank goodness your father is wise enough to stop."

Jenny looked to the floor as she answered. "Yeah, yeah...It's...um...You know—Thank goodness."

"And your mother must be the happiest woman and so, so relieved, I'll bet. I mean, I get that nervous feeling the moment Sean says anything remotely about a mountain. Immediately, I'm thinking, 'No, please don't say you are going to climb it!'"

Kyle, seeing Jenny was desperately hoping the conversation would stop, jumped in. "Oh, excuse me, I found what we were looking for, Jenny."

"Oh, yes, I'm sorry," Claire's mother apologized. "Sorry, you two were reading...but thanks for talking. Come on, Claire, let's read about your Star Mountain, ok?"

Kyle smiled and waved across the aisle at Claire and her mother. Jenny bravely nodded and then leaned into Kyle's shoulder.

"You want me to put this away?" Kyle whispered, holding the journal.

"No, Kyle," Jenny sighed. "I need to hear it, more than ever now." She looked up into Kyle's eyes. "Did you find any entries in 2012?"

"Yeah, Jen." Kyle showed where his thumb was tucked inside the journal.

"Can you read it to me?" Jenny closed her eyes and sunk into Kyle's chest.

Kyle caressed Jenny's face and kissed the back of her neck. She let out a tiny moan-full sigh. He wasn't sure if it sounded like the anticipation of an ache that was to come or the sound of her saying she felt safe enough to listen, so he asked again, "Are you sure, Jen?"

"I need to, Kyle...I really *need* to."

Kyle flipped the journal open and started to read.

April 20th 2012—we are now in the air on our way to Katmandu

Dearest love,

      This feeling of unbelievable just overwhelms me at this moment...This is what it must feel like when you are witnessing a miracle—for tonight, in this darkly lit plane high above the planet, I look at these three young souls sleeping in front of me and I think it's incredible. Troy, Nancy and Philip, they are here! How did this happen? Yes, it's a miracle! So far the flight has been wonderfully uneventful so I have been able to sit here and...well, soak in the reality of what I'm doing with these three.

      I've taken so many students on treks...but this is Everest. Wow! It is going to be an interesting journey and they have their work cut out for them. Creating all those webisodes for almost 200 schools each day...and having so many children's eyes back at home following their adventures...well, that's a job most journalists find taxing. But they started today already by interviewing me at the airport...asking me why do I climb?

      AH, that question!!! How many times have you asked me that? So why...why do I climb? What kind of reason drives me to do this? And you know, love, it seems every time I encounter that question, I always seem to find completely new and different answers...Well, maybe I don't find; it's more like I trip over...and I told them that I climb because, well, because my whole being just revels in this sense of purpose when I'm climbing. Although, I couldn't tell them what exactly that purpose is, but I said that I seem to be filled with it. Is that strange? Is it simply that I'm here to inspire them...Is that my purpose?

      I remember once reading about how most people didn't find it difficult to actually inspire someone; what they found difficult was trying to put that inspiration into action...because if you don't make it active, well, then that inspiration is just a feeling—a feeling without any purpose...and like most inspired feelings, they eventually just wear off...Then Nancy opens her iPad and looks up the meaning of the word (I never really knew this but one of the definitions of "inspiration" is this: the act of breathing life into something. Doesn't that sound great?!) So after Nancy read the meaning I asked them..."Okay then, I guess my purpose is to ask you three this: how can one really inspire and breathe life into someone else so they make that inspiration come to life?" Well, then they all started saying I was copping out and that I wasn't answering the question of why do I climb. But then Troy (Oh, Monique, this kid will forever surprise me), he tells us to all be quiet...and then he said he thinks that the only way we can bring our inspirations into action is to "find motivation for them first." So then he turned to Philip, told him to turn the camera back on. He turned to me and asked, "Okay, Mr. Sanchez, what motivates your inspiration to climb?"

Well, my darling, I was stumped! So I stumbled around with some words, but then Philip said, "I think when you find what motivates your inspiration, that's when you find your purpose! So maybe, Mr. Sanchez, the better question would be: what's your purpose to climb?"(AND I'm the one supposed to be helping them...ha ha...Today I saw how they really don't need me anymore!)

BUT fortunately, I was saved. We were interrupted because we had to board the plane. But that questioning thought is so strong inside me tonight. So here, up above the clouds—with you—I'll try to write about what I think that purpose is. Okay...where to start?

First, I have always felt inspired to help people (I'm sure my mother and you have a lot to do with this). So then, what motivates me to do this? What motivates my inspiration to help others? Is it really so simple? I know helping someone gives me a great feeling of self-worth. When I help others, I feel good about myself, I feel proud of being me and then, ultimately, I feel successful. And all that, I guess, gives me my identity—a reason to exist—and I think once anyone feels their reason to exist, well, then they must have found their purpose!

So maybe that is the reason I climb and have climbed...My purpose has been preparing myself to bring these three up here and pray that having this experience will ultimately inspire and motivate them...and it will hopefully, instill a sense of purpose in them.

So far, in all my journals I have only written about my climbs up on those mountains that we can see on an atlas. But I have yet to write about all the other mountains I have climbed, like these three...So much to say about these mountains. They have been such long and winding roads. But I think that's what I should do on this journey: is write about my life's adventures climbing them. So let's start with Troy. Ah, Troy...

Oh, wait, before I start, do you remember when you told me that at first you didn't like me calling Jen 'Little Rock'? And I told you that the reason I call her that is because she reminds me— that my daughter, Jenny, is one of the greatest, most amazing mountains in my life that I had to climb? That becoming a father was scarier than any mountain I had ever climbed, and maybe climbing all those other mountains was just preparation. An intense training, to help me climb the mountain of becoming a father. Oh, it has been one of the greatest gifts, but also terrified me in many unknown ways. Being a father gave me incredible purpose—a new identity—a real reason to exist! Oh, darling, I should tell you, you've been the greatest climbing partner any father could ever have!

And now, being a teacher, mentor, a friend to these three—climbing these three separate human mountains—has inspired me, motivated me and also given me such a profound purpose of just being. Because through them, I feel all the things I have ever felt during and after any great climb: accomplishment, pride, compassion, achievement, love...

So, my love, let me tell you the story of these three mountains sitting in front me...

Let's see...Troy, we'll start with Troy...

24. TROY

...Maybe it was just before I graduated from high school?
My father, I had never seen him so...

"Roberto, come here." Robert's father sounded angry as he pointed at the chair beside the kitchen table, pulled it out and then demanded Robert sit.

"You have to decide today; tomorrow will be too late! In two months, high school is finished...and the deadline for these is Friday. So you need to choose now!"

"Papa, please, I need to..." His father gestured to the forms that were spread out on the table in front of Robert's mother. "No, you do not need to do anything until you sign one of these."

Robert had rarely seen his father speak with such force. Alfredo Sanchez was a quiet man who owned a music shop where he made and sold all types of string instruments. He also made a little money playing Spanish guitar at Quixote's, the local Spanish restaurant in town. Robert played three instruments—piano, guitar and bass—and would often join his father at Quixote's to entertain the customers.

"Roberto, come sit down." His mother patted the empty chair beside her. "Sit, Roberto. Come on now, please sit."

"I don't know, Ma, *really*, I just don't know." Robert sulked as he sat beside his mother. "Look, it's my whole life, okay? You can't expect me to...well, just decide what I want to do for the rest of my life *today*."

"Come on, Roberto, you were never a good liar! You know that is not the reason you haven't chosen a university yet," his father snapped.

But as he sat down to face his son, his voice became softer, flecked with pride. "Now look! Look at this! Three different universities! *THREE* great places that are all saying they want you. *You*, Roberto Sanchez! And they don't only want to teach you, but all of them are giving you scholarships...money, Roberto! They want to *pay* you to come and learn."

"I know, Papa, I know. It's just..."

"Just what, Roberto?" His father sounded impatient again. "What?"

Robert bowed his head and sighed, "I already told you."

"Roberto," his mother said, raising her hand to calm her husband. "If you don't go this year, these opportunities might not be there when you get back."

"And those mountains are not going anywhere, Roberto. Those mountains will wait for you. You can climb them anytime!" His father tried to be calm, but his voice wavered with emotion.

"And so will these universities, Papa!" Robert answered.

"But they will not *always* be offering money for you to come to them!" Robert's father slammed his hand down on the forms to accentuate his point.

"But, Papa, I may never get this chance to join a climbing team like this again either. Don't you see? No one from this country has ever done it. We could be the first—the *first*, Papa! The first Canadians to ever climb Everest!"

"Roberto, Roberto." His mother laid her hand on his arm. Robert's mother was used to being the calming sensible voice in the room. She worked in Family Services as a social worker and it was her job to go to family homes experiencing any kind of trouble, like abuse, runaway kids or neglect. Robert had seen his mother in action many times when he was a teenager. He would often accompany her to some of her clients' homes whenever she felt a little uncomfortable going by herself.

"Your father and I are really worried, 'Berto. You only started this climbing thing a couple of years ago and also, you have never climbed that high before."

"Ma, I told you, I'll only be going to base camp..."

"Roberto, are they paying you to do this?" his father firmly asked.

Robert shook his head.

"You are paying to go there?"

"Well, that depends, Papa. We are trying to raise money."

"But Roberto, those schools are paying you. They are *paying* you to go and learn!"

"Papa, is it the money you're worried about? Well, *don't!* Don't worry; I'll get a job. I'll make enough to go Everest and go to school when I get back."

"And what if the schools don't want you when you get back?"

"Papa, my marks won't change."

"But what if *you* do?" His father's voice softened. "What if you change, Roberto? What if you come back and then say you don't want to go? Your older brothers and sisters, Roberto, they never had this chance. It's right here—in front of you!. You *must* grab it now!"

"Papa, going to Everest is also a chance!"

"A chance? A chance at what? To risk your life...and for what? What Roberto? So you can say you were one of the first to do it? So what—first, second, third—who's keeping track?"

"Alfredo, please," Robert's mother tried to calm her husband, "there is no reason to raise your voice."

Alfredo turned to his wife. "You tell me then, tell me what kind of future comes to a man who climbs mountains?"

Robert's mother looked at him, to see if he had an answer for his father, but Robert just groaned, "You don't understand...You both, you just *don't* understand!"

"I understand this: Roberto, a mountain is *not* your future!" His father held up the papers on the table. "This *is*!"

Robert jumped up. "Papa, is that what *you* want me to do? I should sign those now because *you* want me to do it?"

"No, because it's the right thing to do. Because it's the *right* thing to do!"

"Was opening a music shop the right thing to do, Papa? Was it?"

"It put bread on this table, didn't it?"

"Then why did Mama have to work too?"

Alfredo Sanchez looked at his wife for support, but she just shook her head and smiled at her husband. "Oh my God, he's right, Alfredo. Remember how your whole family was against you opening up that shop?"

Robert's father paused for a second. "But that was *different*. I did not have these kinds of choices!"

"No, Alfredo, you did not have these kinds of choices, but you still chose to do what you wanted to do, right? We have never stopped any of our children from doing what they choose and we will not start now."

She then turned to Robert. "Roberto, your father and I, we are so proud of you. You are the first in this family to ever get the chance to go to university. And to have three schools that want to give you money...well, nothing could make a parent prouder. But son, what will also make us proud is that you do what you love to do. So that we can tell everyone that our son 'loves what he does.' But do understand, your father is right; the mountains can wait. And maybe it's true—so the schools can wait. But saying you love what you do, well, that should never wait."

Robert sat down and leaned his head on his mother's shoulder.

"But, 'Berto, you must be responsible for all your choices, every single one that is yours to make. Live with the responsibility of that choice. And one thing your father tells me over and over, and I bet he hasn't never said it to you—is that when we speak about what you want to do with your life, music like your father or social work like me—the thing he tells me over and over is this: 'It will not matter, because Roberto will be successful in anything he does.'"

Robert looked at his father. His father smiled as he put a hand over his son's. "And you will, my boy. You will be a great success! I'm sorry, Roberto. I got upset. It's just...well, you know...I'm a father! I have to get...well, you know—upset...Okay, okay. Look, your mama is right. So you decide, do what you love, son...Just...just be careful, okay?"

With the support of his parents, Robert didn't sign those papers that day. And that summer he worked, sometimes around the clock, at three different jobs. He was successful in raising enough money to fulfil his climbing dream. But only four weeks before the team was to leave for Everest, the leader of his team fell ill and the expedition was cancelled, leaving mountain climber Laurie Skreslet to become the first Canadian to reach the top of the world, many years before Roberto Sanchez would ever lay eyes upon it.

Three years later, Robert did stand on the top of something—a stage—where he was handed his diplomas in Social Science and Music.

...So many paths to take. I'm not sure if I chose it or if it was chosen for me. But it did lead me to Troy. Oh, we're landing in a couple of minutes...The three of them are waking, I better go...It's pretty exciting and I can't wait! The journey begins. I'll call when we get to the hotel...Till then...I love you with open arms of smiled joy!

April 22nd, 2012, Katmandu

I wish someday you could come here with me. Maybe Jen, too. This city feels as if it is always in this constant motion, yet you also feel like time is standing still here, even when you are right in the middle of all that crazy hustle and bustle.

There are all these signs of modern technology, yet you are always surrounded by the majestic presence of the past. The city is like...like a deep, tremendously deep, raging river...If you look at it, the water on the top has this constant uncontrollable force to it:

always moving, yet underneath that water it is so still, so unmovable. Like time and memories...time moves so fast, yet some memories just stay, seated in you forever.

After supper we got into talking about the past: families, high school, first jobs. Maybe it was seeing the Pashupatinath Temple. Someone was telling the kids it was built to be the symbol of enlightenment. And that got us talking about some 'moments of enlightenment' that we have felt in our lives. I told them one of my most enlightened moments was when I was in university and I was volunteering with those students. Remember when I was working in those schools, the music therapy stuff I did, and how intense that whole experience was? I always felt like I was meant to be there. It was astonishingly...life changing, not just for me but for so many of those kids too! It still sits so clearly inside me—especially that moment when I told you that working with those students was the reason I existed in this world—it was to do this!!! Remember?

I was so sure after I graduated from university, I would become a music teacher in a high school! Anyway, they asked me what happened with that enlightenment. Must have been a great question because I had no idea what to say and couldn't tell them where that enlightenment even went! I said I thought maybe reality got in the way because when I graduated, I didn't have the money to go to teachers' college right away so I got a job and then got married and then...had a family. And then it struck me again—that question—is that why I climb? Am I trying to find or re-discover that enlightenment again, through climbing? Is that why I kept going, year after year, making my goals and climbs more difficult with each mountain? And then Nancy asked, so simply, "Do you find enlightenment up there?"

I told her I wasn't sure. Then she asked me why I kept going back? Did I think I might find it on the next one?

At the age of thirty-eight, Robert had been happily married for thirteen years. He had a wonderful, talented twelve-year-old daughter and had successfully climbed three of the famed seven summits: Mont Blanc, Mount McKinley, and Elbrus. But after several restless years of working in a variety of positions in the offices of social services, he still hadn't found his calling. That something that would give him a sense of great purpose. So again, he tried something new and this time became a probation officer.

Robert was sitting in his office, a closet-sized room with no windows. His supervisor, Virginia Farrell, was standing on the other side of the desk.

"This morning, you will be seeing three young men. Here are their files."

She dropped three red-coloured files in front of Robert. "Try to read about these young men—well, as much as you can. Just go through the questions on the sheet I gave you this morning, okay?"

Robert tugged at the collar of his shirt. He wasn't used to wearing ties and today it seemed to feel as if it was tightening as the morning wore on.

"Okay, Miss Farrell. I'm sorry, but I must admit, I feel kind of nervous."

"Well, you wouldn't be human if you didn't. Look, if you have any problems, Robert, or you feel uncomfortable for any reason, you call me, got it? And don't worry, Luke is right outside, all right?"

Virginia Farrell stopped at the door. "And keep this open if you want." She then disappeared.

Robert loosened his tie. He opened the file and read, 'Tyrell Williams, age: 21, 9-month probation for possession of drugs and threatening someone with a dangerous weapon. Police arrived at the scene after they had received a call that a group of men were fighting. One man had stabbed another young man, but the victim was nowhere to be found. The only person at the scene was Tyrell, who was found in possession of a large hunting knife. Although there was no victim found in the surrounding vicinity, the knife was stained with blood and three large pools of blood were discovered along the sidewalk.'

"When's this over?" was the first thing Tyrell said as he walked into Robert's office.

"What...What's over?" Robert awkwardly stammered.

"Our little dates."

"I'm sorry, I don't understand,"

Tyrell stood around six feet tall. Long lanky arms with hands that looked too big for his body. His hair was cropped so short, it looked shaved. His dark skin made his eyes look almost abnormally white. He wore a red T-shirt with a small insignia of a hawk on it. And he spoke with an aggressive arrogance, the way someone speaks when they don't like to be interrupted.

Tyrell moved toward Robert, leaned over his desk and scooped up a pencil and then snatched the file from Robert's desk. He slapped it down hard and startled Robert. "*This*, you idiot! How long I gotta come here and do *this*?"

"Probation you mean?" Robert tried to sound calm.

Tyrell placed the pencil directly in the middle of Robert's forehead, and spoke with a snarled chuckle. "You got anything *workin'* in there?"

Robert slowly leaned back in his chair, leaving a small gap between his head and the pencil. He was unsure if he should just take the pencil from Tyrell's hand, or call for help.

With his other hand, Tyrell opened the file on Robert's desk.

"What did it say in here?" Tyrell held the file in front of Robert. "Anything *'bout* my knife? Hey, they didn't happen to give it to you, did they? 'Cause I'd really, *really* like to have my little gut checker back. So, do you have it?"

Robert was scared and tried to remember what his mother told him. "Just remember, if someone was coming to physically hurt you, they would do it right away. It is usually the helpless bullies that like to taunt you. *Yet*, Robert thought, *Tyrell was found with a knife dripping with blood, so maybe he wasn't just someone that taunted.*

Robert had been with his mother many times in the homes of mothers and children that feared their own fathers or husbands. "Never confront violent, aggressive behaviour with the same behaviour," she had told him. "Always answer any mean or violent questions with a question. Always ask the aggressors questions that make them feel like you recognize that they are the one in charge. This usually empowers them, but it can also calm them down as well, because then they see you are interested in knowing something about them."

So with the pencil still pointed at his forehead, Robert asked Tyrell, "Can you help me, please?"

Tyrell's head cocked sideways as if he didn't understand the question. Robert continued speaking. "I'm sure it must be a pain in the ass to have to come here and report to me. I mean, look at me...some new guy who is just learning the ropes! Man, I know I wouldn't want to do it. So...can you help me find a way to make this as easy for you as possible?"

Tyrell smiled slyly. "Oh, so *you* want me to help you?" Tyrell felt giddy; he couldn't believe his luck in getting a rookie as his probation officer.

Robert nodded. Tyrell, still holding the pencil like a weapon, looked behind him and hooked his leg on a chair, then pulled it towards him and sat down.

"You can help me by finding my knife first, ok?"

"I'm sorry, I have no idea where it is," Robert said.

"How the *fuck* you *gonna* help me then?" Tyrell suddenly threw the pencil like a spear against Robert's chest. Robert flinched and made a comical attempt of trying to catch the pencil before it hit the floor. This was his very first case and already he had been assaulted by a thrown object.

Although it didn't hurt him, he was instructed to call in his supervisor immediately if at any time he was approached with any type of aggressive behaviour. Robert picked up the phone.

"So? So how am I *gonna* help you then?" Tyrell snarled again.

Robert looked at the receiver in his hand and asked himself the same question. *How was he going to help me?* Surely calling his supervisor was not going to help the situation. So he slowly put down the phone as he spoke.

"Well, what do you need me to do for you?" Robert then added, "And it can't be about your knife 'cause..."

Tyrell wasn't used to hearing these types of questions. No one had ever asked Tyrell what he needed them to do for him unless Tyrell had a sharp metal weapon firmly wedged against their body. Tyrell's face seemed to soften when Robert spoke, but as a kid that had been in trouble with the law since he was ten, Tyrell was not one to easily trust anyone. Especially not a rookie who was new at his job. So he tested Robert again.

He held up the file and shook it in Robert's face. "Look at this, *this*! Just tell me, how long I gotta do this?"

"Oh, okay. Well, it says right there at the bottom," Robert answered.

Tyrell looked at the file for a moment and then quickly laid it down on the desk in front of Robert and asked, "Yeah...yeah, well, what does it say then?"

"Right there!" Robert leaned over and pointed at a line in the file. "It says how long your probation is right there."

Tyrell looked down at the file and scanned where Robert's finger was. He looked hard, squinting his eyes and bobbing his head up and down. He suddenly pushed the file back at Robert. "I *ain't* doing your job for you! Just answer my question."

Robert gently turned the file around and looked at it. "Let's see...Yeah, here it is, right under 'duration of probation.'" He put the file down and again pointed to the exact line.

Tyrell looked at it and said, "Okay, so how long is that?"

A young voice came from the doorway. "You want me to read it, Ty?"

Robert turned around to see a young boy. maybe about ten years old, leaning behind the door and peeking into the office. Robert was taken aback when he saw the boy's huge round eyes, which were fixed with such an intense fearful look, like he had just seen a ghost and was scared to blink.

"He can't read, mister," the little boy said very matter-of-factly.

"Shut it down!" Tyrell snapped at the young boy.

"He can't read, mister," were the only words I ever heard Troy speak. Even when I would go to say hello, Ty would give his younger brother this angry stare, and Troy would immediately shut right up. That little guy couldn't have been more than ten. Mostly I recall how he would always be scribbling away in that dirty yellow notebook (you know the one). When Troy was busy in that book, his eyes had such a different look. They didn't look scared. It was like his eyes smiled as he wrote, as if another universe existed in that book, one that was alive and hopeful. But it only was alive in that book, because the moment he looked away from it, those fearful frightened eyes came right back. The first day I saw Troy...that kid...he, well, he just rooted himself in me. And those eyes...I could see them in my sleep at night.

The next time I heard Troy speak was probably about four months later in the back of a police cruiser. I helped Tyrell get this job at one of those photocopy places. Troy was leaning against the window, writing in that notebook of his. I said "hi" but all I got was those ominous eyes sneaking a look at me. Just as quickly, they were back in that book again.

As I opened the door, Tyrell was stepping outside to have a smoke. Then it happened! It was piercing, like lightening crashing out of a calm, clear blue sky...happened just as I was speaking to Tyrell's boss. I remember it like it was yesterday.

"Hey, Mr. Braiden. How's Tyrell doing," Robert asked Tyrell's boss.

"Not bad, just wish he wouldn't have to do that every twenty minutes." Mr. Braiden then pointed at Tyrell smoking outside the front door. "I don't mind the *smokin'*. I smoke myself. It's just he keeps *buttin'* out on the window sill and it's getting..."

CRASH!

Broken glass exploded everywhere. Tyrell's huge lanky body slammed against the steel window frame. His arms moved as if he were trying to claw his way back into the store. Mr. Braiden grabbed Robert and pushed him to the floor.

The windows came crashing down. The sound of gunfire drowned out the noise of breaking glass and filled the air with torrential waves at a ricocheting, ear-splitting volume.

"Get down! Get down!"

Screaming. Employees and customers scrambled everywhere.

One last shot. Tyrell's arms were no longer moving; they were gradually sliding along the metal windows structure until he disappeared from sight. It had started and ended in about four seconds—*complete devastation in just four seconds!*

Robert lifted his head. Other than the broken glass, everything else looked the same. It was extraordinary how quiet it was.

"Is everyone okay?" Mr. Braiden called out.

People started to rise from their hideouts, crying and moving cautiously.

Suddenly Robert remembered: *Little Troy was sitting outside in front of the store!* He quickly tore outside the door.

"Troy! Tyrell!" he screamed as he pushed open the store's front door. Some loose glass fell at his feet. Immediately, he froze.

"Oh my God! Oh my God!" he whispered, the sound of complete disbelief evident in his voice.

Troy sat silently on the sidewalk, clutching his notebook to his chest. Beside him was his brother's mangled body, drenched with blood. The cigarette was still burning inches from his opened mouth and bloodstained teeth. Troy did not look at his brother. His eyes just stared straight ahead, as if he was waiting for something to come forward. Robert fell to his knees and put his arms around Troy.

Robert opened his mouth...but no words would come.

The police arrived within minutes and Robert found himself in the back of a police cruiser beside Troy.

"Do you know the deceased?"

"Are you related?"

"Why were you here today?"

Troy just sat silently, never once acknowledging the presence of the investigating police officer. Troy was in another universe, one far away from his pain. The only movement he made was when he pressed his face against the car's window and watched as his brother's body was covered with what looked like a blue tarp, the kind one would use under a tent to keep it from getting wet.

Robert felt anxious and short of breath as he watched the paramedics lift Tyrell onto a stretcher and into the back of an ambulance. His body convulsed and he covered his mouth. He was completely overwhelmed. He'd never seen a dead body before. He answered the police officer's questions as best he could.

Troy kept his faced pushed against the window.

Just as the ambulance closed its back doors, a police officer hit the van with his hand, indicating they could drive off. Robert put a hand on the boy's shoulder. Troy turned to him. Robert looked into the huge, scared and unblinking eyes.

"Don't worry, Troy. I'll come with you to tell your mother."

Troy spoke his first words—the very first words since that time he had told Robert that his brother couldn't read, five months ago.

"Shut it down!" Troy's young voice eerily echoed his brother's tone and hardness; it was as if Tyrell had come back from the dead and possessed his young brother's body.

"It's okay, Troy. I'll..."

"*Shut it* down!" Troy repeated with an almost inhuman cruelty to his voice.

"We have to take this kid home," said the officer in the front seat.

"I'll come with you," Robert said.

"Yeah, sure...Okay...Where do you live, kid?" asked the officer in a routine, uncaring tone that showed little empathy for the kid who had just watched his brother get shot six times in the chest.

Troy said nothing.

"Where do you live, kid?" repeated the officer, just as impatiently as the first time. Troy again stayed silent and stared straight ahead.

Robert had been to Tyrell and Troy's home at least four times so he said, "It's one three four Erskine Avenue, officer."

The officer said something into his radio and they were off. A second police car followed behind them.

Robert liked Tyrell and Troy's mother very much. Mrs. Williams was an animated, heavy-set woman who possessed a rich and contagious laugh. He admired the way she always spoke in such a forgiving way to her sons. She was so accepting and, despite all the trouble Tyrell had brought into their family, she seemed forgiving. Robert closed his eyes, let out a mournful sigh and started to dread what was about to happen. He imagined arriving at Tyrell and Troy's home, their mother dramatically reaching out and clutching her remaining young son tight to her bosom, and then probably falling to her knees and wailing uncontrollably to the God above, screaming for the heavens to return Tyrell back to her arms...back to his home.

Robert looked at the little kid who maybe, in some alternate universe on this very night, would be watching his older brother do something like play basketball. Troy would be watching Tyrell spin and win the game with a stupendous, long, three-point shot, surrounded by celebration and crowds cheering, chanting his brother's name. Instead, the only sound that filled the air was the annoyingly constant police chatter from the cruiser's radio.

The twirling red lights on the cruiser reflected off every window, making it appear as though the houses on the street were lighting up as the cruiser moved through town. Kids and parents sitting on their porches and playing in the street scattered into their homes as the flashing red beacons approached them. In this neighbourhood, patrol cars were a common and not always welcome sight. The cruiser finally pulled up in front of the small, grey, semi-attached house. In a couple of moments, Robert was about to find out just how effective he actually was as a probation officer.

The house had two front windows, and the reflection of a TV's bluish light flickered through an evergreen tree that was much too close to the front of the house.

"Wait in the car," the officer ordered.

He looked around as he walked towards the door. Knocking a little too loudly.

"It's the police. We need to talk to you."

Ten seconds later he knocked again. But his knock was interrupted when the door opened. *There was Troy's mother*. Robert closed his eyes; he couldn't bear to watch the scene that was about to unfold. He found himself holding his breath the entire time the officer spoke to Tyrell's mother. Troy just looked at his mother, shaking his head slightly.

A loud yell was heard and suddenly, there was a bang on the police car's back window. Robert turned to see what had caused the noise. There was no emotional scene of a mother down on her knees, screaming to the empty sky, no begging for the gods to undo what had been done.

Instead, Troy's mother was banging on the car window, yelling at Troy, "I *don't* want no part of this, you young good for nothing...you hear! *Nothin'*."

"All right, Mrs. Williams, step back from the car," said the officer. Two other police officers came out of the second car that had been following the car Robert and Troy rode in.

"Open the door! Get those two out here," the officer snapped at the two other cops.

"I *told* you and your brother if you brought trouble..." the woman yelled as the door opened.

"All right, Ma'am, stand back," the officer said, holding his arm up and moving the mother away from the car.

"Mr. Sanchez, could you bring that kid out here?"

Robert reached over to Troy but Troy just shoved his arm away and began to push Robert out of the backseat so he could get out.

"You tell them, you little brat...you better tell them this wasn't my idea," the woman said, walking with angry strides towards Troy.

"Ma'am, please, hold on," one officer said, holding up his arm again to block the woman from getting to Troy.

"Kid, is this your mother?" the officer asked. Troy just stared at woman and said nothing.

"Kid, *is this* your mother?" The officer impatiently repeated his question. Robert's confused eyes went back and forth between Troy and the woman. "Kid, for the last time, *is she* your mother?"

Almost in a whisper, Troy turned to the officer and said, "No. My mother's dead."

"Troy, what are you saying?" Robert asked.

"No? So this *isn't* your mother?" The officer walked over and looked down at Troy. The boy didn't return the officer's look.

Robert turned and knelt with one knee on the sidewalk in front of Troy. "Why are you saying this isn't your mother, Troy?"

"Because I'm *not!*" the woman interjected and then spoke directly to Robert. "The two of them paid me and said whenever you came around to pretend that I was their..."

"Ma'am, please...Please let me..." the officer cut her off and then turned to Troy. "You and your brother Tyrell, where are your parents?"

Troy then spoke with a take-charge kind of voice. "I told you, my mother's dead and my dad—I don't fuckin' know."

"Which is it: dead or you don't know?" the officer questioned.

"My mom's dead and my dad, I've never seen him, so I don't know."

"Okay, okay," the officer said to the woman and Troy. "You two go with Officers Harden and Birchmont. They'll take your statements back at the station."

"I'm not going! Why should I go?" the woman said defiantly.

"Well, lady, it looks as if you did some things that you maybe shouldn't have, right? So if you want to clear this all up, you better go with them now."

"*Hmmmph!*" the woman spat out. She and Troy followed the officers into the back of their car, which was parked behind the one that Robert and Troy had been in. She never stopped complaining and cursing Troy as they entered the back seat.

"That damn brother of yours...I told you he would end up getting himself shot! You better straighten this all out. I'm not going to jail for—" The car door slammed and subdued her loud cries into a muffled rant. Robert could see the woman's arms still waving animatedly in the back of the car as the police cruiser moved down the street.

Robert stood there with his mouth wide open in shock. The officer laughed and put an arm on Robert's shoulder. "How long have you been a probation officer, buddy?"

"Five months," Robert replied sheepishly.

"Haha..." The officer laughed even louder. "Come on, I'll give you ride back."

"Wait...What the hell is happening?" Robert asked.

"Look, when you're on probation, you gotta have a fixed address right? So this...this Tyrell Williams, well, he told you this is where they were living and you bought it, right?"

"I...ah...well, where did they live then?"

"That's your job, buddy. How the hell am I supposed to know? Anyway, your caseload just got a little lighter, eh? Come on..." The officer started walking back to his cruiser and opened the back door for Robert.

"But I don't get it. Why pretend he had a mother? Why not just find a place of their own?" Robert asked.

"He was on probation, he can't be taking care of a minor." And then the cop stopped. "He probably did that so we wouldn't try to put his kid brother in a foster home."

Robert got into the back seat as the officer closed the door. The officer sat down and started the engine. He looked in the mirror and said to Robert, "Maybe the brother thought he was doing something admirable, but he was just raising another felon. That kid will be sitting right where you're sitting within two years, if it takes him that long."

Robert looked into the mirror and gave a meek smiled sigh to the officer. It all happened so fast. *In one moment, the world changed!* In one moment, a wave of tears washed over him. In one moment, a young man who Robert had connected with for five months was gone—in one moment, a brother was wiped off the planet in a storm of bullets. Change could happen in one moment. A little boy was homeless—*now completely alone, and God knows where he'll end up! How many worlds were changed in that one rifled moment?*

He cried softly, leaning his head on the back of the officer's seat and then looked beside him. There it was, the old worn yellow curled notebook that Robert had always seen Troy carry. The same one he had seen this young boy scribble away in as he spoke with his older brother, Tyrell. Robert picked up the book and looked at the front cover. On it was the scratchy scrawl of a ten-year-old's handwriting:

C U when you get there.

He opened the book and on the first page was written "Coolio's song." Under that title was what looked like the lyrics. As the police car's radio spoke to the officer driving, Robert drifted away into Troy's world.

The book was filled with what seemed to be Troy's attempt to write his own lyrics. It was filled with more scratched marks than words and it was hard to actually follow the sentences, but Robert made out these words:

> *question guns—and your war—and that door that you lock*
> *Home's not a street—that u walk and can't talk*
> *question pain—that you gain—finding fame—in the game*
> *Get a phone—you can moan*
> *but never question Home that's your own*
> *that's your own—Not alone—not alone*

Robert was jolted back to the world around him as the police car came to sudden stop.

"Sorry 'bout that, buddy. Is it okay if I drop you off here? Just got a call, it's in the opposite direction," said the officer.

Robert looked up and saw his car in the parking lot across the street. "Yeah, this is great..." Robert said as he held up the yellow book. "Oh, and I have this..." but then he cut himself off. He was going to ask the officer to make sure Troy got his book back. But he knew it would never make it back to the little boy's hands, so he just put it under his arm and continued, "Ah, nothing...You're in a hurry...Thanks for the ride."

> *Remember when I got home that night, love? You had called my mother and told her what happened. I remember her standing there as I opened the door (it doesn't matter how old you are but when something traumatic happens seeing your mother, well). I just started crying. She grabbed me and held me so tight it almost broke my ribs. You and Jenny were hugging and crying, everybody was crying because I was so close to those bullets— knowing that I could have died, too...My mom telling me how sorry she was that she helped me get that job and I should do something safer, like my music. And all I remember is feeling that incredible gut-wrenching feeling of guilt and overwhelming sadness...Guilt because I had a mother, guilt because there was a mother there waiting for me. And this sadness...well, maybe sadness isn't even really the word for it because what I felt for those two boys, and now for that little Troy, it was like my heart had cracked open and I could actually feel it dripping. I felt like my heart was wet and weeping.*
>
> *Remember Little Rock? How she was so worried about me that she slept in our bed for the next two weeks!*
>
> *"Home's not a street that u walk and can't talk. Get a phone you can moan. Home's your own. Not alone. Not alone."*
> *Troy was ten but his words sounded more like an old solitary warrior*

who had battled a lifetime on the streets of his city, maybe for justice—justice from a world that didn't really seem to care or really even try to listen to him or his brother.

Do you remember that time we sat in that park—you know the one that has those lions on the gate—and we all took turns reading and singing out loud every single thing that little kid wrote in that yellow book?....And in my head that whole time, I had this kind of crazy wish; I was hoping that maybe Troy would hear us—hear his own words—and then like an apparition that comes from chanting some magical words, he would suddenly appear—no longer having to live on the street and be fighting for a home...because you and me and Little Rock, we would give him one.

It had been impossible for Robert to return the book to Troy, or even locate him. The government agency that had custody of Troy thought he might be in danger because he had been a witness to his brother being shot. So, Troy had been put into protective foster care—somewhere that Robert hoped he would at least find a peaceful loving place he could call home, that home he achingly wrote so much about.

Five years later, Robert left the probation office and started doing his safe school workshops in high schools. He would bring that yellow notebook along and read it out loud to the students. He hoped that Troy's innocent expressive words would show the students how a ten-year-old street kid had so keenly identified the loneliness and heartache that so many in their teens deeply felt. And workshop after workshop, Troy's words created a sense of inspiration and painted a picture of someone who had never given up on the quest for hope, home and happiness.

Nine years after Robert witnessed young Troy holding his dead brother Tyrell on the sidewalk, he found himself sitting in a large room with eight inmates at the Milestone Penitentiary. After hearing about Robert success in the high schools, he had been asked by the prison to run a series of workshops for young offenders who had three or fewer months left to serve and were getting ready for transitioning back into society. These prisoners were like the same wayward souls he would have met when he was a probation officer. Robert was so excited by this unique opportunity. This was the reason he had left that job so that he could do something like this. He knew the time these men had with a probation officer was too short and scattered. And Robert thought maybe, maybe by doing these workshops here—before they got out—that he could really make a real difference in their lives.

"This is Robert Sanchez. He'll be working with you today." That was all the warden said before he left the room.

Eight young men in their late teens and early twenties sat in chairs that were roughly formed into a circle. The prison's library was a classroom-sized space. White metal shelves lined the walls and housed maybe a thousand books. Three large wooden desks displayed six ancient computers that were all chained at the back to the wall. Behind the circle of chairs stood three guards, two with the sneering grimaces of dogs you might find tied up at the back of a factory, and another who actually looked interested in what was about to happen.

"Thanks. Hi, my name is actually *Roberto* Sanchez." Although he had just been introduced as Robert Sanchez, looking at the ethnically diverse audience surrounding him made him think being Roberto would gain him greater acceptance.

Of the eight inmates, five were black, one was Asian and two were Hispanic. Most of them looked as if they spent the majority of their time in a gym or a tattoo parlour. Six had shaved their heads and one had spiky, jet black hair. The Asian had shoulder length hair that was tightly tied into dreadlocks. A strange sight caught Robert's attention. One inmate held a pencil and a pad, looking as if he was ready to take notes. The body language of all the prisoners showed complete disinterest. Most were slouching as if they might fall off their chairs. And most did not even look at Robert as he spoke.

"I'm not sure what we can do for a couple of hours each week for the next three months, but..."

Robert was quickly interrupted. An inmate, who had to be close to six foot seven, jumped from his seat and towered over Robert.

"Damn! Nobody said we had to do this every week! Three months? Damn!" This outburst sparked a couple of other inmates to also state their displeasure with the time commitment.

"Sit down, you piece of crap," one of the snarling guards snapped as he put a hand on the shoulder of the tall inmate and forced him to sit. "Go on, Mr. Sanchez," said the guard dog, who wore a satisfied smile at his ability to slam the inmate back in his seat and restore peace so quickly.

Robert looked at the guard. Although he wanted to say 'thanks,' he found it hard to say anything that would empower that self-satisfied smile. He leaned into the group and spoke in a hushed voice, "Okay...wow...Well, if some of you feel like you don't want to be here, let's talk about that."

"Don't bother. They don't have a choice," the other guard barked.

In his years as a probation officer, Robert had dealt with some police officers like this guard, ones who didn't believe in rehabilitation or second chances. The ones who treated every offender as if they had committed their crime against them personally; therefore, it was always the right moment to get even. And Robert knew only too well how futile it could be trying to fight these types of people, so instead he employed the philosophy of keeping his enemies close.

"Thank you. I'm sorry, what is your name?"

"Frank DeCosta," the guard replied with an authoritative nod.

"Thanks, Frank. Thanks for clearing up the situation."

"No prob." Frank smiled, the cynical kind of smile that told each and every one in the room that he was the top dog—the only one in charge.

"So if what Frank tells me is true, that you don't have a choice, then maybe that's where we should start." Robert looked around the circle—all he saw were the same distrustful looks an innocent man sees on the faces on a jury that he knows will convict him no matter what the evidence shows.

"Okay, so what is choice?" Robert asked.

Silence.

He tried a different question. "Okay, how about this? Why don't you feel you have any choice?"

"Are you some kind of moron? We feel it 'cause we ain't got no fucking choice!" said the huge linebacker sporting what looked like a scorpion tattoo on the side of his shaved head.

"Yeah, not *'til* we get outta this shithole," said the guy who was constantly cracking his knuckles.

"Watch your fucking language!" Decosta snapped.

"What choice we got when they tell us when to sleep, when to wake up and what to eat?" asked the Asian with the dreadlocks. "Choice is one of your rich guys' words."

Then six-foot-seven stood up again and said, "Yeah, choice is the word guys like you like to use, guys that don't have to live here." The inmate turned to Frank DeCosta and continued, "Yeah, choice is not having that freak wailing on you if you're like twenty seconds late getting to your cell."

Robert's heart skipped a beat! The last thing he wanted was to provoke the inmates to complain about the guards in the room. Frank DeCosta surprised Robert by not appearing angered at all by the inmate's outburst.

He turned to six-foot-seven and said, "First of all, that never happens here and if it did, I wouldn't be working here, would I?...Would I?!!"

Six-foot-seven looked at the pad writer, who was shaking his head at him in a silent plea for him to be quiet. Six-foot-seven mumbled something in response to DeCosta, but still sat down.

Robert looked at DeCosta and then turned back to the circle, wondering if anyone else was going to challenge the guard. Other than a couple of garbled words of profanity directed at the floor, no one dared catch DeCosta's eyes. The guy with the notepad lifted his hand, and everyone immediately became quiet and still. It was obvious that this young man was their leader. They all watched as he wrote something down then lifted his head and spoke directly to Robert.

"Fucking choice?" he said very calmly. "Do you seriously think anyone one of us here has 'choice'? Let me ask you a question, RobertO." He drew the sound of the 'O' out a little bit longer, which made some of the inmates laugh. But the pad writer held up his hand and they instantly stopped.

"You're here because someone thought you could *help us*, right?" He repeated it a little louder, "*Right?*"

Robert paused and meekly asked, "Am I here because someone thought I could help you, is that your question?"

"No. I want to know, if you even know, what fucking *choice* is?" All eyes were now on Robert; even Frank DeCosta smiled one of those mean-spirited smiles. He seemed to love seeing people squirm.

Robert tried to hide the fear he felt, so he bent over and pretended to scratch the back of his leg. He didn't have an answer so he focused on the question.

"Well, that's a great question! And...well...after hearing everything you guys said, I have to think about it. I mean, because, well, for sure, it *is* different for you. But, I wasn't really talking about what my choices are compared to yours because, well, frankly, most of us would be living in a perpetual nightmare if we constantly compared what others have and measured it against what we don't have. So no, I wasn't really thinking about it that way."

"You talking to yourself? Answer the question! What other fucking way is there?" demanded the pad writer.

No one else spoke. Everyone was now staring hard at Robert, waiting for his answer. The ominous sound of the knuckle-cracker filled the room. Robert felt like he was in one of those movies where the bad guys had you tied up to a chair, demanding that you better spill your guts or they would do it for you—with some very threatening instrument.

"I asked you a question. What other fucking way is there?" demanded the pad writer.

Robert knew what he said next was the key to getting the respect of each of those inmates. He dared himself to look right into the eyes of the pad writer. Then, he kind of arched his head skyward and closed his eyes. He took one long intake of air, exhaling equally as long, then opened his eyes and looked right back at the pad writer.

"Man, you know what? That's an amazing question. So, what other way is there? Okay, okay, don't worry, I'm answering it! Alright, well...most of our choices are dictated by our circumstances right?"

"Quit asking me...just answer the fucking question...You're supposed to be helping us here, right, RobertO?!"

"Alright, alright...Okay. Each one of us...by 'us', I mean all human beings, regardless of our circumstances—well, I think...I mean, it's just a thought of mine and I may be wrong..."

"Will you just fucking say it!" Pad writer pleaded.

"Okay...well, I think each of us always has choices, no matter what the circumstances!"

"What?" The Pad writer threw his arms up in rebellion. "You're *gonna* come here every week for three fucking months to tell us that we all got choices, no matter where we are?"

Robert just looked straight at the pad writer and said, "Okay..." He said it like he had just discovered something. "Okay...What is one thing...*one thing* that is so precious to you, and I mean, a thing that means so much to you, so much that you don't want anyone to ever...even make a joke about it?"

"What?" the pad writer responded. "That's your answer?"

"Yeah...yeah, you want to know what other way there is, right? So please, just answer my question and then you'll find out."

The room got even quieter. Decosta leaned in. Even he knew it was downright dangerous to ever challenge the pad writer.

But the pad writer surprised everyone by actually answering Robert's question.

"What is way too precious to me? So precious that no one can ever make a joke about it?" Robert nervously nodded his head.

"Well...no one ever...ever jokes about my brother."

For a second, the room went dead quiet. But as soon as the pad writer looked around the circle, all the other inmates started speaking, vigorously shaking their heads, saying things like, "no way, absolutely not." They promised that they would never, *never*, never joke about his brother.

The pad writer turned to the knuckle cracker. "Yo, what *'bout* you?"

"Me? Yeah, of course man...you know, no way I'd joke about your bro."

"No, not that, you idiot!" The pad writer sighed in disgust. "What's too precious for you to joke about?"

"Oh, me? Well, my...ah...um...my...ah...mother? Yeah, my mother!"

And then like a teacher in a classroom, the pad writer pointed to each inmate for their answer. Slowly going around the circle, each of these hard looking prisoners spoke about one of the things that they never wanted anyone to joke about: my lady, Jesus, respecting my name, my dream...But when it got to six-foot-seven, he had nothing to say. He just slumped his shoulders, shaking his head back and forth.

"Come on, JJ, think! What's one of yours?" the pad writer asked.

JJ put his hand to his face and looked as if he was thinking hard and then blurted out, "being retarded."

The room burst into laughter. JJ violently swung both arms out, almost knocking the two on either side of him to the floor as he screamed, *"Shut the fuck up!"*

Frank DeCosta and the other two guards quickly moved towards the group to stop what looked like the beginnings of an all-out brawl. But as six-foot-seven stood up, the room became instantly calm. He took a step toward Robert and spoke in a soft boyish, earnest voice.

"My little sister was born with brain problems. I hate when anyone makes a joke about that. They said she always goin' to be like a four-year-old kid her whole life."

The room quickly filled with apologies. "Sorry, man..." "Damn JJ...I didn't know..." "Damn...Sorry, bro...my bad."

"How old is she now?" Robert asked gently.

"She's sixteen." Six-foot-seven sat down. "But man, I mean she's sixteen and she still carries one of those little stuffed things with her all the time. The thing is all smelly and dirty and she won't ever let anyone wash it. Always has to be with her. It's that little green thing from that TV show..."

"Kermit?" asked dreadlocks.

"No, that's Ernie," another voice insisted.

"No, it's that thing in the garbage can...Griefer, I think."

"That's Grover, you ass wipe...and no, it's Kermit."

"Kermit...yeah, that's it, I think it's Kermit," JJ said.

Robert couldn't help but smile a little, watching these threatening looking young men converse about which Sesame Street character was the green one. The playful mood was quickly broken when the pad writer spoke.

"Okay, RobertO," still stressing the O again, "what do these things we don't joke about have to do with choices?"

"Well, look at what just happened. Everybody had a different thing they want to protect. And protecting that thing...that's a choice, isn't it? You see, most of our choices are completely unique from everyone else's. Do you know what the definition of choice is? Well, it's the act of choosing something from all the alternatives."

The room froze with a collective blank questioning stare.

"Alternatives mean...all the choices we have. So, we are like...like these judges, choosing from all the choices we have. And most of the choices we make come from what we value or what we believe in. Someone said respect or their lady, Jesus, their mother...and JJ here, not making fun of his sister who was born with something that stops her from developing like you and me. It is your choice to honour those things you value, right?"

"Yeah, I do value my sister," JJ said.

"And I believe in Jesus," Dreadlocks jumped in.

"See," Robert continued. "It might not be my choice or even anyone else's but no one, nobody, can stop you from making the choice of fighting to protect what's precious to you. Like whether you laugh at something or get angry at something, that choice makes you who you are and says a lot about how you will live your life...and safeguarding what you value is probably going to guide what other choices you make."

Robert felt relieved that most of the eight were scratching their heads or looking thoughtful, trying to understand what he had just said, but his relief was short-lived, because the pad writer spoke up.

"What about you? You can eat when you want and go home when you want. We can't do that. Because we don't have that choice."

The others swiftly joined in. "Yeah, what about that?"

"Well, that's a different kind of choice. That's like your situation choice. You're here because you got in trouble with the law, right? Well, first you made a choice to do the thing that put you in this situation and so now you're finding that your situation ends up making a lot of your choices for you."

"I got here *tryin'* to sell the car I stole," JJ blurted out.

"You see, that's a choice, and how did that work out for you?" asked Robert.

"Not fucking good. I'm here, *ain't* I?" JJ sighed.

"Would you change that choice if you had the chance?"

"Damn right I would."

"So coming here wasn't your choice?"

"My choice would be to be free like you!"

"Our freedom? Well, how much freedom we have to make choices depends on what kind of situation you're in or willing to go in! Sure, I get to go home, but I still have to eat what my wife cooks..."

"Yeah, well, why don't you ask her to cook what you want?" JJ interrupted.

Robert laughed a little. "I do sometimes, but in my situation I choose to let her decide."

"Otherwise she won't *choose* to be married to *ya* anymore," JJ said, and the room broke into a laugh.

"See that? You all *choose* to laugh," Robert jumped in.

"Yeah, 'cause it was funny."

"But maybe it wasn't for me. Maybe saying that might hurt or scare me. Did you even consider that before you chose to laugh?" Robert asked.

"Wait," the pad writer said. "You mean, we gotta think about whether something might hurt..." and suddenly he stopped himself from saying the obvious.

"Yes," Robert said, "and the tough thing is, you can't always know something is going to scare or hurt someone...but see, we all got this thing called choice. We always have a choice and doesn't matter how you look at it; we are responsible for every choice we make. And, in the end, you're accountable for every choice you make. Oh, you can blame someone else—say it was his idea, he hit me first, he brought the gun—but you always have the choice of how to react."

Robert leaned over and pulled his small backpack on his lap. "I want to show you something this kid who lived on the street wrote. And let me say, he wrote this when he was only nine or ten. It has to do with his situation and what he thought his choices were."

Robert pulled Troy's old yellow notebook out. He opened it up and turned the pages and when he got to the page he wanted, he held the book up to read.

"Now, remember this kid is only ten. Okay, here it is: 'My bro has gun, it's never fun, always on the run, home is the night, don't wanna fight so I choose to write...'"

Robert put the notebook on his lap and looked around the circle. A wonderful serene thoughtfulness filled the room as everyone looked at Robert, just taking in the words.

Then the knuckle cracker asked, "Can *ya* read it again?"

Robert picked up the notebook and started reading, "My bro has gun, it's never fun, always on the run, home is the night, don't wanna fight so I..."

"Where the hell did you get that?" the pad writer asked as he leapt from his chair. "Gimme *that!*"

He yanked the book from Robert's hands. The voice that came out of him sounded like a wounded grizzly bear. "Where the hell did you get *this?*"

He then started violently tearing the old yellow notebook into pieces. Two of the guards jumped into the middle of the circle and wrapped their arms around the pad writer and took him to the floor in one quick movement. Still the pad writer continued frantically ripping the pages.

Frank DeCosta yelled, "All right, the rest of you against the wall." They apparently didn't move fast enough for Frank DeCosta, so he screamed his order in such a loud angry shriek that it made Robert shrink down in his chair.

In a split second, DeCosta gave Robert a painful reminder of how limited these young men's choices were. He now sat alone in the circle of empty chairs. To his left, seven young men stood with their faces pressed against the wall. In the middle of the circle laid the pad writer, panting heavily with his face down on the floor and a foot on his back holding him down. The pad writer turned his head to the side to observe the destruction of the yellow notebook, which was now scattered in pieces, inches from his head.

"All right, Mr. Sanchez," said Frank DeCosta, who was standing behind the seven inmates. "Session's up, you better get outta here first."

Robert sat there paralysed, just staring at the pad writer. "Sanchez, I said you gotta go *now*," Frank DeCosta growled.

Robert stood up and took a step towards the door. Then, he turned back and knelt down on one knee as if he was about to pick up the shredded notebook, but instead he bent down to the pad writer and quietly probed, "Troy?"

"I said, *get the hell outta here*, Sanchez," DeCosta almost screamed.

Robert didn't leave. He stood up to face DeCosta.

"Thanks for doing your job, Frank, but please let me do mine. Come on, look around. What happened here? He ripped up an old notebook, I mean the thing was already about to fall apart."

"That's not the point, he was threatening you and he violated your property," DeCosta said very matter-of-factly. Then he smiled and added, "and it was his *choice*, Mr. Sanchez, and he *chose* to...react wrong."

"It's true, Mr. Sanchez," said the guard who had seemed interested in the session. "They all know the rules and with Nelson taking your book from you and destroying it like that, well, we've got no choice; it's our job. We have to protect you."

"See, that's the thing. It's not my book," Robert said, but then stopped himself. "Wait a second, his name is Nelson?"

"Yeah, this is Nelson Dupree," the other guard answered as he took his foot off the pad writer's back.

Robert walked back towards the pad writer who, even though the foot was off his back, still lay prone on the floor. Robert knelt down again and picked up the pieces of the yellow notebook as he spoke.

"So, *Nelson*, then I guess I have to ask you why you would choose to rip up Troy Williams' notebook, a little ten-year-old kid's book. Why?" Robert held out the pieces of the book to the pad writer.

"That kid took a lot of time to write all the stuff he did in this book and it's great stuff. I mean this kid—"

"—That kid didn't know the fuck about life," the pad writer said in a soft voice.

"Please let him sit up?" Robert asked the guards. The guards took a very tentative step away from the pad writer, preparing themselves in case he exploded again, but the pad writer just slowly turned to his side and picked up a piece of the notebook Robert had missed.

The seven at the wall turned their heads to watch as the pad writer sat up on the floor in the middle of the empty circle of chairs.

"That's not my notebook, is it?" Robert asked with a quiet smile playing on his lips.

Everyone looked at the pad writer and waited for his answer. After a few seconds of silence, Robert could almost feel DeCosta's readiness to smack the pad writer, so Robert just gestured, "It's okay," with his hand and winked at Decosta to give the pad writer time to answer.

"That's not my notebook, is it?" Robert quietly asked again.

Then, after another five seconds, a small quiet "No," came out of the pad writer's mouth.

"Well, whose fuckin' book is it then?" DeCosta impatiently demanded.

"Frank, will *ya* just shut up for ten seconds?" asked the other guard.

Robert looked at the plain clock on the wall and said, "Officers, we got thirty minutes left of the session. Is it possible everyone can sit back down and we can finish?"

The two guards standing over the pad writer looked at each other, nodded their heads and then looked at Frank DeCosta.

"No, not until we find out whose book that is."

"It's mine, okay, DeCosta. The fucking book's mine!" the pad writer said. No one moved as they watched the pad writer stand up and sit back down in his chair. Robert sat directly across from him.

The guards then gestured for the other seven to sit back down. DeCosta looked at the clock and loudly broke the silence, saying, "Twenty-eight minutes." The other two guards looked at him and rolled their eyes.

Robert looked around the circle. Every inmate just looked directly at the pad writer, Nelson Dupree. No one said a word, but their looks screamed out loud. Dupree felt the hard and distrustful looks rain down on him. He was their leader. Nelson Dupree was someone you trusted. Nelson Dupree was a guy you fought for. Nelson Dupree was the man you looked up to. Nelson Dupree was the man you wanted to be. But now, all they all wanted to know was, who the hell was Nelson Dupree? And if he wasn't Nelson Dupree, why had he deceived them?

Nelson did not look up. He was staring at the piece of torn notebook he held in his hand. He was delicately trying to smooth it out.

Robert watched him fiddle with the paper as he remembered that little boy outside his office many years ago, scribbling away. Robert, who knew most of Troy's notebook by heart, couldn't help but wonder which piece of paper he had in his hand and what it said. Just as Robert took a breath to speak, Nelson cut him off.

"No, let me speak, if that's okay."

Most of the other inmates muttered back, "Yeah, you better, brother," and, "Damn, better be some truth."

Nelson lifted his head and spoke as he looked around the room at the other inmates. "Yeah, I know, you're all pissed, I know. I wouldn't fucking trust anyone who doesn't say who they are straight up and maybe I *ain't* worth trusting anyway. Yeah, my name is Nelson Fucking Dupree and no one's called me Troy since I wrote this book." He held up the one piece of torn notebook in his hand.

"I didn't change my name, goddamn lawyers and those bitches at 'services' did. They said they were trying to protect me, change my directional course of life." He looked at Robert. "My choices, I guess...but I didn't deceive *ya*. Hey, I'm still here, right? Same fucking direction. Name change didn't do anything..." and then Nelson stopped himself as he thought about what he had just said. He was about to say something, but then turned to Robert. "Goddamn it! You're the doctor, why don't you say something?"

"Okay, well first, what do you want us to call you? Nelson or Troy?"

"Nelson. Troy's fucking dead, man...Yeah, it's my choice. Right? So it's Nelson."

"Then why did *ya* freak, man? Why'd *ya* rip up that kid Troy's book?" The knuckle cracker asked.

"He is Troy, you idiot!" said another. "He ripped up his own book."

"Okay then, great...Why the fuck *ya* do that for?" The knuckle cracker wasn't giving up.

"*'Cause* it had to be done! All right? Now shut it!" Nelson slammed his hand on his thigh.

The knuckle cracker shrugged. "I was just *wonderin'*, bro, just *wonderin'*..."

Nelson turned to Robert.

"You are right, RobertO. Yeah, you're right. We do have choices. Maybe I didn't choose to change to my new name but I did fucking choose to kill the old one."

Robert couldn't help but sadly nod. "Okay, so then you want us to call you Nelson?"

A loud shrieking alarm sounded, which made Robert jump up from his chair.

DeCosta laughed and said, "That's it! Session's over. Line up!"

"Sorry," the other guard said to Robert. "Don't know what it is, usually someone's unaccounted for, but when that thing goes off, we have to get them back into their cells."

The inmates knew the drill. Within fifteen seconds, they were out of the room and halfway down the hall. As the inmates filed out, Nelson stopped, took Robert's hand and placed the piece of book he had in his hand in Robert's.

Only DeCosta and Robert were left in the room.

"Better pick up your bag, Sanchez. I have to escort you out of here. Oh, and listen, I have no choice but to report what that inmate did to your book...It's my job; I have to report it to the warden."

"Yeah, you have no choice," Robert said under his breath. DeCosta must have followed through and probably added some drama to the situation when he reported it to the warden, because the very next day, Robert was notified his workshops at the prison were cancelled.

You remember when I got home from the prison that day? When I dropped all the pieces of that old yellow book on the table? Do you remember what our little girl did? Little Rock...told us the story about her friend Sara, and how they had to all write a poem for class. And the teacher was collecting the poems and was going to read them aloud to the class, but when the teacher was just about to take Sara's poem, Sara snatched it from the top of her desk and just ripped her poem up. And when the teacher asked Sara why she did that, Sara told the teacher she did it because the poem had some bad words in it. But Jenny had found out that wasn't the reason. Sara just didn't want to share her poem with the class...Ah, and how did Jen explain it to us? Oh yeah, she told us Sara had said that the poem was not just from her head, but also from her heart and she said she just wasn't ready to share her heart with the class. But afterwards, Jen helped Sara tape her poem back together and then she let Jenny read it and it was okay because they were friends and Sara felt safe and that was why she could share her heart with Jenny. You remember that? So when Little Rock, saw the torn up notebook on the table, she told me that maybe Troy just wasn't ready to share his heart yet. That wee thing couldn't have been more right...

Two weeks later, as he sat in the small room at the Milestone prison, Nelson Dupree had a visitor. The room was filled with about fifteen rectangular, cafeteria-style tables with a bench on either side that was bolted to the floor.

The moment Nelson walked into the visiting room and saw Robert, he laughed sarcastically. "What the hell you doing here? No wait...don't tell me, you taped that book together and came here to give it to me?"

Nelson's laugh stopped abruptly when Robert actually pulled out that yellow notebook, which now looked more like one of those baby jigsaw puzzles all taped up.

"Yeah, actually my wife and daughter helped me." Robert laughed.

Nelson immediately put his hands up and said, "Are you some kind of fucking freak? Take that fucking thing away from me, man, or I'll shove it down your throat."

"Dupree, sit down!" came a voice from the door. Robert looked up and saw a guard, who had looked up from his Sudoku just long enough to yell at Dupree.

"Don't worry, I'll put it away." Robert put the old yellow notebook back into a plastic bag he had sitting beside him on the bench.

"I know we don't really know each other. Tro...well, Nelson. But it's been so long and I've been wondering...you know, since your brother..."

Nelson's eyes flared with anger. "Shut it...Do you hear me? Just shut it!"

"Last time. Sit down, Dupree!"

The guard pointed at him to sit. Nelson looked at the guard and then back at Robert a couple of times before deciding to sit. He slithered down sideways with one leg straddling the bench, looking as if he was preparing for a quick getaway.

They both sat in silence. Robert didn't know what to say next. He didn't have a plan. He had not really thought how this conversation might go. He just knew he was meant to connect with the young boy that had lived inside of him for all these years. Nelson broke the silence.

"So, what the hell you doin' here?" Nelson spoke with the impatience of someone who had somewhere more important to be.

Robert smiled slightly, remembering the first day he had met him and his brother Tyrell in that closet sized probation office. Tyrell had come in with that same impatient badass attitude that Nelson now exhibited. Yet, Nelson had something his brother didn't have. Tyrell's posturing and talk came off as an act, a toughness he needed to show. But Nelson didn't seem to be acting; his calm self-reassured stance exhibited the same body language one would see in a movie star or a president settling in to be interviewed.

And again, Robert found himself asking Nelson the same question he asked his dead brother nine years ago. "Can you help me, please?"

"Help?" Nelson questioned with a sneering raised eyebrow. "What kind of help could you ever need from me?"

"I'm not a probation officer anymore. I've been working in schools, trying to help kids. Trying to help these kids, you know, to make better choices."

"And why the fuck would you think that interests me?"

Robert fidgeted. He had imagined this moment many times. That if he and Troy were to ever meet again, it would be a joyous occasion. He truly believed the little boy who wrote all those profound thoughts in that notebook would have left the streets, found the home he so longed for, went to university and become a success. In all of Robert's fantasies of this reunion, never once did it take place in a prison visitation room.

"Well, um...do you like it here?" Robert kind of mumbled.

"What? Are you fucking *kiddin'* me? You came to see how I like it here?"

"No...no...it's just...I mean, I'm sure this place is horrible. You see, that's what I'm trying to do...I mean, that's why I left the probation office. I'm trying to help some kids from having to be...well...you know, be here, like this."

"You mean like me?"

"No, well, I mean...Sorry, yeah...that's kind of what I mean, but not like you, you know...you exactly...I'm just trying to help some kids make choices so they don't end up in a place like this."

Nelson looked at Robert for a moment and then back at the guard. The guard didn't look up from his Sudoku. Nelson didn't look like he was planning on leaving, so Robert asked him another question.

"How long have you got left?"

"What is it to you?"

Nelson's attitude and demeanour were so familiar to Robert. He saw it every day in many troubled high school students. But he knew it didn't always matter how the kids responded, because if they were responding that at least meant they were engaged enough to react. *How do you engage someone who comes with so much resistance? Just never tell them what to do,* he thought. *Just keep asking questions.*

"And what's your plan? You know, after you get out of here?"

"Haha..." Nelson snorted. He then leaned into the table and got closer to Robert. His face suddenly became deadly serious.

"Why? You got a job for me, like you did for my brother, Robert*O*?"

"No, Nelson. I've been..."

"And how did that work out?"

"What work out?"

"With my brother. How did that work out?"

"Look, Nelson, that was..."

"I asked you...how the fuck did that work out?"

"I don't know what you want me to say. I'm sorry your brother..."

Nelson cut Robert off by raising his hand. "Shut it! Now you listen to me. I don't care what the fuck you are working on or who you're working with, just get this into your thick skull: you *ain't* working on me. What you come here for? What did *ya* think? Did you think bringing in that little notebook was going to make me cry?"

"No, Nelson, I was just..."

"You think you're going to change my life? I'm *gonna* look at those scrawls on a page and suddenly I'm all changed! Oh, my God, look at me; I was once that little motherfucker who wrote stuff in a book that some old white fart thought was meaningful. Oh, if only I could go back to being that ten-year-old little prick, *Yes*...then my life would be saved!"

Nelson smiled cruelly. He knew exactly how to put someone in their place. And usually after he did that, he was used to people cowering and starting to blubber apologies and forgive me's but Robert didn't respond that way. He just maintained his gaze, looking straight into Nelson's eyes.

"What the hell you staring at? Don't act like you see something I don't,"

Robert calmly shrugged, "It doesn't matter what *I see*, Nelson. It's what you..."

"*What?* What I see? Is that what you were *gonna* say? What I see? Well, fuck you. You hear me? Fuck you! And I don't need your sanctimonious psycho crap. I'm not the one choosing to coming to this hellhole today. So don't tell me, I know what I fucking see!"

Robert tried to calm Nelson. "That's not really what I was going to say..."

"It sure the fuck is! And you know what? You're dead right! It's exactly what I see...and right now I see a man who thinks everyone needs saving!"

"But, Nelson, when I was talking about what I see, I meant..."

"You're not here 'cause of me...you're here 'cause of you!"

"What?" Robert felt as if he had been kicked in the gut. "Me? What the hell do you mean by that?"

"What the fuck you doin' here? Yeah, ask yourself that, RobertO, 'cause it's not like you fucking know me...It's all about you, isn't it? People like you, always saying, oh, they just want to help. Well, look around, I didn't ask for help. You're here 'cause of what? You think you see my future? And now, for some fucking reason, you think I need your help? Well, have you ever asked yourself maybe what *you* see isn't real? Maybe we're not all waiting around for Roberto Sanchez to come and save us?!"

You know, love, right then, in that prison visitation room—suddenly this overwhelmingly anxious feeling took over, making me question every fibre of who I think I am. I couldn't believe what he had said and how much it had hurt me. It actually hurt me to the core. Of course, I know what I'm doing is right. I really think I am helping, I truly believe it. I have to believe it. I mean, I've seen a lot of pain and suffering and I'm just doing my best, trying to, well, trying to make it go away...or lessen it...I mean, look what happened to his own brother. Yet, what he said—is it true? You know, I've never asked myself why am I doing what I do? Why do I do these workshops? Why is it so important to me to care about these kids? Or even care about Troy? Am I'm trying to be some saviour? Even when they tell me they don't want to be saved? What sort of purpose in life is that—helping people who don't want your help?

Or is it all about me? Is that how I want to be seen? A saviour? Is that who I am? Is that how I want people to see me? Have I just become so righteous I don't really know who I'm helping, I just need to save someone to make myself feel good? Is it really all about my own ego?

You know, every day as we journey I think about what I'm going to write in this journal about these three, and I tend to question why I think this is good for them. How does climbing a mountain make anyone a better leader or human being, for that matter? I'm seeing so much on this journey to Everest and today on our three-hour trek to Phakding, Troy and I walked together. Strange thing about the two of us is we never really venture into any conversations we had back in that prison or about his brother. But today, we were taking a break under this incredible magnolia tree and it was just the most magnificent view, and I asked him, "Well, Troy, is it worth it being here?"

133

But he didn't answer me. He just turned to me with that look of his and asked me, "Robert, why do you do this? Is it worth it?" And suddenly my mind was spinning. What the hell does he mean "is it worth it?" How can he ask me that? After all I have done?... And then it hit me. His question—asking me why I came to the prison that day to see him. That question just made me feel so naked, exposed—the same way I feel anytime someone asks me why I climb and if it's worth it? GOD, that question—I just keep living the answer, but never really find words for it.

Then Troy called Philip over and said this should be one of the day's interviews, asking me if it's worth it climbing mountains.

As Philip set up the camera, my mind just kept repeating Troy's question: 'is it worth it?' and all I could think of was you and that time—years ago when Jen was in high school—when you and I were watching her in one of those musicals she was in. The show was called 'Hair' and Jenny was singing that song, "Easy to be Hard." And remember when she got to that part about people who seem to care more about strangers and social injustice...when she came to that question in the song, she fell to her knees in front of her partner on stage and she almost cried the words, asking, 'If he only cared about the needing crowd?' Then she stopped singing and spoke the words, 'What about me, I need a friend?'

I told Troy and Philip how, at that moment when Jenny was singing, you turned to me, looked me directly in my eyes in that dark auditorium and gave me that same look Troy did, that day when we met in prison and he asked me if that was who I was? Someone who cared more for strangers, injustice, bleeding crowds, cared more about mountains than his own family? And was it all worth it?

And, my love, I gave him the only answer I knew—that living life is not easy. Trying to always do what you feel you need to do and want to do and then balancing that with doing what others want or need you to do, who knows? Everybody has different values. Somebody may think it's worth it to run into danger to save someone. Someone else may think scaling a cliff of ice is worth the risk. I mean, how do you measure worth?

So then I asked him, "What is your life worth?" Then, Philip turned the camera on Troy. Oh, Monique, that kid just amazes me with how much he takes in and how it lives inside him. Troy looked right into the camera and told us he's just discovering what worth means. He said back in Katmandu, when I took them to the orphanage and they were asked if they would please write to one of the kids when they got back home. Troy said he was told by one of the instructors at the orphanage that sometimes becoming a pen pal to one of these kids helps educate them, gives them hope and could maybe save them from a life of poverty. But mostly, the man had said, it gave them a feeling of self-worth knowing that someone from our country would take time for them.

Then, with this pained look on his face, Troy told us that afterwards when they were kicking the soccer ball around with all those orphan kids, he kept looking at each one of those orphans and thinking about how he had to pick a kid to write to. He knew he couldn't write to all of them, so how would he decide? Who should he give hope to? Who is worth it? And as soon as he said the word worth, he stopped himself...

In that moment, it was as if that little ten year old boy scribbling away in his notebook had come back to talk to me. Troy said that it seems to be getting harder as he gets older to find the right balance of worth; it just seems to constantly change throughout his life. What he once thought was worth so much, means nothing to him now...and then he told me that was the reason he asked me if climbing a mountain was worth it.

"I'm sorry. You're right, Nelson, that was sanctimonious psycho crap and nothing could be more true. I don't know you and it's true I am here because of me and because of something I see. I mean, maybe half the kids I'm trying to help don't even need help. I just see what I see and..."

"We all are what we see, RobertO. Why the hell do you think I'm here? I'm here 'cause of everything I see and saw. You gotta fucking react to the world you see. Look, I am here because of what I see. And if I don't react to the world I see, I don't survive."

They both turned when the sound of a woman crying filled the room. A young pregnant woman was crying and the inmate she was visiting was trying to console her.

"Is it okay that I ask you a question?" Robert asked.

"Look, I'm here. What you want? Me to hold your hand? Talk already." Though Nelson still sounded impatiently abrupt, Robert couldn't help but feel this was as friendly as Nelson got.

"Okay..." Robert said. "Well, do you think anyone can change from all that they see?"

"What?" Nelson said with a perplexed look on his face. "Can you ask me that question in English?"

"Sorry, all right, okay...Have you ever heard that saying 'Watch your thoughts, they become your words...and your words become actions...actions become your habits, and habits become your character...which becomes your destiny.' Did you ever hear that, Nelson?"

An angry voice interrupted them. "I'm not going to repeat this, Garcia. There is no touching! Got it?"

Nelson and Robert looked over at the guard, who had just gotten up and was berating the prisoner who was holding his pregnant girlfriend's hand.

The guard physically pulled the inmate's hand away from the young woman's hand. She was now crying uncontrollably. Robert gave a supportive smile to the inmate, urging him with his eyes to just let it go and to try not to respond to the guard.

Robert looked back to Nelson. "You want to clock that guard one, don't you?"

Nelson looked as dangerous as ever when he nodded.

"See, that's exactly what I'm saying...You have to watch your thoughts so they don't always become your actions."

"I know, I got that. So..." Nelson clenched his fists a little tighter and watched the guard walk back to his Sudoku.

"You say you have to react to what you see, right? And like the saying goes, if what we see becomes our thoughts and then most likely it becomes our words and then they probably turn into our actions, right?...Like now, if that was your girlfriend crying and the guard did that, what would you do?"

"Fucking label him one."

"And how does that work out for you each time?"

Nelson didn't answer and instead just let out an impatient grunt.

"So, you do what you always do right? You hit another guard? Is that who you have become, Nelson? Every time you see something you think is unjust, you throw a punch and label the guy? *SO*...does all the injustice just come to a complete stop after you do that?"

Nelson's whole body tightened, as a predator's does when preparing to pounce on its prey. He didn't appreciate Robert's question, and his impulse at being challenged was to label Robert right now. But that would mean Robert was right. It would mean that he was someone who answered everything with violence. So instead, Nelson took a deep breath and closed his eyes and leaned his head back.

The sounds of the crying girlfriend suddenly stopped and turned into a happy girlish giggle. Nelson's eyes snapped open and saw the inmate had found a way to make his girlfriend laugh by making funny faces, like a father would make for his young child.

"Argh!" Nelson shook his head in disgust. The inmate was now cupping his hands in front of his face and make childish peek-a-boo faces at his girlfriend. Nelson sharply turned back to Robert. "Yeah...well, right now I'd like to punch that freaking idiot's face for treating his woman like she's some kind of mindless baby!"

"But what made him do that, Nelson? He's reacting to the guard, right? So, what does he see? Does he see a guard on whom he can maybe get in one good punch, or a girl that's crying and needs him? He chose to see that comforting his girlfriend was more important, didn't he?"

"So what? That doesn't make him a man."

"Yeah, then what does it make him?"

Nelson just shrugged.

"Maybe he's like you, Nelson. Maybe he always gets mad in this kind of situation and so he just hits the guard and then...well, then it ends up worse. But this time, maybe...just maybe, he saw his girlfriend was more important to him than his anger towards the guard was. See, he had to change the way he thought about it so he could change the way he reacts to it. By changing the way he saw and thought about the situation, he changed his own actions. In the end, who knows, maybe he changed his destiny."

Nelson looked over at the guard and then at the couple. "So, you think if I stop wanting to beat the shit out of that idiot for treating his girlfriend like some retard, then..."

"No, Nelson, CHANGE...change the way you think about the whole thing! Look farther than you usually do. Try to see something more. That's what he did! Ask yourself why your first thought is always to hit!"

"I don't know why. Maybe that's my destiny! And you know what? Maybe nothing can ever fucking change that." For the first time, Nelson sounded like he was looking for an answer.

"Come on, Nelson; you're too young to believe that!"

"You got no fucking idea what I believe or what kind of choices I have to make! And you know fucking what? Some things...well, some things don't ever, ever change...no matter how much you..."

Nelson stopped himself. Was he going to say "try," or maybe "hope?" It didn't matter, as his ache was obvious. That was the first time Robert had ever heard Nelson complain about his plight in life and thought maybe he did want to change it.

"Look, Nelson, you're right. I have absolutely no idea the choices you have had to make in your life, but I do know...No, you know what? Forget it."

Nelson was looking at his hands as if he was questioning what they were going to do next.

"Look, Nelson, when I asked you how long you have left in here, I asked that because I need some help from someone like you. I've been working with some schools and some groups from your neighbourhood. It's a leadership kind of thing but also something to stop kids from joining gangs and, well, just making it safer out there...and I was wondering if you..."

Nelson's calm suddenly exploded.

"No! You hear me? No! So shut it! You think any of that crap works? Those fucking govern-*mental* programs...those damn programs—they build more gangs than they stop...They make everybody weak...dependent!"

"That's because we don't have anyone running those programs who has actually lived it like you did, leading the...Wait. What did you call it?" Robert asked with a grin. "'Govern-*mental?* I like that, half those programs are mental. Mental because we don't go about it the right way."

"Are you fucking deaf? I said *shut* it!"

"Come on, please...Listen, I honestly think someone like you could change..."

Nelson stood up. "Do you know how everyone sees someone *workin'* for those—"

"—Sit it down, Dupree!" The guard looked up from his Sudoku.

"It's okay, Nelson, please sit down," Robert pleaded, not wanting to lose Nelson like this.

But Nelson continued, "Like fucking traitors, snitches...They end up betraying everyone that helped them survive so far. And how the fuck do they think they all survived? They survived because of their brothers, because of their gangs...and no one has ever died on my watch. *NO ONE!*"

"Sit down, Dupree," the guard sneered. "Don't make me come over."

Nelson leaned over the table close to Robert. "And hear this! Don't think I could ever become one of those...one of those bastards, 'cause I'm no *fucking traitor!*"

Nelson turned and walked towards the guard to show him he was leaving.

"Traitor to what, Troy?" Robert called out. "You think you'd become a traitor by...maybe stopping another young kid from getting strung out on drugs? What, Troy? A traitor by preventing some kid from spending his life here in some prison?"

Nelson took a step back to Robert and raised his fist. Robert flinched. But still said the one thing he knew Troy didn't want to hear.

"Do you think you'd be called a traitor if you helped stop some young kid from having to watch his own brother get shot down in the street?"

"Dupree, don't move!" The guard pulled out his baton and held it against Nelson's chest. He turned to Robert. "Mister, I'm going to have to ask you to leave. All right, Dupree, put your hand down. Come on! Let's move it *outta* here."

Nelson relaxed his hand and smiled to the guard. "Yeah, let's do that. Nothing for me here anyway."

He and the guard started towards the door, stopping only momentarily at the table where the girl was still laughing from the inmate's peek-a-boo faces.

"Stop that shit, man! She's a fucking woman, not some baby in diapers!"

Nelson then looked back at Robert. "See, I didn't hit anybody, did I?" And then, after a perverse and empty laugh, Nelson said, "Oh my God, did I just change my destiny?"

You know, I often think about that jail visit and that word: "destiny." Was I destined to meet these three...or them to meet me? Is there really some hidden power that shapes our future? Can we truly shape our destiny? Because if it is our destiny, aren't we going there anyway???

Strange to think it was only about a year and half ago when Troy stormed out of that visiting room. Sometimes on the journey with him, I've often felt a little ashamed of myself. Could I have tried harder to find him after his brother was killed? Should I have gone back to see him again at the prison? Did I give up on him??? It is kind of like...the climb on Denali, when we were at high camp. And during that whole climb we had such unpredictable weather, but then we got lucky and we had this one window—this one and only chance—to get to the top. But at the same time, another team who climbed with us the whole time had a pretty sick climber and they needed to get him down. They didn't need our help, they didn't even ask for it. And so, as we set off for the summit, they started their decent. We made it to the top and that climber died on the way down. Apparently there wasn't anything anyone could do, but what has always gnawed at me forever is that I didn't even offer to help. If they had asked I would have...but deep down, I was hoping they wouldn't ask me.

It's a question...I wonder what means more: when you are in a hurry to get somewhere, then you see someone slip on the ice and you stop to help them...or when you are just on a stroll with nowhere to be and you see someone slip on the ice and you help them? Does the good deed mean more when you are in a hurry and got somewhere to go?

Anyway...not sure I can answer that any better now, but I know it didn't feel right...

It was called a "block party" and it was in the neighbourhood that Robert had been working in for quite some time. Some of the women from the local community centre started the idea. "Bring the family, bring your barbecue, meet your neighbours," was what the poster said.

The centre had raised enough money to supply hotdogs and burgers and some cold drinks. By eight p.m. there were almost two hundred people gathered on the street and sidewalks. Music played from some of the windows that were left open in the townhouses that lined the street. Kids chased each other with water guns. Young mothers held kids on their hips and gossiped. Teenagers hung out flirting and laughing. A variety of basketball and soccer balls bounced in every direction, threatening to spill cans of soda and knock over condiments in their haphazard flight. The barbecue grills firing up filled the street with that early summer evening aroma, an unmistakable invitation to kick back and relax.

Malvern District was one of the poorest parts of the city, filled with mostly housing projects and tall dilapidated apartment complexes. These streets had more than their fair share of crime and violence and there weren't many festive nights like this one. On a rare night like this, it felt like people were living in the land of plenty: living a life of celebration, music and free food. Everyone was playing in the streets and surrounded by the joyous sound of laughter.

Robert had just set up the barbecue grill he had brought from home with the help of Monique and Jenny. The Sanchez's were not hard to spot in this dark skinned neighbourhood, which consisted of a mixture of Nigerians, Jamaicans, Trinidadians, Pakistanis and Indians. But today, neither colour nor creed mattered, neighbours simply blended together in celebration.

"Where you want this, Robert?" asked Mertle Bolt in her delightful Trinidadian accent. Behind Mertle were her two teenage daughters. They were half-carrying and half-dragging a huge cooler containing meats for the barbecue.

"Oh, here just beside me is fine. Thanks, kids." Robert laughed, seeing the two girls panting as they were relieved of their meat carrying duty. "Oh, hey, Mertle, I'd like you to meet my wife, Monique, and my daughter, Jenny."

Monique put her hand out to shake but Mertle held her arms open for a hug instead. Monique laughed and walked into Mertle's hug. Her tiny body was lost in Mertle's heavy-set frame. As they hugged, Mertle looked at Jenny, opened one arm and gestured for Jenny to join in. "Get in here, girl!" Jenny shyly moved into the woman's arms beside her mother. It looked as if Mertle could have put three more Jenny-sized girls in that hug.

"Well, look at you two," Mertle said, putting her arms around both Jenny and Monique. "Pretty girls you have, Mr. Robert. And I was thinking all this time you were lying about having a family."

Both Monique and Jenny looked at Robert, surprised.

"Oh no, you two don't start letting your minds be playing things." Mertle laughed. "It's just that he spends so much time here helping us and the kids, being with our families, so it was hard imagining he had any time to be familying with anyone else is all. Oh, and these are my daughters, Shania and Tenesia."

Mertle's two daughters raised their hands slightly and waved. "Hey, why don't you two take Jenny and show her around? I'm sure she ain't interested in hanging around with us old folks."

"Okay, you wanna come?" Shania asked Jenny, who looked at her and then her mom and dad.

"It's fine, Jen...Mom and me can do the cooking," Robert said.

"Mom and I." Monique turned to Robert, correcting his English.

Mertle burst out laughing. "Thank God, girl, you said it! I've been wanting to get your man to speak right for months now but always kept my mouth shut 'cause I been afraid he might take it the wrong way."

"Well, you better get going, Jen, before you need to be fixed by these two English majors!" Robert winked at Jenny.

"See you later Mom, Dad." Jenny and the two girls drifted down the street into a throng of teenagers who were playing a game of basketball without nets. The girls stopped the game and were introducing Jenny. In a matter of moments Jenny was on a team and playing a game that looked more like keep away than any kind of basketball.

"Well, nice meeting you, Monique. I've gotta get some more meat for Jessie. Look around Robert, will you? Look at *'em*, a lot more people than we expected...We did good, Robert...We did real good..." Mertle smiled as she waddled off.

Monique turned to Robert. "She's exactly like you said, Bobby, and you're right about those hugs. Even though I thought she might cut off my air supply, when you're in her arms, it really feels like it's your mom hugging you after a bad day."

"And I can't tell you how many times she has helped kids who don't have mothers to feel that way, Mon. I really don't know what Malvern would be like without Mertle Bolt."

"Hey, you got anything ready, mister?" came a little voice behind Robert.

Robert turned around and saw a little boy holding a baby. The boy couldn't have been more than eight and the baby looked to be maybe six to eight months old. Monique squeezed Robert's arm tightly to suppress her reaction. Although the image of this little boy holding his baby brother might be cute, it was the way he was dressed in dirty clothes and the fully stained blanket his brother was wrapped in that had Monique grabbing her husband's arm.

"Well, my friend, it'll be about seven minutes. Think you can hold on till then?" Robert asked.

"'kay." The little boy nodded.

"What's your name?" Monique asked as she knelt on one knee so she was face to face with the boy.

"Martin," the boy answered.

"And who is that your holding? Your baby? I don't know, you look too young to be a father," Monique teased the little boy.

"This is my brother, Luther, but I'm kind of like his dad too because mamma says his dad is dead to her and Luther now…and she needs me to help him grow up."

"Oh, so you both have different dads?"

"Yep."

"And who's helping you *gr*—" Monique stopped herself and just asked, "so where is your father then?"

"He's dead…He was shot before I was born."

"Shot?" Monique quickly recovered from the boy's frank reply. "Oh…I'm sorry." Monique thought of how little Martin could probably use a lot of those Mertle hugs. She gave Robert an I-can't-believe-this look.

"Hey, Martin, where's your mom now?" asked Robert.

"She went to pee."

Suddenly a loud thumping sound was heard in the distance. As the noise grew nearer, you could almost feel the pounding of the beat quake under your feet; it drowned out all other sound. Robert immediately saw that it was coming from a dark green Hummer that had just parked on the side street. The moment the car's engine was turned off, the harsh pounding ceased. Everyone stopped whatever they were doing. All eyes focused on the Hummer. Anxious murmuring filled the street. Watching and waiting in anticipation for the doors to open, almost as if royalty had arrived.

The car doors opened, six black men emerged onto the sidewalk and made their way into the party. Three went in one direction and the other three moved towards Robert and Monique. Even the kids stopped playing. Everyone seemed to part in order to make a path for the royal six as they walked around. You could feel a palpable mixture of awe and angst as they mingled. Some people were clearly not too happy about these guys showing up and yet there were many that excitedly gathered around to follow and welcome them.

"Oh my God! I can't believe it," whispered Robert.

"What...What's wrong, Bobby?" asked Monique, standing up from where she'd been leaning over to talk to little Martin.

"It's Troy...or Nelson...whatever he's calling himself now," Robert said as he mindlessly turned a burger over.

"You mean your Troy, the yellow notebook Troy?" Monique asked.

"Yep, Mertle told me he got out of prison a couple of months ago. But I haven't seen him since then. By the looks of the way he seems to be parting the sea, he here for a reason."

"Bobby, he seems to be walking right towards us."

"Yeah, it's okay, Mon." Robert looked at little Martin, who was still waiting for his burger. "Hey, Martin, is your mum coming soon?"

"She said to go back home after I get something to eat," Martin said.

"Okay, my man, only two minutes left, okay?" Robert looked up from the grill; Troy's eyes met his.

Troy was only eighteen but had the kind of presence that gave off the impression of someone much older. His deep set eyes could either be menacing or have the look of one with undeniable purpose. Beside Troy were two younger kids that walked with an almost synchronized swagger and they tilted their heads in an obvious rehearsed attitude. There wasn't anything natural about them. One could see they were gangsters in the making and Troy was their teacher.

"RobertO...nice to see you." Troy spoke as if the two had been old friends. There wasn't any of that attitude Robert had seen him show in prison. He didn't need it because here he was a king; all that attitude was left for the young guards in training. The two mini-gangsters eyed Robert with a healthy disdain.

But the way Troy had spoken and welcomed Robert eased Monique's worry, so she spoke with a smile. "Troy, it's so great to finally meet you."

Troy just tilted his head and gave Monique a sinuous wink. Robert quickly chimed in, "It's Nelson, love...Nelson! Hey, Nelson, I'd like you to meet my wife, Monique."

"Hey, you did well for yourself, Roberto." Troy purposely made an effort to slowly look Monique up and down.

"I like what you're doing for my people, Mr. Sanchez. I like this..." Troy said as he looked down the street and the party was slowly getting back to normal. "Yeah, you did good...and who's this little man?"

"That's Martin and his brother, Luther. They are just waiting for their food which is—ah, finally ready!" Robert said as he started to put the burger into a bun and handed it to Martin. "Here you go, Martin!"

"No, that's okay. He can have mine...I can wait," said Martin pointing at Troy to take his burger. It was painful to witness the fear that little boy had for Troy. Why did he even think he should fear him? Robert wondered.

Troy reached out for the burger and snatched it from Robert's hand and said, "No way, Martin, this is yours. You gotta take what's yours...Okay? You gotta learn to do that, okay?"

"Okay," Martin said in a smallest voice. But as Troy leaned down to hand the burger to Martin, it was impossible for him to take it and hold his brother at the same time.

Monique saw this and reacted. "Here, let me take little Luther and hold him while you eat your hamburger."

But Troy handed the burger to one of his young henchman and commanded, "Hold this." Then he reached down towards Martin and took Luther from his hands. "Us brothers have to stick together. Give him his food, Dog." Troy's henchman quickly obeyed and handed the burger to Martin.

Troy held Luther with one arm and rubbed the little baby's head with the other.

"What'd *ya* say his name was?"

Martin, who had not touched his burger, answered him. "Luther...his name is Luther."

"Martin and Luther..." laughed Troy. "What's your daddy's name, King? Haha..." Troy laughed out loud and the two henchmen awkwardly joined in and laughed as well.

Troy quickly shut them up. "Do you even know why I said that?"

The henchmen lost all their attitude and looked sheepish for a moment until one said, "'*cause* you said king...and...well, look at the kid, he's kind of dressed like a bum?"

"Shut it!" snapped Troy. "Martin Luther King was The Man, he..."

Pop! Pop! Pop! Troy froze as he instinctively squeezed Luther to his chest. At first it sounded as if the kids were popping some of the balloons that were tied to the fence, but as the fourth pop sounded, screams filled the air. Suddenly, as if a tornado had hit, waves of people were running scared in every direction.

Jenny came running frantically towards her parents in a fearful panic. "Daddy, someone's been shot...People are shooting..."

Then the sound of a motorbike came roaring down the street, weaving its way through the throngs of people. Within seconds, it came closer and closer, driving directly at them. The driver reached inside his jacket and pulled out a gun.

"*Down! Down!*" Robert screamed. In one motion, he pushed Monique to the ground and then grabbed Jenny and Martin by the wrists and yanked them down behind the barbecue. Jenny let out a painful cry as she hit the concrete. Robert lay straddled over Jenny and Monique, who had pulled Martin as close to her as humanly possible.

Pop! Pop! Pop! The popping got louder and faster as the motorcycle gunman fired towards them. It was complete hysteria! People were still running crazy, hiding in every little place they could find.

The whole incident took maybe twelve seconds. Little Martin was curled up in a ball in Monique's arms. Robert held all three of them tightly.

The sound of the motorbike disappeared as quickly as it came.

He looked into Jenny's terrified eyes. "Baby, are you okay?" Robert whispered.

"Just my arm, Daddy. It's okay, I just hit the sidewalk."

The entire neighbourhood was completely still. There was no movement from anyone. Robert helped Monique sit up. Martin clung on to her. "Heart, are you all right?"

She nodded slowly to say she was okay. But as she stared straight ahead, the look in her eyes—that look that can mark a life forever, made Robert turn to see what she saw.

There, four feet in front of the barbecue lay three bodies: the two young henchmen, their bodies all twisted in awkward positions and showing no signs of life and between them, Troy, lying face down.

"My brother...Where's my brother?" Martin cried. He jumped up, but Robert quickly stopped him from running into the street, for fear that someone might still be shooting. "Shhh...hang on, Martin...You wait here, I'll go check on your brother."

Monique took Martin's hand and hugged Jenny. Robert dragged himself around the barbecue towards Troy, using his elbows to pull himself forward, as if he was a soldier moving behind enemy lines.

Troy moved his head and moaned.

"Don't move!" Robert whispered loudly. "I'm coming to you."

Robert looked around as he crawled. The street had become a war zone. He could see the terrified faces of mothers and children hiding in their own private foxholes, behind fire hydrants, picnic benches, barbecues, behind cars and fence posts. No one moved, afraid that the slightest movement might cause more gunfire.

"Don't move, Nelson, just let me see if the baby is okay."

Robert saw Troy's face. A large gash was dripping on his forehead and creating a small pool of blood on the ground. He raised his arm, stretching to grab a handful of napkins from the barbecue. When he reached Troy, he put the napkins over his open wound.

"Here, hold these on that cut," Robert whispered to Troy.

"Now, lift up."

Troy moaned as he lifted his shoulder. There was tiny Luther! No sound. The baby was lying motionless underneath Troy.

"Just lift up a little more." Robert reached under Troy and delicately slid the baby towards him. So lifeless! He uncurled the blood soaked blanket from Luther's body. "Come on, little guy." Robert touched the baby's lips. "Come on, little one...Come on..." But Luther didn't stir.

Seven months later. Robert, Monique, Jenny, Mertle Bolt, her two daughters and many others from the block party that night sat together in the high school's auditorium with nine hundred other Malvern students. They watched a young man stand alone on a stage and talk about destiny.

"...and when Mr. Sanchez took him, I looked at that baby...he didn't move. That little kid...so small...he hadn't even really started living yet...and thank God, hadn't even started hating yet...but that little..."

Troy started to get a little emotional, and he wiped his eyes with the sleeve of his shirt—but tears were not going to stop the words he needed to let go of.

"That little guy had a brother, eight years old and he was there...Yeah, he was there all right. He was lying on the ground crying after all the shooting. And you know what? I knew exactly...I knew exactly what he felt like...

"I was almost the same age when I saw my brother get shot down, right in front of me. I still see it every day, one minute he's ragging on me about something, and the next second...and I'll tell you, in one second your whole life can change. Really. I know that now...but you know, sometimes it's in that split second, that you gotta make a choice. That's *somethin'* I learned: there's *always* a choice. Yeah, really! Most of the time you have a choice! My God, your whole destiny is sometimes based on you making one choice...and that's what I found out that night.

"You see, right after the shooting, the only thought I had was...was *vengeance!* Yeah, I had murder on my mind, just pure hatred. I wanted to get those guys who did this. I was *gonna* burn those motherfu...but then, here's this little kid I was holding. He's right there in my arms. He was shot...I mean, he's no bigger than my arm. All I got was a big cut on my head. But this little guy got a bullet in him and he's bleeding bad and...and his little brother's now crying—a crying that you feel more than hear...Everything went so fast and suddenly there are ambulances and cops all over. They rushed the baby and me into an ambulance. They thought I was his father or something. And they're asking me a lot of questions. But my head was just filled with how to get even, but then the baby's mother showed up and she was screaming. One guy patched me up real fast while the other guys hooking that little baby to all these machines and they're telling me this baby's going to die. He needs blood...I yell to them...well give it to *'im*. They say he'll never make it to the hospital...and I say then give him blood here...but they say they can't...they don't have any...and it's against procedure...Then the baby's mother comes into the ambulance, yelling with all her life, 'Save my baby...just please save my baby'...and then one of the paramedics...he tells his partner...don't worry...and he's asking about the baby's blood type?...What's his blood type?...The baby's mother, she yelled over and over, 'B negative! B negative!' She kept repeating it until I just said, 'That's me, too...' 'Are you sure, sir? Are you sure?' The paramedics are yelling at each other...and one just says 'You don't even know if this guy's blood is clean..." I tell them I have to do blood tests every month because of my probation...and they ask the mother...she looks at me and she says 'I trust you...Please save my baby.'

"And there I was, blinded with this burning desire to take down some lives that night, to get revenge. But as I looked at this kid all hooked up to these machines, looking so small...and in all that commotion—it was weird—cause in my head I just kept repeating this one question..."

Troy stopped. Wiped his face once more.

"All I'm thinking is...is this his life? And in that second, it hit me. About the same split second it took to wipe my brother from the face of this earth, I thought if only there was someone there that day that could've made a choice to save my brother, maybe by doing something like just pushing him down, or even maybe the guy who shot him, that he would choose to not shoot my brother...save him instead...And it was in that moment I made a choice. I thought I could do that...

"I could *be* the guy who didn't shoot.

"I could be the guy that's *gonna* save that guy I was going to get even with...

"I could be the guy...and save this kid...

"It took a few minutes and then they hooked up this tube, hooked my blood to his, and suddenly the kid was crying, his brother was crying, his mother was crying...but a crying I'm not used to hearing. It was like, joyful crying. Probably for the first time ever, I started to cry too. But mine wasn't joyful, though. Mine was like...a cleaning out. All the shit...Sorry about that word...All that anger and hate that I had built up inside of me, garbage kind of stuff that I chose to keep inside me. Seeing that mother hug her two little boys...well, then I started to cry it all out of me. Guess I still am 'cause I've done lots of things I ain't too proud of. I mean here's this paramedic risking his job, doing something he might get fired for...and that mother...they both trusting me...trusting *me*...ME?

"Anyway, there were tons of people all watching from outside the back of the ambulance and when they heard that baby cry, they all just busted into a cheer and for once in my life, I made a choice that caused somebody to cheer!

"But I wasn't no hero. Two of those kids that were with me that night, they were shot. They died 'cause they were with me...They died because they chose to be with me. And I was leading them."

Troy took a couple of steps to the edge of the stage to get as close to the audience as possible

"Is that what I wanted to do? It's crazy, you know. But somehow this made me realize I actually had a choice of what I could be. So I asked myself: is that what I wanted to be? This kind of leader? Someone who led people towards their deaths? To drugs? Led them into a hopeless world?"

Ah, my love...I don't know if I ever told you this. I know you and Little Rock went through a lot with me, especially with Troy and...

"Wait a second, Jenny." Kyle stopped reading and looked at her. "Oh, my God! You were there too?"

"It's okay, Kyle. My dad would never have let anything happen to us."

"Yeah, but you actually saw people get shot! You could've been killed!"

Jenny kissed Kyle's cheek. "It's okay, baby...Please, could you read some more?"

Jenny looked calm but inside, she felt time was moving too slowly. She needed to get to her father. She looked down at her watch. Only twenty minutes had passed. Jenny couldn't shake the thought of her father having bought a gun. *Why did he need this gun?*

"Oh," she sighed.

If only this plane could go faster...faster...faster than a speeding bullet, to save her father.

25. 4 WEEKS AGO – SEEMA'S OFFICE

"Is anything wrong?" Monique was standing at Seema's door.

Seema lifted the light blue scarf off her head and lowered it to her shoulders.

"Benny said you wanted to see me after I dropped Robert off. Is there something wrong?"

"No, no, Mrs. Sanchez, everything is fine. Please, could you close the door and sit down. And please, don't worry. Really, I just thought it had been a while since we last spoke and if you had a couple minutes this morning, we could connect."

"Oh, okay. Yeah, sure." Monique closed the door. As she walked to the chair, she stopped to look out the window.

"A nice view you have here."

Seema chuckled slightly. Monique noticed her smiling and asked, "Is that funny?"

"I'm sorry, no it's not funny; it's just...well, I smile because that's the first thing your husband does every time he comes into this room. He looks out that window. Oh please, would you like to take off your coat, Mrs. Sanchez?"

Monique put her purse on the floor beside the chair in front of the desk and then unbuttoned the dark blue cotton jacket she had on. "Thanks, but I'll just open it. I've still got a bit of a chill."

Seema smiled and leaned back in her chair. "And how are you doing, Mrs. Sanchez?"

"Oh, please just call me Monique, okay?"

Seema watched Monique unbutton her jacket and couldn't help but notice the dark circles under her eyes. But despite Monique's weary appearance, she spoke with a very cheery, upbeat energy.

"And you can call me Seema. So, how has everything been going for you, Monique?"

"Well, I'm sure Robert's told you everything that's going on, hasn't he? About my company and the talk he is going to give?"

Seema raised her eyebrow in question. "No, I'm sorry, Monique. What talk is Robert going to give?"

"Oh my gosh, I can't believe he didn't tell you." Monique forced a laugh. "You see, my company is expanding, three companies are going to become one. We have this big...well, huge event next month and Robert is going to be our keynote—you know, the guest speaker."

Seema tried to hide her surprise at the news. "And what is your husband going to speak about?"

"Mountains. Oh, Robert, he's done a lot of talks. Has he not told you that? He's quite amazing, you know. He can make climbing a mountain, well, he can make it relate to anything. It was all arranged before, you know, before..."

"Before the accident, you mean?"

Monique smiled feebly and nodded. "Yes. Oh, it was planned well over a year ago."

Seema looked completely dumbfounded. "And Robert, he's agreed to do this?"

Monique's smile vanished. "Why? Did he tell you he wouldn't?"

"No, no, not at all. Really, it's just...Well, I guess I'm a bit surprised. He's never mentioned it. This is the first I've heard of any talk."

Monique's smile returned and she leaned forward, speaking in a confidential tone. "You know, I wasn't sure if he still wanted to do it after the...you know...the accident. And because—anyway, I put all the slides and music together so all he has to do is be there and well, of course, talk! And you know, I think it'll be good for him, don't you think it will, Seema? 'Cause I really do. I really think it will be good for him."

The more Monique spoke, the more shock Seema felt. Was Robert two different people—one at home and one with her? She just couldn't comprehend the Robert she had been seeing for the past months being capable of such a feat. So she questioned Monique further.

"And how does he feel about it? This talk. What has Robert said?"

Monique answered with the same forced upbeat energy that she had come into the room with.

"You know Robert. Right now he's not, well, to be honest, he doesn't really want to talk that much now. But I think...well, maybe I'm kind of praying actually..." Monique tried to make everything sound as hopeful and bright as possible. "But I hope once he starts talking about what he loves so much, I think, I really do...that the old Robert will just jump right out, right back out to all of us. Don't you, Seema? Don't you think it's what he needs?"

"Well, I've never met the old Robert," Seema said.

"I think it might...it might really help him. He loves that, you know, talking about his climbs. Oh, he really does. You can't believe how many people want to hear all his stories. He just...he just comes alive when he's up there."

"Well, that's great, Monique, but how does Robert feel about doing this talk?"

"You know, it is getting hot in here. I think I better take off this coat." Monique stood up and removed her jacket very slowly, folding it four times over and then balancing it gently on her lap as she sat down.

Seema smiled politely. Seeing that Monique had twice avoided her question of asking how Robert felt about the talk, she changed the subject. "And so how have you been adjusting with everything, Monique?"

"Hmmm...how have I been adjusting? Well, of course, it's not easy. I'm sure you know that. But who am I to complain, eh? I mean, he's the one that has to do almost all of the adjusting."

"Well, Monique, I'm sure you have had to adjust your life around Robert's needs as well."

"You know, Miss Pourshadi, Robert has always been a man who takes care of himself, he's always been that way. I mean, I try to help him. Like when he first had to take a shower and had that cast, or even now. Helping him...get in and out of that wheelchair. But he's so independent...he just...just refuses to ask for or accept my help."

Seema noticed how Monique's body stiffened and that she was calling her Ms. Pourshadi again.

"And how does that make you feel, Monique?"

Monique suddenly lowered her head and looked at the floor. Seema waited a moment and then asked her again, "So how does that make you feel, Monique?"

Monique raised her head, looked directly at Seema and sighed. "I don't know."

"You don't know how it makes you feel?"

Monique shook her head.

"Does it make you feel hurt, resentful or angry?"

"I don't know, Miss Pourshadi. I simply don't know. I just don't have time to think those things. And anyway, I can't be spending too much time being angry or hurt—and well, look, I just don't know how I feel, okay? I really don't. It's just a lot has changed and—when someone you love, someone that you're spending your life with, and this happens to them—you have to try. You have to try to do your best, to be there for them..."

"And what kind of support do you have?"

"Oh, Robert's parents and family came by and so many of students wanted to see him, but...but, he asked everyone to give him time and not come over for a while. And of course, he has this place...Benny's been great and of course, you too."

"And what about you, Monique?"

"Oh, I'm fine. Fine, really!" Monique looked at her watch. "I'm sorry, but I have to leave soon. I have to be at work in twenty minutes. Is there anything specific about Robert I need to know or do for him?"

Seema sadly smiled to herself. She had seen Monique's same reticence to talk about herself in so many other family members that were taking care of a loved one: people who had the same life-changing experiences as she and Robert. Whenever Seema saw this kind of selfless behaviour, she knew it was the beginning of the end of most relationships. What she discovered was that when most of these parents, siblings and partners became helpers they neglected their own lives and feelings. Soon, they became lonely, angry martyrs. Their selfless behaviour towards the one who had been hurt usually created a wedge that eventually destroyed even the strongest relationships. Yet, the five minutes Monique had left this morning would not be enough to address this, so Seema tried another angle.

"I'm sure you are doing everything you can. But Monique, just don't forget yourself, okay? Concerning Robert, I do have a couple of questions. How do you feel he is sleeping lately?"

"I'm not sure. You see, he sleeps in the guest room 'cause it's closer to the washroom. He was worried I might roll over on his leg, so when he first came home, I would only lie beside him until he fell asleep. But, he said, I always fell asleep before him and then he would have to wake me so I could go back to my bed—I mean, to our bedroom where we used to both sleep until...Anyway, so now after he gets into bed, he...well, lately he just locks the door. And it's okay, I get it. I mean, I really do. I see he needs his space, so...so you know, I try to give it to him."

Seema tried to smile as compassionately as she could. "And affection, Monique? How—"

Monique shot a scornful look towards Seema. "—Affection?"

"Yes, do you and Robert share—"

Monique's voice became strained. "—You mean sex?"

"No, I'm just asking—"

"—Sex? How can you ask me that? I think that would be the last thing on his mind. Don't you? He's got enough to deal with, don't you think?"

"I'm sorry, Monique, really I was only asking about affection, like a hug, hand holding, maybe a morning or goodbye kiss. That's all."

"Do you know...that I haven't even seen his legs yet?"

"You mean since the operation?"

"Ever since we got back from Katmandu. I think he purposely keeps me from seeing them!"

"Really? Have you asked him to show you?"

"What? No! He has enough doctors and people probing and touching them, he sure doesn't need me doing the same. But you would think after this much time—I'm sorry. I should be the last one to complain."

"It's fine, Monique. It's not a complaint. Do you ever talk about how—"

"—We don't talk!"

"I'm sorry. You don't talk?"

"No...Well, not right now. He's dealing with a lot. We never had a problem. We used to talk about everything, but now—look, it's okay. I'm sure he would talk if...if he needed to."

"Of course. I was only asking about affection because I was just wondering how much has changed or maybe even has got back to normal between—"

"—I'm not sure what normal you are talking about, Miss Pourshadi. Do you know how long Robert would be gone when he went climbing? Sometimes almost three months! Believe me, we've gone through long periods of time not sharing affection. So it's not such a big deal now. It's going to be okay, I'm sure we can last through this!"

"Of course, of course you can." Monique's constant avoidance and responses gave Seema a sad glimpse into the Sanchez household—a home barren of communication and affection with a wife living as if her husband was still far away, scaling some mountain. Again Seema changed the subject. "And how about his prosthetics?"

"I'm sorry, his what?"

"His prosthetic legs. Does he try to wear them at home at all?"

"Well, um..." Monique looked truly lost and she stammered, "You see, um...the truth is, we never brought them into the house. They've been in the car for a while now. I wanted to bring them in but Robert, well, he said they don't fit right. That they were going to make him new ones."

"Okay." Seema smiled and nodded. Benny had already confided to her that he was at his wit's end with Robert and his prosthesis. Robert was abnormally resistant to working with the artificial limbs and always voiced a variety of complaints about how the prosthetics didn't fit properly or hurt too much. Benny had over twenty-five years of experience working with amputees and fitting them with artificial limbs and he told Seema he could not find any legitimate reason why Roberto Sanchez wasn't already walking out of the centre on his own. But seeing how distraught Monique was, Seema didn't push the issue.

"Well, Monique, has there been anything of note that you might want to mention. That you think might be helpful to us?"

"Note?" Monique creased her eyebrows. "Note? I'm sorry, it's just that word, it just sounds...kind of strange. "

Seema smiled. "I'm sorry, you're right, the word 'note' does sounds strange, doesn't it? No, I mean is there anything different, something Robert does or hasn't done that concerns you?"

"You mean other than everything?!"

Seema's eyes opened wide. It looked as if Monique's defences had failed her and she was now going to finally let it all out, spill the hurt and reveal everything she felt. But Monique quickly let out a laugh, "Ha...no, I'm sorry, I'm just kind of tired this morning. Look, forget I said that."

"Really, Monique, would you like me to forget that?"

"Yes, please, I just...oh, okay! Okay, do you want to know something Robert did that I'm concerned about? He bought a gun. That's right, a gun! He did. I know for a fact he doesn't even like guns, but he brought one home a week ago. Well, I think it was a week ago. How on earth was he able to get it? I don't know. He didn't show it to me, it was hidden under the mattress. I only found it when I changed the sheets. A gun...a gun? And did he tell you why he bought that gun, Miss Pourshadi?"

Seema sat back in her chair and tried to hide her concern. "No, Monique, he never mentioned it. What did you say to him when you found it?"

"I didn't say anything. I was too afraid to ask him. I just...just put it back under the mattress. But then just last Friday, I came home early because our daughter, Jenny, was coming home for a visit and there he was. When I opened the front door, there he was, sitting there holding that gun. He saw me looking right at it, but he didn't say anything. He just put that gun on the coffee table beside him like it was a magazine that he had just been reading. And then, he looked at me and saw me staring at the gun. And then he said, as simple as can be, 'We need it for protection now,' and I just didn't know what to say! I was so shocked! So I said, 'Okay, just don't leave it on the coffee table, Jenny's coming home tonight.'"

Monique looked back at her watch. "I'm sorry, Miss Pourshadi, but I really do have to get to work now."

Seema looked down and realized she had mindlessly pulled her scarf from her neck and was now nervously winding it tightly around one of her hands.

"Monique, I think we should—" A knock at the door interrupted her.

"Excuse me, Monique." Seema then called out, "Yes, who is it?"

The door opened and there were Benny and Robert.

"Oh, hi Mrs. Sanchez." Benny smiled. "Sorry, I didn't know you were in here."

"What is it, Benny?" Seema asked.

"Sorry, Miss Pourshadi, I saw on the calendar you were free this morning so we came up. I should have called first. It's just Robert wanted to switch his afternoon appointment to first thing this morning."

Monique stood up and started putting on her jacket. "That's okay, I was just leaving, Benny."

Seema stood up and walked from behind her desk and held out her hand to Monique to say goodbye. "Thank you for the talk, Monique."

Monique completely startled Seema by hugging her instead of shaking her hand. Monique's hug was so strong and powerful, it was hard for Seema to lift her arms and hug her back. This hug said everything Monique couldn't speak out loud, Seema thought. Or was it that, for these past six months, Monique had just simply needed some affection from someone? A hug, because for last six months she had felt alone, waiting, like she had done so many times—waiting for Robert to come back from another one of his climbs.

The moment the two finished the hug, Robert was in the room, a couple of feet behind his wife. In one fluid motion, Monique turned, briefly touched her husband's shoulder, gave it a quick squeeze and then walked out the door without sharing a look or saying a word to him.

26. NANCY

Namche Bazar, 3:30 pm
Dearest Love,

I'm sitting on top of the highest hotel in the world—the "Everest View" hotel. Unfortunately, the only view is my pen on the pages of this journal. The clouds have decided to wrap themselves around us. I can't even see who is sitting at the end of this table as the fog is so heavy. Today was newly-born with so many firsts...Today, these kids made me feel as if it was my first time ever seeing a mountain. With all the planning, weather gauging, the schedules and timing the breaks...I think I've been guilty of putting all my focus on watching where my feet are going, and completely forgetting to see where I am...

We're travelling with three Sherpas—Ang (you know, Mr. Happy Feet, always finding a reason to dance. He's the same one who summited with me three years ago), Mingma (kids call him 'the silencer' because he just doesn't like people talking and he can give you this look that just tells you he wants silence and so you better shut up immediately!) and Mingma's teenage son, Satya (can't figure him out yet, strange young man). I must say, even though Mingma doesn't like too much conversation, he still smiles a glorious smile and in his own odd way he has made our gang feel welcomed and safe!

I think Troy feels guilty every day watching the Sherpas carry his stuff and he keeps wanting to carry more than he should. Ang is constantly taking things out of Troy's sack and putting them back on his yak during breaks. This hasn't stopped for two days: Troy filling his backpack and Ang taking things out. Really makes the breaks quite entertaining with all that tugging back and forth between them.

Satya must take after his father. He doesn't talk! Seriously, we have not heard him speak ONE word! Yet we were told he speaks very good English. Nancy walked beside him most of the day, talking his head off. But he doesn't say a word and he definitely doesn't have his father's wide-open smile. He's such a sad looking boy, it's impossible to make eye contact with him. I think Nancy's trying to get him to smile as I write...I can hear her at the end of the table; can't see them though. REALLY, the fog is that thick! Lots of filming and interviews with the village folk and climbers today...I think Philip will have a tough time editing all of it into a half-hour clip to put on the web site for the kids back home. I'm really proud of the way they've been taking turns talking into that lens and exposing themselves so far.

There is an old song that sits inside me today. Found myself singing it as we trekked, Story of a Life *it's called. It's an old Harry Chapin song and I find as I'm attempting to start Nancy's story in this journal, well...I just can't seem to recall how it all began with her and what words best describe her. It kind of reminds of a line from Harry's song: something about words can work so well...sometimes words belong in hell...because sometimes— words—they don't do much of anything at all...and that's definitely how it started with Nancy.*

The phone rang. It was two thirty-seven am on Thursday.

Every Thursday for the past year Robert had been volunteering at the Scarborough Crisis Centre. He sat in a small windowless room in St. Teresa's church basement. There were two phones on a bare wooden table with a couple of binders and an odd mix of paper pads. Against the back wall was a bookshelf filled with telephone books, an assortment of magazines and a variety of paperback novels that had seen better days. The generic light green coloured walls were empty except for a list of local emergency phone numbers and a map of the city that had some key emergency locations circled in purple.

Robert sat in a leather chair with upholstery that was held together with silver duct tape. He leaned far back into the chair as he answered the phone.

"I'm not going to do this anymore," a young girl's voice said in a very matter-of-fact tone.

"Hi, my name is Robert. I'm listening."

"Yeah, well listen to this: I'm not going to do this anymore."

"Do what anymore?"

"Living."

"Living, did you say?" Robert wasn't sure he heard correctly because the music in the background was quite loud.

"Yes, living!" the girl shouted over the music.

Robert quickly sat up and leaned onto the table, picked up a pen and drew one of the paper pads towards him. In the last year, only one call had alerted him enough to call for emergency help. It was a college dorm party. A female student had mixed drugs and alcohol, fainted and wouldn't respond. The partygoers had explained they were too afraid to call 911 and get caught so they called the crisis hotline instead. The students were quite disappointed when they found out the only thing Robert could do was to call 911. That had been the only real crisis he had ever responded to. And he never did find out what happened to that girl because after one quick 911 call, the crisis centre was completely removed from the situation.

Most of the calls the centre received were from lonely people that just needed someone to talk to. So when he heard someone didn't want to live anymore, he sprang into action. First, he needed to find out how serious the call was since, unfortunately, the crisis centre was not immune to a good number of annoying prank calls.

"And why wouldn't you want to live anymore?" he asked. And then the voice started singing into the phone something about being almost dead, and a drummer drumming as they carried her body. Her voice was a bit slurred and sounded as if maybe she had been drinking.

"You have a great voice. I'm not sure I've heard this song before. Who is it?" Robert asked.

"Red Hot Chili Peppers. And you couldn't have heard it 'cause it hasn't been released yet. Okay, I'm going...*Goooood* bye. " The voice sang the word 'goodbye.'

"Why do you like it?" Robert quickly jumped in, hoping to get the caller to stay on the line.

He repeated the question.

"Why do you like it?"

There was no response, but he could still hear the music so he repeated the question once more.

"Just wanted to know why you like this song?" Again, there was no response, yet the music became louder. It seemed the caller had put the phone right on the speaker. Robert held the phone a little away from his ear but listened intently. The song did not have a sad sound to it at all. Despite the dark sounding lyrics and the words the girl had just sung, the music actually sounded rather upbeat and positive.

The music became more and more frenetic. It was building to a finish. Then, the girl started singing along with the repetitive lyrics, getting louder each time. He couldn't make out the exact lyrics. But the words were something about someone being almost dead, someone being almost gone.

Was she also preparing for a big finish? he wondered. Robert didn't know what to do. He rocked a little in his chair and then just tried singing along with the girl on the phone. Guessing the lyrics as he sang and singing loudest on the ones he could definitely make out. Almost dead. Almost gone.

They sang together in time with the lead singer, ending the last line with purpose, slowly giving each word its full meaning.

The song ended. Silence. *Had she hung up?* He panicked. No. There was a faint sound of breathing. He waited for a full thirty seconds, listening to her breathing, and then she broke the silence.

"Okay, I think I'm ready. Bye."

"Hey, wait! What's your name?" Robert almost yelled.

The caller's voice was now a little more slurred, yet pointed. "What does it matter? I could tell you any...name...would you believe me?...No!...Wait...Okay, I could tell you...Yeah, I'm...No, I'll tell you who I really am...I'm Lady Gaga."

Robert looked at the receiver and scribbled down the caller's number on the pad. He then drew the other phone closer to him in case he needed to make an emergency 911 call.

"Hi, Lady Gaga! It was great singing with you. Quite the privilege actually! Never in my lifetime would I have thought I would have the chance to do something like that: sing with Lady Gaga. So is anybody there with you tonight?"

"No, you think I'd be calling you if anyone was here?" Her voice changed. It got hard and angry.

Robert didn't react; he knew enough to stay quiet in order to let the caller vent anything else she might want to.

"My goddamn family is never here, all right? Oh, did Brad have another big game tonight?" she said in a mocking tone. "Oh no, wait, maybe Suzy has another one of her freaking tutu recital?" And then she screamed into the phone, "No...no, okay...No one's here...No one's ever here!"

The phone went dead.

Robert waited ten seconds to see if she would call back. *Nothing!* He glanced at the pad and called the number he had just written down.

It rang four times and then went to voicemail. "Hi, this is the

Archer's residence. No one is home at the moment, so could you please leave a message?"

Robert hung up and called again but got the same voicemail.

He stood up, wringing his hands together and paced behind the chair.

"How bad did she sound?" he said out loud.

I mean, she was singing...Yeah, but what was she singing? Death. She didn't want to live anymore. And her voice sounded like maybe she had been drinking. Had she also taken some drugs?

He took a deep breath and made his decision. Picking up the phone, he hesitated for a second. *Yes,* he thought, then quickly jabbed the numbers 911. He quickly explained the circumstance to the man who answered and relayed his reasons for suspecting a potential suicide. Then, he hung up.

A restless energy surged inside him. He jumped up and stretched his legs, all the time staring at the phone. He wanted to call 'Lady Gaga' again, but he knew the procedure. The moment he gave her number to 911, it was out of his hands. Because of privacy laws, he was never going to know what happened with the girl named Lady Gaga.

Oh, my love. I felt so goddamn helpless! My words? My words were the only thing I had to try to save her. But what were they? My words...they were probably nothing more than a listless noise to her, like the sounds of someone annoyingly tapping their fingers on a table. And she just wanted me—the noise—to stop. And the other words of the 911 people, did they save her? Or at least stop her?

Sitting here tonight, looking at the legion of stars that seems to multiply each time I look up into the sky...I can't help but wonder, who would want to leave this—this world of incredible, spontaneous, curious adventures? What is that moment really like, that precise moment when someone decides they are going to leave all THIS...and they choose to end their life? What is that moment like—the moment they actually decide to choose death?

Does their mind start to wander into some parallel world beyond all those stars? Do they think that after killing themselves, they are going to some death world where they will still be alive?

Are they choosing death because they are finished with living or do they do it because they think they will live on somewhere else...as someone new? Do they think life will be better in the death world? Or is this their way of trying to make their mark somehow?

Somehow believing they are making the mark that they were unable to make when they were living. Perhaps by killing themselves they think they can create a new identity, one that will scream out to the rest of the universe, "SEE, none of you could ever see the true me. Well, LOOK, this is who I am!!! I am someone who decides to die...leave your world. YES, I'm in control and I choose death!" Or...do they do it just to spite the living, 'cause they must know suicide always leaves a mark on those left behind?

To choose death...is it because they don't feel needed? Is that what can save us, feeling needed? Do we need to feel purpose to live? This girl, this Lady Gaga—a teenage kid that had wandered deep into those thoughts of hopelessness, thoughts of not living...What question is she asking? To live or not to live...Maybe the real question she was asking wasn't "why do I want to kill myself?" but rather, "what would make me choose to live?"

Oh sorry, look, I'm climbing up that unanswerable mountain again!...Back to Nancy's story. Well, two weeks later, I had another late Thursday at the Crisis Centre.

"Hi, my name is Robert. I'm listening."

"What the hell did you have to call the police for?" a young girl's voice questioned.

"Hi..." Robert said. "I'm sorry. Can I help you?"

"Why did you do that? You're all the same. Now I know why you call this a crisis hot line. It's because that's what you do, you cause a fucking crisis!"

"Hi," Robert felt a huge relief. *It's her again!* She didn't kill herself...didn't choose the death world. *She's alive!* "Oh, I'm so happy to hear from you!" he said.

"Why? *Why?* Now I'm...Now I'm—" and then she started crying. "That's all they wanted, you know? Something to finally show them that their loser kid..." She paused and then started crying harder. Wet painful sobs.

Robert closed his eyes and nodded his head slowly in rhythm, listening to her as if he was rocking her in a cradle. He waited until the sobs and loud sniffles subsided and then said, "You have a nice voice, Lady Gaga."

"Well, I don't trust you...Why did you call the police?"

"I'm sorry, but you kind of left me no choice."

"Is that all everybody ever does? Nancy cries, call a doctor. Nancy

162

yells, give her some pills. Nancy says she's hurting, call the police...*How the hell* are the police going to help me?"

"Is that your name, Nancy?"

"What do you think?" And suddenly her childlike pout abruptly switched to an impatient teenager's voice. "Did you *really* think Lady Gaga was calling you?"

"No, I thought a sensitive, beautifully creative young girl was calling me and she didn't want me to know her name."

"How the hell can you know I'm beautifully creative?" she asked with slightly less attitude than before.

"That song, I looked it up after we spoke. It was a bit hard to find but I found it. I listened to it and thought probably only a creative person could really understand it." Robert had found that song and once he read the lyrics he realized that maybe he was too quick to call for emergency help. "It's called Brendon's Death song, right?"

"Yeah," she sniffed.

"Well, you know that line...about wanting to live and when I'm dead the Reaper will cry?"

"Well, that's not the exact right words."

"Okay, but it's about death, right?"

"Yeah."

"Well, that whole idea about the Reaper crying. Well, you see, I didn't get it right away."

"So what did you get?"

"Well, I think it means that if a person lives a life so great, when Death finally comes to take them, it would make Death cry because...because Death would have to take them from such a great amazing life, right? You see, I think most people hearing all this stuff about Death and then the Reaper, well, most people probably think it's a depressing song about dying. But I think creative people—well, they listen in a different way. And they probably understand that the song was actually meant to be positive and not really about death at all, but more about celebrating a wonderful life."

Robert waited for her to comment but all he could hear were more sniffles.

"So, I see now. It's positive song. I'm sorry I didn't get it before...I guess I didn't really listen that good."

"*Well.*"

"Well what?" Robert was puzzled.

"It's not you didn't listen good, it's *well.* You didn't listen *well.*"

Robert chuckled a little at having his grammar corrected.

"Haha...yeah, I'm sorry about that. How about we start again, okay?"

Suddenly, Nancy erupted into loud gasping sobs. "That's how...how I feel...every day, every day...I just feel like I want to start all over again."

And that was how I got to know Nancy Archer. We did start over again and what I learned in the next hour about this absolutely lost sixteen-year-old girl was really difficult to listen to. But, you know, love, it made me realize that this choice to leave the probation office and a steady paycheck to start my own work— following this passion of mine—trying to help young people...It definitely was the right choice. I'm meant to be here! Thank you darling, for supporting me, for helping me live such a rewarding life...and I remember thinking that as I listened to her cry over the phone. Thank God, she is still here to talk to.

Robert knew that was the first step towards hope.

Nancy Archer came from an affluent family. Her father owned a very successful head-hunter company and her mother was high up in the ranks at the largest pharmaceutical company in the country. Both had to travel extensively. Her nineteen-year-old brother, Brad, was on a university basketball scholarship and her sister Suzy, at fifteen, had already been chosen as a full-time apprentice for a professional ballet company in the city.

Nancy, Brad and Suzie were brought up by many full-time nannies and Nancy had always felt the nannies favoured her brother and sister over her. And now, at sixteen, with her brother and younger sister already on career paths, she felt extreme alienation from her parents because she didn't know what she wanted to do with her life. So, she started slowly carving her identity into her body with a razor and became the family's problem child. She had been cutting herself for the last year, but the experimentation with drugs and alcohol started when she was fourteen.

"Nancy, did you say that every day you wish you could just start all over again?"

"Yeah, kind of wish...Well, not just that day but my whole life. I just want to erase it and start all over again."

"Do you ever laugh?"

"Yeah. Of course."

"No, I mean *out loud*...like, as if your whole body is laughing and you couldn't stop it even if you tried."

Robert was sure Nancy had just smiled. He heard her make that oh-yeah-I-remember sound and then she spoke with such a happy animated spark.

"Yeah, well, there was this one time my mom made this treasure hunt for my birthday and...and she made these clues. God, they were so funny. I couldn't believe she took the time to do that—all that—for me."

But then in an instant, Nancy's happy sound abruptly vanished and her critical voice again appeared. "But she never did that again."

"Okay, so...do you want to erase that birthday celebration, as if it never happened?"

"No, but what's the use of having something fun if you never get it again? If you can't even hope that it will ever exist again?"

Robert smiled. This girl was quite clever. He wasn't sure how to answer her question so he did something Monique had taught him. His wife had gone to one of her company's training workshops and she learned a technique called the *Five Whys*. It usually worked when someone came to you with a problem that they believed was unsolvable. The *why* questions usually wouldn't fix the problem, but they might get you closer to why the problem existed. Every time the person gave an answer, you were to just ask them why. And by repeatedly asking the question "why?" you could peel away the layers of symptoms and get to the root cause of the problem. So Robert started.

"Why can't you hope it will ever happen again?"

"Because I know it won't!" Nancy quickly answered.

"Why are you so sure it won't ever happen again?"

"*'Cause* my mom is too busy now."

"Why do you think your mom's too busy now?"

"She's always too busy for me!"

"Why do you think she's too busy for you?"

"Because she doesn't care about me anymore, okay?!" Nancy's voice sounded exasperated, as if she were hoping the questions would just stop.

Ah, the root of the problem was exposed! There was a long pause. Robert waited, hoping Nancy heard what she had just said. It was simple. Every child wants the same. *SHE wanted to be cared for by her mother!*

And then Nancy surprised him and asked,

"Aren't you going to ask me why she doesn't care about me anymore?"

"You know, Nancy, I once learned that sometimes when we have a question we don't know the answer to that it often helps to ask a better question."

"Like what?"

Robert was silent so she asked it again with even more impatience.

"No, really, like *what?*"

Robert stayed silent.

"Are you going talk or *what?*"

"I'm sorry, Nancy, I was hoping you could find the better question since it's your question, not mine."

"Well, I don't know any better questions about why my mother doesn't care about me anymore. Do you?"

"No...but...Okay, do you want your mom to care for you?"

"Duh, yeah...Who doesn't want their mom to care about them?"

"That's a good question, Nancy. *Who* doesn't want their mom to care about them?"

"I don't know...Crazy people, bad people...killers!"

"And are you any one of those?"

After a little pause, Nancy said quite loudly, "No, what the hell do you think?"

"Well, Nancy, I think you want and need your mom to care about you, right?"

"Yeah...okay, *so*...?"

"And I'm pretty sure your mom needs *you* to care about her. So, tell me, when was the last time you showed your mom you cared about her?"

"But *how, how, how?* After you called the police that night, my parents actually let them search my room. I'd never seen my parents so freaked. They found some alcohol and some pills and stuff. And then they brought me to the hospital in an ambulance! My parents hadn't seen my bare arms for the longest time, so when the nurse told me to take off me shirt...then they saw all the cuts and scars...and they...well, they just lost it. I mean my dad starts yelling, 'Who did this to you? *WHO* did this to you?' And then my mom quickly picks up my shirt and she is telling me to put it back on... *'PUT IT back on!'* She's almost yelling at me, like she was worried that someone might see *her* own daughter all wrecked up. And my dad is still asking me, 'Who did this to you' and I lose it and then I start screaming and swearing at my parents. 'I don't know who fucking did it, Dad...Do you know...*DO YOU?*'"

She stopped to take a breath. Robert could hear a cry welling up, but she swiftly suppressed it.

Nancy needed to let this out.

"And then...then they take me to this other room. Three different doctors ask me all these questions, stupid questions. Like I'm some brainless idiot and then they do these crazy kind of psyche tests on me. My parents are standing right behind me the whole time and every time I look back at them, they just look away. Yeah! They do! They turn their heads like they might throw up if they look at me or something. And you know what? They don't...they don't even try to touch me. They can't even touch me! You know, like parents do when their kid is—"

Nancy stopped. She didn't want to cry, so she took in five or six heavy, deep breaths and continued.

"And then my mother, as one of the doctors spoke with them near the door, I heard my mom tell the doctor she was sorry. And then I hear her tell him how embarrassed she was. And then she starts crying. *She cried!* I mean like, not a little cry. I mean she cried, like weeping, and then everyone starts consoling her. But she's not crying for me, she's crying as if it was all happening to her! Not to me. Crying like it happened to *her!*"

Nancy stopped to gulp down another sharp cry, keeping it from coming out. "And for the last two weeks, she hasn't even said a word to me. Not one! She avoids me like I have some kind of contagious disease. No, worse! Like I don't even exist! So you tell me...how...how is that 'care'?"

"Care?" Robert spoke softly and slowly. "That's kind of hard to answer. I mean, care is something different for every person. Everybody shows it in so many different ways. Look at you, Nancy. You showed you cared enough about yourself to call some crisis hotline, right? But with your drinking and cutting yourself, how is that showing care for yourself? Or that you even care about how that affects your parents?"

"I'm the one who is bleeding, not them! How does that affect them?"

"Nancy, you're their little girl! And now they see their little girl is all cut up and—"

"You *don't* understand. Have you ever cut yourself?"

"Well, not on purpose." Robert knew about teenagers cutting themselves, but he had never actually spoken to anyone who had, so he asked her, "But Nancy, let me ask you a question. Have you ever cut yourself when you were laughing or happy?"

"No, of course not. That's not the point."

"What *is* the point, then?"

Nancy got furious and screamed into the phone, "I'm *not* happy, okay?! I'm not happy! Isn't it obvious?"

"Maybe not, Nancy. Maybe it's not so obvious. Maybe no one else knows you're not happy. I mean...Do you cut yourself in public so everyone can see you're not happy?"

"*Shut up!* You don't understand at all, so just shut up...and *stop* talking about it."

Robert was silent. The last thing he wanted was to rile her up. He could hear her breathing and for a full minute they both sat quietly, waiting for the other to speak. A little sound of crying came first and then Nancy broke the silence.

"Look, I do it alone, okay...because I am alone...all alone, okay?!"

Robert waited a moment and listened to Nancy's crying. "No, actually it's not okay, Nancy. I know I don't like feeling alone and I'm pretty sure being alone and feeling alone is never okay for anybody. I'm sorry Nancy, really I am. I'm so sorry you feel that way. But can I ask you one last question? I promise, no more, alright?"

He listened to her sniffle into the phone and could just imagine how huge her tears were and how wet her face must be, so he asked the question with as much care as possible.

"Nancy, please ask yourself this. Are you willing to change? And how much, how much really, do you want to stop being unhappy and feeling alone?"

The phone went dead.

Robert's eyes opened wide in shock. Had he gone too far, pushed Nancy to where she wasn't ready to go?

It was impossible for him to call her back as Nancy's number was now unlisted. He had only one hour left on his shift at the crisis centre. He sat staring at the phone, willing it to ring, trying to cast some magic spell to get her to call him back.

Five minutes passed. Ten. Half an hour. *Bringgggg.* The phone rang. He went to it so quickly, attempting to answer it, that he fumbled the phone around like he was trying to catch a hot potato.

"Hello, Nancy?"

"No, no, dear, just me, I'm feeling a little sad right now and I was wondering if you could help me?"

It was the old woman who called every Thursday, always complaining about her children not visiting her, and how they never called her. Today her complaint was no different.

Usually Robert would just listen and every now and then acknowledge the woman's feelings, but tonight, just as the woman said, "They don't care about me. These kids, they just don't care anymore," he couldn't hold back his question.

"Well, Ma'am, how do you show your kids you care about them?"

The old woman got flustered and angrily repeated exactly what Nancy had said. "Well son, you just don't understand, do you? You really don't get it, do you? I have cared for my children all my life. Do you hear me? *ALL MY LIFE!* I think it's time they showed they cared. It's only right! It's only right!"

"Well, if you have been caring for them *all your life* and you're still alive, doesn't that mean you should still be doing it?"

"You don't understand. It's them, not me! I think it's time they showed they cared. It's only right!"

"But when was the last time you phoned or visited them?"

The old woman's voice became bitter and indignant.

"I'm their *mother,* they are supposed to come to me. I shouldn't have to run all over the city to see them. I'm the mother. Don't you have a mother, son? Don't you go and visit her?"

"Sure," Robert answered, "but my mom also comes to see us, too."

And then the phone went dead.

Not again! Twice tonight! Robert knew the old woman just wanted the same thing he gave her each week, to feel listened to. But somehow, after Nancy's call, he just couldn't let the old woman off the hook. *Parents need to show their care to their children too, no matter how old they are.*

Great! he thought, *what kind of crisis centre gets the callers more upset after they call?* The crisis centre had the same oath as the doctor's oath: "First, do no harm," and now Robert was wondering how much harm he had done Nancy and the old woman.

What could I have done differently? They both felt no one cared. They both felt so alone. Yet, neither Nancy nor the old woman could ever tell the people who they cared for how they felt. You know, I never thought about it then, but almost everybody that called that centre…what was their crisis? They all had one thing in common. They were all confronting the same thing: change. A change they wanted desperately to occur. Some didn't even know what that change would be or could be and most had no clue how to change. Some were hoping the change would be that everyone else would change and, well, most just didn't have enough courage to do it themselves. And sadly, some people are so completely without hope that they can't believe a change could ever happen for them.

You know darling…I must say it's so strange every night writing about all these things that happened in the past with Phil, Nancy and Troy…because the present is so amazing up here. Every day, small little adventures of finding!

Tonight after supper, Satya was as quiet as always. I don't think I've mentioned it before, but he always wears this yellow coloured scarf around his neck. It's not a bandana. It looks more like one of those prayer flags we see flying around everywhere. He ties this scarf real high, right under his chin, completely covering his neck. He kind of resembles some rich guy you could see having a butler and a British accent or wearing an ascot. The boys tease him and call him 'Richie Rich,' after that kid in the comic books. Well, after we ate, Ang had turned on that old tape recorder he has and was showing us this funny dance step of his: something between what you'd see a highland dancer and one of those Russian folk dancers do, with his arms crossed and kind of squatting and kicking. Philip thought the kids back home might want to get a little taste of Sherpa dancing, so he took out the camera and started filming. Then Troy joined Ang and all of us got a good laugh watching Troy, this muscular street kid, fumble his legs around like a tangled up marionette trying to learn Ang's step. Then Ang got Nancy to get up and as she got up, she took Satya by the hand and tried to get him to try the step as well. And for the first time, Satya looked like he was actually smiling. But just as he started to rise, he glanced at his dad and then he just pulled his hand away from Nancy's and quickly sat back down. So then she asked Satya for his scarf to use it in the dance, but just as she reached her hand out to Satya, his dad, Mingma, violently swatted Nancy's hand away! He hit her so hard that she let out a loud yelp. Then Ang and Mingma started shouting in their native tongue, pointing the whole time at Satya and the scarf. Ang grabbed both Mingma and Satya and took them outside to continue their yelling match.

Ang came in and apologized and said he had fired Mingma and his son for their behaviour and told us he knew of two other Sherpas in Namcha that would take us the rest of the way. But Nancy said it was her fault and Mingma was just being protective, and he didn't hurt her at all. She'd overreacted, and she begged Ang to please give Mingma and Satya another chance? Ang asked the four of us if that is what we wanted. Troy and Phil tried to make light of it and joked that if they do come back, Ang had to promise them that...that Mingma would have to refrain from his non-stop chatting as it was driving them crazy! Ang laughed so loud, nodded his head and said, "You good people...must make parents happy with proud." Phil and Nancy both looked at Troy, knowing he didn't have any mom or dad and then Phil said, "Ang, it's more important we feel happy and proud first."

Four months later, the crisis call centre ran out of funding and was disbanded. Robert never heard from Nancy or the old woman again. Yet for those last four months, Robert still had at least one or two mysterious hang-ups each night. A couple of times he found himself questioning into the phone, "Nancy, is that you?" but it would always end with the same dull ache of a dial tone.

The only change that old woman wanted, Robert thought, *was probably to find someone else she could complain about her children to.* Yet Nancy, Nancy...He tortured himself with questions. *Where was she now? Had her wish for change become more permanent? Had she maybe overdosed or just cut herself too deep this time and help had come too late?*

For months he spoke of his concern for the girl at home. And one night at supper, Monique had finally heard enough and said, "Stop, Bobby. Stop torturing yourself! My God, you see hundreds of kids a week and some with tons of problems a lot worse than this girl. Why is she bugging you so much?"

"*'Cause* I think she killed herself! Because of me. I failed this kid because of what I said."

"You don't know that, Robert, not for sure...You don't know that!"

Robert opened his mouth to speak but instead let out a troubled sigh. He pushed his plate over to the side and lowered his head onto the table.

Monique reached over to her husband, put her hand in his hair and gently stroked his head. "Okay, what did you tell her? What, Bobby? That she needed to change? To be more happy? How can that be so bad?"

"It's bad if the change she chose was death!"

Then Jenny put her hand on her father's and spoke to him simply and directly, like a mother would, comforting her child after losing a big game.

"Daddy, it's not the first time you have ever failed, is it?"

Robert turned his head to look at his daughter. She was almost twenty and was blossoming into such a bright, beautiful young woman.

"What?"

"Dad, you once told me that if there were a hundred kids and you could only get through to maybe sixty or seventy of them, you would know you hadn't failed. Remember that?"

"Yeah, but Jen, this is—"

"Different, Dad? *Why?*"

"Because this girl might have killed herself and I couldn't help her."

"And I'm sorry, Daddy, but maybe she did. You can't save everybody. *YOU* were the one that told me that Dad...*you!*"

Robert sat up, staring at Jenny with a look of awe as she continued

171

on.

"You said that sometimes the only thing you can do is help the core get stronger. That you can only help make the world they live in more positive. And you said doing that would help the other thirty who you couldn't reach. That the core you did get through to would be the support for the others—the ones you couldn't help—because then they would always have a positive place to go to, right? So, Daddy, just keep doing *that!*"

Monique gave Robert one of those listen-to-your-daughter nods. Robert took his daughter's hand in his and gave it a kiss.

"When did you get so smart, Little Rock?"

"Oh, and while I'm being so smart, Dad, here's something else you said: that everything happens for a reason. And that no matter how dark something might seem, it's up to us. Right, Dad? We all have to try to find the light or positive in that reason." Jenny paused, smiled at her father and asked, "So what's the positive reason for this, Daddy?"

So just like Troy's yellow notebook, the adventure of Nancy Archer found its way into the high schools throughout the city. *'How do we deal with personal failure?'* was now part of his high school workshops. Robert would speak about his failure to listen and help out this one caller at the crisis centre. He would stand there. Surrounded by the young participants. Sitting in a huge circle in some gym. And there he would speak about the girl he had failed to help. He spoke of his guilt and his inability to move forward. He would never use Nancy's name, but the isolation and pain of her story was easily recognizable for many of the teenagers.

Seven months later at Dufferin High School, Robert stood before eighty grade eleven students. "I'm human and I failed," he confessed. "And you know what? I also failed at being a probation officer. My very first case was a young man named Tyrell. He was shot—on the street, in front of me and his ten-year-old brother. And then, there I was, volunteering as a crisis counsellor, and again, I failed. I failed this girl so miserably. But that's not enough. No, because then I also ended up failing myself and my poor family and friends who tried to help me cope with my failures. You see, I was totally unable to see anything positive to learn from my failures."

He then asked the students, "What could I have done differently? What would you do to help this girl?"

These questions really engaged the kids. They would all break off into small groups and share stories of their own personal failures and how they would do things differently the next time. For some it was a welcome relief to have this unique opportunity to say the words out loud, *"I failed. I'm human."* For many, this journey was difficult and awkward. Yet it never failed that the hushed tones would soon melt away and the volume and energy in room would build with the open sounds of *"Yes...I did the same,"* or *"Man, I'm sorry, I did that too!"*

The gym came alive with purpose as these young human beings suddenly felt the unbridled freedom to say to their peers, "I failed. Can you please help me to find something positive to take away from that experience?" One could almost feel the four walls of the large gymnasium let out a great exhale of grief and misery and then take in a huge lung-full of hope.

There were always those who had their reasons to not join in and today was no different. Robert could see one girl sitting far in the corner by herself, looking like she was being scolded by one of the teachers.

Robert walked towards them and asked, "Can I help?"

"I'm sorry, Mr. Sanchez, but she refuses to join a group," the teacher loudly said, knowing full well she would be heard by the other students.

Robert calmly put a hand on the teacher's shoulder and motioned for her to step away so he could talk to her in private.

"It's okay, lots of kids have difficulty with sharing. Maybe later she'll decide to join, but if she wants to just sit around, that's good too. At least she's here."

It was obvious as she spoke that this teacher was personally fed up with the girl, "Well, she never joins in and it's not like we don't try. She's a new student this year and all of the staff have tried everything to help her. You can't believe how many times we...Oh, never mind, Go ahead, you try talking to her!"

Robert took the teacher a couple of steps further away from the girl. "It's okay. She's here in this room. That's a good start. And, I'm sorry, what's your name?"

"Penny, Penny Mooreland," She seemed pleasantly surprised by Robert asking for her name and her harsh tone suddenly changed into that of a shy girl.

"Well, Penny, I want to thank you for being here, too. Believe me, it's appreciated. You know, a lot of teachers don't even like to be at these workshops. They like to treat it as a day off but look at you. Here you are, showing the kids you support them. They don't act like they appreciate it but, believe me, they need you!"

Penny Mooreland became apologetic. "It's just, Mr. Sanchez...I mean, she's one of the most at-risk kids we have at this school. That's the reason we brought you and this workshop to our school, because of maybe ten students like her and, *big surprise*, five of them aren't even here today. And her—"

Penny Mooreland stepped closer to Robert and whispered, "Look at her arms. I haven't fully seen them, but we think she is...well, you know!"

Robert didn't turn to look at the girl, he just shook Penny Mooreland's hand and said, "Let me talk to the girl, okay? And thanks, Penny!"

The teacher walked away smiling, but still found a strategic place in the gym to keep a watchful eye on the girl. Robert grabbed a spare chair from against the wall and sat beside the girl. She was dressed completely in black except for yellow socks. She had short red hair and porcelain white skin that was coloured with as many freckles as it was blemishes. She wore a zippered sweatshirt and her arms were tightly crossed. But just as Robert sat down, she reached behind her to pull the hoodie over her head. As she lifted her arm to yank it over her head, Robert saw what Penny Mooreland was talking about: the reddish scars etched into her wrists just above her hands.

Robert purposely looked away from the girl, surveying the students in the gym instead. No matter how many times he did these types of workshops, it never ceased to amaze him how this room, which was mainly built for competitions of the chosen few, had now come alive with a different kind of sound. Usually, these gyms echoed the sounds of the cheers and chants and were a place where the jocks and the pretty cheerleaders sang and soared. But he also knew how many students hated this room. Because it was in gyms like this that they were constantly reminded how they were not the pretty ones. It was usually in gyms like these that many had to face the failure of their own physical inadequacies— a daily reminder that they were not and would never be the chosen ones.

But today this gym transformed into another world—a world that was listening. A world filled with little groups of teenagers huddled in circles, leaning in to hear, straining to listen to each other—listening to how being the chosen or unchosen really feels.

Robert turned to the girl and said, "Could you excuse me for a second? I have to say something to everyone."

The girl looked down at the floor and sneered with a sour face, but as soon as he started speaking, her eyes glanced his way and he could see she was listening.

"I'd like everyone to do something. Think of someone you know who is a really, really bad listener. Don't say the name, just think of them. Now think of the top three things that really annoy, piss you off or even hurt you about how they listen to you. But don't say anything. Just think of those three things."

Robert watched the students. Some of them looked serious, some started to giggle and some even pointed at someone in the room.

"All right, let me hear some of things that piss you off or hurt you about how someone listens to you." Robert walked around the room and as he pointed at a student, they would get up and speak.

"She's always texting while I'm telling her something."

"He never looks at me when I'm talking."

"He cuts me off before I even finish."

"...telling me it's not such a big deal. Get over it!"

"No matter what I tell her, something worse has always happened to her!"

"He doesn't even look up from the computer."

"Always has to give me advice."

"Tells me they know what I'm going to say."

"No matter what it is, they...they just try to fix it."

With each statement, the room reacted, acknowledging how they too had felt the hurt or annoyance of not being listened to. Ten minutes later, Robert then asked a question to everyone in the room.

"Okay, now stand up if you have never and I mean never, listened in any of those ways we just heard?"

No one in the room stood up.

"Look at us. We have all these things that hurt us, piss us off about others and how they listen to us, yet we do the same things to someone else! I know one thing I had to change in my life was how I listened. I wasn't a good listener at all! I think I hurt a lot of people who came to me wanting me to listen to them. Someone just mentioned how it hurt them when someone just wanted to fix them. Well, that was me. My daughter and I always send each other the new songs that we like. Anyway, one day she sent me this Coldplay song called 'Fix You.'"

The gym filled with some clapping and cheering, showing they knew and loved the song too. Robert put up his hand to quiet the room.

"I like the song too. But when my daughter said the song reminded her of me, well, at first it made me feel great. Then after listening to it a couple of times, it kind of hit me. Is that how she sees me: someone who is trying to fix others? Am I the fixer?"

Robert let the question reverberate in the room for a second.

"I was. It was true! When it came to listening, that's who I was— the fixer. Because if anyone ever came to me with a pain or complaint, what did I do? I was always so quick to give them advice. *YES*, I was going to fix them! Maybe I was brought up to think that if someone was telling you something, you better have a reply for them, and it's your job to fix it or change it. I didn't know that people just wanted to be listened to. I think the thing I didn't realize was that most people weren't coming to me for an answer. They weren't looking for any judgement; they didn't come to be fixed. They just wanted to let something out and have it heard."

Robert's eyes momentarily made contact with the girl. But she quickly pulled her hoodie up to mask her face when she saw him.

"And another thing I didn't know. I didn't find out what it meant to *feel* listened to until my sister died. I was already twenty-two years old. It took me twenty-two years to find out how much I really needed someone to just listen to me!"

Robert pulled another chair from the wall and sat on the back of the chair so everyone could still see him.

"You see, I wasn't living at home at the time. I was in university about three hours away... I remember it was five am. I was in this deep, deep sleep and the phone rang. It was my mother and she was telling me that my sister had just been killed by a drunk driver. Man, it was all so surreal! There's just no preparation for something like this. How do you deal with someone you love getting killed?"

All eyes were now on Robert.

"So I went home for about a week. I saw my sister before they put her in a coffin. I'd never seen anyone...you know, dead. She looked so... not her. I touched her hand and suddenly there was this overwhelming feeling that I didn't know anything anymore. It was like I was an alien and I had just beamed down on this strange planet. Over the next few days, I was like this otherworldly being watching these strange human creatures cry and hug. It was like I was removed from the reality of it all. Her funeral, lowering her into the grave...I mean, if you saw me, I was crying. There were tears. But inside me, nothing! I felt numb. Anyway, a week later I went back to school."

Robert looked over to the girl in black. She had taken off the hoodie and sat tall in her chair. He wondered what loss in her life had affected her enough that now she looked so engaged.

"Now, when I got back, I thought it was strange how no one really spoke to me about what had just happened to my sister. After a couple of weeks, I was getting really angry with my friends. One day, about four of us were sitting having a beer after class. When I saw everyone just sitting around laughing, talking about something that had happened at school, I just *lost* it. I couldn't take them ignoring this...this horrible thing that had happened *to me*. So, I stood up and told them how heartless they all were and cruel. I screamed at them, 'For God's sakes, my sister had just died! And not one of you,' I told them, 'has really talked to me about it...and you call yourselves my friends?'"

Robert got up from the chair.

"Then, I just ran, not knowing where I was going, but man, I was running hard, so hard, until I just couldn't run anymore. I completely collapsed right in the middle of this huge empty parking lot."

Robert walked towards the wall and leaned against it.

"When you feel this kind of pain, it's like you're in a play or a movie; you're just acting everything out because you can't seem to connect with the horribleness of it all. You feel so alone...like you want to be touched, but a hug is not enough. You feel like you need someone to reach inside of you and...well...I just sat there and screamed and I didn't know what I was screaming for. Maybe I thought my screams would somehow connect to something that made sense. But all I remember was the more I screamed, the more pain I felt. And I was so alone...so, so alone."

Robert wrapped his arms around his body.

"Then I heard my name being called out and there were two of my friends on their bikes. They peddled towards me and got off their bikes and said, 'Robert, we're sorry, really...but when you came back from the funeral we tried to talk but you kept saying, 'I'm okay,' or changed the subject. We didn't know what to do and thought you knew how to deal with it and...' Well, then they tried to explain to me about me being the 'fixer.' They said, 'You gotta know Robert, it's hard talking to you 'cause no matter what anyone tells you, you always have an answer for everything. We didn't know how you felt 'cause you really don't ever expose yourself to any of us or really tell us how you feel!'"

Robert looked directly at the girl. She didn't turn away. He then walked away from the wall and sat down on the back of that chair again.

"And there we sat for the next two hours in the middle of this huge parking lot emptying out all the miscommunications and feelings that were, for so long, unspoken. And I can tell you, I learned what the greatest gift of life was that day. I learned to have the courage to talk about myself and how to appreciate that wonderful gift of feeling listened to. But I also know it's something you can lose just as fast. You have to constantly be working at it: talking, listening, listening, talking. That's why it's called connecting. Once one side stops—doesn't listen, doesn't talk—you break the connection!"

Robert then stood up and smiled.

"So, how many in this room can give that connection to someone else here?"

And at that point, Robert asked the students to go back into their little circles and simply go around and tell everyone in their group something about themselves, starting off with, "One thing you probably don't know about me by just looking at me is..."

And very quickly, the room was buzzing again with young people sharing with each other. The room felt so alive with purpose. Listening with purpose. The room soon filled with sounds of great open laughter as someone obviously shared something funny about themselves. In other groups, you could see hands reach over and comfort someone who'd just shared something delicate.

Robert looked over at the young girl. She was quietly mouthing the lyrics to the song Robert had playing in the background. Natasha Bedingfield had found a fan in this girl and she seemed to know the song as if it was her own—that we are all a blank page and our story is always ready...ready to be written.

Robert sat beside her. The girl suddenly stopped mouthing along to the song, turned to Robert and asked, "Do I want to stop being unhappy and feeling alone?"

"I'm sorry, what did you ask me? Do I want to stop...feeling alone?" Robert was puzzled.

"Don't you remember you asked me that?"

"You mean, when I was talking about my sister dying?"

"No, on the phone...On the phone *to me*. On the phone, you asked me, 'Do you want to stop being unhappy and feeling alone?'"

"Oh my God." Robert's eyes opened wide with disbelief. "Nancy...Nancy?"

"Yeah, don't be so shocked. I *do* go to school, you know!"

"But I checked, the school you told me you went to was—"

"Big shock! I *lied*. And anyway, even if I told you, it wouldn't have mattered because I had to move to this school this year."

"Nancy...Wow! Nancy, I...I'm just—"

"—Happy I'm *not* dead?" she sarcastically asked with a knowing smile.

"That night after I spoke to you and you asked me if I wanted to stop being unhappy and feeling alone...well, I did. So, I told my mom about talking to you and calling. And do you know what? You were right; my mom actually listened to me for once. I told her about things and how people at my school were so mean and...Do you know what she did? She actually helped me go to this school and, anyway, here I am at a new school!"

"That's so great Nancy. I'm just so—"

Nancy cut Robert off. "—Only it's not so great, really...she's thinking everything is solved 'cause I'm in a new school, but guess what? *Big surprise!* Nothing's different, all the same, the same assholes...*Nothing* changes! People are all the same!"

Nancy then tugged her sleeve up a little to hide the multiple scars on her arm that mapped the pain she held inside. "See, nothing's changed, and trust me, *no* one cares!" And then she got up and started to walk out of the gym.

Penny Mooreland immediately popped up from her chair to stop

Nancy from leaving, but Robert darted in front of Nancy first. "Okay. No one cares, same assholes and so now you still want to cut yourself...I got that, Nancy. And that's how you feel because that's how you think, right?"

"It's not how I think or feel, it's how *it is!*" Nancy then put her hands up and pushed Robert away from the door so she could exit.

Robert could see Penny Mooreland and another teacher making their way towards them. From angry looks on their faces, it was clear they felt very little compassion for Nancy after seeing her physically push Robert.

"Nancy, please...please just stay for one more hour and if you still think that's how it is—" Robert was interrupted by Penny.

"—Ms. Archer, we have tried to be patient with you for two months and—"

It was now Robert's turn to cut Penny off. He knew what these two teachers were about to say were the same words Nancy had heard her whole life. That people had tried to be patient, but now they had had enough and that she needed to be punished for not playing along with everyone else.

"—Oh, I'm sorry, Penny. One moment please. Nancy was just showing something to me."

"Mr. Sanchez, I just saw her push you."

"Oh, no no no." Robert had thought he had lost Nancy forever, so he wasn't about to lose her again because of a little push.

"Well, yeah. You saw her push me, but that was because she was showing me something I had asked her to do. I asked her to demonstrate how she feels when people don't understand why she..."

Robert then pointed meekly to his arms, leaned towards the two teachers, and then whispered, "You know, cutting herself." Then he spoke a bit louder. "So I asked her what that made her feel like doing. So she pushed me. You see? Because that's what she feels like: like pushing people away."

"Oh." Penny was at a loss for words. She looked at the other teacher, who also stood there, baffled, and just repeated what Penny Mooreland had said. "Oh!"

"So, thanks for your concern." Robert smiled.

But Penny still felt the need to be in control of the situation so she pointed at Nancy's chair as she spoke.

"Still, we don't need any more pushing or shoving. And if there's nothing else to show Mr. Sanchez, could you please go back and sit down?"

"Oh, there is one more thing," Nancy said. She slowly drew one of her sleeves up as high as she could, exposed the multitude of scars, then simply turned to the two teachers and said, "My arms...I wanted to show him my arms."

Penny Moorland had obviously never seen the full scope of the scars that lined Nancy's arms and she immediately let out a little gasp.

The other teacher blurted out, "Oh, my God!" and quickly turned her head, pretending something else had suddenly distracted her.

Although seeing Nancy's arms caused Robert to wince a little, he also could not hold back a smile at Nancy's shocking boldness. He knew she wanted to shock her teachers into some kind of reaction and he couldn't resist playing along with her. So he turned to the two teachers and said very softly, "Yeah, we just wanted to do it in the hallway away from everyone else...you know, in private."

The two teachers sheepishly backed away and murmured, "Of course. We're sorry...Go on."

"Look at them run away!" Nancy mocked.

Robert took a step closer to her. "I don't think they are running away. They just reacted because of your arms, Nancy."

"Yeah, these are the adults that say they care for us and the moment they see something bad, they run away. Nothing ever changes!"

"Well, maybe something did change. You finally showed them your arms."

"Yeah, and they ran away!"

"You have to give people a chance to react first. They didn't realize how bad it was. How can you expect them to care about something or someone they don't know anything about? Look Nancy, you say nothing has changed; it's all the same, even coming to a new school, right? Because that's how it always is, right?"

"Yeah...so?" Nancy hesitantly asked.

"Well, I'd like to make a deal with you. Just stay for one more hour, and after that, if you still think that's how it all is and nothing has changed, well, then I'll talk to your teachers and you can go home, all right? I promise I won't stop you from going home and cutting yourself some more."

"*What!* You don't care if I do this?" Nancy said in a hurt voice while holding her arms out.

"Nancy, I think you'd cut yourself whether I cared or not."

Nancy's face was filled with disbelief. She opened her mouth wanting to respond, but nothing came out.

"Listen, of course I care, Nancy. But no one can help you if you don't want to be cared for and are just resigned to thinking you're all alone. And you know what? You'll feel even more alone if you never tell anyone what is hurting you."

"Well, I am alone...I've always been all alone." She turned to the gym looking at all the small groups of people sharing and pointed at them.

"See, look at them. They all have someone listening to them. Who have I got?"

"Well, who do you listen to, Nancy?"

"What?"

Robert questioned in the kindest and gentlest way possible, "Really Nancy, who do you listen to?"

"It's hard to listen to anybody when you're always alone!" Robert heard a little cry in her voice.

"A lot of times being alone is a choice. Look around you, Nancy. Here's a whole room of people to listen to! Usually if you want someone to listen to you, you have to listen back. So, Nancy, tell me, who in this room have you ever listened to?"

Nancy put her hands on her hips and stood there looking at Robert, then sarcastically smiled and waved at the two teachers who were watching the whole conversation. The teachers turned away as soon as Nancy waved.

"Okay, good point, professor, and what the *hell* are you anyway? A teacher? A counsellor? *What?* And why do you do this? I'm sure you're not getting rich doing this!"

Robert chuckled. He could see a tiny glimpse of hope that Nancy might be coming back into the gym. He thought about what she had just asked.

"You know, that is a very good question, Nancy. Why do I do this?" He thought for a second and simply said, "Well, it makes me feel proud of myself. Oh, and you're right, I don't make much money. So, will you stay?"

Nancy raised her head and let out an exasperated sigh, the kind you make when you know you have just lost an argument to a worthy opponent. She turned to Robert and said, "Okay, one hour and really, I mean one hour, so it *better* be good."

"It'll be as good as you make it!"

Nancy went to sit back down on the chair near the wall, but Robert quickly snatched her chair up and started walking it over to a small group. Nancy nervously pulled her sweater over her hands as she followed behind him.

When he got to the nearest group he asked them, "Excuse me, this girl, Nancy is her name. She thinks she's ready to join a group now. Any of you mind if she joins you?"

Nancy looked down to the floor, tugging at her sleeves. She did not want to see the signs of rejection she was so sure would come. But the kids were all smiles and moved their chairs to make space for her. Robert put the chair down for her. She awkwardly sat down and looked up at Robert with a little fear in her eyes. But her focus immediately changed when Adam, a Brad Pitt look-alike—one of the school's chosen ones—a gifted athlete, repeated what he had just shared with the group.

"Hi, Nancy, I was telling everyone that one thing you wouldn't know by looking at me is that it hurts me that my dad refused to let me miss a game last week when my hand was badly bruised. But then he really got furious when he found out that the real reason I wanted to miss that game was so I wouldn't hurt my hand anymore because of the talent show. Because I needed to play guitar...and my dad thinks football is...is more important."

Nancy looked up at Robert with a look of pure disbelief. How could this guy be hurting? This talented, good-looking...

Dearest love,

Arrived at Tengboche. Although there is this wondrous, building excitement the closer we get to Everest, today turned out to be kind of scary for the three. They had a lot of trepidation walking along these cliffs lined with incredibly steep drops. All these stunning views surrounding us, yet they spent most of the day looking down and watching where their feet were. And when they did look up, we were being circled by vultures! Despite their ugly reputation, vultures really are quite beautiful. Their wings are so long! Picture Icarus leaping from his cliff. Their wings are more like his feathered arms flapping...But from how these birds are depicted in all those movies back home, Troy and Phil said they were getting worried that they were following us for a reason...and then Ang joked, saying these birds can always detect the weak ones and usually know who will be their next meal. Everyone laughed except Nancy. I told her Ang was just trying to make a joke...but, when she told me that's how she always felt at school. Scared of the vultures flying around her...getting ready to pick at her bones, I...

Robert got the room to stand up and put all the chairs along the wall. Earlier in the day, he had them all draw pictures of themselves with their eyes closed. This experiment always had the room laughing playfully. He told them that the reason for having them close their eyes was so everyone had the same disadvantage. No one was asked to be perfect or show a talent. Just like when they were small children, they just drew what they instinctively thought or felt about something. They didn't worry about how good they were at drawing.

Robert asked everyone to take their portraits and put them in the centre of the room, side by side, in one long line down the middle of the gym floor. It was quite the sight with all those strange looking, Picasso-like faces sitting side by side. The artwork definitely had everyone seeing each other in a new perspective. In many ways, this next exercise was about to do the same thing.

Everyone was standing on one side of the line. "I'm going to ask you to do a simple exercise, allowing each of you to tell your story in silence. I'll ask a question and if your answer to that question is yes, then please cross over the line of faces to the other side of the room and then turn to face the rest of us. I'd like to ask you to listen to everyone's answer by watching. It's quite simple. For example, cross the line if you have blonde hair."

With that said, every person who had blonde hair crossed the line and faced the rest of the group. There were only about eight kids that crossed the line until three dark haired girls giggled their way across, telling the room they had dyed their hair for years, but they still believed it to be blonde.

Once the mild laughter settled, Robert said, "You see, sometimes it's a simple thing like hair colour that makes us different or separates us from everyone else. And those of you that crossed all share something in common and you're not alone! Okay, all you blondies cross back again, please."

Once they got to the other side, Robert said, "Cross the line if you or your parents were not born in this country."

Over half of the students crossed the line. The room was filled with comments of "I never knew that." There was a touch of amazement in their voices, as if they were marvelling over how many of their classmates were not from this country.

"You know, I have been doing workshops in other schools across this city where I found kids treating other kids like the enemy, simply because they or their parents were not born here. They were being picked on, hurt, because of something they didn't have any control over." Robert turned to the group of kids that hadn't crossed and said, "Look at these people who have crossed over. Ask yourselves, is there any reason to make them feel like they don't belong just because of their background? And those that have crossed, do you ever do that to each other?"

At that moment, Robert saw Nancy still standing about ten feet behind everyone else, looking like she was just waiting for the hour to pass.

"Okay, everyone cross back please."

As they did, one kid dragged his feet and stepped on a couple of portraits on the floor, kicking them two or three feet away from the rest.

"Hey, don't step on that! That's Fiona's face," a tall black girl shouted out as she quickly walked back to the line, gathered up Fiona's portrait, along with the others, and put them back in the line. There was a little commotion when a couple of the feet-dragging kid's friends playfully slapped his back, showing they didn't like him disrespecting the portraits either. The small gesture of rescuing the portraits caused the room to break into a mini applause and the girl took a moment to turn around to the group and bow. Then Fiona and another tall black girl went to hug their friend and thank her for protecting her picture.

Robert walked in front of the group. "And could you imagine if we all stood up for each other like this girl did for her friend's picture? How many would have done that?"

"Yeah, my bad," apologized the feet dragger.

"Wait a second." Robert then questioned the foot dragger. "*My bad?*"

"Yeah, my bad, okay." The foot dragger shrugged and drifted behind one of his friends.

"I think it's great you kids have this expression that acknowledges you did something...well, bad. Yet, how many of you have friends that are quick to say 'my bad' but then they go and do the same thing over again?"

"Look, I'm...sorry about the pictures. It was an accident, okay. It's not that big of a deal. Sorry, okay?" the foot dragger said as he tried to take the focus off him.

"I'm sorry all the attention is on you. What's your name?" Robert asked as he moved beside the boy.

"Franklin."

"Well, Franklin, I think it was just a careless accident, but just because you say that it's not a big deal doesn't mean that it isn't a big deal to someone else. Accidents hurt people. Our carelessness hurts people. It's all about perspective and being open to listening to how others see things. What hurts them may not be something that would hurt us. That's why I do this exercise: it's a way for all of you to show each other what affects each of us."

Robert looked up and saw Nancy had moved closer to the line, and though she was still focused on the floor, she was almost, *oh, so close* to being part of the group!

"Okay, next. Cross the line if you are an only child."

Only four kids crossed the line.

"Cross the line if or you or any of your family have to deal daily with someone who has a handicap, that has to use a wheelchair, a cane, or is autistic, anything...something that needs special care."

Seven kids drifted across the line.

Robert walked behind the seven students and said, "If you ever see one of these seven in the hallway, maybe looking tired, remember, these seven are dealing with something none of the rest of you have to deal with. Handicaps don't go away, heal themselves or get fixed. To love or care for someone who is dealing with that reality each and every day is not always easy. In many ways, these kids have to sacrifice things that none of the rest of you do."

Robert looked directly at the group across the line and asked, "Is there anyone on the other side of the line that would come over to someone here and say, 'Hey, if you ever want to talk about it, I'm here.' Please go and get that person and bring them back across the line."

Slowly, one by one, someone came to each one of the seven. They either took their hands or hugged them and then brought them back over to the other side.

"Okay, notice how it feels to cross the line. And when you are there, look to see who is with you. There is always someone who is going through something like you. And yet there are always others who are on the other side. Notice how we get separated so easily by these things—these simple differences that cause us to cross the line. Some of these differences cause us pain. And you have to do something with that pain right? You can't just will it away. No one can truly out-smart hurt."

Robert looked at Nancy. *Yes!* he thought with hope. She had not crossed yet, but she was now up front with all the other students. Standing beside the same people she said would never change. And discovering that so much of the pain and aloneness she thought was unique to her wasn't so unique at all. It was becoming clear that no one in this gymnasium was alone in their hurt.

"Cross the line if you have ever had someone you love walk away in anger; ever felt excluded because of your looks; wished you were someone else because it would be easier or make you feel happier or more loved; felt betrayed by someone close to you; called a slut or a whore; been whistled at, felt violated, called gay, a fag, a homo; insulted or teased by someone in this room; lost sleep because you were worried for the safety of someone you love; struggled with an addiction; fallen asleep to the sound of violence..."

The questions were alive! The room was electric! Teenagers were standing up for other teenagers. Nancy still had not crossed the line. But Robert knew the next question was hers: the next question would ask her how honest she was and how much courage she had. Yes, when he asked the next question, she would get her chance.

"Please cross the line if you or a family member or friend has ever thought seriously of hurting yourself, or has ever attempted or even committed suicide."

I remember trying to wish Nancy across that line! But no one moved! 'Come on, Nancy, seize your moment!' my heart was screaming to her. I waited for what seemed like eternity. This was her chance...but she didn't budge. Not one student even looked around the room at each other to see if anyone would cross. The question was just too risky for the group, I thought. Maybe seizing the moment wasn't going to happen today!

We hear that line so often in life, don't we? Seize the moment. And we hear of how everything can change in a split second—people talk about the moment that changed their life...Is it true? Can one moment—whether it be one blessed golden moment or one frighteningly raw moment—can that really be the reason for a WHOLE LIFE to change?

Well, Love, I wish you could have been here today. Because up here, under the shadow of Everest, an unexpected line was crossed and I think I saw one of those moments. Nancy had...

Nancy came up to Troy and asked if he could help her the next time they stopped for a break. If he could ask Mingma to help him do something, she could talk to Satya alone.

"I didn't know Richie Rich was your type, Nance," Troy laughed.

"Come on, Troy, can you just do this for me? Keep his dad busy for the break, can you?"

"Nance, Mingma doesn't even like it when we talk to each other, so how the hell am I going to keep him occupied for a whole break?"

"I'm sure in your past you had to cause some diversions. Like, how about when you were out stealing...you know, whatever?"

Troy didn't laugh. "I never stole anything, okay."

"Well, then what did you go to jail for?"

"Is this how you go about asking for favours?"

"I'm sorry, Troy. Really, I'm sorry. It's just Satya...I think I know why he never talks."

"Yeah, it's no big surprise...look at his father!"

"He's not like his dad. Come on. Please, Troy, trust me. Can you please just get Mingma away from his son for the break?"

Troy put his arm over Nancy's shoulder. "Easy there, girl, easy. I'll get Phil. I'm sure he can help me come up with some way. You know, I think Satya just doesn't want to be climbing mountains and he's trying to piss his dad off by wearing that scarf, looking like some rich kid that doesn't belong here and—"

"No, Troy, I do think he's wearing that scarf for a reason, but it's not that!"

Troy put his finger to Nancy's forehead. "Man, you got a lot of stuff goin' on in there!"

"Please?" Nancy begged.

"Okay...*OKAY*, I'll keep his old man busy for the break." Troy then called out, "Hey, Phil! Come here! Nancy's got an interesting challenge for us!"

Nancy watched Troy walk over to Philip and put an arm over Philip's massive shoulders. After they spoke for a minute, Philip looked back to Nancy, held out his arms and made a "what?" gesture. Nancy just smiled and nodded her thanks.

A couple of hours later, Ang stopped the yaks, which were about a hundred yards in front of the group, and told everyone it was time for a water break. Robert was talking to some people from another party of trekkers who were travelling with them. Nancy watched Troy and Philip speak to Mingma. Mingma threw his arms up in the air in disgust, but then walked the boys over to one of the yaks. As usual, Satya sat by himself behind a big tree, sipping from his water bottle.

Nancy waited until she knew for sure Mingma was occupied with Troy and Philip and then she walked around the tree to where Satya sat.

"Hi there, Satya."

Satya looked at Nancy and nodded politely.

"Would you mind if I sit with you?"

Satya's face filled with surprise at Nancy's request. Like a proper gentleman, he quickly stood up to let her sit. Just as he gestured for her to sit, he abruptly stopped and looked around the tree. He saw his father was with Troy and Phil, unloading one of the yaks.

"Don't worry." Nancy smiled. "Your father is helping Troy and Philip."

She plopped down and leaned against the tree. "Come on, sit down, Satya."

Satya looked again, hoping his father hadn't seen Nancy sitting with him.

"Don't worry, sit down. They can't see us! And I asked Troy to keep your dad busy so we can talk." He gave her a questioning look

"Because I want to show you something. Okay?"

He hesitantly sat down. Nancy smiled at him as she pulled her left arm out of her jacket. Satya shyly looked away.

"No, Satya, could you please look? I just want to show you this."

Satya lifted his head slightly and looked at Nancy. She rolled her sweater sleeve up to the elbow.

"What happened?" he gasped.

Those were the first words Nancy had heard Satya speak.

Nancy let out a small laugh as she rolled down her sleeve.

"I knew you could talk, Satya. I knew you could. I'm sorry if that scared you, but I'll tell you what happened if you take off that scarf."

"Why?" Satya nervously put his hand over the scarf and pulled it closer to his chin.

"Because I think—"

He then pleadingly whispered to Nancy. "—No, no, I cannot do that. Now, please...please go away before my father sees us."

"Look, Satya, look at your father." She pointed at the path almost thirty yards away.

"Your father's helping the boys and by the looks of it, it might take a while."

Satya looked and saw his father slowly and meticulously untying the supplies on the back of the animal. It sometimes would take the Sherpas over half an hour to load and tie the supplies. And Mingma always showed great compassion for the four-legged carriers, making sure the load was completely balanced. He often said that five pounds more on one side than the other could maim an animal for life.

"Please, my father asked me not to speak. So please, I must try not to."

"But why, Satya? Why would your father ask you to do that?"

Satya just shook his head, stood up and started to slowly walk away. Nancy got up on her knees and almost shouted, "I think I know why you wear that prayer flag around your neck!"

Satya turned to her and put his finger to his lips to ask Nancy to shhh! "It is not a prayer flag. One does not wear a prayer flag."

"Well, whatever it is, I think you wear it because you don't want anyone to see your neck."

"What? How can—" He swiftly looked towards his father, who was still untying the bags, and then quickly looked around to see if anyone was watching them. He knelt down behind the tree, facing Nancy, and whispered, "Please, please, Nancy...please understand I should not talk."

"Okay, I'm sorry, Satya. But why would your father ask you to not talk? Come on, you can tell me. Trust me, I won't tell anyone, I *promise!*"

Satya checked again to make sure no one could see them. He held the yellow scarf around his neck as he spoke.

"I must wear this to heal me." He started to stand. "And that is all you need to know."

"But wait, Satya. You wanted to know what happened when you saw my arms, didn't you?"

He smiled sadly at Nancy. "I'm sorry I asked. I know it is not my concern."

"Well, I'll tell you! I cut myself. *Many times!* I cut myself, Satya. Me, I did it because...well, because every time I didn't feel like anyone cared, I cut myself. And I cut myself every time I didn't want to be *here* anymore."

"Here on the mountain?" Satya questioned.

"On earth, Satya. Here! Anywhere really. I cut myself because I didn't want to be...be alive anymore."

Satya let out a faint, "Oh."

Nancy looked at Satya's hand on the scarf. "Okay, when I said I know why you wear that scarf, I said that because, okay, forgive me for saying this, but every time you reach up and tug at that scarf, it reminds me of all the times I pull at my sleeves to hide my scars."

Satya bowed his head and put his hand over his mouth. "Oh no! Does everyone know then?"

"Know what?"

"My...ah...the scarf, why I wear it. Is that why the boys call me Richie Rich?"

"Oh, those boys, Satya, when they see that yellow scarf around your neck, they just tease you because you remind them of some kid in a comic book. They don't mean any harm by it. Mostly they're teasing you to get you to talk. And me, well, I think you wear it because...because, I thought you were trying to hide something. Like I do." And then she corrected herself, "Well, like I did. I try not to hide it anymore."

Satya looked amazed. "You mean...you show people...your arms?"

"Well…" Nancy tilted her head in thought and wondered how to answer his question.

Satya then knelt back down again. "You don't care if anyone sees your...your arms?"

"No, Satya, I really do care. That's why I was always pulling at my sleeves to hide them. And to be honest with you, I still hide them sometimes, but not as much as I did. You know what? Because I always wear long sleeves shirts and sweaters, my parents hadn't seen my arms for two years after I started cutting them. They never knew what I was doing!

And then the day they saw them...and, they freaked. Treated me like I was some kind of, I don't know...some kind of hideous monster! I thought they wanted nothing to do with me ever again. So I just kept cutting myself and hiding my arms. I can't even count how many times I did it. And sometimes when I cut myself...sometimes I wished I died."

Satya watched Nancy as she stopped to catch her breath. It seemed like the altitude was affecting her. "Who stopped you from...you know, being dead?"

"It was the strangest thing, Satya. Every time I took that razor and cut myself," Nancy lifted her arm and made a gesture of a razor cutting herself open, "and I would watch the blood drip...it was strange, because as I saw it coming out of me, it was like I was watching someone else's arm bleed, not mine. And then, I would just look at that arm bleeding and this feeling came over me. It was as if I was looking at myself, as if I was another person and...and I was talking to the girl who was bleeding, 'Oh, you poor girl, is no one helping you? Doesn't anyone know your bleeding?'"

Satya looked at Nancy with such compassion and sympathy. "And so...what did you do then?'

"Well, I met Mr. Sanchez and he had asked me a question, Satya. He once asked me if I ever cut myself in front of people or did I just do it when I was alone."

"What did you tell him?"

"Well, almost a year after he asked me that, Mr. Sanchez came to my school. He was doing this thing where he would ask a question to all the students and you had to cross this line if the question he asked was true. Like something you did in life. He asked lots of questions about if we did this or felt that, but I never crossed, even though I did do most of those things he mentioned. But so many of the other kids would cross. It was like all those kids could tell the truth...they could tell the truth about themselves to each other, but I just couldn't. I kept wanting to cross. But I just couldn't tell anyone, you know?"

"You didn't want to show anyone you were weak...right?"

"Yeah, maybe...Well, no, not really. It was more like I was terrified someone would find out and know who I was or how I really felt. Isn't that crazy? I cut myself because I felt alone but I was scared to tell anyone I felt alone."

Satya smiled sadly as he nodded.

"And this was my chance, Satya, but I didn't move! I just kept letting all the other kids do it. But then Mr. Sanchez, he asked this one question and no nobody crossed. Absolutely nobody moved after he asked it."

Satya leaned closer to Nancy. "What was the question?"

Nancy was starting to struggle to breathe and had to slow down. The effects of the altitude were more noticeable today and so, as her heart rate increased, it became more difficult to speak. Satya put up his hand to stop her from speaking.

"It's okay, Nancy, you need to stop talking now. Your breath is almost gone." He picked up his water bottle and held it out to Nancy. "Here, drink."

"Thanks." She took a sip. "It's okay. I want to tell you." She put her hand to her chest and smiled. "Really, Satya, I'm okay. The question was...he asked if anyone ever cut or hurt themselves on purpose. Or even tried to kill themselves."

Nancy now paused every couple of words to take in a breath.

"Well, I looked around and nobody budged. And my heart was pounding. Mr. Sanchez even knew what I did. He knew I cut myself...but he never even looked at me. And then I remembered his question from a year before...did I ever cut myself in front of anyone?"

Nancy stopped and looked directly into Satya's eyes.

"No, Satya, No, I didn't! I didn't because I'm always, always hiding! I hide everything...everything! But, after nobody moved to cross the line, Mr. Sanchez was about to ask another question and all the sudden I just yelled, 'ME!' I don't know how it came out! I just yelled, 'ME!' It was real loud too! I knew I didn't want to say anything, but there I was yelling, 'ME!' And then, Satya, I just started moving across that line. I was the only one moving in the whole room. And that line—that line—it looked so far away. But then something happened. It was like this great magic moment: I looked at that line... I was so scared. And I knew everyone was watching me. But when I got there, I turned to face all those kids and then suddenly, don't ask me why, but I...I pulled up both of my sleeves and showed my arms to everyone. I couldn't believe I was doing it. I didn't even think of doing it...I mean, why was I doing it? I know I was frozen...completely afraid to move. I know I was frozen, but someone was moving me."

"You think it was Mr. Sanchez?"

Nancy smiled, and continued panting as she spoke. "He couldn't. He was standing twenty feet away. But later I asked him how did I do that? And he told me it was probably that same little girl...that same girl who was always watching me cut my arms and watched me bleeding and...that same girl who wanted to help me to stop cutting...and stop me from hiding."

Satya looked puzzled.

"Me, Satya...*me!* I was the *little girl!*"

"Oh!" Satya laughed at himself. "You saved yourself?"

"Well, a part of me did, but then, oh Satya, the greatest thing happened! When I was, standing there all alone showing my big, ugly scarred up arms..." She stopped and took in a long slow breath. "And you know what happened? The whole room just started clapping!"

Satya shook his head in disbelief.

"Yeah, clapping. Me too! I was thinking how weird it was. The cynical part of me was thinking, 'Are they clapping because I wanted to kill myself and they wanted to see me dead?' But then this one guy comes beside me...and this guy is like one of those hero jock guys...everybody loves him. He looks like some movie star guy. Well, then he rolls up his sleeve. He has scars too, like me...and then he takes my hand. All of a sudden another girl comes to us; she does the same and takes my other hand...More kids came, until there were about twelve or thirteen of us all holding hands...holding hands because...we tried to kill ourselves...and everyone's clapping."

"They are friends then?"

"No, Satya, they never were my friends. But maybe now."

"You make friends?"

"Oh, Satya, I hope so! But, by telling these kids...all of a sudden I'm not alone any more. Everything's different. I haven't wanted to cut myself and if I did, I'd tell someone. I talk now and...and you know what, Satya? It's like I got this new reason to live, 'cause now I'm the one...me...kids come and talk to me when they feel—"

Satya interrupted Nancy by grabbing her hand with both of his hands. "—My father thinks I shouldn't talk because—"

A deep voice suddenly came from behind the tree and cut Satya off.

"Satya, go. Help your father. We need to start moving." Ang poked his head around the tree and barked at Satya.

Satya let go of Nancy's hands and jumped up. He bolted so fast towards his father and the two boys that he tripped and fell awkwardly on his knee. Troy and Philip helped Satya up. Nancy also ran to help, but the moment Satya saw her, he held up his hand, signalling her to please stay away. She took a few more steps but stopped when Satya squinted his eyes and shook his head in a desperate and intense no.

Satya's pant leg had ripped and his knee was bleeding. Ang pulled out something from his backpack and tended to Satya. As Mingma walked towards his son, Ang shook his head and spoke about how he might need to replace Satya when they got to Tengboche if the bleeding didn't stop. Troy said it didn't look that bad, but then Ang explained the dangers of getting a wound in high altitudes, describing how wounds tended not to heal when one was up so high.

For the next three hours of the trek towards the village of

Tengboche, Satya limped close beside his father. Neither one of them said a word to the other. Troy and Philip had asked Nancy if she got Satya to talk. But she lied and said he just nodded hello, as he usually did.

"Then why the hell was he running back to us like he was a crazy man?" Philip asked her.

"Oh, Ang scared him." Then Nancy stopped to tie her shoe, telling the boys to go ahead and not to wait for her. Philip and Troy walked ahead, looking behind them every now and then. But Nancy never noticed them. She was lost in another world of thought.

At supper that night, Ang, Mingma and Robert sat facing Troy, Nancy and Philip. Satya was not there. The other group travelling with Robert's had just finished their supper and had said their goodnights, leaving the six of them alone in the sparse supper room at the lodge where they were staying.

No one spoke as they ate their egg noodles, which were drowned in garlic. The garlic helped with breathing at such a high altitude. Nancy poked at her food, then broke the silence and asked, "Where is Satya, doesn't he need to eat?"

Mingma shot Ang a very hard and stern look but then smiled at Nancy.

"Satya needs to stay off leg. I bring him food."

"I can bring it to him if you like," Nancy said.

"No," Mingma said very sharply.

"No need, Baba. I'm here," Satya said, standing in the doorway.

Troy and Philip looked at each other in total surprise. This was the first time they had ever heard Satya speak. The cook, who saw him walk in, quickly filled a plate and placed it on the table beside Robert.

"Wow, the man talks! Hey, Phil, look...little Richie Rich can talk!" joked Troy.

Mingma put his finger in front of his lips as he looked at his son. He then picked up Satya's plate and stood up. "Satya, come, you need to rest leg. We go room, you eat there."

"Come on, Mingma. He just started talking. This is the most we have heard the two of you say all week. I think we'd all love to—" said Troy.

Robert, sensing something serious in Mingma's behaviour, put a hand on Troy's arm. "Maybe we should let them go if they want, Troy."

Ang said something in Nepalense to Mingma and Satya, which caused Satya to lower his head and nod.

Troy didn't argue. "Oh, yeah, sorry guys, I didn't mean anything. Just go ahead."

Mingma had one hand on Satya's plate and the other on his son's shoulder as they walked towards the door. Ang was now standing at the table and said good night.

Mingma let go of his son to open the door. As he did, Satya rushed back to the table and leaned over the table, facing Robert.

"I want to line cross too...Please, Mr. Sanchez, I want to cross it too!"

Robert had no idea what Satya was asking him. "Satya, you want to cross where?"

Mingma called out, "Satya, now!"

Ang put a hand on Satya's back. "Go with your father now."

Satya then turned to face Nancy. "No! Nancy. Please tell Mr. Sanchez I want to cross line too."

Robert looked at Nancy. Mingma yelled for his son to come. Ang repeated for Satya to go with his father. Troy and Philip now looked at Nancy, awaiting her response.

Nancy stood up, feeling a little anxious, not sure exactly what to say. She then looked at Robert and stammered. "He wants...he wants to do...what I did because of ..." Then, not knowing how to explain, she just held out her arms and said, *"This!"*

"Yes." Satya turned to his father. "Yes, Baba, I want to do this."

And as he said the word "this," he undid his scarf, pulled it off and dropped it on the floor. A faint red scar circled Satya's neck.

"No, Satya!" Mingma took a couple of steps and reached to pick up the yellow scarf. Half of the noodles and garlic fell off the plate and onto the floor. "Stop talking now!"

Ang quickly knelt down to clean up the food that fell off the plate. He looked up at Mingma. "Mingma, no trouble...No trouble!"

"Come, Satya, *now!*" Mingma ordered.

Satya looked at his father, shook his head and sat down in front of Robert. "No, Baba, *please!* Listen to Mr. Sanchez, he will explain. Please Baba, please, come listen."

Mingma took a step towards the table. Ang stopped cleaning and they both looked at Robert.

Robert scratched his head and raised an eyebrow. "Ah...explain what, Satya? I'm sorry but...what am I explaining?"

Satya held his hand out to Nancy, gesturing for her to speak.

Nancy smiled meekly as she spoke. "I kind of told him about that time I crossed the line, Mr. Sanchez."

"And he wants to do that *here? Now?*" Robert asked Nancy.

"I don't know...I don't know. Today I was..."

Satya took Nancy's hand. "Please, can I show my father?"

"What? Satya, what do you want to show him?" she asked.

Satya then gently touched Nancy's arm where all her scars were. "This," he said. "*This.*"

It took Nancy a moment to comprehend what Satya was asking. As soon as she realized he wanted her to show her arms to his father, she looked at Troy and Philip. They both knew and had seen the damage Nancy had carved into her arms. Troy kind of shrugged as if to say "why not?" and Philip just smiled in support. Nancy then looked back at Robert, who just stared pensively, awaiting her decision.

She then held both her arms out and simply said, "Okay!"

Satya got up from the table and stood facing Nancy. He then delicately drew Nancy's sleeves up high. "Thank you, Nancy," he said. He then turned and looked at his father as he held Nancy's arm out for his father to see.

Mingma and Ang both took a step towards Nancy and looked at her arms. The two Sherpas had seen many scars in their travels, but had never seen such unnatural ones as these.

Mingma looked at Ang who spoke first. "Who has tortured this girl in such a way?"

Nancy answered Ang's question immediately. "I did."

Mingma looked disturbed and shouted at his son, "Satya, put sleeve back on, girl!"

Satya adamantly spoke back to his father. "No...no, look, Baba, look!" And then Satya let go of Nancy and pulled his shirt collar down to expose the reddish marks around his neck.

"This Nancy, she tried just like me, but she is also alive, just like me. Because she talked, Baba...because she talked."

Mingma put the plate of food on the table and firmly grabbed his son's arm. "Son, we must go before we bring trouble, come."

"No, Baba, I already bring all trouble to you and Aama. I am sorry, Baba, I am sorry. Please just let Mr. Sanchez ask the question...and when I cross the line, you will see."

Robert rubbed his face. "Um...well, Satya. I'm not sure this is the place to do that and—"

Nancy shot up from the table. "Sure we can do it, Mr. Sanchez." She then turned to Philip and Troy. "Help me, please."

They both watched her walk around the table and pull it about eight feet away from where they were sitting. Troy quickly grabbed a couple of chairs and moved them as she yanked away. As Phillip joined in to move some chairs, he asked Nancy, "What are we doing?"

"Just make some space," Nancy said as she finished pulling the table away from Robert. There was now a twelve-foot vacant space between the two tables.

Ang stood beside Mingma and watched the three kids move the room's furniture about. Robert got up and walked to the cook, who had come out of the kitchen after hearing the commotion, and told him not to worry because they would move everything back before they left.

"Philip, can I have your headphones?" Nancy held out her hand. Philip then pulled out a long wire with two earplugs from his pants pocket and handed it to Nancy. She unrolled the wire and laid it down in a line in the middle of the space they had created.

"Okay everyone, stand on that side of the line," she said, gesturing at the wire on the floor. Troy and Philip were the first to move to a spot facing Nancy. Satya quickly followed them. Then Robert put a hand on Ang's shoulder and the two of them stepped up beside Troy. Mingma was the last to move. He shuffled awkwardly until he stood beside his son. They were all standing in a line, facing Nancy, who was on the other side of the headphones.

"Ah...what are we doing, Miss Nancy?" Ang asked.

"It's a game, Ang. Come on, we tried all those dance steps of yours. Just play with us, okay?"

Ang looked unsure, but Robert put his arm around Ang's shoulder and said, "She's right, Ang...We all tried your dance last night. Now it's your turn. Come on, try it a little."

Ang shook his head in disapproval. "All right, but soon this boy needs to get off his leg." Ang then settled in beside Troy and Mingma.

Nancy then explained, "Okay, Mr. Sanchez is going to ask a question. And if that question is something that you do or you feel, then you have to cross over the headphones to the other side of the room, okay?"

Nancy then walked over the headphones and stood in line with all the men. Robert walked away from the group, and shook his head in amazement as he smiled to himself, thinking, *Well, this will be a record: the first cross the line ever done at this altitude!* But as he walked to face the group, he felt a sudden shiver of emotion come over him. Images of Troy as a kid, in prison, shot at in the street; Nancy screaming, crying, singing over the phone; Philip's whole body shaking in uncontrollable anguish. And now here they all stood together—halfway up the tallest mountain on the planet—standing in this chilly, barren eating room with some headphones creating a makeshift line; standing with three Sherpas and waiting for one son to have the courage to cross a line because he wanted to show his father something.

Mingma and Ang both stared at Robert with distrust on their faces. Satya stood between them with his eyes closed, as if he was lost in prayer, wishing for some kind of miracle to descend into this tiny little room.

"Okay," Robert started. "Cross the line if you ever thought of—"

Nancy stopped him. "Oh, Mr. Sanchez, please don't start with that one right away. Do some questions to warm us up first."

Robert chuckled loudly. "You don't ask for much do you, Nancy? Yeah...okay then. Let's see. All right, let's start with...Cross the line if you don't have any brothers or sisters."

Satya opened his eyes and turned to his father. "Baba, that's you! You don't have any brothers or sisters...Go, Baba. You have to cross over that wire to Mr. Sanchez."

Mingma looked at his son and muttered something, but still crossed over. Then Philip crossed and stood beside Mingma, who gave him a sheepish smile.

Robert then walked over to Mingma and put a hand on his shoulder and said, "Okay...see, this is one thing you two have in common, but is different from the others. Look, see Mingma, you're not alone in this, right?"

Mingma shrugged a so-what.

"Okay, cross back over." Robert patted Mingma on his back as he left.

"All right, cross the line if you...Hmmm...okay, I know. Cross if you never thought of climbing or never really wanted to climb a mountain."

All five exchanged questioning looks. Then Troy walked across and faced the group. "Let me tell you, this is the last place I ever thought I'd be!"

Nancy and Philip laughed and just as Robert was about to speak, Ang walked over and stood beside Troy.

Mingma then said something to Ang in their own language. Ang just shook his head.

Troy looked at Ang and asked, "Are you kidding us? You never wanted to climb a mountain—*you*, the greatest Sherpa around?"

Ang's weathered face had a serious look as he simply replied, "No."

"You never wanted to climb a mountain and yet you do it every day?" Troy asked in utter disbelief. Then Mingma said something in Nepalese again, but Ang just looked at Mingma and repeated another even more firm, "No."

Robert took a step towards Ang with a questioning look. "Really Ang? So, you never enjoyed climbing?"

"You did not ask if we enjoy climb, Mr. Robert. Sometimes I enjoy the climb and I enjoy the people like you very much, but you asked if we ever *wanted* to climb. And I have never wanted to climb." Ang bowed his head reverently to Robert.

Then Philip spoke up, "Okay, Ang, so you never wanted to climb but you enjoy it?"

Ang turned to Philip and smiled. "A man can always find joy in something he does not want to do."

Philip thought about it and then shrugged. "Yeah, I guess you can. This is the last place I ever wanted to be too."

Ang then crossed back over and stood beside Mingma. He raised his arm and placed it on Mingma's shoulder as he spoke.

"My uncle, my father and my brother died climbing a mountain. I climb the same reason Mingma does: so his son will not have to."

"That is so incredible Mingma. You're such a great dad!" Nancy gushed.

But Mingma didn't turn to acknowledge what Ang or Nancy had just said. He looked incredibly intense, as if he was about to explode. The small room was very still and quiet. Satya took a step to stand directly in front of his father and broke the silence.

"Thank you, Baba. Thank you, Ang." Satya then started to clap his hands. Nancy quickly bounced beside Satya and clapped as well. Troy, Philip and Robert immediately joined in. The applause grew in rhythm and became increasingly louder. Mingma just stared at the floor and Ang looked a bit embarrassed at everyone applauding them. But Ang's face soon broke into a huge toothy smile and he bowed to show his thanks. Across the room, the cook joined in and was banging a large wooden spoon on a pot. As soon as everyone saw this, they broke into a heart-felt laugh.

"Does he even know why we're clapping?" Philip asked.

Troy quickly seized the moment and said, "Okay, everyone cross the line who wants to thank the cook for our food!" Everyone crossed over and faced the cook, with the exception of Mingma. The group applauded the cook. Ang walked over to the cook and explained what Troy had said and why they were clapping for him.

"*Tank*...you, *tank* you," he said in his broken English. Then he spoke in Nepalese. Ang turned to the group and translated what the cook had said.

"We live to find joy, he said. And he thanks all of you for bringing joy to his kitchen." Everyone except Mingma applauded the cook again.

Robert walked back over to the other side where everyone stood and whispered something to Nancy. She smiled and nodded back to him. Robert then moved to the middle where the headphones were and spoke.

"All right, let's do the question Satya wanted."

Satya squeezed his eyes shut once again. Mingma was still brooding and staring at the floor.

"Cross the line if you have ever thought of...or tried to hurt yourself...or even attempted suicide."

Nancy took a step towards the line, but stopped and turned back to look at Satya. Satya opened his eyes. They were now filled with tears. He took four long strides and crossed the line, but kept his back to the others. Nancy swiftly followed him and took his hand. She raised her arm to wipe some of the tears off his face with her sweater.

"Okay," she whispered. "Let's turn around."

Satya sniffed and smiled meekly. "Okay."

As they turned to face the group, Satya looked directly at his father, but Mingma had not raised his head and was still staring at the floor. Philip started clapping, and Troy and Robert joined in. Ang looking confused and clapped hesitantly.

Mingma threw his head up and exploded,

"Stop! Please stop!" Everyone did. Mingma continued speaking angrily. "This is not for clap!...This is not for proud!...*Come now*, Satya!" Mingma then stomped his way towards the door, his old boots pounding on the wooden floor.

Nancy ran in front of him, beating Mingma to the door. "No, wait, Mingma, don't get mad at Satya, He just—"

Mingma turned to Nancy and pointed at her. "You are bad for boy. This is not for clapping! You are bad for boy. Come now, Satya!"

Ang walked behind Satya, put his hand firmly on his back and started walking him to the door. "Satya, go with your father now."

"*NO!*" Satya pulled away from Ang and stood between the two Sherpas. "*NO!* Baba, this Nancy is not bad." Satya then looked at Troy, Robert and Philip. "They clap for me, Baba, because now I am not alone. This Nancy is not bad."

"Come, we go, now, Satya!" Mingma opened the door.

"Go with father, Satya!" Ang pointed to the open door.

"To where, Baba? To where do I go, Ang?"

"We go. Rest your leg. Come, we prepare for tomorrow." His father waved his hand for Satya to go through the open door.

Satya slowly walked out the door, but just as he passed through the threshold, he quickly grabbed the door handle and shut it before his father could follow him. Mingma tried to open the door, but outside Satya held the door handle tight so his father couldn't open it.

"Satya, *open door!*" Mingma shouted to his son.

"*NO*, Baba, you must listen," Satya yelled through the closed door. "I know, Baba, you ask me not to talk. That if I don't talk, it will heal my life. But Baba, each day I don't talk, I feel worse. I think more of how much I hurt you and Aama. Baba, you climb this mountain to make my life better, to make it not like yours, right?..."

"Satya, come open the door! Talk no more!" Mingma pulled at the door. "Satya, *talk no more!*"

"I want to talk, Baba! I need to tell you and Aama...I am sorry. I'm sorry I'm not smart enough. I'm sorry I can't be a doctor. That I lose all your money."

Mingma pulled mightily at the door handle but it wouldn't budge. He banged on the door to get Satya to open it, but Satya held tight. He looked back behind him. Robert, Troy and Philip were now standing beside Nancy. The cook came back out and was standing near Ang. No one was doing anything to help him open the door.

Mingma pulled one last time, yelling, "Talk no more, Satya! *Talk no more!*" Satya let go of the handle and Mingma fell on his backside as the door flew open.

The cold night air quickly filled the room. Satya stood at the door and saw his father on the floor. He took a couple of steps into the room. Nancy ran to close the door behind him. He walked over to his father to help his father sit up. Then, he sat beside him on the floor. He never once looked at his father as he spoke.

"Baba, you always say with the animals...you must get the weight just right for the load they carry. That it must be right or animal be hurt for life. Baba...this..." He then touched the red scar that lined his neck. "This...is now something I have to carry...this. This is my load that I carry, Baba, and it...is not weighted right."

Mingma raised his hand and spoke softly. "Satya, please, no more words."

Satya turned his body and looked directly at his father. "No, Baba, I don't want to hurt for life. What do you say to all these people who come to climb Sagarmāthā? One step then the other. You teach them that when they climb, Baba—you always say: First they must want to be there before they take even one step, right, Baba?...They must want to be here first before they climb. And so, that's what I need to do, Baba. I want to be here with you. So then...my step...my step must be to talk, Baba. To tell you..."

Those were the words Satya used: "My steps must be to you..." Tears fill my eyes as I write this, darling. Tonight must have been one of the most difficult and humbling situations for Mingma and Ang. These Sherpas are always so completely generous in spirit, yet they are not much for sharing anything too personal. But Sherpa pride was not going to stop Satya tonight. The dam inside him had finally burst and he just let it all flood right out of him. Sitting beside his father on that bare floor, telling us all how he tried to kill himself because of shame! Shame?! His father, Mingma, had saved for many years to send his son to medical school, but Satya failed his first term and was dismissed from the school. When Satya got home, apparently he lied and said the school was on a break and told his parents he had great marks. He didn't know how to tell his parents he had failed the one and only hope they had for him. It was at the beginning of the Dumje festival (something the Sherpas celebrate—prosperity, good health, and general welfare of the Sherpa community) and he knew his parents and almost everyone in the village would be out singing and celebrating. That was when he tried to hang himself. His mother unexpectedly came back because Mingma had forgot his hat and she was the one who saw Satya hanging there. He was unconscious but still breathing, but she couldn't get him down so she grabbed onto Satya's legs and tried to hold her son up as she shouted and screamed for help. Fortunately a couple of neighbours were leaving late for the festival and they heard the screaming. They came and helped cut Satya down...thirty more seconds either way, he'd have been dead.

Tonight, after we did the "cross the line" and Satya holding the door, we all tried to leave the dinner room (especially Ang) to give Satya time with his dad, but Satya begged us to stay. Must have been so hard for Mingma, he is such a proud man. Must have been a living nightmare for him—first to bear the shame of having his neighbours witness his son trying to kill himself, and now the shame of all of us hearing what his son had done. Ang had known about it. It was partially his idea that Satya come on this trek and to not talk. He was supposed to use this climb as some kind of silent penance...and rehabilitation.

Oh my love, there was such agony in Mingma's face as he listened to his son! He is such a big muscular looking man, but there on that floor, he looked so...so...completely helpless. Yet, the miracle Satya looked to be praying for must have come because you could see that, no matter how helpless his father felt, Mingma was listening. It was so beautiful, you know, that wonderful moment when a parent starts to understand that their child has a need to be heard. Well, it happened right in front of us. With every breath his father took in, you could see he was filling himself up with his son's words. And even though as Satya spoke, we could see this unbearable pain on his face—it was incredible watching this strong, strong man use every ounce of his mighty strength to just let his son talk. And you know, as a father, all I could think of was you and Jen. I'm not sure how much strength I would have or what I would do if Little Rock tried to take her life, or even felt that desperate.

Jenny put her hand over the journal. "Kyle, I'm sorry. Look beside you. I think that little girl—Look, Claire is listening. I'm not sure she should be listening to this."

Kyle looked across the aisle. Jenny was right—Claire was leaning over her armrest. The moment Kyle's eyes met Claire's, she asked him, "Can you read louder please? I keep missing stuff."

27. PRESENT DAY – AT THE HOTEL

K'naan's "Waving Flag" was still playing. Greg gave Lou a thumbs-up. Good old dependable Lou had gotten a group of his employees to sing along, which slowly encouraged the staff of the other two companies to clap hands and sing along as well. Greg sighed in relief. The presentation was going well. The response was not as critical as he anticipated. The morning's schedule had changed a couple of times already. Robert would speak before lunch—then after lunch, but since Linkup's president had still not arrived, it looked as if the plan was going to have to change once again. Greg walked over to Monique and told her the change of plans.

"Look, Monique, I'm sorry but we have to change the schedule again. Mr. Romano is still in transit and won't be here for another hour. So, I'm wondering if it is possible to have Robert start his talk now?"

"What *now?*" Monique's voice was full of panic. She hardly had enough time to sort out her fears. First, there was Jenny's frantic voicemail, which was abruptly cut off and second, because of Robert's behaviour all morning, she was becoming more and more afraid of what might come out of Robert's mouth during his talk today. And now she felt terrified of how Robert might react to the sudden change of plans.

"I'm so sorry to do this to you, Monique, but we now have some time we need to fill before lunch can be served. I think it's best if we have Robert speak now and delay the lunch a little. What do you think?" Greg said.

Monique stood up quickly, trying to find some excuse to delay. She looked to Amir and said, "But I don't think Amir has had enough time to set everything up."

Amir, overhearing the conversation, quickly took a step towards the two of them. With a smile and reassuring voice, he said, "Oh, don't you worry, Miss Monique. I am as ready as a man can be. When would you like to start, Mr. Wong?"

"How about five minutes?"

Monique felt a little faint. Her thoughts were racing. Jenny's voice was still echoing, *"Why does Daddy have a gun now?"* in her mind. She looked at Robert, who was still staring off into space and clutching that brown leather bag. A voice inside her screamed, W*hat is in that goddamn bag that no one is allowed to touch?*

But before Monique could say a word, Barbara Pouge was up on the stage and interrupted the conversation.

"Good news, Mr. Wong. I just got the okay from the kitchen. We can start lunch early."

"When?" Monique sounded panicky.

"Oh, no later than fifteen minutes." Barbara smiled. "Does that help you at all?"

"Well, of course it does." Monique said in a tone that was a little condescending.

Greg put a hand on Monique's shoulder and apologized for her rudeness. "I'm sorry, Barbara, she is a little nervous today. You know, the stress of the three companies coming together today and, of course, her husband's talk...So, okay, yes, that will be great. Let's have lunch in fifteen minutes. I'll announce it and tell everyone to take a moment to go out and freshen up so your staff can get the tables ready for lunch."

Barbara Pouge thanked Greg and hurried off.

"Well, there you go, Monique. Right after lunch, we'll hear Robert's talk," Greg said with a relieved looking smile. Then he pulled himself closer to whisper to Monique, "I've never seen you so jumpy. Don't worry, the presentation went really well and I'm sure your husband will do great!"

He gave Monique a supportive pat on the back and then turned to Amir. "Oh, Amir, I'm going to make a quick announcement and after that can you play some more of that happy music you just played? You know, something that gets people to sing along? It will be about fifteen minutes until lunch, okay?"

Greg then picked up the cordless microphone from Amir's table and informed the room of the lunch plans.

Monique stood there, flushed with emotion. She politely nodded her head to Amir, thanking him for being so prepared. She then walked over to Robert and stood directly in front of him. She waited for a long moment, but Robert would not return any eye contact.

"Bobby, did you send Jenny your journal?"

Robert said nothing.

"Robert, did you send Jenny your journal?"

Still nothing.

"Why would you do that? Come on, Robert, don't do this! Speak *please!* Okay? All right, can you just say okay?"

"Okay," he said without moving.

"Please, Bobby…Can you please…just look at me?"

Robert didn't budge.

She now spoke with the most direct, firm voice she could muster, "Look at me."

Robert turned and gave her an annoyed glance and then just turned his head away again.

"Oh God, Robert! I *can't* take this anymore!"

Monique's eyes started to well up with tears. She held up her hands, her fingers clenched like an eagle's talons, ready to snatch up her prey. Her hands kept rotating as she searched for the right words.

"You," was all she said. Then she took another breath and again said, "You." But when this one came out, her voice started to crack with emotion. "You…You…" and each time she said 'you' her voice became more strained. She repeated each 'you' as if she was an actor practising how they should start a scene, making each 'you' completely different and unique from the last.

But in between each of those you's, was a full, storied sigh that told the sad tale of the last six months between the two of them. Yet, Monique's emotional ache did not seem to stir Robert enough to even glance at his wife. He just sat there, head on his chest and clutching that brown leather bag closer to his body.

"Come on, Robert, I know you, this isn't you. I thought maybe you being here might change things. I don't know, maybe help you get over this. Come on, Bobby, I know you. Please, please just…just snap out of it!"

"Snap out of it? What the hell am I supposed to snap out of, Monique?"

"*This!* Is this how you want the day to go? Like this?"

"This? What '*this*' are you talking about?"

Monique took a step closer and loudly whispered, "*This*, Bobby. I mean, just look at us! Every day, more and more, and it just gets worse! Can't you see it? This…this… death we live!"

Robert rolled his eyes and mocked his wife, "Death, Monique? Really?"

"Yes…Yes! Look at us! Six months ago, Robert, they told me you were dead. I honestly thought you were dead. Do you know what that's like? *Dead*, Robert. We all thought you were dead. And now—"

"—Now, what?"

Monique crouched down on one knee to get closer to her husband. Tears were now streaming down her face. "Do you have any idea what that was like? Do you? 'Your husband's dead, Mrs. Sanchez,' 'Jenny, your daddy's dead.' But you weren't, Robert, you weren't! You were alive...but now...now—"

"Now, what Monique? For Christ's sake, *what?*"

"Now I actually feel you *are* dead!"

Monique's body suddenly convulsed and she quickly put her hands to her mouth as if she was about to vomit. She turned quickly, ran down the steps of the stage, opened the doors out into the hallway and disappeared. Her sudden departure caused a commotion at the foot of the stage and several colleagues were asking each other what was wrong.

Amir had witnessed the emotion that sparked between Monique and her husband. But he did not wish to make the situation worse, so when the onlookers looked up to the stage to ask what happened, Amir made motioned toward his stomach, indicating that Monique was just a little sick.

Robert didn't say a word. He brought the leather pouch to his chest and then slowly slumped over. He dropped the pouch on his lap as his hands slid down his thighs to the end of his stumps. He started rocking slightly in his wheelchair. He knew all too well the 'this' Monique was speaking about and the 'you' he had become. And the words, "No wait, I'm not dead!" were as far away and foreign to his lips as his amputated limbs were to his body.

Amir smiled sadly as he watched Robert rock in his wheelchair. Although he had no idea what had happened between this husband and wife, he was sure it must have been painful to both.

The song was just ready to end and Amir found himself a little panicky as he tried to decide what song to play next. He knew Greg wanted a spirited sing-along song, but he didn't have the heart to ignore the rocking man in a wheelchair clutching at his lost limbs. So he played a song that started slow, but always made the crowd to start singing along. The Proclaimers had never failed to bring a positive spirit into a room.

As the room started singing along with the song *500 Miles*, Amir's eyes suddenly opened wide with panic. *Oh my God!* he thought. *What have I done? Playing a song that reminds a man he can't walk!*

28. PHILIP

Dearest Love,

I hope my heart will always strive to be hungry, hungry to explore—to always find that "more" that makes me feel the way I do today. We arrived at Dingboche much later than planned. We became part of a rescue mission today. We helped a Sherpa and this woman pull her husband up a cliff after he had become tangled down below (mostly "tangled" in his own ego and stupidity). Apparently, this man wanted to cross an old bridge that Sir Edmund Hillary probably crossed sixty years ago! The river we were crossing has these new metal suspension bridges (even these will have your heart firmly planted in your mouth). Anyway, this new bridge is built directly above one of the remaining old wooden bridges. The old bridge is in such disrepair and is about five hundred feet underneath the new one. The rotten wood lath and frayed rope has made the old bridge unusable, but this guy was still attempting to climb down to it so he could cross over and, as he said, "Walk in Hillary's footsteps." As noble as that might sound, it was pretty damn foolish. Anyway, as he was lowering himself to the old bridge, his rope got so tangled around him that he was unable to move. Satya, who had a lot of experience rock climbing, had to harness up and climb down to untangle him. By the time Satya got down to him, that guy was getting ready to slice off one of his own ropes to get untangled. And if he had done that, he would have either hung himself or fallen to his death for sure!

Troy, Nancy and Philip really felt like they were saving someone today and they filmed it all for the kids back home. But they got a little depressed after interviewing the guy's wife as she was totally ungrateful to everyone. She said we were interfering and felt her husband could have untangled himself. She then told us they had just fired their Sherpa because he had unnecessarily panicked by asking for our help. We had a great discussion about it at supper tonight. Specifically, the question of how to save someone that doesn't want to be saved.

Mingma (who, after last night's adventure with his son, is no longer "the silencer") He was the most adamant about answering the question. He just simply said, "Life is to live...Save life when can." It was quite simply beautiful. He turned to his son and repeated, "Save life when can," and then Satya put his hand on his father's. Mingma shocked us all when he leaned over and actually kissed his son's cheek. Philip pulled out the camera and asked him to do it again, but Mingma wouldn't repeat the kiss for Philip to film. He really made us laugh when he said to Philip, "Some things happen when they do, NOT when we want them to happen!" And then the moment Philip put the camera down, he kissed his son again, making us laugh even harder. You know, love, that laughing felt so...well, it was that kind of laughter that makes you feel free, full of YES! It has only been twenty-four hours since our "cross the line" last night and it's like someone has turned a switch on inside of Satya and his father. They seem to shine now.

Oh, darling one, each day of this journey holds such wonderful reasons to be here!

Today—there is such a missing of you...Everywhere I hear your sounds—our sounds. This feeling has been inside me all day. It started at breakfast. Nancy wanted to read a poem she had written the night before called "The Word 'Heart' Starts with HEAR—there are two kinds of 'here's—you must be here to hear!" Then she gave me the poem as a present.

> *Listening is the sound that love makes,*
> *Love, knowing it can exist and thrive,*
> *Never becoming a faint feeling of 'remember when'...*
> *But is here to hear,*
> *And understands...*
> *That the only love that endures is a love that listens...*

Ang actually stood up and clapped real loud and told Nancy how she must have been from China in one of her last lives. When she asked him why, he took out a pencil and a scrap of paper and drew out the Chinese word or character for listening. He showed us that the Chinese word for hear is made up of five different symbols: you, the heart, the ear, the eyes and undivided attention. All five are equally a part of listening! Then the boys thought it was getting too heavy and made a joke and asked Nancy that if the only love that endured is a love that listens, did that mean deaf people could never have love?

But, you know, darling, that line about "The only love that endures is a love that listens" really came to be lived today...

Kyle stopped reading when he heard Jenny let out long sigh. "What's wrong, Jen? Do you want me to stop reading?"

"No, Kyle, it's just I thought of my mom and wondered if she ever read this."

"Why?"

"Well, it was always so weird whenever my dad came home from one of his climbs. There was always this...well, this really big tension between them. And it was so strange because, I mean, my mom was completely supportive of him going—she'd help him plan and pack, and she'd help him with so many things before he left. She even said how much she loved those drives to the airport with him. And when he was gone, she'd constantly be checking her e-mail for letters and run to the phone when it rang. You should hear how they spoke! Oh, they would talk so...so...well, like teenagers in love. But then, when my dad got back home..."

Jenny stopped.

"Yeah Jen, what happened when he got home?"

"I can't explain it. Even when I was just a little kid, I noticed it. My mom and I were always so excited when he came home. We would get all dressed up and talk all the way to the airport about Daddy....and I...I was just so, so happy when—you know, those big glass doors at arrivals? Well, when they opened, and my father would come walking through, I was like a cannon ball—I would just throw myself at him and he would catch me. But my mom would always act so strange. Like it wasn't special seeing him, like we were picking him up from shopping or something."

"Why do you think she acted like that?"

"Well, she told me last time I was home for a visit that it was hard for her. Even though she was happy to see him, she couldn't help feeling resentful. Things like, why did he leave, why make her worry about him, his safety? Anyway, it always took her a little time to warm up to him and get back to normal. But, I always knew when it happened. Mom would say something like, 'we need to do something as a family,' and it didn't matter what it was—going to movie, playing a game, or even going downstairs to watch TV together—but I'd always notice that my mom would take my dad's hand. And it didn't matter where we were or what we were doing, they would always be holding hands for the rest of that night. That was the signal. It happened every time. And do you know what I always said to myself?"

"What?"

"I'd always say, 'Ahhh...Daddy's home...Daddy's really home now!'"

Jenny wiped a tear from her eye. Kyle kissed the hand that brushed the tear away.

"Do you want me to keep reading?"

Jenny took Kyle's hand and kissed it. "Yes, please."

> *All day the glorious mountain, Ama Dablam, towered over us and it was framed by one of the bluest skies. We could see every detail, every curve of this massively impressive mountain. During the day, there was this moment I stood behind Philip with the same sky framing him, and I asked him for the camera to take a shot of him just walking. He looked so majestic—I could see why Troy sometimes calls him "our walking mountain."*
>
> *Tonight after supper, Phil waited until everyone left because he said he had to ask me something. He said he had heard I was writing about the three of them in some book. I told him it was just my journal and I was just about to start his story tonight and that when I've finished it, I'll let him read it. He said he didn't need to read it; he just wanted to know if it was good or bad. And he hoped I didn't really remember too much about the first time we met because of how he...*

The music came out of a small black speaker in the corner of the old high school gym. The day was almost over. Seventy-five teenagers stood in an odd-shaped circle. Seventy-five lives had just spent the day laughing, singing and dancing. Seventy-five souls had just spent their day sharing and unmasking themselves.

A song played—"Man in the Mirror". Robert slowly walked inside the circular human chain, making sure to make eye contact with each and every student. Some smiled back, some just stared and some were silent. Some had tears they kept wiping away, yet you could see they didn't want the tears to overcome them because they wanted to be here. They wanted to be standing in this circle of life and feel proud of this shedding.

"Before we started today, I know a lot of you were skeptical. Some of you were dreading having to be here, wishing you could be anywhere but here. But look what happened! Today I saw some of you open a door—the door of possibility, the door to a new understanding. Some of you opened a door of trust, one of friendship, one of kindness. Look, if you have the courage to see. Because every door you want to open is almost always waiting, waiting right there in front of you. Even the door of forgiveness."

Robert paused a moment. "Okay, maybe it sounds corny, but try...like that song we just heard...try to take a look at yourself and ask yourself what change you want to make today? Today, a lot of you said there were people in this room that made you feel hurt, like you didn't belong, bullied you, or just didn't understand you. Well, today...here is a chance to open that door of hope. Here's your opportunity to tell someone in this room you're sorry. Maybe say to them, 'I'm sorry I hurt you,' 'Sorry, I didn't understand,' 'Sorry, I didn't listen...I didn't see.'"

Robert turned on a song that Jenny had sent him in an e-mail about two years ago. She sent it to him because she wanted to say she was sorry about an argument they'd had. She'd yelled at her father about a message concerning a singing audition that he forgot to give her. She got so angry that when she ran out of the house and slammed the front door, the glass broke.

> *I remember sitting in my car in the driveway. The tears came so easily when I played the song. I never could stay angry at Little Rock for very long. But oh, that song helped. Coldplay. The Scientist. Someone trying to say they were sorry and wanting to start again. That song has really worked for me in the schools...*

And then, inside an old gymnasium, it happened. Doors opened. And it almost always happened, because these kids longed for a different kind of connection. One that was impossible to get inside the world of Facebook, iPods and Blackberries. Although most had been born into a world full of technological miracles—a world that bragged how human beings were more connected now than at any time in human history—yet, despite that, these teenagers still desperately longed to connect. A connection they would never find from any electronic devices. So, slowly, those young souls would wander in that old beat up gymnasium, some gathering their friends with open arms—friends that didn't need words, just a hug. Some looking for that kid they had teased so they could try to open a door of forgiveness.

As beautiful as all this connection was, Robert noticed there was one student who stood alone. Although he was a big boy, easily weighing over three hundred pounds, he looked so small standing by himself with his hands deeply wedged in his pockets.

Robert made his way to him. "Hi."

The boy was silent.

"What's your name?"

Still *nothing!* The boy just looked at him with a pair of big vacant eyes.

"Did you find anything helpful today?"

The boy's face got red and flushed, he pulled his hands from his pockets, lifted his shirt and wiped the sweat off his face. "Emotional intelligence?" he said. "What the hell *is* that? Look, no matter how hard we try, people are people and you can't change people."

Robert moved closer and gently reached out to put his hand on the boy's shoulder. The moment he was about to touch him, the kid pushed Robert's arm away with such force that it almost knocked Robert to the floor. Without another word, he stormed out of the gym. Robert looked back at the other students and saw that no one had even noticed. Right at that moment, the next song, about an ordinary day and feeling all right, started. This song held a special place in Robert's heart. It was the first song Jenny sang in that bar not so long ago—the day she leaped out of her depression back into her life.

There was a joyous feeling in the gym as most of the students who knew the song sang and danced. It felt like there had been an explosion of openness and, just like the rock band's name, the room felt like a Great Big Sea of sharing for everyone except the kid who had just run out of the gym. The boy who had slammed the door shut on the hope that people could ever change.

Robert listened to the radio on his way home. An advertisement came on: *"Your brain just got brighter!"* It was a commercial for a new web site, advertising how they could help build the power of one's memory. Their slogan was *"If we change our thinking, we change our life!"*

Yeah, if only it was true that we could do it all in a simple game on the computer! You know, that day when I first met Philip, I remember it being such an exhilarating and healing day, but I just couldn't let go of the image of that kid pushing me away and walking out. And then I heard that "Your brain just got brighter!" commercial, and all I could think about was that kid whose brain must be so dark. Was there any way to get some light in there? How do you retrain a brain to hear something new? Listen to the positive when it is already filled with something so overwhelmingly negative? And his reaction to "emotional intelligence" made me feel kind of foolish...

The year before, Robert had taken a night school course called "Emotional Intelligence." The course was focused on how everyone needed to build a stronger emotional intelligence in order to help cope with the many emotional situations they would encounter in their lives. And he found himself using some of what he learned from that course in his workshops.

"Add up all of the time and money you have spent on how you look. Think about it. How much time and money did you spend on your hair—your clothes – your looks? How much time working out at the gym? And now think of all the time or money you have spent on your emotional health."

It's crazy, isn't it? We spend so much time and money on how we look, but how much time and money do we really spend on making our insides look or feel better? And all the time we spend at school in classes training and strengthening our brains...but "emotional intelligence" was just a new, fancy, empty word to this kid. Like that commercial: "If we change our thinking, we change our life!" How do you get someone like him to listen in a new way? And what kind of listener was I?

Monique and Jenny had often teased Robert about his inability to multi-task. If Robert was doing something that needed any type of even mild concentration, he was unable to listen to anyone and do his work at the same time. He would always have to stop what he was doing and listen. *Was that bad?*

It struck him as strange that in all his schooling throughout the years, he never came across a course on listening. He was taught to write and speak but not really how to listen. And when working as a probation officer, the most common complaint was how someone wasn't listening to them and how that pissed them off, made them mad, hurt them and somehow ultimately caused them to do the things they were doing. 'It sometimes sounded,' Robert thought, 'that the real reason they turned to a life of crime was because they felt no one ever listened to them.'

It's true, isn't it? When we come into this world, we can't talk, we are just these needy observers that are constantly listening and responding. So we listen in order to survive. If something scares us, we wail and seek protection. So, I guess we listen to feel safe. Yet, if that's true, then maybe we also don't *listen to feel safe as well!*

All these listening questions excited Robert, as they gave him new ideas for topics in his workshops. Whenever he had these ideas, he would go to Virginia Farrell.

Virginia had been Robert's colleague at the probation office. All four foot eleven inches of Virginia was pure drive and energy. It was strange the two of them had become such good friends as they were complete opposites. Robert was playful and impulsive; Virginia was a tough, no-nonsense kind of person. The probation office always assigned her all the difficult cases. Like the many young girls who had fallen and were barely hanging on to the cliff of life—the lost ones that would do almost anything to survive—abused, pregnant at fourteen and selling their bodies to feed a serious drug addiction.

Virginia possessed a true love for her work at the probation office. She was great at it until an incident eight years ago made her question her ability and whether she was really making a difference or helping anyone.

It happened on the final day of probation for a seventeen-year-old, Louise Parks. Virginia had just signed Louise's court papers for her last probation visit. They talked. Everything felt positive and hopeful for the future as Virginia walked Louise outside. Just as they reached the parking lot behind the office, Virginia opened her arms for a goodbye hug but was greeted with a small, sharp-looking knife.

"I'm sorry, Miss Farrell, but I need your purse," Louise said.

Virginia didn't flinch. She didn't say a word. She just took her bag off her shoulder and handed it to the girl. She then watched Louise put the knife back in her coat pocket and run down the street.

Virginia stood there stunned, with her arms still wide open, preparing for that goodbye embrace. For almost a full minute she stood there. Then suddenly, she dropped her arms, walked to the front of the building and picked up her almost empty purse. Virginia noticed her cell phone was still in the purse. She pulled it out and made a call. She didn't call the police. She called back upstairs to her office and asked for Robert Sanchez.

"Do you have a client right now? 'Cause I need to talk," Virginia said in a calm, unnerving voice.

"Virginia? Why are you calling? Didn't I just see you here in the office?" Robert questioned.

"I'll be back in thirty seconds. Do you have some time?"

"Sure, I got about half an hour."

"Great, see you. Bye." Virginia went back into the building and walked into Robert's office. She closed his door, told him what had just happened and then asked him to help her write a resignation letter.

"Do you want me to call the police?"

"What am I going to tell them, Robert? I just got robbed at knife point by a girl I have been meeting two times a month for the past year...*and* I just signed off on her last probation visit. Tell them that I just signed a document stating she has officially paid her price to society and is now ready to be welcomed back?"

"Yeah...Doesn't sound that good when you say it that way."

Virginia sighed. "I care, Robert. God knows I care, but every year the list gets longer, the girls get younger. How big is your case load this year?"

"It's...umm...well, it's doubled."

"It's *killing* me! I want to do something so it's not always doubling."

"But Virginia, there have been a lot of cut backs."

"Really? Robert, really? Count them. Seriously count them. All the cases from last year, compared to this year, or the year before. How much time can you spend with each case? Oh God, what the hell am I'm doing with this life of mine?"

Virginia put her face in her hands and looked as if she was about to break down and cry. Robert suddenly felt uncomfortable seeing his mentor, his role model—the one he always came to for advice and ideas—look so defeated. She was the probation office's guiding light; she represented its strength, courage and never-say-die attitude. And now, Virginia Farrell was giving up! He was speechless, not knowing how to comfort her.

Virginia reached over to the shelf behind her, grabbed a tissue and then wiped a tear from her face. Robert quickly stood up, awkwardly took the tissue box and held it for her, but it slipped from his hand onto the floor. Robert knelt down to pick it up, then almost comically put his arm out to comfort her. He found himself unsure where to put his hand. *On her knee? No, that would be too intimate*, he thought. *Her head? No, that would seem like he was patting a child.* Robert ended up putting a hand on her shoulder and as he knelt beside her chair, he said, "I know how you feel. Is there anything..."

"Robert, please stand up and don't look at me like that. I'm quitting here, but I'm not giving up. I've been thinking about this for a long time now and it's about time I do it."

"Do what?" Robert asked slowly and suspiciously, while looking at Virginia as if she was about to do something she might regret.

"Oh my God, what's wrong with you? *School*, Robert, I'm going back to school to teach elementary kids. If I'm going to make any difference in these girls' lives, I need to start working with them when they're younger."

And as Robert walked into Warden Elementary School, he thought of that day, the day Virginia Farrell changed her world and gave him the inspiration to change his as well. It just took him a few more years.

Robert walked down the overly decorated hallway that was filled with massive celebrations of the student's artistic endeavours. Virginia walked out of a classroom and Robert immediately opened his arms to give her a welcoming hug. Virginia put her hand up and stopped him in his tracks.

"No," she said. "Roberto Sanchez, the answer is no if you're coming to get me to climb another one of those mountains with you. I'm still limping from the four thousand blisters I got last year!"

Two years ago, Robert had convinced Virginia to join him and a team of twenty-five people that included principals, teachers and some parents, to climb Mount Kilimanjaro. Their goal was to raise money for safety awareness programs at their schools.

"Nope, let those blisters heal. Just wanted to know how your class is this year."

Virginia smiled at Robert with a questioning look. "Really?"

"Okay. I just want to know if you could lend me your class for a couple of hours. I have this idea and I was hoping I could test it out." Robert gave her his please-help-me smile.

"All right, come here." Virginia reached up and gave Robert a welcoming hug.

"Now get in," Virginia said, laughingly pointing to her classroom door. The two of them talked about Robert's listening questions and ideas as they walked into Virginia's grade three classroom.

Virginia's classroom looked like a garden in full bloom. It was filled with so many colourful drawings. There were some classical pictures of pyramids and pharaohs and some pretty outrageous cartoon figures of Greek gods.

Pointing to the neat rows of desks, Robert asked, "Hey, Virginia, I thought you liked to group the kids' desks?"

"I do, but this week is independence week, so each desk is a place on its own. Look at them! Each student had to identify themselves as a country or place. It can be real or completely made up. Then they have to write their own laws, code of conduct, and beliefs. Look at all their flags. They had to design and build them out of anything that was found in the recycling bins here or at home."

Robert laughed in amazement as he looked around each desk. Paper, cardboard, milk cartons and some metal things he thought might be old computer parts—all transformed into flags with names mounted on the top of each desk: The Grand Cameron, Los Angela, Argen-Tina, Eiffel Tyrone, Cheri-ton Hotel, United States of Amelia, Niagara Frank Falls...

All the desks were uniform in shape and size except for one in the middle of the last row of desks. It was an adult-sized desk that had a simple, conventional looking flag made out of gold paper. On it was written, "Manny's Place."

"Is this your assistant teacher's desk?" asked Robert.

"No, that's Manny Moulder's desk. Oh my God, Robert, you wouldn't believe this child's story. He has a background just like so many of those kids down at the parole office: father ran off, mother in jail for drugs. Oh, and on top of all that, he's twice as big as all the other kids his age."

Robert sadly smiled. "Must be hard for him."

"Well, maybe at first it was, but Robert, you can't believe—"

The bell disrupted Virginia. She told Robert to wait in the classroom as she went outside to get her class. Virginia poked her head back through the door. "Oh. Robert, look at the *BE* wall, I think that helped Manny the most."

At the back of the classroom were photographs of every student in Virginia's class. They were tacked up in one big circle. In the middle of the pictures was the word BE. Under that BE was what looked to be a poem titled: BELIEVE + BELONG = BEHAVE. Robert read it out loud to himself:

> To BE or not to BE depends on what you BElieve. If you BElieve you BElong, then that is how you will BEhave! BE-cause that is what you BE and have. So help others BEhave by helping them to BElieve they BElong. And then, everyone can always say they BE-LIVED!

Of course I immediately thought of the big kid from my workshop who didn't believe people could change, and how he probably didn't believe he belonged, and perhaps that was why he behaved the way he did—pushing me away.

I don't think I've ever told Virginia how really proud I was of her. She had a purpose: she wanted to make a difference in younger people's lives. And look at her now, she was actually doing it! Virginia was doing something very few ever seem to be able to do: she was living her life with a purpose and making a living doing it!

The halls of the school quickly came to life. Robert looked outside in the hallway and watched all the children enter their classrooms. Soon, Virginia's class was passing him by, laughing and talking as they made their way to their desks. Robert greeted each child; some smiled, and some asked right away who he was with intense, suspicious faces. At the end of the line came a child who looked to be twice the age and size of the other children. The boy passed by Robert and went into the classroom but then suddenly swirled around to face Robert, bowed slightly and said, "Manny Moulder, and who do we have the pleasure of meeting?"

Robert was completely taken aback and looked at Virginia, who just chuckled and said, "That's him, that's the authentic Manny Moulder style."

But Manny didn't move. He was waiting for Robert's response. So Robert bowed his head slightly and said, "Robert Sanchez."

"A pleasure to meet you, Mr. Sanchez," Manny simply said, before he made his way back to his desk.

Although Manny Moulder was taller than every other kid and was probably close to a hundred pounds heavier, no one seemed to pay any mind to it. Robert watched as Manny made his way to his oversized desk. Even while he was walking past all the same-sized desks that fit everyone but him, Manny seemed perfectly at home. He was just there. *He believed he belonged and so that was how he behaved!* Despite the obvious differences to every other child in that class, Manny seemed to just "be" another kid in that room. As he watched Manny fiddle a little with his flag to make sure "Manny's Place" was prominently displayed, Robert couldn't stop himself from thinking, *What does it feel like to not fit into something everyone else fits into?*

"All right, class, please sit down. I'm going to time you starting...five, four, three, two, one...*now!*" Virginia had a stopwatch and pressed a button. Robert was astonished, for, magically, the room was suddenly silent. Robert gave Virginia a questioning look but she just held up a finger, signalling for him to wait.

Robert looked around the room. Some kids had their eyes closed, some with faces all squeezed up and some with cheeks ballooned out. Suddenly, gasps could be heard from each part of the room. Some kids were sucking in air like they had just run a mile.

Virginia let out a gasp too and then said, "We're practising holding our breath." As she looked around the room, some kids appeared to still be holding their breath, so she waited until the last of them gasped for a precious intake of air.

"Well, today, it's Linda at twenty-three seconds! And that will be our goal tomorrow, to beat Linda's twenty-three seconds."

Robert raised his hands and was about to clap but then, noticing how quiet the room was, he gave a silent applause to Virginia, acknowledging her always unique ways of getting kids to quiet down.

"Well, kids, I'd like you to meet Roberto Sanchez."

She walked over to a large picture that hung between the colourful words "Perseverance" and "Goal." The picture was of a large group posing on top of a mountain. The picture was a strangely animated shot, as most people in the group had their hands reaching out in front of them, looking as if they were ready to jump. Virginia pointed to the picture. "Mr. Sanchez was the one that organized for all of us to be on top of this mountain."

A little girl quickly raised her hand and Virginia asked, "What is it, Thelma?"

"How come he's not in the picture then?" Thelma asked curiously.

"Good question! That is because someone had to take the picture."

Thelma's hand immediately went back up again. "Was he that someone?"

Robert jumped in. "I was! But one thing your teacher didn't ask was why most people in the picture all have their hands reaching out and pointing. See?" Robert pointed at the picture. "The top of the mountain isn't that big and we had a pretty large group. Is it okay if I take your class's picture, Miss Farrell?"

219

Virginia smiled and nodded her agreement. Robert pulled out his cell phone and brought it to his eyes. Then he started backing away from the class, pretending to relive the moment and acting as if he was trying to take a picture of the class.

"Wait...Can everyone push together?" Robert backed up a little further.

The kids quickly responded by getting out of their desks and gathering into the centre of the room.

"No...not yet, I don't have everyone..." Robert backed up further and three feet behind him was a rickety looking, three-legged easel filled with math equations.

"Wait!" Robert stopped. "I almost have everybody. Could you all just snuggle in a little closer?" Robert backed up a little further and he could sense that the kids in the class were noticing him backing up into the easel. Although they were posing, their mouths started to open and their hands lifted as he backed up. And then, just as Robert was about to back into the easel, most of the class jumped up and screamed, "No, watch it! You are going to..."

Robert quickly turned to all of them and yelled, "*FREEZE!*"

The kids were so shocked that they all froze with their warning hands reaching out. Robert then snapped the picture.

"*And* that's why everyone's hands were reaching out. They were trying to warn me because I almost backed up off the mountain while trying to take that picture!"

The kids all melted into laughter at finding themselves frozen in the very same poses as the people in the picture on top of Mount Kilimanjaro.

"Robert Sanchez has climbed some of the biggest mountains on Earth and next year he is going to climb the biggest mountain in the world. Who knows what that is?" Virginia asked. All the hands in the class flew up, except Manny Moulder's.

Virginia motioned for the class to put their hands down and then looked directly at Manny. "Well, Manny, it seems everyone knows the answer but you. Everyone want to help Manny out? The biggest mountain in the world, is...?"

Everyone looked at Manny to see if he would get it first. They looked at him with disbelief that he wasn't answering what seemed so obvious to the rest of them. Some kids were slowly mouthing and whispering the answer to him. "Ev...er...est!"

That's when Thelma just exploded with, "*Everest*, Manny, the biggest mountain in the world is Everest!"

Most of the kids chimed in that, yes, Everest was the biggest mountain in the world.

But Manny stood up and just shook his head and then said in a very polite quiet voice, "No, I don't think it is."

The rest of the class all chimed in, reassuring Manny that, yes, of course it is, *everyone* knows that!

Robert was just about to add in something similar, reaffirming that, yes, Everest is the biggest mountain, but somehow Manny's elegance of not bending or following the overwhelming opinion of the class made him question himself. *He must really believe he belongs if he can stand his ground when every single one of us disagrees with him*, Robert thought. But, sadly, he had to tell Manny he was wrong. So he repeated Virginia's question.

"Manny, I'm sorry to inform you but, the biggest mountain in the world is..."

And then, Robert suddenly stopped himself. "Oh my God!" he exclaimed. "Manny's *right*, it's not Everest!"

Together, the class gasped a huge "What?"

"Well, your teacher didn't ask what was the highest mountain in the world was. She asked what was the biggest and Manny's right, Everest isn't the biggest; Everest is the highest. The biggest mountain in the world is Mauna Loa. It's in Hawaii and it's the biggest because if you lifted Mauna Loa up from the earth and you lifted Everest, Mauna Loa would be bigger in size. *Good work*, Manny, not only for answering a very tricky question but for standing up for what you thought was right even though every single one of us thought you were wrong!"

Manny then held up his flag and proudly waved it.

BE...how could two letters describe something so profoundly huge? Virginia made it seem so simple. Man, what confidence that kid had! It was un-BE-lievable! Here he was, three times the size of any other child his age; he could have been a target for such ridicule, yet Virginia found a way to make him and all his class believe and feel he belonged and so he behaved as such...

29. 4 WEEKS AGO – SEEMA'S OFFICE

"It's all right, Benny, leave Robert here." Seema quickly unwrapped the blue scarf from her hand and neatly placed it on her head.

"Thanks, sorry about not calling first. I hope I didn't interrupt your conversation," Benny said as he walked towards the door.

"That's fine. Mrs. Sanchez was just getting ready to leave." Seema then gave a little wave to Benny as he closed the door behind him.

Robert did as he always had done and wheeled himself to the window.

"I just told your wife how you do that every time you come into my office," Seema said as she walked around the other side of her desk to sit down.

It was a grey day and too early for recess, so the yard was empty except for what looked to be a school janitor carrying a green garbage bag. He had a pole in one hand and was stabbing it down to pick up odds and ends, mostly paper, that had blown and gathered in the corner of the play yard.

"And how are you today?" Seema asked as she opened a folder.

"What was my wife here for?"

"Oh, I just asked her to stop in, so we could touch base."

"What base needed touching?"

Seema shook her head and smiled at Robert's question. "Well, Robert, I wanted to see how she was doing."

Robert looked back over his shoulder to Seema. "And that concerns you, how?"

"Well, Robert, you are my concern, and since she is..."

Robert cut her off. "Yeah, okay, I got it...Sorry I asked."

"Robert, why did you want to see me this morning?"

"Well, it's just..." Robert stopped. "No, let me ask you a question."

"All right, sure, ask away."

"How long have I been seeing you?"

"Well Robert, I don't have the exact date. Would you like me to check?"

"No. Please don't! We both know it's been over three months, right?"

"Okay. Three months. That sounds right."

"And what's changed, Miss Pourshadi?"

"I'm sorry Robert, what do mean what's changed?"

"Is it working? *This?* Is this working?"

"Well, I think that's something I should ask you."

"*Damn!* Can you ever just answer a question?"

"But Robert, I'm not here for me...I'm here for you. What's the use of me telling you if I think it's working and you don't think it is?"

Robert let out a loud sigh. "Ahhh! Look, I just can't do this anymore, all right?!" He grabbed the wheels of his chair and charged towards the exit.

"No, wait! Please Robert, wait! Please?" Seema almost begged.

He stopped a couple of feet near the doorway, but didn't turn around.

"Just tell me what you can't do anymore, Robert. Please? Is it me that you—"

"It's me! *Me!*" Robert started to turn towards Seema but stopped halfway. "I tried. I did! Maybe you can't see it...but I tried. It's just...It's just, I don't want to be this anymore...I'm just so...tired of feeling this...You know? This way! I'm just sick and tired of waking everyday feeling like...like this!"

Seema walked over to Robert. She almost touched his shoulder, but stopped herself. "Robert, I know it's hard to hear this but I think maybe that's probably a good thing."

"A *good* thing? How the hell could feeling like this be good?"

"Because now maybe you know how you don't want to feel...Maybe you can change that."

"How?...How?...How?" With each 'how,' Robert's voice lost strength until the last 'how' was only mouthed.

"We all need something to help us move from a place we might be stuck in—like a catalyst. It could be something or someone that helps us out of that dark place—to help us find some light. It doesn't take much. Sometimes all we need is a little tiny light far off in the dark somewhere."

Robert slowly turned to face Seema. "Yeah, and where is that something or someone with my light?"

Seema smiled to herself. She was finding it hard to suppress the joy she felt at hearing Robert finally opening up. She quickly reached over and took the chair Monique had just been sitting in. She pulled it beside Robert and sat down.

"When I was a little girl, my mother had some kind of nervous breakdown. She couldn't do anything. She just stayed in her room for days. She closed the blinds. She didn't want any light at all. My father tried everything he could, but she wouldn't come out. Then, one day, my grandmother came over. Anyway, she had these books for my mother to read. And slowly, day by day, my mother got better. Well, we kept bugging our grandmother, we wanted to know what those magical books were, but Grandma would never tell us. She would just say, 'It's private; they are your mother's books!'"

Robert looked directly at Seema. "So what were they...these books? Did you ever find out?"

"Well, of course, being kids, we soon forgot about the books and stopped asking about them. But when I first started working and had this really difficult case, it was my mother who helped me. She reminded me of those books. And do you know what they were? The books were her diaries. She had forgotten about them and they were still at her mother's house. That's what my grandmother gave her. And she told me it really helped her. She found that reading about all the thoughts, the hopes and dreams she once had gave her that light. Even reading about all the simple daily boring things helped her. She said it helped to just—well, to see herself again."

Robert put his head in his hands and rubbed his face roughly.

"So Robert, I just wondered...Have you ever kept any diaries or journals—any kind of past writings?"

Robert didn't answer; his head was still lost in his hands.

"'Cause maybe you wrote something...You know, things to yourself. Things that you may not think would be relevant but sometimes, these things we write...Well, some of our past thoughts or insights can be the very thing that gives us a perspecti—"

"Well, sorry, I didn't. I don't have anything like that. I'm sorry...Look, I'm sorry but I need some air. Good bye, Miss Pourshadi." Robert swirled around and was out the door before Seema could say another word.

30. PRESENT DAY – AT THE HOTEL

Down the hall of the hotel in a brightly neon lit washroom, Monique Sanchez was emptying her stomach into the toilet, trying to expel every sorrow that had filled her life in the last six months since Robert's accident.

How could I have said that, her conscience echoed, *told him he was dead? Dead! Oh my God!* She threw up again.

She gagged six or seven more times, trying to force all her pain into that toilet. But other than the tears that trickled down her face, nothing more came. She yanked off some toilet paper and wrapped it around her hand as if she was making a mitten out of it. She stood up, looked into the bowl and shook her head in disgust, knowing she that even if she threw up for months it would still never be enough. Her sickness, the painful throbbing bruise in her gut, couldn't simply be flushed down a toilet. She pushed the lever and then slapped the seat cover down. She gently wiped her mouth with the mitten of paper as she sat.

Monique had not thrown up like this since that early morning phone call she received from Mt. Everest, telling her that Robert and his crew had been in an accident—a freak avalanche. After searching for two hours with no sign of him, there was little hope that he survived.

"So he's dead?" she asked.

"Well, we can't confirm anything yet, Monique, but you know it just doesn't look good," the voice on the phone said.

"What would good look like?" was all Monique could say.

"I'm so sorry, Monique...but we um...we will keep you updated. Okay?"

Jenny, who had been visiting her mother for the weekend, poked her head into her mother's room. It was the usual time for Robert to be making a call from Everest.

"Is that Daddy?" she asked, and sleepily reached out her hand to take the phone from her mother so she could speak with her father. Monique stopped her from taking it.

"What about the students?" Monique asked.

"We are not sure. Nothing's been confirmed. It's crazy up there and all I received was the news about Robert. We'll keep you updated. I promise, Monique."

"No, don't keep updating me, just find him alive."

"Look, I'm sorry, Monique. You know I wouldn't be calling you if I thought there was any—"

The voice stopped mid-sentence and then said, "It's just that...well, I just don't want you to be finding out about him on the web or the news."

Monique hung up the phone and ran past Jenny to the bathroom. She threw up for five minutes straight. She was kneeling on the floor in front of the toilet when Jenny leaned against the door.

"Mom, you okay? What's wrong? Mom, what's wrong?" When her mother didn't answer, Jenny opened the door to find her mother sitting in between the toilet and bathtub.

"Mom, are you sick? Who was that on the phone?"

Monique just held her arms open to her daughter and said, "Daddy's dead, baby...Daddy's dead..."

While Monique sat in the hotel washroom only fifty feet away, Robert was still sitting on the stage. Twenty men and women dressed in white shirts and black pants were busy setting the tables for lunch. Lou had a pretty strong chorus of employees' chanting, "I would walk 500 miles" going. And sure enough, Amir's fear that the song might upset Robert looked to be coming true as he was now quickly rolling his wheelchair across the stage and straight in Amir's direction. As Robert pushed forward, he made a gesture to Amir that indicated he wanted to speak to him.

The moment Robert arrived, Amir desperately tried to apologize.

"I'm so sorry, Mr. Robert. I...I just did not think! I realize the song is not really appropriate."

But just at that moment, Amir was interrupted by Lou, who was leaning over the lip of the stage and telling Amir to turn up the volume. There was a group of other happy singers gathered around Lou and singing loudly. They were also clapping to encourage this one guy, who was jumping up and down, to jump even higher.

Amir shrugged his shoulders. "I'm so, so sorry, Mr. Robert."

"Turn up the volume," cried out one of the happy singers.

Lou was still looking at Amir and pointing his finger up into the air. He repeated, "Louder! Turn the music up."

Amir just kept shaking his head and opening up his arms, trying to convey how sorry he was to Robert.

"No, you should turn it up. It's a good song and always sounds best when it's loud," Robert said.

Amir jerked his head in shock. That was the last thing he thought Robert would say.

"But after you do that, can you please help me down off the stage?"

"Of course, of course." Amir pushed a lever up. Lou and his happy gang gave him the thumbs-up and Amir walked behind Robert until they got to the top of the stairs that led off of the stage. Then he grasped the handle grips on the back of the wheelchair firmly and leaned Robert towards him as he guided Robert down the stairs.

"Thanks, Amir," Robert had to say in a loud voice so he could be heard over the music. But then he motioned for Amir to come closer. Amir leaned close to Robert's face as Robert asked him, "Did you see which way my wife went?" Amir pointed to the double doors nearest to the stage. "She went out those doors. But would you like me to find her for you?"

"No," Robert replied.

Amir watched Robert push his wheelchair through the crowd of people. Because of his height in the chair, he looked like a young child moving in a world of adults.

Amir could hear the song was about to end, so he ran up the stairs towards his table. When he got there, ready to play another song, he noticed Robert had changed direction and was now about to go through the door at the side of the stage that led to a couple of storage rooms. The door was clearly marked 'STAFF ONLY.' Amir thought about stopping Robert, but then decided against it. He wouldn't be in anyone's way and he knew the storage rooms were locked. 'And maybe Robert needed a little time for himself,' he thought. After all, he had looked quite nervous to be speaking today and it also seemed like he had an unpleasant fight with his wife. So Amir smiled and actually said out loud to himself, "Yes, yes, let him go. The man must need a little space right now."

31. PHILIP

It must have been the way Virginia got that little Manny to believe he belonged despite his obvious differences that led me back to Philip—the boy who slammed the door shut on the hope that people could ever change...I can't remember the year I started doing those high school transition workshops, but I had never done a project like that before. My arrangement with the school and the leadership teacher was that I could video the journey and use it as a tool to raise money for future workshops. They would supply a couple of their media and communication students to help do the videotaping and the editing.

I was at Westmount High, Philip's school. I was waiting in the office of the vice principal, Mr. Bosco, to meet the media and communication students that were going to help me. It had been about three months since I'd had that incident with Philip, but the moment he entered Mr. Bosco's office, it was clear that he recognized me.

"Oh man, *damn!*" were the first words that came out of Philip's mouth.

"Is there something wrong, Philip?" Mr. Bosco asked.

"No, sorry...I was...um...Look, I'm...I'm sorry," Philip said in a voice that was barely audible.

"Well, where is Andrew Hunter?" Mr. Bosco asked.

"I don't know, sir," Philip quickly answered.

"All right, then. Mr. Sanchez, this is Philip Kong. Mr. Sanchez needs to speak with you, Philip. Why don't you two talk? I'll find out where Andrew is." And with that, Mr. Bosco exited his office.

"Hi, Philip," Robert said, smiling. Philip said nothing. He kept his eyes glued to the floor like a kid who knew he was about to receive punishment.

"Would you like to sit down?" Robert said, pointing at the empty chair in front of the desk.

Still nothing. It was a strange sight, seeing this huge-sized human being try to make himself small enough not to be noticed in a room that probably couldn't have held more than five people.

"'Kong.' What nationality is that?" Robert tried to engage Philip.

Philip stayed silent. He seemed to be working on his invisible act by edging closer to the wall. Pushing one foot into the floor as if he hoped a secret trap door would suddenly open and he could escape.

"So, Philip, I'm not a psychic or anything, but I can tell that maybe you don't want to do this?"

"Look, I'm sorry! Okay, I'm sorry. I didn't mean to push you...I'm sorry, okay?! I just couldn't take it." His voice sounded like a man who had been held under water for too long; every word came out in a gasp.

"Whoa, Philip...easy. It's ok. I'm not here because of that."

"Please! I'm sorry! And Mr. Bosco, if he tells my parents, you got no idea! You got no idea...I'm sorry, Really! I didn't mean to push you! It's just, they all lie, they do! They *all* lie. Please, sir, my parents are already ashamed of me enough."

Robert took a step to put a hand on Philip's shoulder, but the moment he reached out, Philip's arms flew into the air and almost hit him.

"I'm sorry...Oh, God, I'm so sorry!" Philip pleaded like a little boy. "Look, see, I did it again! I'm so sorry, sir. I'm just not used to being touched. It's just—"

"Philip." Robert spoke as sternly yet compassionately as he could. "Philip, listen to me. I'm not here because of what happened at that workshop. Mr. Bosco asked you to come here so I could talk to you about filming and editing some of my workshops at this school, that's all."

Philip looked stunned. He wiped the dripping sweat from his forehead with his hand. His white T-shirt was becoming soaked and he looked as if he had been doing laps for the last hour. Even though he was extremely overweight, his face somehow did not reflect that. He was handsome with long hair. Robert thought he looked a little bit like Jackie

Chan did in that Shanghai Knights film.

"Look, Philip, I never told anyone about what happened. Why would I? I think you probably had your reasons..." Robert tried to calm the boy by making light of the situation. "But, I am going to ask you not to push me again, okay, Philip?"

"I'm sorry, sir. It's just...you know...well, nobody ever—" Philip stopped.

"Ever what, Philip?"

"No, it's okay. I just sometimes...I'm sorry, sir, would you like to tell me what you want me do?"

"Okay...well, Philip, I'm working with the grade twelve leadership class and I'd like to film it. And I asked those students who would be best to record and edit this thing and most people pointed me in your direction, you and Andrew Hunter. And that's what I wanted to talk to you about: to see if you're interested in working with me. Your teacher has confirmed that you will get credit for all the work. So what do you say?"

"Are you kidding? Really? Some other kids said I would be good at this?"

"Yeah, Philip, I asked the students first and at least six or seven mentioned your name."

Philip stared at me and it looked as if he was about to smile, like it made him proud that some kids had thought of him, but just as quick, he revealed the pain that surrounded this young man. A hurt so vividly spelled out...

"My name? What did they say...the fat kid will do it. Phil-huge-jo...Summo Phil...Chop-Phil-suey? I don't think anyone even knows my real name and the stupid part of all is that all those names are Japanese or Chinese."

"What are you then, Philip?"

"Korean. Well, my parents are...I was born here."

"Philip, honestly, I never heard any of those nasty names. They just said just your name, Philip."

"And it's not like my last name is doing me any favours."

"Oh!"

What could I say to that? It was true. No one would expect someone named Kong to be small. I remember wanting to make light of it, maybe make a joke of it, to lighten the moment. But I'm sure he'd heard every possible spin on his name, so I just smiled and told him I was hoping he would do the filming for me.

"What do you need me do?" he asked.

"Just come to the workshops and film them. Shoot some interviews and then help me edit them into something I could use as a promo for the workshops. So what do you say? I really need your help. Seriously, I could really use it, Philip."

Philip wiped his sweaty brow once again and then, thinking Robert didn't notice, wiped his hands dry behind his back on his T-shirt. He looked at Robert, still not letting go of those suspicious eyes.

But suddenly blurted out,

"Okay, I'll do it. But wait, I don't have to do anything but film, right?"

"Yeah, that's right, Philip. But I really need to speak to you about something you said to me before we do this. Okay?"

Philip looked away but nodded.

"Look. The first time we spoke, you said to me that, no matter how hard you try, you can't change people and that people can't change. Now, since you will be working with me and what I'm actually trying to do is to get people to do things that require some kind of change...well, I really need to know what you meant and why you reacted the way you did."

It took Philip no time to reply. It was clear that the thoughts he had about people and change had already been implanted in him many years ago. It was also clear from the moment he opened his mouth that these festering thoughts had created some type of ticking time bomb inside of him—an explosive device that had already been turned on and had started its countdown.

"Look, I know you're trying to get people to care about others and kind of try to understand each other better...But even after all that stuff at

231

your workshop, you know, kids crying and saying stuff like they are sorry...well, you know what? It didn't matter 'cause in the end, they still all act the same. *No one* is changed!"

I remembered having to take a breath before I responded; Philip's response was a bit of a punch in the gut.

"Are you sure about that, Philip? No one's changed? No one changed any of their behaviours towards each other at all?"

Philip stayed silent, busy wiping his brow and no longer trying to hide what he was doing by drying his hands on the front of his T-shirt.

"Have you spoken to anyone since then, Philip? Have your friends said anything?"

"*Ha*, friends?" He tried to laugh, to look as if he didn't care, but the next thing out of his mouth was painful to hear. "Look, no one wants to be friends with the Asian fat-freak kid, okay!"

His voice was starting to get loud and I didn't want any of the office staff busting into the room, asking him if everything was okay...because frankly, it wasn't. Nothing was okay for this poor kid! I wondered when the last time he could actually say he felt okay.

Robert tried asking him, in a soft, reassuring voice, "Well, Philip, I just want to know why you think nothing's changed if no one ever talks about it?"

Philip pulled his T-shirt up over his head and rubbed, as if he wanted to pull it off. It seemed evident by the way his hands focused on drying his eyes that he might also be crying. His hands came down, and he tried to straighten out the T-shirt, apologizing. "Sorry, that must be kind of gross. Sorry, no one needs to see my whale of a stomach. Sorry...it's just that I sweat a lot."

"Ah, that's okay, Philip. I do it all the time. My wife is constantly telling me to stop using my shirt as a napkin." This made Philip smile. "But Philip, really, I need you to help me and if you think what I'm doing is not helping anyone, that there is no change and kids are still treating each other—"

"No," Philip interrupted. "I'm sorry, I can't speak for everyone. Look, what I mean is, no one is treating *me* any different, okay? I was wrong to say that. I can't speak for anyone else. All I know is, I'm still Summo-chunky Chink, Phil-huge-jo...Blubber Butt!"

"Really, Philip, kids actually call you that?" Philip slowly nodded. "Well, that's got to hurt! I don't know what I'd do if someone called me those names. I can't say to you that I know exactly how that feels, because I don't. But I do know the pain, 'cause I've felt it, too. It kind of happened to me too."

Then came that wonderful, magical moment that can happen when two strangers find they have something in common! Just telling him I felt that same pain of name calling, too...Well, all the suspiciousness and anger in Philip's face just melted away. And then I thought about Virginia's class—those simple words on her classroom wall. BElieve plus BElong equals BEhave. And I wondered, how could I help this boy BElieve he BElonged?

Robert asked him to sit down. Philip almost fell into the chair across from Robert. He came down so quickly and heavily that Robert momentarily found himself holding his breath, praying the chair would catch his voluminous weight. Because the last thing he needed was for the chair to remind him of his oversized body.

"But Philip, let me ask you something. When was the last time someone called you one of those names, or any name that hurt you?"

He closed his eyes and took in a large breath, then let it go. When he opened his eyes, he didn't have an answer right away. He had to think for a moment but then said, "I'm sorry. What did you ask me? It's just, I can't believe anyone ever called you names."

"I asked you when was the last time someone called you one of those names or any name that hurt you?"

Robert noticed Philip's face becoming suspicious again, so he quickly explained, "The only reason I'm asking you that is because of something I found out when I was around your age, when I also felt picked on."

"Why, you were fat, too?" Philip was hopeful that maybe he wasn't alone in this world of his.

"No, Philip, I was never really fat. My thing was my nose and forehead. They grew bigger than my face did. And it didn't help how my dad cut my hair then either. A bowl cut, I think they called it—short and straight in the front. And because I had this real big forehead, kids started calling me Frankenstein, or Eagle Face...well, any bird name they could think of because of my nose. But also, you see, I come from a big family and have two older brothers. When they were in school, they hung out with the bullies—the tough kids—and all the kids they picked on ended up picking on me when I got to that school. Well, picked on isn't really what I would call it. I was pretty well hunted during recess, every moment of the day when there wasn't a teacher in sight. And they were mean, Philip, really cruel and mean. I thought they were all so...well, not only physically but also mentally evil to me. So for every day in my eight years at elementary school, I had this feeling of being hunted down, hurt. But then, before high school, my family moved to another town where no one knew me. I got a fresh slate, you could say. But you know what? When I started high school, do you know what was on my mind each and every day, Philip?"

It was obvious Philip had never had an adult share with him in this way, so he leaned forward in his chair and, for the first time, his eyes opened wide. "What, sir, what happened?"

The door to the office suddenly swung open. "I'm so sorry, Mr. Sanchez, it appears that Andrew Hunter is not available to work on your project. Would you like me to see if there are any other students who wish to participate?" Mr. Bosco was oblivious to the intimacy being shared in that moment.

Robert quickly stood up. "No, that's okay, Mr. Bosco. Thanks for all your help, but Philip here believes he can handle all I need. And he looks pretty trustworthy."

Mr. Bosco raised an eyebrow slightly and smiled, playfully giving Philip one of those you-better-not-screw-up looks. Philip awkwardly pulled himself out of the chair and because he was leaning forward, as he stood, the chair tipped over. He turned around to settle the chair and tried to put it back at exactly the same angle it was before.

"Well, Philip, that's great." Mr. Bosco smiled. "I'm happy for you, Mr. Sanchez, because you have one of the best technical minds at this school working with you. Did Philip tell you how indispensable he has become to our staff and that we sometimes ask him to come down to the office to help with our computer troubles? Now I hope, Philip, even with this work you are doing with Mr. Sanchez we can still count on you to help us here in the office?"

This should have been a moment for Philip to be proud of, but he looked preoccupied with a whole new bout of perspiration that needed attending to, so Robert jumped in.

"Don't worry, Mr. Bosco. From what Philip has shown me, I can see he is very responsible. So I really want to thank you again for your help and your school's commitment to the workshops."

Mr. Bosco shook my hand and was just about to put his hand on Philip's shoulder and usher us out. I felt like I was caught in one of those slow motion moments where something is about to happen and you have to leap into the air and jump across the room and yell, "Noooo...don't touch him!!!" But then I saw Philip had anticipated that pat coming near his back and so he quickly took three steps to avoid any contact with his principal.

"No problem. You're doing some great work with our students, Mr. Sanchez, I only wish we had more of a budget so we could actually pay you." Mr. Bosco shook Robert's hand one more time. "So, okay then, I know you'll be in good hands with Philip. I'm really looking forward to seeing the finished product!"

Mr. Bosco closed his door. Philip and Robert were now alone in the hallway. Philip turned around and stared at Robert. His face looked full of a hunger for an answer to the question he'd asked before Mr. Bosco had come into the room.

"What did you think, sir? What happened when you went to high school?"

He asked it in such a childlike way. Like he wanted to know how the fairy tale ended. What was the happy ending? What did I think after feeling I was being tormented and bullied throughout my childhood? What did I think when I was transported into a brand new world without any of my tormentors or bullies around?

Robert motioned Philip to follow him to the other side of the hallway where they could have a little more privacy.

"You want to know what I thought, Philip? Well, remember I told you I felt like I had been tormented for so long and always heard so many ugly things said about me?"

Philip nodded anxiously.

"But none of those people were at that high school. So was it still really happening to me? I mean my father stopped cutting my hair in grade four. That was the time of the Beatles and rock and roll and I wore my hair longer for years after that. And who knew it would be wavy, just like my mom's? I surely didn't resemble Frankenstein anymore! And my nose, well, it's big and curves down, but would you say it's freakishly huge or bird-like?"

Philip actually squinted and moved closer to Robert's face to survey his nose. "Well, it's a prominent nose sir, like on those Greek statues in the library. And no one makes fun of those!"

Robert shook his head and laughed. "Thanks. I never thought of having a Greek god's nose! Okay, anyway, so I'm this complete stranger to everyone at this new school, no one knows me, and there I was. I had this long wavy hair like a rock star and a Greek god's nose and yet, you know what?"

"No, I don't know. What?"

"I didn't hear any of those bird or Frankenstein comments, Phillip! Not one. I can't remember anyone ever calling me names in high school, *And yet,* that didn't stop me from thinking they did! See, I didn't trust anybody. So, it was impossible for me to make any friends, right? I mean, how could I? Because I thought all these new people, well, they already didn't like me. So, Philip, when I asked you when was the last time someone called you those names, I guess I was just wondering if maybe you are doing the same thing I did."

Philip didn't turn away. He didn't look at the floor, but rather straight into my eyes, like he was in a trance. But it wasn't a vacant stare. His eyes almost seemed to flicker. It was like I was watching a computer screen boot-up—flashing all sorts of different things. Once he blinked, he simply asked me, "So, Mr. Sanchez, what did you do then?" I smiled, because it was the very first time he actually addressed me by my name...

"Well, Philip, remember what you first said to me few months ago, that people are people and people don't ever change? Well, that's exactly what I thought! See, back when I started high school, I was still hurting so bad and I always felt so...ugly...and just plain lonely because I always assumed everybody was still thinking bad things about me. And you know what, Philip—they probably did think I was a bit of freak, but do you know why?"

Philip shook his head slightly.

"Imagine the way I must have acted to them? I was so paranoid of every person I met and I had cast everyone around me—all the kids passing me in the hallways, all the kids in every class—as the bad guys. I was acting as if they were all horrible people who bullied and hurt me. Yet, they did nothing! Do you know who my biggest tormentor was? Me, Philip, *me!*"

Philip lowered his head and pulled at his T-shirt.

I could see he heard me, from the way he tugged at his shirt, meticulously trying to fix the creases he had put in it from wiping his hands and face, as if with each crease he straightened, something became clearer.

"You see, Philip, I think people can change. But usually they only do it if they find a reason to change. And, back in high school, my reason was that I wanted to be happy. I wanted to have friends! And if I wanted that, well then, I had to stop being my own biggest threat. You see, I'll bet those kids probably stopped bullying me years way before high school. And you know, if you asked me, I probably couldn't even remember the last time I was called Frankenstein or Bird Face after grade four! But then, it didn't matter because it had already made such a...such a profound lasting imprint on me—that I remained the victim—not to anyone else, but to ME. I was a victim to my own thoughts for so long. So that's why I asked you when was the last time you heard someone say hurtful things to you. And ask yourself, Philip, how many are doing things to you? Is everyone doing it to you?"

Philip was still tugging away at his shirt; you could see his mind was now computing as his eyes were darting back and forth in thought. This was a lot of new information to take in. His face contorted with every passing thought. Where does it go? What file? Under what document? I could see he was getting more anxious with each thought so I asked him something else...

"Okay, Philip, let me ask you a question which might help you sort this out. As we left the office, what did you think Mr. Bosco thought about you?"

Philip looked at Robert and sort of twisted his face. Then he finally spoke out loud the thoughts that had always been only his thoughts for as long as he could remember—the thoughts that he trained himself to think.

"Well, I know I almost dropped his chair on the floor...He was probably thinking I'm so fat that I can't even get out a chair properly. Probably hoping I didn't leave my gross sweat all over his office and...I probably disgusted him because when he shook your hand, you probably noticed he couldn't even touch mine. "

"Okay, Philip...Let me tell you what I saw and heard. Mr. Bosco says you are the best technical student at the school, I'm in trusting hands with you, that you are indispensable to his office staff and when he went to pat you supportively on the back, well, you went into turbo drive and jettisoned yourself out of that room before he could even touch you. So what's the truth? Who saw what really happened, Phillip?"

And then Philip did something that very few of us ever do when confronted with the truth. Instead of defensively denying or running away from it, he became what I call 'the hero of his life'— that same hero we see in every fairy tale we knew as kids.

He didn't even pause for a split second. He just looked me straight in the eyes and asked, "Can you help me? Can you help me change?"

"I'd be glad to help you in any way I can, Philip. But you have to know something first *and* I want you to hear this. Don't just let your brain hear it, but let your heart listen and feel the compliment I'm about to give you. What you just did was one of the most spectacular displays of leadership I have ever seen! You just found out you may be doing stuff that's wrong and bad for you and others too...and what did you do?"

He looked stunned. "I'm sorry Mr. Sanchez. I'm sorry. What did I do?"

"You *asked* for help. Only the bravest, strongest of leaders have the courage to ask for help, Philip. So do you want to start that change right now?"

I remember Philip nodding his head. And then I held both my arms open wide to give him a big hug but right away, I could see the look of terror in his eyes, so I said, "Okay, I get it; hugging may be too much of a leap for now. How about you and I shake hands then?"

Philip quickly wiped his hand on his T-shirt and hesitantly reached out. I took his hand. And I remember having this crazy little thought as I shook his hand—how people have shy hands, and Philip's hands were about as shy as they came. Because his hand was limp, I put my other hand over both of our hands to feel some connection.

"Thank you, Philip, thank you!"

"For what, Mr. Sanchez?"

"For trusting me to help you! Oh and also for all the work you are going to be doing with me."

"So, how do I start or prepare for that?" Philip asked, as if this was a course and he wanted to know the curriculum we were going to study.

"Well, Philip...Okay, what kind of stuff do you like to read?"

Philip suddenly looked embarrassed and then said, "Well, you might think it's kind of *kiddish.*"

"Philip, I just read *Dora the Explorer* a couple years back, so if you can beat that for *kiddish,* try me."

"Well, okay, *Harry Potter.*"

"Great series! I didn't read all the books but I read the first two. What is it you like about them?"

"I don't know...I'm just sort of interested in that world 'cause...Well, I guess 'cause the world has...I don't know—Yeah, I'm sorry. I'm lying—I do. It's 'cause there's magic!"

"Great reason! And if you saw yourself in Harry's world, who would you be?"

"Neville Longbottom," Philip said without hesitation.

239

"Hang on, isn't he that timid kid in Harry and his friends' room at that school?"

"Yeah."

"Why him, Philip? I mean, he doesn't really do anything, does he?"

Then Philips eyes glistened. "That's 'cause you only read the first two books. You have to see how he changes in the end. This kid that nobody really notices...I mean, they all think he is kind of...well, a *nobody*. But without Neville, Harry's as good as dead. Actually, the whole world would be dead without him!"

It wasn't hard to see why Philip liked Neville Longbottom
and I guess after being called names like "blubber butt," the name
"Longbottom" was maybe something he identified with.
"So he's kind of the hero of the story?" I asked.

"Yeah, no one expected it...I mean, not even me."

"You know, Philip, you just reminded me of this old saying by another British writer named Chesterton. It goes something like this: 'Fairy tales do not tell children that dragons exist; children already know that dragons exist. Fairy tales tell children the dragons can be killed.' So if you want to be a hero, Philip, try slaying some of your dragons."

"What do you mean, sir?"

"Slay all your negative thoughts, Philip, all those dragons breathing fire in your head every time you see someone and think they are thinking bad things about you. slay them! You know what? I got an idea: try something real simple just for the next week. Every time you see someone in the hall on the street and you have one of those negative dragon thoughts, take a mental note of it. At the same time, note if they actually said something negative or reacted negatively to you. And then see how many times you were right about that person. What did they do? Were they were actually calling you names or shunning you. Make a mental note of whether or not they actually did anything bad to you."

"And that will help me?"

"Just try it out, Philip, okay? Look, I have to go now but let's meet on Friday right after school to go over the plan of how we should start shooting the workshops. I'll be going into the leadership class a week from today, next Monday, alright?"

"Should I write these notes down?"

"Yeah, we'll plan it out on Friday and you can take notes then."

"No, Mr. Sanchez. I mean those other notes...You know, the dragon thoughts I have."

Wow, this kid is really serious! He might actually do this, I thought.

"Sure, Philip, write it down if you can, anything that will help you."

Robert held out his hand again to say goodbye, but right at that moment, Mr. Bosco opened his office door and walked passed them.

"So everything worked out, Mr. Sanchez? Are you sure Philip will be enough for what you need?"

"Yep, he'll do great."

As I started to walk away I noticed a little of Harry's magic world coming to life. Mr. Bosco started to walk away from Philip but as he did, he said, "Thanks, Philip, I knew I could count on you." Then he patted Philip on the back, and Philip didn't move!!! He still looked miserably uncomfortable, but he didn't move.

Philip and I did meet that Friday and we went over what was the least intrusive way for him to film the workshop. He was all business at our meeting, asking me questions and taking notes on his computer. I didn't ask him anything about slaying his dragon thoughts. I just waited for him to bring it up, but he didn't say a word about it. Then, at the end of our discussion, Mr. Bosco came into the office to say goodbye to both of us and he shook my hand. Then Philip ACTUALLY SHOOK HIS HAND! He did wipe it on his T-shirt first, but he surprised me because he was the one that initiated the handshake.

The next Monday was amazing! I did have a little fear of how the students would react to being filmed and having Philip moving around in the small classroom. But the leadership class was a joy to work with. They seemed quite committed and even with someone of Philip's size moving around the room with a camera, not one student blinked an eye or made a comment. Philip was incredibly sensitive to these kids sharing and baring their souls to each other. He seemed to know exactly when someone needed him to back away or when they didn't want the camera on them at all. It was a sight to see how he moved with that camera—with such agility and grace, like a real professional!

241

After all the students left, Philip hooked his camera to a monitor to show Robert some of the day's footage. He asked if he could show him something else first. He pulled out his own laptop and opened up a document he had titled "Neville's Dragons." The page opened up, displaying what looked to be a very complex, coloured graph and statistics.

"Look, Mr. Sanchez." He pointed at the screen. "I did what you said. I took notes."

I looked at the screen, but all I could see was what looked to me to be a mathematical equation with notes. Philip had charted each and every person he passed for the last week. Names were included, if he knew them, or if not, descriptions of the person. Beside each name or description was a time and a location. There was colour coding as well, which he explained to me...

"Red, I use that colour to show when I felt someone was thinking bad stuff about me. Green was for when they said nothing to me. Yellow was used when they looked at me. Blue was where they actually said something bad to me. Purple was when they said "Hi" or nodded. Pink is where they didn't look or notice me."

Philip explained his chart in such a detached, scientific way. As if he were presenting his thesis—you wouldn't think he was talking about himself!

"Oh, and I added something else, aqua. That's for when I felt scared. So, as you can see, Mr. Sanchez, in the first four days I met or passed three hundred and ninety-three people. Please note there may have been more but these were the ones I charted. Now, look: there are two hundred and eighty-seven red marks, which means I think you're right, I'm like you were. Because seventy-three percent of people I passed...well, I thought they were thinking bad things about me. Okay, out of three hundred and ninety-three kids, there were three hundred and sixty-one 'green kids' that said nothing to me; hundred and twenty-three 'yellow kids', where I thought maybe they looked at me; two hundred and seventy pink, where they didn't look or notice; and thirty-two blue, where they said something bad...but actually, if you take out Kevin Forester, who has been...well, you know, not nice, it is only seven blue."

"What about the aqua—being scared?"

"Well, twenty...but again, seventeen of those are Kevin Forrester."

"*Wow*...You recorded all that? How on earth could you keep count?"

Phillip was just about to explain when Robert stopped him.

"No, I'm sorry. That's not important right now. I'd really like to know how this makes you feel, Philip?"

Philip got so excited. "Wait, wait, that's just the first three days! Look at how it changed in the next three days." Philip closed that document and opened another.

"Look, Mr. Sanchez, look! The overall number is a bit down, but that's because it was only two days of school and then the weekend, and I didn't really go out. But *look*, look! Out of two hundred and thirteen people, only one hundred and six red! One hundred and six! Do you know what that means? Well, after I did the chart for the first three days I thought, 'I gotta try to stop thinking everyone's thinking bad stuff about me,' and look, I was eighty-eight percent and then, in only two days after, I went to forty-nine percent. I bettered it by almost thirty-nine percent!"

"So how do you feel, Philip?"

"No wait, Mr. Sanchez. Remember, I had thirty-two blue, people saying or doing bad things to me? Well, look, Kevin Forrester wasn't at school the last two days. *Look!*" He said this as if he was a stranded on the ocean and had just seen land or he had discovered the cure for some incurable disease.

"Look! Two blue. *Two* blue! And I don't even care about that guy. He hates everybody."

Robert smiled. "Well, Neville, I think you found your Voldemort."

Philip laughed—a real, genuine laugh! It's amazing how a simple laugh can be so inspiring!

"Voldemort, but we shouldn't say his name, Mr. Sanchez! Hahaha...I'm just kidding! That's a good one, Mr. Sanchez. Yeah, you know what? I think I noticed that when Kevin Forrester is around, he makes the other kids turn blue...you know, in the chart...say mean things. Oh, I'm sorry, Mr. Sanchez, I'm really taking your time, right? Sorry. Okay, let's look at some of the stuff I shot today."

"Philip, Philip, don't be sorry. I'm so...man, I don't know what to say to you. I'm so impressed. I think it is amazing what you have done."

"Thanks."

I could see he was feeling a little embarrassed, so I let him start showing me some of the day's workshop footage.

Philip switched on the monitor. This was really exciting for me because I had never seen one of my workshops on film, only photographs; I was so pleased with what Philip had shot. His creative angles, zooms, and some quirky camera effects—as if it was shot for the six o'clock news! At first, he showed me bits and pieces and then fast forwarded to something else. But after about ten minutes, he stopped on this one girl and let it play much longer than the rest. She was talking to her group about how a friend of hers tried to kill herself two weeks ago and how that friend was saved by this mysterious stranger who called himself "P.K. Phoenix" on Facebook.

As soon as she said that, Philip froze the screen. He bowed his head and bit his lip as if he was about to say something. Then he rolled both of his hands in his T-shirt and started furiously wiping his hands.

"What's wrong, Philip?" He didn't bring his head up, but he lifted his eyes to Robert. "Philip, what is the matter?"

He took a laboured breath, released his hands and in a very timid and shy voice he asked, "Can I show you something?"

I nodded and put my hand on his shoulder. But I let go as soon as I felt him stiffen up. He grabbed his laptop and logged on to Facebook. He opened a page and in place of the usual profile picture, there was a colourful drawing of a majestic bird in flight with wings of flame. Beside the picture was the name "P.K. Phoenix."

Philip looked up at me and pointed at the screen. "That's him."

244

"Wow, this is the guy that saved that girl's friend? And he's a bird on fire?"

"No, that's a phoenix. It's a mythical fire bird."

"Thanks, Philip. But where is this guy's photo?"

"I don't know. He doesn't have one. But listen, Mr. Sanchez, I have to tell you this: She's lying. It wasn't 'a friend' who was going to kill herself, it was her!"

"And you know this? How, Philip? How do you know this?"

"Okay, I don't want you to think I'm strange or anything..."

Robert smiled to himself, thinking that it was going to be hard not to think of Philip as a little strange, given the incredible colour-coded chart of his thoughts he had created.

"You see, I follow these chat lines, you know, with Twitter and stuff. Well, two weeks ago, Megan...Oh, that's the girl's name there, Mr. Sanchez. Megan Moregenstein..." he pointed at the frozen screen, "and you see, Megan was going out with some guy from university. They thought they were destined to be forever together but she had just caught him with another girl."

Robert must have looked at Philip with a questioning look because he got all apologetic.

"Oh, please, Mr. Sanchez, don't think I'm some freak spying on her...I'm not! I know all this 'cause she wrote it on her blog."

"That's okay, Philip. Go on."

"Well, she was writing how she didn't want to live anymore. She said she was had been mortally betrayed, that the pain was beyond anything she could live with. Anyway, she wrote that she went to her parents' medicine cabinet and pulled out a bunch of pills...Wrote she didn't know what they were, but she was taking them...But the weird thing, Mr. Sanchez, was that most of the kids' writings to her, well, they weren't telling her to stop. A couple kids cared and wrote 'Think about it', 'Wait 'til tomorrow you'll feel better'...but most...most of them just told her, 'Yeah, go for it...do it,' telling her that they would do the same, and 'The world's a fucking dying place' and...oh, sorry, Mr. Sanchez."

"That's okay, Philip, I've heard people swear before. Go on."

"Okay, well, she starts taking the pills and, like, she started bragging about what she was doing. She started to write the name that was on the bottle and how many she's taking. It started to become like a game and kids were writing to her, telling her they thought she was brave and that they wish they had the courage to kill themselves. They kept writing and urging her to take more pills."

"Then what happened?"

"Well, that's when P.K. Phoenix started writing to her. He told her to stop but she wouldn't listen. The other people writing were telling him to go away. Some said that she was a hero for what she was doing. And some were getting impatient and saying things like, 'Die already,' and, 'Quit talking about it and just do it.' Some said she was worthless and who needs anything worthless? We throw those things away. So she started getting more and more hurt. Her responses became, well, they sounded real desperate. And this P.K. Phoenix started telling her all about what he thinks is worthless and what is a hero is. And he started writing this story about when he was in Africa where he saw all these kids without parents—kids raising kids, kids raising each other up. He told her how these kids have nothing, absolutely *nothing!* They maybe eat once a day and they live these lives that seem so hopeless. And then he asked her, what worth does she think their lives have?"

Robert leaned in. "And what did she say?"

"She said, probably not worth much, *BUT* then he went on and said maybe they don't have much, *YET* these kids never, *never* ever think of suicide as an option. They never do. Then he asked her why is it always the people that have so much that are the ones who can so easily take their lives when they confront their first challenge or sorrow? He said to her that these kids, they are the heroes we should look to when we start crying about some pain we might have in our life."

Robert was blown away listening to Philip. He spoke with such clarity and passion about this mysterious P.K. Phoenix.

"So what happened, Philip?"

"Well, she said those kids in Africa could never know the love she felt and then said she was taking the last bottle of pills and she had taken a bottle of vodka from her dad's liquor cabinet and was drinking that, too."

"So how did she survive then?"

"Well, this P.K. Phoenix guy, apparently he looked up her address and called 911 and the police and ambulance came. Her parents were downstairs watching a movie the whole time and she said they had no idea what was going on. But those ambulance guys saved her life. They said in a couple of hours she would have been dead from the mixture of drugs she took."

"Okay, but how does she know it was this P.K Phoenix guy who called 911?"

"Well, apparently he wrote her to ask her if the help came on time." Philip turned the video back on and the screen came to life with Megan talking:

"He saved my friend. When everyone else was telling her to kill herself, he cared. I mean, really, guys, how...I mean how did he know my friend's address? And my friend tells me that his words when he writes to you...it's like...it's like he knows all your secrets." Then a voice asked her if her friend has met this Phoenix guy yet.

"Listen to her, Mr. Sanchez."

A close up on Megan as she spoke filled the screen. "No, he says that night when she wanted to kill herself, he cried for her. And now they can never meet because when you're touched by the tears of the Phoenix that saved you, you can never see the bird again. But then he said, don't worry, they will always be connected and he will always be there for me...I mean her...my friend...Listen guys, seriously...so now I've connected with him, I'll send you his Facebook page. Write him if you have anything bothering you. Write him. Write him, he listens!"

Philip froze the screen again. "Mr. Sanchez..."

"Yeah, Philip, what?"

Philip turned to me and started to cry and then, in a small little boy's voice, one that I could hardly hear, he said, "I don't know what to do." But by the time he got to the last word, his body shook hard and his small cry erupted into thunderous sobs. He shook so hard I was worried he might fall off the chair, so I turned a chair around and sat down, facing him. I put my hands on his knees. He didn't pull away; instead he bent over, lowered his head into my hands and wept.

It lasted for a couple of minutes. Every few seconds it looked as if he was about to stop, but like a thunderstorm, he surprised me by booming into the next cry. I didn't say a word. He held on to my hands the way a man who has been hanging onto a cliff for hours would grab you as you tried to pull him up.

Slowly, his hands let go of mine. He let them go as if at that moment he might need to grab them again, much like a child letting his mother go and trying to take his first steps. His raised up his hands, grabbed his T-shirt and wiped his face. But he was delicate, unlike the last time in Mr. Bosco's office. He took his time to wipe his face dry and when he lowered his T-shirt, although his face looked swollen and red, his eyes were peaceful.

I waited a moment to see if he wanted to speak first, but he just kept staring at me with that look, as if I should be the one to say something. But I wasn't sure what caused Philip's wailing. Why was he telling me he didn't know what to do? Did he want to kill himself as well? Was he feeling remorse that he didn't do anything that night when Megan was taking the pills? I just didn't know so I just simply asked him, "What is it that you don't know what to do?"

And, as calm as Robert had ever seen Philip, he smiled the smallest of guilty smiles and said, "I don't know if I should tell Megan...that... I'm P.K. Phoenix."

"What?" Robert shook his head in disbelief. "Philip! What?"

Philip shyly nodded his head.

I had to take a moment to think about this whole scenario. Who was this kid? Questions were mounting in my head. Who was this kid that took the time to write down and colour code every person he confronted for a week to find out who was hurting him? Who was this kid that was so afraid to be touched, had felt abundant abuse from so many bullies in his life, and yet he still asked for help to change, to make it better? Who was this Philip Kong? And then it hit me: "P.K. Phoenix"...

"Oh, P.K...is...Philip Kong," I said aloud. "But...why a phoenix?"

"Well, that's the book where Neville finally comes to life in the series, Mr. Sanchez, *Harry Potter and the Order of the Phoenix*," Philip explained in his I'm-very-sorry voice.

"Oh, well, that makes sense, I guess," Robert said, still a bit stunned at the masquerade Philip had gone through in order to save a life. He looked at Philip for more explanation, but Philip just looked at him like a little boy waiting for his dad to come up with a plan to help him out of the mess he had gotten himself into.

"Okay, Philip. First, let me say I'm really proud of the way you saved a life. It's a pretty awesome thing to do. Yet, you can get into a lot of trouble disguising yourself and pretending to be other people on the internet."

"But it's only for good, Mr. Sanchez, it's only for good. I mean, lots of people do it. Why do you think every superhero have a disguise? Like Batman and...Superman, Green Lantern and—"

"Philip, Philip, those are comic books!"

But Philip just became more animated in his defense of a secret identity. "Okay, then how about all those phone help lines...or 911? Those people don't tell you who they are! And what about all those other help sites on the internet? They ask for money to help you, but they never show their faces either! See, I don't get it, Mr. Sanchez, I'm only trying to help. I'm not asking for money. And, imagine if all those people knew it was me, *Blubber Butt* Kong, trying to help her, do you know what they'd say? Do you know, Mr. Sanchez? They'd say, 'Leave her alone and go kill yourself, fat ass!'"

Philip didn't say that last line with any anger or hurt. He just said it like he was discussing the result of some mathematical equation.

And sadly, the truth was, I knew Philip's formula might be the reality of the world. Who wants to be saved by a Knight in rusty ill-fitting armour? She was the beauty to his beast. And even though he was fighting for a better position in his young teenage life at school, he definitely knew the uselessness of certain equations. And big overweight kids didn't have the right to save pretty girls. The Prince Charmings saving damsels in distress were not the Philip Kongs of the world. And so, if he was going to do any saving, he would have do it as the mysterious, undefined PK Phoenix.

"Wait, Philip, have you or PK Phoenix ever done this before?"

Philip twisted his arms between his legs and tilted his head like someone who had done something wrong and was about to admit it.

"Yeah, kind of. But this is the first time anyone has ever really tried to contact me."

Robert silently nodded his head and looked at Philip. *Well, he's got a point. I mean, he's not a trained professional, but is he really doing any harm? Using a secret identify to help others, how harmful could it be?*

"Okay, Philip, maybe you're right," Robert said. "But I'm not sure about all the laws on the internet and I think if you're going to be helping people and that's the only reason for that identity, I think you have to say that right on your —You did this on Facebook?"

"Yeah."

"So, do you want people to know what you did Philip?"

"Well, I told you."

"Yeah, but Philip, if you're going to disguise yourself to help people and then you start feeling you need to get recognition for your good deeds, well, you could become frustrated and maybe it could become something bad."

"Yeah, Mr. Sanchez. That's it! I don't want it to become bad, that's why I'm asking you what I should do."

"All right Philip, then answer this question first. Why are you doing this? Are you doing it to meet girls? Make friends? Be a hero? Ask yourself, why are you doing this?"

There was a quick knock on the door and then it opened. It was a middle-aged Asian woman who bowed slightly as she spoke.

"Oh, excuse me. I was told to come and get Philip in this room. I am so sorry. So sorry to interrupt but, Philip, your father has been waiting now for ten minutes in front of the school."

Then she bowed to me. "Please...I am sorry. Please excuse my interruption. I am Philip's mother."

I stood up and shook her hand and told her who I was. "Wonderful to meet you, Mrs. Kong. I'm Robert Sanchez. Philip is doing a special project for me. I'm sure he has told you about it."

She shook my hand and let go of it as fast as she could. It wasn't hard to see where Philip got his shy hands from.

"We are so grateful for you tutoring our son, Mr. Sanchez. We are so grateful. I'm so sorry to interrupt, but we are late."

Philip had gathered his things and was already standing behind his mother.

"Mrs. Kong, may I have one moment with Philip, just a second please?"

"Of course, Mr. Sanchez." She bowed and walked out of the room, but stood beside the open doorway, looking in. Robert took a step closer to Philip and smiled. "Tutoring, Philip? How many disguises do you have?"

"I'm sorry, Mr. Sanchez, but if my parents knew what I was doing with you and, well, for your kind of workshops, they would never approve. We're not that kind of people," he whispered. He glanced at the door and we both saw his mother smile at us. But you could tell it was not a patient smile.

"Okay, Philip," Robert said in a louder voice. "We will see each other in four days. Please come with the answer to that question. Why you do this? Okay? See you then, Philip, and nice to meet you, Mrs. Kong. Great boy you have there!"

Philip bowed his head as he exited the room and his mother backed her way out of Robert's view, all the while smiling and bowing. They both vanished from the office, leaving him with an uneasy feeling.

Unfortunately, there were some scheduling mix-ups at the school so the next time Philip and I met was almost a month later. We didn't have any time to speak before he was in the room with me filming the next step in the student leadership workshop.

Philip was just as amazing as last time—moving from group to group with such ease—his presence was almost undetectable. Yet today, Philip seemed even more at ease; at times I saw him silently communicating with a couple of students as he went by their groups. And I'm sure that some students were nodding back to him to say hello. It wasn't as if at the last workshop any of these leader students were in the slightest way mean or disrespectful towards Philip, but I never noticed any real signs of him being acknowledged or engaged. And at one point, as some students were standing up and moving from group to group, I'm sure I saw Megan Moregenstein, the girl Philip saved, I was sure I saw her wave into the camera as if she was waving to Philip.

Something had changed in Philip, for at one point in the afternoon he came behind me and actually touched me by tapping me on the shoulder. He just wanted to ask me a simple logistic question about closing a window blind because of the light, but I couldn't help but notice he had actually touched me.

After the workshop was over, Philip said he had to pick up something from one of his teachers in Mr. Bosco's office but would be back in fifteen minutes to go over the footage. Robert had to go to the washroom and as he walked through the halls and down the stairs to the washrooms, he started to notice all these handmade signs hanging in different places. One said, "Someone saying 'hi' saved my day," and another said, "Make someone feel like they belong," and "No one should feel alone, just say 'hi.'" Another said, "You don't need to save your hellos." There seemed to be no particular special movement going on in the school, but it was nice to see some kids actively trying to say positive things and leaving them for others to read.

Between the two of us, I'm not sure who was more anxious to talk. My curiosity about how Philip had handled his situation with PK Phoenix and Megan Moregenstein was quite strong. But the moment Philip walked into the classroom, he closed the door, leaned against it and immediately said, "Guess what?"

Before I could say anything, he came around the desk, opened his computer and started talking with the energy of a news reporter who had just received the greatest scoop ever.

"Okay, Mr. Sanchez. Okay...there are just too many things to tell you. But don't think I forgot your question. First, I'm sorry about my mom and me having to tell her you were tutoring me. You see, I don't know what would happen if they knew I was being a part of something that has people talking about their feelings, especially at school! If they knew I was missing some classes to be doing this, well, I'd probably be grounded forever. Not that it matters about being grounded 'cause I don't really go anywhere—" Then he cut himself off. "Sorry, look, I just wanted to say, don't think badly of me for telling my parents you're tutoring me, 'cause I think what you're doing is great but my dad and mom, they still live with the old country rules. They wouldn't think you are a bad person for what you do, but they don't like the Western ways. They are always suspicious. But please, I hope you don't think I was being disrespectful, it's just—"

Robert had to stop him, for it seemed the apology was going to last forever and he really wanted to hear about his guess what!

"Philip, it's okay. I know sometimes it's difficult to appease what our parents want and what we want. But please, tell me what happened."

Philip was almost overwhelmed with excitement as he spoke. "Okay, okay...Well, first, let's see...Okay, first the project you put me on, you know, the one about what I think when I see anyone? Well, I haven't been able to do it every day 'cause..." Then he paused as if he needed to think it clearly out. He thought for a second and said, "Okay," and pulled out his laptop and opened up that same coloured chart he had before.

"So look, see...it's so working, Mr. Sanchez. It's so working. See...look, the red just keeps going down. Remember, red is where I think bad stuff about what people think of me. Okay, look...I still have to forget about Kevin Forrester and whoever he's around because I'm still...well, you know, fat and everything to him. But look. I don't know if you remember but purple, purple is where someone says hi or even waves or nods. Well, I don't know if you noticed but when I first did this I never had any purple, but now every day—purple...*Purple!* Mr. Sanchez. Look, it just started last week. A minimum of *at least* three purples a day!"

It was incredible witnessing Philip's simple happiness! So many of us take these things for granted, but for the last week there were at least three people that said 'hi' to Philip Kong and for that, he was on a purple cloud nine.

"That's great, Philip! So great! And if anyone deserves it, you do! So do you know how this change happened?"

Philip slowly closed his laptop computer and stared at the floor. Robert waited a moment, but he wasn't moving and still stared at the floor.

"Is there something you want to tell me, Philip?"

He slowly lifted his head and said, "The thing is, Mr. Sanchez, now hearing you say great, well...maybe now I'm not so sure I do deserve it. You see, I thought about what you asked me. Why did I help Megan and why did I do something like that. And do I want people to know it was me that helped her? I really thought about it and you know what? Really, I don't need her to know it was me."

Robert moved a chair and sat beside him. "Truthfully, Phillip?"

"Yeah, really. Honest. I think I just like doing it. It made me feel great about me. It was the first time in my life I felt good about being me and doing something that I wasn't doing for my parents' approval or as a career move for them... I was doing it because it made me...me feel good."

"So why would you think you don't deserve people saying 'hi' to you then?"

Philip scrunched up his face and became that shy little boy again. "Well, Mr. Sanchez, I...I did this thing. Well, more than one thing, I guess...You see, after that night we talked—about a month ago—when I got home I had about eight messages. Well, I should say, PK Phoenix did. One was from Megan and three of her friends...The other three, I don't know them, but I recognized their names. And the last one...I don't know this guy at all. Don't think he goes to our school. He writes that he heard about me helping people like him. Says everyone picks on him and that he couldn't do it anymore. He actually wrote that he was pretty sure he was going to kill himself. Anyway, so I wrote him back and told him to try doing what you told me to do. That maybe what he thinks is everybody picking on him might actually be only a few people. He needed to start believing that he belonged just like anybody else. And I told him to start keeping track of every time someone says 'hi' or doesn't do anything to make him feel like he doesn't belong. And guess what, Mr. Sanchez? For the next week, he wrote to me every day and said it was amazing that what he thought was 'everyone' was really just a couple of people. And Megan kept writing to me asking me how she could repay me for saving her life. So, well and this is why I'm not so sure I deserve it. See, I told her the way to repay me is... is for her to save someone else."

"Well, Philip that sounds great!"

"Really? I hope so. She asked me how to do that. I didn't know what to say to her, Mr. Sanchez."

"So what did you write then?"

"Don't know why I came up with it, but I told her try saying 'hi' to people that you normally never speak to. And then, Mr. Sanchez, unbelievably, the next day, the *very next* day...I was standing in front of my locker and then I get this little tap on my back—oh don't worry, I didn't push anyone. Do you know who it was? Megan Moregenstein and her friend Talia! I was shocked. Anyway, I turned around, I'm sure I wiped my hands on the back of my T-shirt twenty times, and I just stood there frozen like some kind of zombie, I'm sure. Then I thought...*oh my God, she knows!* She knows that PK Phoenix is me! And all I could think of was 'How am I going to get away? Where can I run?' But then she just smiled and said, 'Hi, I'm Megan and this is my friend, Talia. I don't think we have ever said hi to you and I'd like to change that. Okay?'"

"That's so wonderful Philip. It must have made a big purple mark on your graph!"

"But I didn't know if she was joking, Mr. Sanchez. I thought that maybe she knew everything and this was a joke. That she was just waiting for me to tell the truth."

"So did you?"

"I was too scared to think. I just said, 'Okay, hi.' Then she handed me a little piece of paper with PK Phoenix's Facebook address and told me, 'If you ever need someone to talk to, try this guy.' Then she walked away. But...Mr. Sanchez, then her friend Talia turns around and she walked directly back to me....and so now I'm thinking she knew it's me...she knew...and she's going start yelling in the hallway what a freak I am."

Phillip then rose to his feet. "But I was wrong! That didn't happen, Mr. Sanchez. It didn't happen at all! No, she came close to me, real close.

And then she put her hand on my arm." He then lightly touched his arms to show Robert how she touched him.

"Oh, and I didn't pull away! And then she just asked me my name! And I told her, 'Philip,' and she just kept her hand on my arm the whole time, Mr. Sanchez, the whole time! Then she said, 'Look, Philip, Megan almost died about a month ago and this guy, the one on that piece of paper she gave you, it's true, he really did save her. I just wanted to make sure you knew, he's one of the good guys...and he's for real.'"

Wow, I was absolutely blown away. I know that feeling of complete exhilaration. I know what it feels like to stand on the summit after a difficult climb. I thought I knew what that strong sense of accomplishment felt like, yet what I witnessed that day in that classroom was beyond anything I ever have experienced on any mountain. It had only been a couple of months ago when he asked me to help him change. And here I was, thinking I'm helping this boy, but it was unbelievable what this kid was doing on his own. Just look at what Philip had accomplished in those last two months! He saved the life of a girl who had already decided to kill herself; he created— completely on his own—a help line for others in need; he initiated a movement in his school, urging all students to acknowledge one another by just saying hi; and, during all that, he actually found a way to escape the prison of his own sorry perspective of how others viewed him.

And now, only a short year later, he's here on the highest mountain in the world, talking to thousands of kids online each day, asking everyone he meets the question, "Why do they climb?" But look at what this incredible boy had the courage to climb? And now he's helping others scale down their mountains of misery...and climb to make a safer, happier school (world) to live in...

Well, my love, my eyes feel so heavy....A hug, oh, feeling you tonight would be so glorious! Soon we will be together. Tomorrow is our last day here...Everyone's all excited that we will be able to broadcast live—talk to almost six thousand kids back home—first we'll do that little journey to the ice fields...

And so I ask myself that question again: why is it that I climb these actual mountains when I'm able to witness the greatest change I have ever seen any human being go through—climbing MT KONG.

I love you. Open arms coming soon...
Robert

32. PRESENT DAY – AT THE HOTEL

Monique sat on the toilet, removed the paper mitten she had wiped her face with and stood up just enough to lift the lid and put the paper in the toilet. She opened her purse, pulled out her phone and pressed a number.

In a complete daze, she listened to the ring and got a voicemail. She disconnected and tried another number. "Please pick up," she whispered. Two rings and, "Hello, Leaside Art and Music Academy. Could you please hold?"

Monique heard a couple of women enter the washroom. She didn't want to be having this conversation in a washroom stall for others to hear, but after all the crying and vomiting, she had no idea what she looked like and didn't want anyone to see her and ask her what was wrong. So she just stayed seated. After about thirty seconds, the voice on the phone came back.

"Thanks for holding. May I help you?"

Monique spoke in low voice. "Hi, this is Monique Sanchez. I'm wondering if my daughter, Jennifer Sanchez, is at work today. I really need to speak with her, please."

"Oh, you're Jenny's mom? Hi Mrs. Sanchez! Jenny has told me so much about you and her father. Oh, and how is Mr. Sanchez doing? Jenny told us all about—"

"He's fine...fine. Sorry, but I really need to speak with Jenny. It's kind of an emergency." Monique was still half whispering so no one else could hear her in the washroom.

"Are you okay, Mrs. Sanchez?"

"Yeah, I'm sorry. I'm in a meeting so I'm trying not to disturb anyone. So please, could you check to see about Jenny?"

"Yes, I know. I have to do that all the time in this office."

"Please, could you check about Jenny?"

"Oh, yes, I'm sorry...Okay, hang on, Mrs. Sanchez, I'll check."

"Oh wait, Mrs. Sanchez, I have a note right here. But it's not from Jenny. It's from Mr. Le. He said there was an emergency and both he and Jenny would not be in today and possibly tomorrow."

"Mr. Le was the one who called the school, not Jenny?"

"Yes, Mrs. Sanchez."

"And who is this Mr. Le?"

"I'm sorry, Mrs. Sanchez. Has Jenny not mentioned him at all?"

"No, no, she hasn't. Who is he and why is he calling for my daughter?"

"I'm sorry, I don't know if I should be saying this. But Jenny and Mr. Le are dating."

Jenny had yet to tell her mom about Kyle. Even though Monique had many questions about who this Mr. Le was, she didn't have time to get into it, so she lied to the school's secretary. "Yes, yes, I'm sorry. When you said Mr. Le, I was thrown. Yes, I know they are dating...but please tell me, did he say what the emergency was?"

"No, I'm sorry, I didn't take the message. Kyle spoke to Ruth, she's the morning secretary and she had to leave for a dentist appointment this morning. Oh, that woman and her teeth...Do you know it's her third appointment this month? Oh, I'm sorry, you're in a meeting; you don't need me blabbering away. So, would you like me to have Ruth call you when she gets back this afternoon?"

"Yes, please have her call this number. Thank you."

"Excuse me for asking, Mrs. Sanchez, but is everything okay?"

Monique wanted to just tell her the truth. She wanted to scream it out to the world that "No, everything is *not* okay and I don't know if it will ever be okay again. Jenny's father and the only man I have ever loved is dying right in front of my eyes and I can't do anything to save him!" But it seemed the truth was something not to be spoken out loud today.

"I'm fine...fine...Please have Ruth call me when she gets in."

"Okay, Mrs. Sanchez. It was great speaking to you. Oh, and I have to tell you we all love Jenny here. She adds such a wonderful youthful energy around here...Really such a...what's the word for it? Um...oh, 'life.' Both her and Kyle. Yeah, such a new life to this school, which I don't think we've had in years. And do you know what? She...oh, I'm sorry, you're in a meeting. Anyway, great to speak with you and goodbye. Have a nice day! And don't worry, as soon as Ruth walks through that door, I'll ask her to call you. Okay, *buh-bye.*"

"Bye," Monique said, but she wasn't sure the woman even heard it as she had dropped the phone on her lap as she spoke. She then listened for sounds of movement. Nothing stirred. It seems the women had exited and so Monique wandered out to take a look at herself in the mirror.

Her face looked puffy, coloured with blotchy spots of red. The little makeup she wore had all been rubbed off by the paper mitten. She turned on the tap and held her hand under the water. She leaned down, cupped the water and then wet her face. Mindlessly, she brought her hand to her face and touched her lips. She looked at herself in the mirror. Raised her hand and slowly traced her lips with her wet fingers. As she exhaled, out came a long agonizing sigh. She closed her eyes.

Unexpectedly, it struck her. She couldn't remember the last time her lips had been touched, touched with any gentleness, touched with any thoughts of love.

Was it just six months ago? It seemed like another lifetime when she had received that call. A nervous man's voice telling her about an avalanche...Robert was buried in a crevasse in the ice fields of Everest. There was no chance of survival. He was *dead!* After crying nonstop for hours upon hours, she had then gathered water onto her face, just like now, looked in the mirror and touched her face. And the same agonizing thought held her captive—the man she loved would never touch her lips again.

Back then, looking in the mirror, she imagined her hand was Robert's hand saying his goodbye as he always did—so slow, so gentle—a caress only her face knew. Love felt so deep and, oh, the way he smiled at her, eyes making her feel *more alive, more there*. It always felt like one of those once in a lifetime moments. His warm hand, tracing his finger across her lips and always, always saying to her, "Home...These lips will forever be my reason to come home."

But at that time, she had just heard he was dead under a mountain of snow. She knew Robert was not coming home. She tried everything to hide from the haunting visions she had of his body, tangled and entombed under a huge avalanche of ice and snow. Was he curled up or did he die trying to claw his way out? The images were too torturous to go on imagining. She begged the nervous voice on the phone to do everything they could to find his body. But they told her that the possibility of recovering Robert's body was very remote because of the dangerous location he was buried in. And although Monique was not a religious woman, she prayed that night in front of her bathroom mirror. She prayed out loud to whatever god would listen. *Please let them find Robert, find my husband's body. Just please bring him home—to see, to know, to bury...*

And some gods must have heard, for the moment she asked, her bathroom prayer was interrupted.

"Monique, Monique!" The voice on the phone was out of breath.

"Monique, it's Robert, Robert...They found him!"

Despite living in this dark, desperate sorrow, both she and Jenny had already taken actions to deal with Robert's death. When the news first arrived, they immediately booked flights to Katmandu, clinging to the hope Robert's body would be recovered and they could bring her husband and the father of her only daughter back home.

So when she heard, "They found him," Monique said, "Thank God! Oh, thank you, whatever God heard me! Thank you! Thank you! Listen, we are taking the first plane to Katmandu to bring him home."

"Oh, that's so great, Monique. I can't tell you what it's like. It's like a freakin' miracle! A freaking *fantastic*, incredible miracle! I have to tell you, I never thought it was possible to find him under all that ice and snow."

"What shape is his body in? I mean did it look like he suffered a lot?"

"Well, prepare yourself and your daughter, Monique, 'cause when you see him...Well, his legs are pretty banged up."

"But do you know if he suffered or was it quick?"

"Oh, it was quick all right, Monique. That ice and snow can hit you in seconds. He probably didn't even have time to react. And I'm not going lie to you, his legs don't look good. Look, it'll be about ten minutes and you can talk to him yourself."

"*What!* Are you crazy?" Monique pulled the phone away from her face with disgust. *What kind of sick idea this was—having me talk on the phone to my dead husband's body?*

"Monique, I'm sorry I didn't hear what you said. *Whoa*, wait a second..."

Then she heard the voice shouting out some commands. "Over here, I have his wife on the phone...Just lift him...Hook it up to your walkie...Monique? Monique? You still there?"

"Yeah, I'm here."

"Okay, hang on a minute. They are hooking up the phone to a walkie."

"Jenny," Monique called out. "Jenny, come here quick..."

Jenny slowly entered the room. She moved as if her being was void of any life. She sat on the edge of her parents' bed, her heavy head hanging as if it might fall off. Monique sat beside her daughter and whispered, "Jen, I'm talking with base camp. They found Daddy's body."

"Oh, Daddy." Jenny said in the tiniest voice and then started to cry. She fell on the bed and started to wail. Monique lay back beside her daughter and pulled her close.

"I know, baby...I know..." She couldn't hold back her tears either. "But now we can at least bring Daddy home."

"Monique?" the voice called out on the phone. "Monique...You still there?"

"Yes, I'm here...so is my daughter."

"It's a miracle that's for sure...A *goddamn* miracle!" The voice on the phone continued. "All right, you guys ready? Okay, we got the walkie hooked up. Monique? Monique, you can speak now."

Jenny stopped crying. Her wet face looked at her mother wondering what was happening and wondering what the man on the phone was talking about. Monique gently put her hand on the receiver and caressed it. "Jen, Jen, listen...They are putting a phone on your father's body so we can talk to him."

"Mom, *what?*"

Monique then delicately put the phone on the bed between the two of them. They looked at each other, silently crying. Then they looked at the phone as if they were looking at Robert's body in a casket. Jenny reached out to touch the phone, but couldn't stand the pain, so she buried her head into the bed as deep as she could get it. Her mother put her head on her daughter's and just stared at the phone on the bed.

Then a faint sound came from the phone. "Monique...Baby...You there? Little Rock? Girls...are you there?"

Jenny's body jerked and she turned to face her mother. It was like the voice came from inside her head, as if in a dream. Jenny even smiled to Monique, wishing her mother could hear her father's voice. So Jenny reached out her hand to touch the phone again. But this time the voice was louder and obviously not in Jenny's mind.

"Monique?"

Then Monique turned her head to the phone as she could now hear what was, unmistakably, Robert's voice.

"I thought you guys said this was hooked up to my family?" Robert's voice shouted out.

Then the other voice came back on the phone, speaking to Monique.

"Monique, are you still there? Monique?"

She picked up the phone. "Yes, I'm here."

"Well, Robert's trying to talk to you...Hang on, let me try the connection again."

"Wait," Monique almost screamed, as if she had been caught in one of those video comedy pranks. "Wait, the body you found was a...alive? Are you telling me he's alive?"

"Monique, what did you think the miracle was?"

"Oh, God!" Monique loudly wept with complete abandon. "Yes...yes...Please, please let us talk to him. Oh, let us talk to him!"

And then came the moment few get to experience in a lifetime: Monique and Jenny got to speak to someone who had risen from the dead.

Jenny leaped, bouncing on the bed, shrieking in a voice that went from crying to laughing, laughing to screaming, and screaming to crying. Finally, saying, "Daddy, Daddy, Daddy, Daddy, Daddy..." She didn't know what else to say. Monique pulled her daughter as close to her as it was humanly possible. She had to put her hand over her daughter's mouth. "Shhh..."

Both of them sat there staring at the phone in Monique's other hand. They listened to crackling. Tears, joyous tears, washed away the dark grief that had surrounded them for the last twenty-four hours. First there were more crackling sounds. Then they froze and in total unison, they inhaled, devouring all the air in the room. And then, they held their breaths—creating a perfect silence that only his voice could break.

"Baby...Little Rock...I can't believe I'm talking to you." Roberto Sanchez spoke. His story had not ended.

And yet, a mere six months later, Robert had completely stopped talking to his wife and daughter. But he was alive! So how did it happen? He was alive! So how did they become this story? One that was only filled with questioning silence, a guessing game of who felt what and why? He was alive, but no one dared to question what was happening for fear of what the answer might bring.

So now, today, as Monique traced her lips in the mirror, she tried to remember how the joy of that moment felt. That moment when she had found out he was alive, a joy that was still so indefinable. How could that joy have turned into this?

Monique knew the mountain did not take her husband's life, but in her heart she felt he was still buried somewhere deep within its womb. *He must still be there*...because the Roberto Sanchez, the husband, the father, the man she knew and loved, did not come home six months ago.

It took two long days of travelling for Jenny and Monique to get to Katmandu. Those two days were filled with an anticipation neither one of them had ever experienced before. They came directly from the airport. The moment the cab stopped, they shot through the doors into the clinic where Robert was, forgetting all their luggage. Fortunately, the cab driver caught them before they started up the stairs.

"Ah, just put their luggage behind my desk. It will be safe there," said Doctor Tiber, a young man who was dressed in a plaid shirt and jeans and possessed a Grizzly Adams lumberjack beard that matched his outfit. "Ah, it's great to meet you, Mrs. Sanchez, and you must be...Little Rock?" He reached both his hands out to Monique and Jenny and shook their hands at the same time.

"Robert has told me so much about the two of you. Now, your husband is doing well but when you go in, he might be a bit groggy because I had to give him something for the pain."

"Pain?" Monique asked. *Pain?* Somehow in the euphoria of the miracle, Monique had not thought of pain, only joy and rebirth.

"Yes, he is in quite a bit of pain. His leg—"

Monique interrupted the doctor. "Oh, yes they had told us that he hurt his legs."

"Well..." The doctor sort of grimaced as he said that. "Well, yeah, the hurt is quite extensive. But, look, I'm sorry, we can talk about this later. You must want to see him. Please follow me."

Katmandu was not a rich city and its hospital clinic reflected that. But Jenny and Monique took little notice of the doctor, who looked as if he had just been out chopping wood, or the walls and their peeling paint. They were so excited as they walked down the little hallway toward Robert. They approached a white door with a small, scuffed window in the middle. Doctor Tiber stopped as he put his hand on the doorknob.

"Just give me a moment, please. Robert would never forgive me if I didn't help him look presentable for you two."

"It's okay." Jenny smiled. "Believe me, I've seen my Dad at his worst."

"I'm sure." Dr. Tiber smiled. "But I promised him. Just a second, okay?"

Dr. Tiber walked through the door. Jenny tried to look through the little window but it was quite scratched and blurry, so all she could see was a shadow moving across the room.

Pain? thought Monique. *Extensive hurt?* She shook her head with a little quirky smile. It was strange hearing these words because pain and hurt just hadn't been in her vocabulary of thoughts for the past two days.

It was only a moment later when Dr. Tiber opened the door.

There was her husband, propped up in almost a sitting position. Half of Robert's face was discoloured from frostbite. His legs were under some kind of dome and covered with a sheet. He looked terribly tired, like he would fall asleep at any moment. His eyes were not fully opened and his head was rolling like he was in a bit of a drunken stupor. Yet, he had a smile that said it all. He was *alive* and was smiling.

"Daddy," Jenny screeched with delight.

Robert lifted both hands, as if he was a blind man reaching out for something in front of him to hold on to.

Jenny ran to her father and grabbed his hand. Monique took the other.

"Oh, my *girrrls...Mmmy* girls," Robert said with a bit of a slur. "I *looove* you..."

"Oh, Daddy...I love you so much!" Jenny said as she kissed her father's hand and pulled it to her body, clinging to it.

Monique put her hand in Robert's hair, which was greasy and matted. She kissed her husband's forehead three times before she rested her head on his and closed her eyes. "I love you, Bobby...So much...I love you so much," she whispered as tears rolled down her face.

"Oh, Daddy, how are you? How are you?" Jenny tried to smile but her voice cracked with emotion and her tears started to flow as well.

"Well, I'm *nooot* dead," Robert said. "So you can stop crying." Robert then clumsily pulled both his wife and daughter to his chest. "Thank God, *you'rrre* here...Thank God, *I'mmm* alive!"

Those words had haunted Monique for six months now. She reached over to take a couple of tissues from the Kleenex box on the washroom counter. If she was going to get back into that Leaning Tower of Pisa room, she had better make herself presentable again.

She wet the tissue and ran it under each eye to clean up the mascara that had made black half circles there. *Alive?* she wondered. *What kind of alive is this?*

They stayed in Katmandu for eight days. For most of that time, Robert was quite drowsy or asleep. Dr. Tiber told them that the clinic could do very little for Robert.

"I can't really give you any more information, Mrs. Sanchez. I can only fix Robert up enough for him to get back home to a much better equipped hospital."

"But, in your opinion, Doctor, how long will it take for his legs to heal?"

"Really, I feel your question is best answered after you return home. I can only tell you both his legs have been badly broken. I have set them enough for travel but they might require surgery to repair the damage. And the frostbite, I'm still not sure about. I'm sorry—it will be wise to wait for your specialist back home to tell you about any procedures."

"Why's he sleeping all the time?" Jenny asked.

"Well, it's a combination of things. One reason is the pain medication."

"And what's the other?" Jenny sounded worried

"Well, frankly, the real reason is that when the body goes through a major trauma, such as your father's has, it shuts down, trying to save all its energy for healing. I know at the moment he seems mostly out of it. But don't you worry, Jenny," Dr. Tiber smiled, "your father will come back to you. You will see soon enough after I start to wean him off the morphine tomorrow."

The next day, Dr. Tiber had Robert taken off the morphine. He gave him a new pain drug that didn't dull his senses as much, which made him a lot more coherent and mentally present. But it also brought alive a Robert that was now terribly irritable and negative.

This wasn't what the doctor promised, she thought. The husband coming home with her was a different man, one that she had never seen before. This Robert had little patience and was mostly quite distant. Both Monique and Jenny found themselves constantly apologizing for every little thing they said around him and avoided all talk of the accident and the state of his legs.

"Jen, he just needs time. Daddy doesn't mean some of things he's saying now. He's just dealing with a lot pain, but don't worry honey. If anyone can handle it, we both know your father can!"

"I just wanna be home, Mom."

"Me too, baby, me too."

"When Dad gets home, it will all get better, right?"

"Of course, baby, but for now we need to be patient with him, okay?"

"Okay, Mom."

"Good. We just have to accept he's not going to be himself for a while and maybe he just doesn't want to talk. Okay? So let's just give your father a chance to get all healed up and then he'll be back to normal. It'll get better when we get home. Now come on, let's try to sleep, okay?" Jenny laid her head on her mother's shoulder and tried her best to get some sleep during the long flight home.

Robert could not live at home right away. He needed to be put in a medical facility that could care for his legs until it was determined what treatment was needed to get him walking again.

Because of the extent of his injuries, he had to have two different specialists looking after him: one was a frostbite specialist and the other was a doctor who specialized in breaks and fractures. That meant they had to find a hospital that provided these treatments. The only hospital for this was Mount Sinai.

"I'm sorry, Monique, but I'm not going to any place called *Mount* anything!" Robert firmly said.

"We don't have a choice, Robert."

"Well, why can't we just go to two different hospitals?"

Monique knew that in his condition it was impossible to be transported back and forth between two different hospitals so she joked, "Mount Sinai is a great hospital. And look, for years you got to pick which mountain you went to, so it's time for me to choose one." But Robert found very little humour in it.

"Well, Robert," Dr. Sarah Schwartz said. "I spoke with Dr. Hussein and he says the frostbite in your left leg is manageable and he thinks you might get close to fifty percent of the nerves back and working. Unfortunately though, your whole knee joint and fibula bone—the bone below your knee—was splintered and broken in too many pieces to recover naturally. So we will have to try and surgically repair it with rods and screws. Since the frostbite damage is very limited, I'm very hopeful that you will recover and have a working leg."

"*Working*, what the heck does that mean 'working?'" Robert snapped back at doctor.

Doctor Sarah Schwartz was a tiny, elf-like woman with short, spiky, grey hair. She was about sixty years old but spoke in a very youthful voice.

"By 'working' I mean you should be able to put your full weight on it and walk and maybe do some light running. But you will likely only have fifty percent feeling in your lower leg and foot because of the nerve damage."

Robert let out a loud, disgusted sigh. Monique half smiled, trying to excuse Robert's behaviour. But Dr. Schwartz knew Robert's sigh was nothing compared to how he might react to the news of his right leg, so she smiled and said, "Oh, it's okay, we should all be allowed our reactions. Robert's legs have been through a lot of trauma."

Then the doctor retrieved a huge yellow envelope and pulled out what looked like some kind of x-ray of Robert's leg. She held it up in front of her and starting talking.

"Now, this is your right leg and if you notice here, just below the knee...all that white area? Well, Robert, your right leg was broken and bent ninety degrees in the wrong direction. On top of that, because it was exposed to the ice for a long period of time, the frostbite started here. Look at this area, just below your knee. Because it got very little blood flow for such an extended period of time, all the tissue and the nerves there died. There is no chance for tissue renew—"

Robert interrupted the doctor. "So what can you do then?" Without waiting for the doctor to answer, Robert continued, "I know, I've heard. You remove all that muscle and tissue and replace it with other parts of my body, right? Yeah...I hear you take it from my behind." He then looked right at his wife and joked, "Great, I'm going to have a bum knee."

Monique tried to laugh, but then noticed the doctor was not putting the photo of Robert's leg down. She must have more to say.

"Well, Robert, I wish I could do that for you, but I'm sorry, I can't," the doctor said. "Your leg has been without blood for too long and gangrene set in. That is the white area below the knee."

"How can you heal that?" Monique asked.

Dr. Schwartz put the photo down. She looked at Robert. The two words every climber works fiercely to avoid had just been said: "frostbite" and "gangrene." Robert dropped his head into his hand and muttered, "Ah, damn!"

Monique looked at her husband and then back to the doctor. "Well, what...What can you do then?"

Dr. Schwartz took in a deep breath. "We have to amputate the leg just below the knee."

Monique felt faint. She grabbed onto Robert's hand and spoke to the doctor in a panicked voice. "*Amputate?* Cut his leg off? Is there nothing else you can—"

Robert took Monique's hand. He patted it a couple of times then brought it to his lips. He gently kissed her hand and then put it onto her lap. If Monique had known this was to be the last time her husband would ever bring his lips to kiss her, she would have memorized it. She would have emblazoned the memory of that kiss with something more profound. Maybe she would have turned to her husband and kissed him back.

But instead, Monique turned to Dr. Schwartz and asked, "Isn't there anything? Some kind of experimental treatment? Anything?"

Robert raised his arm and gently said, "Shhh" to his wife.

Monique abruptly turned and faced Robert. "Shhh?" She stood up and almost screamed, "Shhh is all you can say? They are going to take your leg off, Robert! Come on, *fight* for it."

She turned to the doctor. "You don't understand, Doctor. They said he was dead...*dead!* But he survived! Do you know how many tons of ice fell on him?" She turned to her husband. "Robert, *say* something!"

Again, Monique looked directly at the doctor, waving her hands as she spoke. "They said it was the size of small apartment building. An apartment building! Can you imagine that falling on top of you? He can't have survived all that...all that...only to lose his leg! Please, please...there *has got* to be something else?"

Monique's question was left unanswered. Dr. Schwartz gave her a sympathetic smile. The doctor had witnessed this desperate scene many times and knew it was best to allow people time to react. Monique felt a little weak from so many emotions, so she reached behind her, grabbed the arms of the chair and slowly lowered herself down.

Robert spoke the moment she landed in her seat. "When?" was all he asked.

"Tomorrow, Robert, tomorrow at the very latest. I would like to admit you tonight." Dr. Schwartz then looked at Monique and said, "I'm sorry it is such short notice and, believe me, there is nothing else. What's going on below your knee is endangering your life; the tissue inside you has been dead for too long and is starting to spread."

Dr. Schwartz then smiled as she spoke about rehabilitation and all the latest developments in prosthetic limbs. She even mentioned a double amputee who had just competed in the Olympics. She said, depending on the surgical progress on Robert's right leg, he could be walking in months.

Neither Monique nor Robert responded. Monique just held out her hands as the doctor handed her pamphlets, each displaying smiling people showing off their artificial limbs.

Within three hours, Robert was lying on a hospital gurney and being wheeled into a small shower room by Bruno, a male nurse with long dreadlocks. Monique followed them and was just about to enter the room when Bruno said in his faint Jamaican accent, "I'm sorry, lady, this room is only for the gents. But don't you go worry, I'll get him all fixed up in no time."

"Fixed up?" Monique asked.

"Oh yes, we need to shave his leg all pretty for tomorrow. You can wait down the hall in room two thirty-seven. Lots of chairs there. We'll be fifteen minutes. Okay?"

"Mon, go home," Robert said.

"No, it's okay, Bobby. I'll wait."

"Please Monique, just go home."

"No, Bobby, it's okay. I'll stay."

"Why, Monique? There's no reason...*Please* just go home."

"It is okay, man. It will only be fifteen minutes, not long. Your lady can wait just down the hall," Bruno said with a smile.

"No, it's not okay," Robert said, showing a bit of frustration. "Please, Monique. Could you go home please? I'll be fine."

Monique paused for a second, not knowing what to say, then she blurted out, "But Bobby, we need to talk!"

"About *what* Monique? What? They're cutting my leg off...No talking is going to change that. You heard the doctor, it's dead. It's gotta go." Robert stopped, took in a long breath and then spoke gently to his wife in a more pleading voice. "Look, Monique, could you please just go home? You heard the nurse, they are going fix me all up. It'll be all right."

"*But*, Bobby, this is all happening too fast! We should—"

"Monique, *please!* Could you please listen? I don't want to talk about it, okay? Don't worry, they are just shaving the leg tonight. Now, please just...just come tomorrow after they fix me all up. Please?"

Bruno reached into his pocket, pulled out some tissues and handed them to Monique as he saw her eyes welling up with tears.

"Take your time, I'll just stand over there until you two are finished," Bruno said. He then took a good fifteen steps away from Robert and Monique and leaned on the wall to give them some privacy.

"Oh, Bobby, Bobby..." Monique sighed as she gently laid her hand on his right leg.

Robert winced in pain. "Ahhh, don't, please that hurts."

"I'm sorry. I'm so sorry. I just wanted to touch it before—" Monique couldn't hold it in any longer so she put her head on Robert's chest and cried softly.

Robert waited a little, then lightly patted his wife on the back and said, "Mon, I just need some time alone, okay? So please, could you go home?"

Monique wiped her face with the tissues and desperately forced a smile. "Of course, Bobby, of course. You need some time alone. It's just so much to take in...and I'm not as strong as you Bobby. I mean, you're amazing how you're able to...Oh, I'm sorry for crying. I know if anyone can handle this, you can. I know. You're the most—Oh, I'm sorry. It's selfish of me to be the one crying. It's your leg...and you must be going crazy with all this. But I just don't know what to say. I'm so sorry, but I...I understand. I'll...I'll go home, okay. Just promise to call me before you go to sleep then?"

"Okay, sure." Robert said as Monique leaned over to kiss him. But Robert tilted his head so that only his forehead was open for the kiss. Monique held her lips on his forehead for a few seconds and she slowly whispered, "I...love...you..."

As her lips let go, she looked at her husband and he looked at her. Robert raised his hand to touch his wife's face just like all those times at the door when he would trace his fingers along her lips, telling her they were his reason for coming home. But instead of the caress and words of coming home, he just reached out with his index finger, tapped her nose and said, "Don't you worry. You just come back when I'm all fixed up, okay?"

She tried her best to smile. "Okay...Okay, Bobby."

Monique looked at the nurse to indicate she was leaving. Bruno started walking back to the gurney to push it into the shower room.

"Thank you for waiting and please, please take care of him," Monique said.

"Like he was my own father, I will. So, don't you go worrying yourself," Bruno said as he opened the door to push Robert inside. Monique stood there, watching Robert being wheeled into the room. Just as the door was ready to close, she pointed at her heart and waved at Robert, who smiled meekly. He did not return the romantic gesture. Instead, he gave her a thumbs-up as he passed through the door.

Monique stood there for a long time in front of that door, listening hopefully for sounds of her Robert. Maybe he would talk to the nurse, say something about how he felt about what was going to happen. But those sounds never came. Instead, the only sounds she heard were those of water and the instructions Bruno gave about why he had to shave his leg. Then she looked at her hand and noticed she was still holding on to those brochures the doctor had given her. She held one up and looked at the smiling people modelling the latest artificial legs or arms. The smiles stirred an aching question inside her: *How long does it take to start smiling again after something like this happens to you?*

Damn it! Damn it! she cursed as she lined her eyes in the hotel washroom. *Nothing has changed since Robert's accident. I'm still living with those same damn questions today. When do we start smiling again?* She checked her watch and started to move with a little more purpose; she knew she needed to get back to the Leaning Tower of Pisa to see how Robert was doing, especially after her explosion.

The door to the washroom burst open, followed by laughter. Monique felt suddenly panicked, so she snatched up her purse and scurried back into one of toilet stalls. She still didn't want anyone seeing her. Even though she was hidden behind the door she recognized the voices immediately—Kalinda and Dee, both from sales.

"Hahaha. Oh Greg...I'd pay anything to see him on that basketball court today."

"Yeah, I bet he'd probably be playing in his suit and those precious shiny black shoes of his."

"It was good though—Greg's speech, wasn't it? You know, I never knew he grew up in Hong Kong, did you?"

"Nope, me either. You know, I wasn't really looking forward to this day but it's been really fun so far."

"Yeah, and I guess Linkup's head of sales has made it a little more fun for you."

"Ah, him! Well, Kalinda, don't worry! Apparently he's quite happily married and his wife just had twins."

"Twins? Ah, I'm sorry, that's too bad. I was really hoping for you, Dee!"

Monique leaned against the stall door, wishing she could enjoy that simple banter her co-workers were sharing. But just as she thought that, the happy sounds changed and shifted into those of concern.

"But, oh man, that was so weird seeing Monique's husband, wasn't it?"

Monique's body suddenly became stiff.

"He looked so different in that wheelchair...I almost didn't recognize him. Have you seen him since the accident?"

"No, I don't think anyone has. Don't you remember they were supposed to host the barbecue this summer and then Monique cancelled it at the last minute?"

"Oh yeah, we didn't have one this year, did we? I guess he wasn't ready to face all of us yet."

"I don't know what I'd do if that had happened to my husband."

"Your husband, Kalinda? Hell, I don't know what I'd do if that ever happened to me! I don't think I could handle that—losing *both* my legs!"

"Does she ever talk to you about it?"

"No, every time I ask her how things are, it's always fine, she says, always fine. Well, you know Monique."

"Yeah, oh God, I felt so bad seeing him like that. But then he must have really recovered quickly...I mean it's pretty impressive coming to do the talk today. I don't think I could do that. Talk about climbing mountains if that had happened to me."

"It's just sad! Did you see how he acted when we all said hello? He just looked so—I don't know. I mean I remember him always telling these jokes and being so...I mean, that man, anytime you met him, he was always so...so up...you know, he just had that energy."

Monique felt a little short of breath. It was true she cancelled the barbecue, but it was completely her idea. Robert didn't say anything. Monique made that decision without ever consulting him.

"You know, I've always envied them—the way they were together. Don't you remember how they'd always be at the parties and he'd always be holding her hand...Must be weird now, I mean, holding hands with him in that wheelchair."

"Yeah, well, one thing for sure, those two must have the most incredible relationship to deal with something like this. I mean, that's a huge change, right? I just don't know how Monique does it—coming to work every day and she never complains...She never even talks about it."

Monique put her hand on the door handle. She felt such a strong urge to bust through the door and tell Dee and Kalinda they didn't know what the hell they were talking about.

"And Monique never talks to you about it? I thought you guys were best friends."

"Yeah, we were, but she doesn't talk to me much anymore...Anyway, come on, we better get back. *And* let's not say anything because Monique and Robert are actually sitting with us. Oh Dee, and who knows, maybe Mr. Linkup has a brother who isn't married with twins."

Monique didn't burst through the door. She didn't tell Dee and Kalinda they didn't know what the hell they were talking about. She just listened and waited until the two women exited the washroom.

Then she slowly opened the stall and walked to the sink, tossing her purse on the shelf, not caring that some the contents flew into the sink below. Mindlessly, she picked up the mascara to do her eyes. She couldn't tell Kalinda and Dee that they didn't know what they were talking about because they did—they were absolutely right! Monique didn't talk. Monique always told everyone that things were fine, not to worry, everything was going great. And everyone bought into Monique's disguise. Even today she was providing more evidence of how wonderful things were. *Hey look everyone, my husband Robert is good enough that he is actually coming to do this talk today, despite everything that's happened to him.* Yes, everyone saw how the Sanchez's had handled their adversity and triumphed!

She looked in the mirror and a stranger was looking back at her. It was the same stranger who, for the last few months, had been wearing her clothes and was using her name. The stranger that told everyone things were fine. But at this moment, the stranger looked at her in an intense and accusing way. Monique leaned on the sink to get a closer look and then slowly started to rock rhythmically back and forth until she exploded with rage at the stranger. She ranted like a guilty person who desperately needed to purge themselves of every last detail of their crime so they could finally be at peace with all they had done.

"This?" she spat. "*This*, how did we become *this?* This? It's all a big *goddamn* guess! We're living this one big, horrible guess!!!"

She held on to the sink tighter and confessed to the stranger, "And there I am, there we all are, telling him he can do it. If anyone can handle this, Roberto can. Damn it! All I've been wanting to do is *fix* it...and...and...I *can't* fix it! He's lost his legs. He's in a wheelchair...and what did I do? Oh, I tried fixing it, all right! I tried to do everything—I got that ramp, the doors, the bathroom. I changed the whole goddamn house!"

Monique froze for a second. The rage ceased as another realization came to her. "Oh my God, everything's changed but me! I just couldn't...I just didn't want to believe or accept that *this* had happened to us."

The moment she finished the word 'us,' Monique put her hand on the mirror and the stranger stopped rocking.

This was exactly what happened after my father died!

Monique was only fifteen when her father died after complications from a heart surgery. Afterwards, Monique would never mention his name or talk about her father to her mother. Monique never asked how her mother felt because she didn't know what would happen and what she would do. So Monique spent months avoiding any conversation about what happened to her father. No matter how many times her mother would casually mention him, Monique always found ways to escape the conversation. Until one day on her ride to school, her mother couldn't take it anymore.

"Monique, we have to stop this," her mother said as she slid the key into the ignition.

"What, Mom? What are you talking about?"

"Honey," Monique's mother didn't turn the car on, "it's okay to talk about Daddy. It is."

Monique responded defensively, "I never said it wasn't. Why you saying this now? Come on, Mom, drive. I'm going to be late!"

"No, Monique, *no!* I can't live like this anymore. We just go on every day, never saying anything...pretending like Daddy never existed."

"Ah, come on, Mom, we don't do that. Please, can we go? I have that test today."

"No, Monique. No, honey. I'm sorry, but I can't live like this anymore. I'm sorry, but we have to talk."

"Mom, we talk."

"About what, Monique? About what? How can we go on living if we just avoid talking about Daddy?"

"Mom, please. I just...well okay. You know what? Maybe, maybe I just don't want you to cry, okay? Or be upset or anything."

"But this is worse, honey. This is worse. Of course I'm going to cry. Of course you're going to cry...We can't just hide from what happened. What about us, honey?"

Monique cried out, "But Daddy's gone! We're not us anymore, Mom. We're not! He's gone! He's gone!"

"But you're still here, Monique, and I'm still here. We have to talk about it...We have to."

Monique threw off her seatbelt and crawled as close as she could into her mother's waiting arms.

"I know, baby, I know, everything's changed...so I need my little girl now, more than ever."

Over the weekend, her mother and her just talked and cried. Cried and talked. They asked each other all the painful questions left unasked over the past months. Why? Why? Why? Yet with each aching question of 'why,' they discovered new hopeful ones: "How?" How can you...? How can I...? How can we...go on? And today, standing in front of that mirror, her mother's voice came back to her loud and clear.

"I don't ever want to lose you, honey! No matter what happens, all the difficult things you are going to face...if you really love someone and they love you, don't try to do it alone. Don't hide from it. Talk about it! Once you stop talking, that's when it's over. How are you ever going to know anything if you don't ask? We need to face it together. You have to have the courage to be able ask all the hardest questions. What's stronger, honey? What's more powerful? Love or fear?"

Monique quickly opened her mouth to say "Love," but then stopped herself and looked painfully stunned.

Her mother laughed. "It's not an easy question, is it? Do you know who asked me that question, Monique?"

"Dad?"

"No, and his answer would have been love too. But you did, honey. It seemed almost every day you came home asking your father and I those questions. Oh, you liked this friend but were afraid they didn't like you. You loved volleyball but were afraid you might not be good enough. And that first boy you had a crush on but were afraid he thought you were too short for him...Remember?"

Monique laughed with each memory.

"And Monique, what did you do each of those times?"

Monique spoke slowly. "I didn't let what I was afraid of...be more important?"

"Yes, honey. Never let fear be more powerful than who or what you love. Never be afraid to ask anything. Don't let fear guide you, Monique."

Monique tried to convince herself that she let the questions remain unasked in order to protect Robert—to spare him of any pain or bad feelings. *But it's me, isn't it?* she thought. *I'm the one afraid to face the truth— afraid to face the answers to those questions—just like I did with my mother. Oh God! Why do we keep forgetting the things we learn?*

There were so many questions alive in her now. *Why did I never ask him why he didn't call that night before his operation? Or, when he said he needed some time to be alone, why did I never ask when that alone time was going to be over? How long did he still need to be alone? What's it like to lose your legs? How does it feel in that chair? When is Roberto Sanchez going to be fixed? When is everything going to go back to normal?* The questions started coming fast and furious, screaming inside her. *What is normal? And Robert, do you still want me? Desire me? Need me? Love me? Are we still "us"? And how did everything change into this? Will we ever get over this?*

Focusing on the word "this" produced another question that echoed so loudly inside her that it caused her to drop her mascara brush into the sink. The brush bounced around, making little, black, dotted smudges all over the white porcelain. She stared down hard at the odd dark marks, looking at them as if they formed some kind of secret code she had been trying to crack for years. Then, in an almost instinctive effort to clean the sink, she found herself putting her finger on one black mark and then connecting it to another mark until they all formed the word "this" in the sink.

Monique suddenly turned away from the mirror. She bent over, leaned on her knees and shook her head with a wild sound. "Ha...well then...I just have to ask! We have to talk about *this* because *this* doesn't work. Because *this* doesn't work!"

She turned back and the moment Monique looked into the mirror, the stranger vanished. *I don't know anything. I really don't know anything at all. Is it really that simple?* she wondered. *Is it really true that if you don't simply ask then you'll just never know? So much has changed and we never, ever talk about it! No...I never talk about it! I want to stop guessing. I want to just talk. I want to start making plans again- I want to smile again- I just want to hold hands...I want to be us again.*

The glorious new feeling of that wanting caused her whole body to rise and straighten. Suddenly, she felt a smile coming on. She felt that smile coming from deep within her. The smile was in her legs, in her chest. She could even feel it in her fingers! She could now taste that smile as it spread across her face. She smiled—hope.

Monique reached over across the counter, pulled a couple of tissues from the box and then wiped the sink clean. It wasn't as triumphant as she had wished because she didn't wipe the word "this" away in one fell swoop. But after a couple of swipes and slight twirls of her hand, the sink was restored to its former shining white sparkle.

Can I...Can we?

Yes, she thought, *yes, I can change 'this.' I know we can change this!* She laughed to herself out loud. *What good is any question if it is not asked?* She laughed at herself even louder. *How could I not have seen this?* She looked back in the mirror. *Because...because you were afraid! Don't let fear guide you!*

Monique felt roused and filled with a determination to face the truth and the consequences of those questions. She quickly opened her mouth and traced her lips with a Tuscan red lipstick. She reached behind her head and pulled out the beautiful African pearl hair clip that held her hair in place. She shook her head until her hair fell evenly on her shoulders. After all that crying, she decided that it would be best to hide her face a bit. She gathered all her cosmetics and put them in her purse. On her way out the door, she picked up each stained Kleenex like a chicken pecking at its food, forcefully balled them up in one hand and finally, like any good basketball player would, tossed them a good eight feet across the room right into the trashcan.

She wasn't sure what she was going to say to Robert. She had no idea where to start or what question she would ask him first. All she knew was that if they had any chance at being an "us" again, she had to stop this guessing. Come hell or high water, they were going to start talking and listening to each other. And if it was over, at least she would know it was over!

33. PRESENT DAY – AT THE HOTEL

Monique flung the washroom door open and almost ran down the hall to the Leaning Tower of Pisa. With each step, a new confidence grew inside her and a smile of determination started to blossom on her face. Why, why had she been so afraid to talk to her husband? Well, today it all would change. She decided that even if Robert didn't want to speak at her company's event, it would be okay, she would understand and she would do it herself. *Heck,* she thought, *I put that whole talk together in the first place—I know it by heart!*

As she opened the doors to the Leaning Tower of Pisa, she saw everyone was seated and eating. The room had a wonderful serenity to it and matched the mood of Pachelbel's Canon in D Major, which was drifting from the sound system.

"Hey, Monique, over here!" Lou called out to her, waving his hand in the air. "Sorry, but you're eating with us lowlifes." A couple of laughs came from the table.

Monique quickly glanced toward the stage. She couldn't see Robert. 'Good,' she thought, 'he must still be behind the curtain.' She quickly walked over to the table and saw that there were two empty places for her and Robert. She stood behind one of the empty chairs as Lou made the introductions.

"Monique, this is Norman who is...No, no, don't tell me...Ah, yes, the network architect, and Bettina, the...oh my God, what was it? Oh yeah, telecommunications specialist, both at Linkup, and over here we have Metronome's whiz kids, the newly appointed application engineers, Mickey and Minnie...Okay, okay...Manuel and Margarita."

Everyone smiled, waved or said hello to Monique as Lou went

through their names.

"And everyone, this is Monique Sanchez, Elevation's senior and by that I don't mean age. She's actually our chief communications older person...ha ha! Oh, but seriously, our guest speaker today is Monique's husband. He...oh, I can't remember...What did he do again, Monique? Didn't he climb up some little hill?"

"Very funny, Lou. My husband's name is Robert and the hill Mr. Zheng is referring to was Everest," Monique said as she started to turn but was called back.

"Oh my God, really?" Margarita from Metronome exclaimed. "My husband and I both started to rock climb last year. Is he going to eat with us?"

"Of course, I told you we have the most interesting table, didn't I?" Lou chimed in.

"Yes." Monique politely smiled. "And if you'll excuse me, I'll go get him."

"Can't wait!" Margarita called out as Monique turned away from the table.

Monique waved to the occupants, but she had no intention of bringing Robert back to their table. There were too many things she needed to speak to him about now.

She looked up at the stage. Amir was sitting by his table and eating. She felt a little nervous—an excited nervousness. What was she going to say first? What were those magical words that would open the door, which had been shut so tight for so long? She stopped at the bottom of the steps, closed her eyes for a moment to settle her nerves, then opened her eyes and started to make her way...'To begin,' she thought. 'Yes, to begin!'

Monique climbed the stairs, walked onto the stage and pulled the curtain aside, but Robert was not there. She crossed to the other side of the stage but didn't find him there either. Her heart jumped a little.

She turned to Amir who looked up from his lunch and the magazine he was reading.

"Amir, where is Robert?"

Amir wiped a little dressing from his chin as he spoke. "Oh, he said he wanted to get off the stage for a while. I think for quiet."

"How did he do that?"

"I helped him down the stairs."

"Did you see where he went?"

"Oh yes, and don't worry yourself, Miss Monique. You see those doors on the side of the stage? He went in there."

"Where it says staff only? And what's in there?"

"Oh, just a small hallway connecting some rooms, but all the rooms are locked. There's nowhere to go, so he must be still sitting in the hallway there. Would you like me to bring him back up here?"

"No, it's okay. I can go and get him. Thanks, Amir."

Amir's easy going demeanor calmed her heart. Monique crossed the stage but when she was halfway down the steps, Greg stopped her.

"Ah, Monique, I was looking for you. Oh, you look different. Did you change your hair?"

Monique touched her hair. She felt a little self-conscious and wondered if her face still showed signs of crying. "Yes, it—um—it felt too formal, I thought."

"Well, looks good. Okay, a couple of things. First, did you and your husband get a chance to eat?"

"No, I'm just going to get him."

"Great, I just wanted to see if you'd be ready to go at twelve twenty-five?"

Monique looked at her watch. It was five to twelve. She felt a little relieved that she still had about half an hour to at least start to talk to her husband.

"In a half hour?" she asked and Greg nodded with a smile. "Sure, Greg, no problem."

Monique started to walk away but Greg quickly called back to her. "Oh, Monique—"

She stepped down as he walked over to her. He put a hand on her shoulder and spoke in a confidential voice. "Please forgive me, Monique, but I changed your table. You're sitting with Lou now. It's just I noticed some...well, you and your husband seemed a bit—you know...tense. So I thought maybe a little Lou might help."

Oh my God, was it that obvious? Normally Monique would have thought of some kind of excuse for what Greg saw, but at this moment, being inspired by this new sense of purpose, she opened up to her boss in a way she never had before.

"Greg, I'm your senior advisor of communications right? But do you know that I have never even asked my husband what it's like to have no legs? What kind of communication is that?"

Greg let his hand fall off Monique's shoulder. His mouth opened, but no words came out.

"And we don't talk Greg. My husband and I, we simply *don't* talk. There's this huge change happening in our lives and we just pretend it's all going to go back to normal. Can you believe it? We don't ever talk about it!"

There was now the look of terror in Greg's eyes.

"What does this mean, Monique? Why are you telling me this now?

Is there not going to be a presentation?"

"No, I'm so sorry, Greg. Don't worry. I'm just telling you that that was the tension you saw and...and I—Oh God, I'm so sorry, I didn't really need to tell you all that. Please, don't worry, Greg. I mean, look around you; it's going great today, isn't it? People are talking and that's what we wanted, right? So, don't you worry! There will be a presentation. Sorry about all that. Look, please go back and eat."

She looked at her watch. "And don't worry...It's twenty-seven minutes to show time!"

Greg smiled, although he still looked a bit uneasy and perplexed. "Okay, good. Sorry about you and your husband not...um...you know what you said—not talking...so...Well, good, twenty-seven minutes then? Hopefully Mr. Romano from Linkup will have arrived then. Okay, good. Um...I'll come up and do a little introduction before Robert starts, alright?"

"Wonderful." Then Monique did another thing she had never done. She opened her arms, hugged her boss and said, "Great work, Greg. It's wonderful working with a man like you."

But before Greg had a chance to respond, Monique let him go, turned around and hurried to the door on the left side of the stage. As her hand touched the knob, she stopped herself and thought, *What am I going to say to Robert first? There are so many questions!* She laid her head against the door, but in a second, she smiled knowingly as the first question came to her. She leaned against the door, took a deep breath and then opened it.

34. 2 WEEKS AGO – SEEMA'S OFFICE

"Have you ever felt nothing?"

Seema put her pen down and looked at Robert. "What exactly do you mean by nothing?"

"I mean nothing. Being...feeling...void, vacant. Feeling absolutely empty—like there is no reason to think or to even have any thought."

Seema let out a smiled sigh. "Hmmm...you know, Robert, I'm not sure if there really ever is a *nothing* because, even as you describe it, well, it sounds like something. Sounds like you're feeling the absence of something—"

Robert threw his arms up. "—No, please don't! Don't get all linguistic about it. When I said 'nothing' I meant—Ah, you know what? Forget it."

He put his hands to the wheels of his chair to push himself away, but then stopped suddenly. "No! Okay, remember after my last operation...I sat right here. Right here by this very window. And out there was a woman, a woman with a dog and she threw a ball...and that dog ran with all its life to get that ball. Remember? And then he brought it back to that woman and dropped it right in front of her. Remember that?"

Seema nodded with a questioning look.

"That dog had one purpose. And that purpose was for her to throw the ball again so he could chase it—so he could get that ball and give back to her. Remember how he sat there, waiting? The dog's whole body was starving to do it again. He was so excited and filled with a purpose—his purpose to relive that whole experience again, right?"

Seema's whole face smiled. It made her feel an unexpected joy to hear Robert speak so willingly and openly.

280

"Yes, I remember it very well," she said.

"Well, that's the 'nothing' I'm talking about. You see, I've come to understand that...that dog—that dog who is simply chasing that ball—has something I don't. That dog is able to get pleasure from something so simple. I don't have that either! You see, that dog has more purpose, more purpose than I think I'll ever feel again."

Seema's smiled face fell, "But, Robert—"

"No, Seema, don't say it. Please don't! I can't bear to hear about all the things I can still do. I just can't stomach it anymore, okay? It's just...well, all my life it seems...all my life I've been—do you know how many lost souls I have helped? Helped to find a reason, an excitement to do something? Helped them discover a purpose—helped them to simply be happy? To feel that simple thing—that...that reason to exist?"

"I'm sure it has been many, Robert, I'm sure."

"And you know what I've found? Just because I've helped all those people, that doesn't mean it's going to help me, does it?"

Seema suddenly sat up. Her hand went over her mouth. "Do you mean like, do we really listen or follow our own advice?"

"Yeah, but it's deeper than that...more—it's something even more profound than listening to our own advice."

Robert turned his wheelchair away from the window and looked right at Seema. "Like you. You told me when you worked in that prison, you had to leave because you felt, well, I am not sure exactly what you felt, but you said something about how you left that prison job because you thought there were some people you just couldn't rehabilitate, right?"

Seema pulled her chair close to the desk and leaned toward Robert. "And?"

"So you're here now, helping, rehabilitating, working with all sorts of people who lost their arms, legs...lost—"

Robert stopped for a moment, looked away in thought and then continued, "Lost parts of themselves, parts that they'll never ever get back. They will never get it back, no matter how hard *you* try, no matter what Benny Tucci or Seema does, they'll never get their arms or legs or whatever they lost back. It's lost to them forever, right?"

"Yes, but that doesn't mean I don't keep trying to—"

"—Really, Miss Pourshadi? Ask yourself this: if you lost your hands or both your legs and then you came here to this centre, with whatever you lost—do you think that what you do, all the therapy and techniques you employ for all your patients, all the things you say to them—everything Seema knows—would that be enough for you? Would your ways actually *help you?*"

Seema wasn't prepared for the question, so she repeated what

Robert asked. "Lost my hands or my legs?"

She waited for a response but Robert stayed silent.

"Well...Maybe, I...you know, each one of us deals with loss differently, Robert."

"Yeah, we do! But can you answer the question? Could everything you know and do help you—Seema Pourshadi?"

Seema looked down at the desk and blinked nervously as she spoke. "I...I guess it's one of those things that I'll never know unless it actually happens to me."

"But I know, Seema! Not about you, but I know about me!"

Seema was a little confused so she waited a beat and then asked, "Okay...Well, what is it you know, Robert?"

Robert turned around, faced the window again, and spoke without emotion. "Some years ago, I did a workshop and there was this boy. Jake, his name was. Jake didn't want to have anything to do with what I was doing that day. He looked as miserable as a human being could. And Jake had good reason to, because you see, eight months before I met Jake he was drinking a bit much and dove into his friend's pool and broke his neck. And now Jake was going to be in a wheelchair for the rest of his life. Oh and I...I tried everything I could to engage that kid that day. But about halfway through the workshop, Jake started opening up—he was now talking, he was sharing...And near the end of the day, I did this exercise where people had to cross this line I put on the floor. They cross it if they feel or believe they are the answer to something I ask. Well, I asked if anyone, no matter how many people were around them, no matter how many friends they had, if they still felt alone. Well, Jake wheeled himself across the line. Everyone watched him slowly roll his chair...and about ten full seconds of looking at him sitting in that wheelchair on the other side of the line, the whole room, suddenly just crossed over to Jake and some girls hugged him, guys high-fived him and they were all saying 'Don't worry, Jake, we'll make sure you never feel alone again.'"

Robert stopped. Seema wasn't sure it was the end of the story so she added, "Well, that must have felt great—being in that moment—seeing all those students supporting Jake!"

"Yeah, you're right, Miss Pourshadi, I felt great about that moment. I felt so good about what happened. I told my wife and daughter all about it that night at supper. And my daughter actually got up from table and kissed my forehead, telling me how proud she was of her father. And I really...I really felt I helped create a difference in that kid's life. Until...until I heard from the principal the next day. She told me that Jake shot himself with his father's shotgun that night."

Seema gasped, "Oh no!"

"You see, it didn't matter what *I did*, Miss Pourshadi, or what any of those kids did. Jake had lost something and none of us could make it better. We couldn't fix it for him. We couldn't rehabilitate him. We couldn't make him feel—Yes, that's it; we couldn't make him feel like he had any purpose to live. We didn't succeed at giving him enough of a reason to exist."

Seema was speechless. She tightly pulled at her scarf and watched Robert wheel himself away from the window and start going toward the office door. He stopped and turned his wheelchair around, but only halfway, and then, without looking at her, he said, "So you can stop trying now, Seema. You can finally stop trying to give me a reason."

35. PRESENT DAY – AT THE HOTEL

Monique's new sense of purpose had her flying towards the door at the side of the stage. She flung the door open, fully expecting to see Robert sitting in the hallway. But he was not behind the door.

It was just a small, empty hallway about twenty-five feet long. There were three doors. One door was at the end of the hallway and the other two were on the right, side by side, connected to the stage.

She went to the first door and again she took a breath and prepared a smile to greet her husband. But as she turned the doorknob, it wouldn't budge. It was locked. She quickly put her hand on the next doorknob, still ready and smiling, but it was locked as well.

The doors being locked made her feel a little anxious and she quickly walked the ten feet to the door at the end of the hall. She didn't pause to take a breath or to smile this time and just quickly grabbed the knob, only to find it locked as well.

She spoke in a half-whisper as she knocked on the door. "Robert? Bobby, are you in there?" She waited and listened, but there was no response. She knocked on the door again and spoke a little louder.

"Bobby...Bobby, are you in there?" Nothing! She moved back to the other two doors. This time knocking louder and speaking in a full voice.

"Bobby, are you in there? Please, if you are, open the door."

She knocked on each door and repeated, "Bobby, please...please...Bobby, if you're in there, please open the door. I'm sorry about what I said! Please come out. We need to talk."

Monique started to feel a little panicked but quickly calmed herself, thinking maybe this wasn't where Amir said Robert was. So, she walked as fast as she could back out to the front of the stage and got Amir's attention by waving her hands at him.

Amir left his table and came down to the front of the stage. "What is it, Miss Monique?"

"Robert, he's not in there."

"Are you sure?"

"Yes, I checked. And all the doors in there are locked. Are you sure he didn't come back out?"

"No, I think I would have seen him, Miss Monique."

"Could he have gone into one of those rooms back there?"

"I doubt it, I was back there this morning and I am sure I locked the rooms."

"Well, maybe one was opened and he went in and locked himself inside."

"Didn't you knock on the door to see if he was in there?"

Monique lied and said, "No, sorry, I just checked the door."

"Okay, I have the keys to the two rooms along the stage, please let me check the music first and I'll come down with you and see."

Amir went back to his table and Monique looked out into the room, scanning every table, but Robert was not there. When Lou caught her eye, he waved and held up a full fork of steak to her in an obvious gesture of showing her what she was missing. He then pointed at the empty chairs beside him. She smiled tightly and held up her index finger to indicate she needed to do something else first.

Amir tapped her on the shoulder, which made her jump. He leaped down from the stage and stood beside her. "Okay, Miss Monique. Come, let's check."

She followed Amir, who was jingling the keys as he walked. "I don't know why he would go into these rooms even if they were open. It's just a lot of sound equipment and lights. And the other is just filled with extra chairs and tables."

"I don't know, maybe he just wandered inside and got locked in?" Monique was becoming more and more anxious and was starting to imagine why Robert would lock himself in a room and not answer.

Amir slid the key in the lock and opened the first door. It was pitch back.

"Ah, I don't know why they put the light switch behind the door!" Amir said as he walked behind the door and switched the light on.

Bright white, fluorescent lights emblazoned the room.

Monique was now breathing short quick breaths as she looked in the room. It wasn't very large and had two tables that were covered in monitors, mixing boards and microphones. Six speakers were stacked on top of each other and coils of extension cords hung on the walls. Monique felt a little momentary relief.

"Well, he's not in here, Miss Monique."

Monique's looked at the corner of the room where a couple of huge signs were leaning against some lecterns. *High enough to hide a man in a wheelchair*, she thought to herself.

"What's behind there?" she asked Amir.

Amir laughed, "Unless your husband's playing a game of hide and seek, he won't be over there." But as he spoke, he saw that Monique was not smiling. "But, okay, I will look. Just need to move some of these lights first."

Amir moved aside a couple of long black light fixtures that were in the way and then took a couple of steps and looked behind the signs. As Monique watched, she found herself holding her breath. Amir reached the signs and pulled them forward so Monique could see there was nothing behind them.

"Thank you, Amir. I'm—" She stopped as she didn't know what to say next.

Amir looked at her and smiled politely, but as he walked back towards the open door, he had to stop and ask her, "Miss Monique, I do not want to pry, but is everything all right?"

"Yes, yes, Amir. Thank you. It's just—" Once again she couldn't fill her sentence with any more words.

"Miss Monique." Amir's friendly happy voice was replaced with a concerned tone. "Forgive me, but it's just...we are looking for your husband behind a sign in a locked room?"

Monique reacted to the bare facts of what Amir had just said, as if someone had just thrown a bucket full of freezing water in her face. "I'm sorry, Amir, no, it's not all right. It hasn't been all right for a long time. I'm looking for my husband here because...because he doesn't want to be here today. To be honest with you, I've been so worried about him because I don't think he wants to be anywhere today!"

Amir put his hand on Monique's arm and squeezed it gently. "How long has it been since his accident?"

Monique didn't answer. She just reached out to Amir's hand on her arm and clutched it.

"How long has it been since he lost his legs? Maybe he just needs—"

"You don't know Robert, Amir...the man he is...All the things he has done in his life. This just *isn't him*. He's seen people die right in front of him and...He's helped so many people in situations—hopeless situations! He's just...the most positive, optimistic man I know!"

"Yes, yes, I'm sure he *still* is. Maybe he just needs a little more time to find his way...his way back to being that positive man."

"No, Amir, my fear is that he has worked himself onto this ledge and now there is no turning back."

"I'm sorry, I don't understand. What *ledge* do you mean?"

"He used to warn me about climbers that climb themselves into places where there is no return. Oh, I'm sorry—it's just I've never seen Robert give up on anything or anyone. But it's like now—he's just stopped. It's like he's stuck somewhere and can't find the way back. He never talks anymore and I actually have to ask the people at the rehabilitation centre how he is doing. They told me he has these new legs but he shows no interest in trying them. And that they can do nothing more until he starts trying. But he doesn't try any more! That's why I was praying that this talk might help...I thought maybe talking about this great love of his..."

"Well, maybe your husband is fearful of talking in front of strangers."

"No, Amir, no. He has been doing for years—working with strangers, helping them in their lives. Many people call him—the healer, the hope-giver. This just isn't him!"

The look on Amir's face grew sullen and serious. "And forgive me for asking but...are we looking for him back here behind a sign because you think your husband might want to—?" It was Amir's turn to not know how to finish his sentence.

"I don't know what I know anymore! It's just that—Two months ago there were some break-ins around our neighbourhood and Robert told me he was worried about being able to protect us and so he bought a gun."

"Oh dear!" Amir groaned.

"Remember when you were helping him up the stairs and that brown leather bag dropped on the floor? Remember how angry he got when you went to pick it up? He won't let anyone touch it." Monique waited a beat. She didn't want to say it out loud. She did everything she could to erase these thoughts. These were the words she tried painfully to burn out of her mind. But it seemed they could no longer be hidden and so, finally, they were spoken...

"I think he has a gun in there."

"Oh my! Oh my!" Amir put his hand in his pocket and pulled out the keys. "Come, let's check the other room."

Amir didn't bother to close the first door before rushing to open the next one. His hands were a bit nervous as he fit the key in the lock. Once again, the room was dark and he quickly went behind the door and switched on the light. The room was stacked with chairs and tables all along one side of the room. Monique stepped into the room and it was obvious that Robert was not in there.

"He is not here," Amir said. Then they both jumped a little as Monique's cell phone started to ring inside her purse. They looked at each other in relief as Monique pulled the phone out. She looked at the number that was calling and said, "Oh, thank God!"

"Is it your husband?"

"No, it's my daughter. Excuse me." Monique clicked on the phone, "Jen, Jen, I've been trying to call you."

"Mom, where have you been? I've been leaving messages all morning."

"I know. I had the phone off. I'm just glad you're safe and—"

"Mom, where are you?"

"Honey, I told you last night, I'm at the hotel for the conference today."

"Yeah, Mom, I know, but where are you and Daddy now? I'm here looking for you."

"*What?*"

"Mom, I'm at the hotel."

"What? You're here? Why, honey...What on earth are you doing here?"

"Mom, please just tell me where you are. I'm in the Leaning Tower of Pisa room now and I'm standing in front of stage. Where are you and Daddy?"

"Just wait there, baby. I'll see you in a moment—Just don't move, I'm coming, okay?"

"Okay, Mom. Bye."

$36.$ 2 WEEKS AGO – SEEMA'S OFFICE

Seema was speechless. She tightly pulled at her scarf and watched Robert wheel himself away from the window and start going towards the office door. He stopped and turned his wheelchair around, but only halfway. Then, without looking at her, he said, "So you can stop trying now, Seema. You can finally stop trying to give me a reason."

"No, wait, Robert!" Seema shot up from behind her desk and started to plead with him. "Please, let's talk about this."

Robert calmly turned his wheelchair to face her. "I thought we just did that? Didn't we just talk?"

"No, that wasn't a talk; you just told me things. And if it's true you feel no reason or no purpose to...well, then I think we have to talk now, Robert." Robert looked blankly at Seema. His eerie calmness disturbed her greatly. "Please, Robert, please. Can you stay for a little bit? Let's discuss this."

"Discuss what? That all the things I've done in my life to help others don't seem to help me?"

"But that was just one boy, you can't hope to—"

"It's not about Jake. It's just—It's like I've spent all this energy, all this time, so much of my life reaching out, helping others and now when I need it—Now when I'm so desperately searching for it, well, now it...it just doesn't seem to help me!"

"Then maybe it's time for you...to let us help."

"You? I'm sorry, I didn't mean for that to sound cruel. But, do you know every day I pass through these doors and I look at those words written on the door, 'Rehabilitation Centre.' And, no matter where I look, keep seeing that word '*rehabilitate*' *on* every sign and pamphlet you have here.

I see that word so...so many times every single day. And do you know what? It's funny—because I realized I don't even know what it means! That's right! I'm coming here every day to be rehabilitated and I don't even know what that means. Do you know what that word means?"

"Well, Robert, sometimes words—"

"No, please don't do that. Do you know what *that* word means, Seema?"

"Well, um...Rehabilitation is a treatment designed to facilitate the process of recovery."

"Yeah, yeah...Okay. Do you know what I did? I looked it up! Do you know what it says in the dictionary about that word? It says: to restore someone's *useful* place in society."

"Yes, Robert. Useful! That's why I like the word. I like to look at the word as re-habit-ing. Helping someone change to discover what new habits they need in order to be useful."

"Well, I can't find it!"

"Find what? What is it you can't—"

"I can't find that useful place anymore!"

"You realize, Robert, many—"

Robert interrupted Seema, "I went through my journal."

"Your journal? I thought you told me that—"

"Yeah, I lied. I know you asked me if I kept one and I said I didn't. But I did...I kept one for many years."

"And?"

"You said sometimes when we look back to some of the things we wrote in the past that maybe—Oh, damn it! You know what? I believed you! I did. I really, really thought it would be in there. I did!"

"What would?"

"An answer."

"Answer to what?"

"Something. *Anything!* That's my life in there! I wrote about it. I wrote about *everything* I've done, that I said or thought...I really was thinking it would help me now."

"So reading your journal—"

"It didn't do a thing! I still feel this way. Do you know how hard it is to feel that? After all the things I did to help those kids. And some of them—their lives, I mean some...they were so lost, so hurt, so...broken...and so close to being...being...lost forever. And...I just thought I could find it in there."

"What did you find?"

"That it means nothing to me now."

"What, Robert? What means nothing to you?"

"My life! *My whole goddamn life!*"

"Robert, you may feel that now, but—"

"No! Don't you get it? I'm that kite."

"What kite?"

"That kite! That kid's kite we saw flying around that day—the one that's crashed, all mangled. Remember? Remember when we talked about what you would do after it got all wrecked up? And...that I said, sometimes it's better to just leave it? Remember? Don't try to fix it—just leave it there. It can't be fixed...so just walk away!"

"But those kids, Robert, those ones you said were almost lost forever. They were broken but you didn't walk away from them, did you?"

"No. I didn't! But I looked in my journal and I saw...look, I know I was there with them along the way. But did I really help them? No. Somehow they all...they all were able to find this...this something. Like somehow they all had this moment and this moment just changed everything for them. And me, what did I do for them? Well, I wasn't *their* moment. Don't get me wrong, Seema, I know, really I do...I know I helped them...even like you are trying to help me. But they all found this moment—How? This moment it just came to them, like it was some kind of place they suddenly knew they had to get to. Like...like some kind of line that they all crossed over—and they got there—all because of that moment."

"And what do you think that moment was, Robert."

"I don't know...Obviously I haven't found it."

"Or maybe it hasn't found you."

37. PRESENT DAY – AT THE HOTEL

Monique clicked off the phone. *Jenny's here! Thank God.* She hadn't realized how much she needed her daughter at that moment. She was mid-way through bolting to the door to see Jenny when she stopped herself.

"That door, Amir, at the end of the hall, what is that?"

"That's the back entrance to the Taj Mahal room." Amir walked to the door and checked the doorknob. It wouldn't budge. "It's locked and I don't have a key for it, only the front desk does. They have it. But it was locked this morning, so Mr. Robert could not have gone in there."

Monique looked up. "Oh, please! Where is he?"

Amir put his hand on Monique's shoulder. "Come, let's go to the front desk. Someone is sure to have seen him. How far could a man in a wheelchair have gone?"

That question echoed in Monique's head as they walked back down the hall and into the Leaning Tower of Pisa room. *How far? How far? How far could he go?*

Monique saw Jenny the moment she opened the door. Jenny's back was to her but she could see she was with a young man, a woman and a little child.

"There he is! There he is, Mommy. I see him, Mommy. There's *Daddy!*" Claire said, jumping up and down in excitement.

"Okay, honey, come on. Let's go and surprise Daddy." Claire ran between the tables towards her father, who was sitting at a table in the middle of the room and talking to Greg.

"I better go too before she knocks something over. Thanks for sharing the cab with us. And really it was wonderful that we were both coming here today!" Claire's mom turned back to Jenny and Kyle. "Oh, and thank you for keeping my Claire so occupied on the plane. She hasn't seen her father for two weeks and she was so excited that I thought she might try to jump out of the plane! Anyway, thanks for reading to her. I didn't hear too much but from what I did hear, your father sounds like quite a man and we are really looking forward to hearing him speak today. Okay...well, bye."

"Bye," Kyle and Jenny said, just as Monique reached them

"Jenny? Jenny, what are you doing here?" Monique opened her arms and pulled her daughter tightly to her. "Oh, baby, it's so great to see you!" Just as Monique's head rested beside Jenny's, she whispered, "But what are you doing here?"

Jenny pulled out of the hug and put her hands on her mom's shoulders. "I left you messages all morning, Mom. Dad sent me his journal." She then pulled it out of her purse to show her mother.

"I can't believe he did *that!*" Monique looked at the worn book in Jenny's hand. Monique knew full well about Robert's promise to his daughter. Jenny had begged countless times to read it, but Robert's comment was always the same. The book was her inheritance. 'You'll get to read it when I'm gone,' he would say. "Oh my God, honey, that must have scared you."

"Why wouldn't you answer your phone, Mom? I got so worried. I had to come. I called everywhere, Mom. Why did he give this to me today? *Now*, Mom? So when I couldn't reach you, I just...well, I just had to come. Where is he? Where's Daddy?"

Amir, sensing a scene was about to erupt, tapped Monique on the shoulder and quietly said, "Come, let's go out into the hallway, okay, Miss Monique?"

"Yeah, that's a good idea. Come on, Jenny." Monique put her arm around her daughter and they started out the door. Kyle walked closely behind.

Jenny looked terribly worried as they walked out. *Why is no one answering where my father is?*

The hotel hallway was quite empty. Monique looked up and down the hall for any sign of Robert. Then she immediately turned towards the wall to speak privately to Jenny.

"Jenny, this is Amir and—" Monique then noticed Kyle standing with them. "I'm sorry, can I help you?"

Before Kyle could open his mouth to speak, Jenny quickly grabbed him by the arm and pulled him into their little circle along the wall. "Mom, this is Kyle. Kyle, this is my mom. Kyle's with me, Mom."

Kyle opened his hand to greet Monique but was interrupted by Jenny's question to her mom. "What's happening, Mom? Where is Daddy?"

Amir interjected, "I am sorry, Miss Monique, please excuse me. It's better you speak to your daughter first. I will go to the front desk and ask for the key to look in that room." Amir nodded politely and hurried down the hallway towards the front desk.

"Jenny, I went to the washroom about half an hour ago and when I got back, your father was missing."

"*Missing?*" Jenny almost yelled out. "Missing, Mom?"

"I'm sorry, I didn't mean missing. I meant, he left and we just don't know where he went. Apparently, when I was in the washroom Amir told me that he wanted to get off the stage and he went into the back hallway behind the stage to be alone."

"Well, come on, let's go and look for him."

"We did, Jenny. He's not there."

"Does he have his cell?"

"No, Jen, you know he hasn't used that for months."

"Maybe he went home, Mom."

"*How?* He can't drive."

"This isn't like him, Mom. He wouldn't just take off. Something's wrong with Daddy."

Monique put her hand on her daughter's head and stroked it. "I know, baby, I know."

Kyle spoke for the first time, "Maybe he took a cab, Mrs. Sanchez."

"Well, that's true, he could have—No, his wheelchair isn't collapsible. Did you see an empty wheelchair when you came into the hotel?"

"Well, we weren't really looking for that when we got here, but let me go and check in the front of the hotel, okay?" Kyle shot down the hallway.

Mother and daughter stood there alone.

"Oh, Mom, where is he?" Jenny hugged her mom tight. "I'm scared, Mom. Why would Daddy send me his journal?"

"I don't know, baby, I really don't know..."

Amir came back running and was a bit out of breath. "No one at the front desk has seen Mr. Robert pass by but I have the key for that other room. Come, let's go back in."

The three of them walked back into the Leaning Tower of Pisa.

"One second, I must change the music." Almost without making a full stop, Amir ran up the steps, went behind his desk, quickly pushed a couple of buttons and then leaped off the front of the stage and walked to the door leading to the rooms off the stage. Monique and Jenny followed him.

As Amir entered the hallway, he walked directly to the door at the end of the hallway that led to the room called the Taj Mahal. Monique and Jenny followed closely behind.

"Why would my dad come here?" Jenny asked Amir as he put the key into the lock.

Amir looked sheepish as he turned back to them. "I am so sorry, this is my fault. He said he wanted to get off the stage for a while. I thought he just wanted to move about. And when I saw him come in this hallway—well, I...I just didn't think anything of it. There was nowhere for him to go. The doors were locked. I thought maybe he just needed some time alone. I am sorry, I should have told him not to come in here."

"It's okay, Amir. It's not your fault. Please just open the door," Monique said.

The door opened and the three of them walked into the Taj Mahal.

Despite feeling nervous and apprehensive, both mother and daughter were immediately struck by the warm magical presence of the Taj Mahal and spoke in unison, "This is *beautiful!*"

Even though the lights were off, the sun brightly lighted the room. The radiant yellow beams that came through the huge windows bounced everywhere. They reflected off the glass chandeliers, which created hundreds of tiny rainbows that seem to happily dance in every direction around the room. The richness of the red carpet and the beautiful green-hedged gardens outside the windows gave the feeling of walking into a castle.

The three of them quickly scanned the room. Although the tables and chairs were all set up, they were without tablecloths.

"Your father is not here." Amir stated the obvious.

Jenny noticed a Starbucks coffee cup sitting alone on a table with one chair pulled away.

"What's this?" she asked as she walked to the table. "And look, someone was definitely sitting here."

"More than likely a cleaner left it behind," Amir said.

"No, it's still warm," Jenny said, picking up the cup. "Mom, did Dad have a coffee?"

"No, I don't think so. Come on, Jenny, he's not here," Monique said as she touched her daughter's arm.

"Well, someone was." Jenny was still hopeful as she looked around the beautiful room.

The three of them left the same way they came. Amir followed behind and locked the door to the Taj Mahal. Jenny asked about the other two rooms. Amir patiently told her they had already checked and her father was not in there...

The moment they entered back into the Leaning Tower of Pisa, they saw Greg standing with Claire, her parents and a man at front of the stage.

"Ah, there she is!" Greg pointed at Monique. "Mrs. Sanchez!" Greg called out to her. Monique tried her best to smile, grabbed her daughter's hand and squeezed it for a little strength as she approached the group.

"And here's the face behind today's magnificent event, Monique Sanchez! And, oh my gosh, Jenny? We haven't seen you at the office for years. It's wonderful you came to hear your father speak today!"

It was Jenny's turn to squeeze her mother's hand now as she nodded her head in reply to Greg. Amir caught Monique's eyes and made a gesture with the key to her, signaling that he was going to return the key and he would be right back.

"And Monique, our late arrival is happily here. Mario Romano, as you know, is the CEO of Linkup."

"Pleased to meet you both," Mr. Romano said as he extended his hand to Monique first. Monique had to let go of Jenny's hand to shake his.

"I'm sorry about the mix up and that you missed your flight this morning, Mr. Romano, but it's great you're here now," Monique said.

The door swung open and Kyle came running in. "I checked the front, no wheelchair. And I asked all the front office staff if anyone saw him but no one had. I asked everybody and no one noticed anyone in a wheelchair going out the front door." Kyle stopped for a brief second to catch some air. "So he probably hasn't left the hotel. But has anyone even checked the washrooms for him?"

"Oh my God!" Monique hit herself on the forehead. "I didn't even think of that."

"I'm sorry, who are we looking for?" Panic and confusion was in Greg's voice. It was only ten minutes ago that Monique had told him about how she and her husband never spoke.

"Oh yes, I'm sorry, we're just looking for Robert," Monique explained. "You see, Mr. Romano, my husband left the stage for a moment to ah...go to the washroom...and so we are just trying to locate him."

What! Kyle thought. He was still out of breath and gave Jenny a disbelieving look. *Have I really been running in such a panic for no reason?*

"Yeah, excuse us," Jenny said, immediately taking Kyle's arm and swinging him about face. As they started walking out of the Leaning Tower of Pisa room, she called back to her mother, "We'll go and find him, Mom."

"Can I come too?" Claire called out. Jenny and Kyle stopped and looked back and before they could reply, Monique quickly and firmly said,

"No!" She couldn't shake the horrible image of what they might find. Everyone looked a bit taken back by Monique's reaction to little Claire, but Jenny quickly stopped and covered for her mother's hostile reaction.

"No, Claire, *you* have to stay here and find us the best seats to watch from, okay?"

Everyone looked at the little girl until she simply said, "Okay, Jenny."

"Well, great!" Greg smiled but then gave Monique a steely look. "We're all looking forward to hearing that better half of yours, Monique, and we start in ten minutes."

Monique saw Greg's serious look and smiled back. "Oh, don't worry, Greg. And nice meeting you, Mr. Romano."

"All right, please let us three go over the final presentation," Greg said to Mr. Romano and Claire's dad. He then looked at Monique with a pleading look. "And don't forget, ten minutes, Monique."

Monique watched the three of them walk up on the stage and go to the back where there was another table filled with handouts and gifts that they were going to give out to everyone at the end of the day. She then surveyed the room once more. Perhaps Robert was sitting at a table eating. But there was no sign of him, only the sound of happy, carefree people eating desserts and sipping their coffee and tea and Elton John singing, "Can you feel the love tonight?"

Monique had never doubted this day would be good for Robert, but seeing the three presidents together jarred something in her. That meeting when they went over all the possible speakers. The newspapers had just announced the school's initiative with Robert—Mt. Everest and the students he would be taking. And it was at that meeting that Lou asked her how he was doing with all those "mountain virgins." It had been that comment that gave Greg the idea that maybe the best speaker would be someone connected to the company. Someone, who was doing something new, something ground breaking. Robert certainly fit the bill. His idea of bringing some at-risk students to Mt. Everest and filming their journey for thousands of kids back home definitely sounded like something original and courageous.

Oh my God, what have I done? she thought. *We have never once spoke about that journey after he got hurt. Never! He has never even mentioned anything about Troy, Nancy or Philip. And now...now I'm asking him to do a presentation on it? My God, no wonders he's not—*

Amir interrupted her thoughts. "I have asked the security to check the building and see if anyone has seen your husband, Miss Monique. They are looking and will get back to me." Amir looked up on the stage and saw the three bosses talking. "Oh, I'm sorry, but I have to get back up there.

The security chief is Alex Lattimer. You can contact him at the front desk. I'm sorry I let him go in there. Miss Monique, I'm so sorry."

"It's okay, Amir. Thank you for helping." Suddenly, she noticed Jenny's head poking around the door beckoning her to come. "Okay, Amir. I have to go."

"Good luck, Miss Monique...and God bless...God bless." Amir voiced trailed off as he watched Monique walk as fast as she could towards the door. Kyle and Jenny greeted her with anxious looks.

"Mom," Jenny's voice sounded ominous. "Mom, we checked the washrooms. He wasn't in there, but—" Jenny stopped, almost collapsing into tears.

"What? What?" Monique asked worriedly.

Kyle put his hand on Jenny's shoulder as he spoke. "It's okay, Jen. It's just a locked washroom door."

"What...*what* door is locked? What is it?" Monique started to panic.

Jenny started frantically, "There's a handicap washroom down the hall. It's locked. We kept knocking and knocking on the door but never got an answer. What if—what if Daddy's in there?"

"Did you ask someone to check it?" Monique questioned.

"No, not yet, Mrs. Sanchez. We were just going to get a janitor or someone to open it," Kyle said.

"Please, Kyle, go to the front desk and ask someone to check it. Come on, Jenny, show me this washroom."

Kyle ran in the opposite direction while Jenny and Monique hurried about two hundred feet down the hall. When they got to the door, Jenny was too frightened to touch the door. She just pointed at the door with the handicap sign. "There—in there."

Monique looked hard at the symbol on the door. She stared at it, as if it was the first time she had ever seen it. She had probably seen that symbol a million times but she never really took much notice of it: it was a man in a wheelchair. And then it hit her. She had been so busy trying to change everything in the house for him, yet she had never once asked him how he felt—being the man in the symbol. *What does he think when he sees that now? Does he think that's him? That sign is him now?*

Monique turned the door handle. It didn't budge. She then knocked firmly on the door three times. Nothing!

Jenny then came beside her mother, started knocking on the door and calling inside. "Daddy, Daddy. Please, if you're in there, say something!" She knocked harder and more furiously. "Daddy, please just come out." Monique grabbed her daughter's hands to stop her from knocking.

"No, Mom, stop it! *Stop it!* I know he's in there." Jenny pulled away from her mother and pounded the door. "Dad, come on, open the door! We want to talk to you."

Monique pushed herself in front of Jenny and held both of her daughter's arms back.

"Baby, *stop!* Stop it! It's okay, Jenny. It's okay. He's probably not even in there."

Jenny threw her mother's hands off her.

"Why did you have to do this, Mom? Why? Daddy wasn't ready. You knew he didn't want to talk, you knew he didn't want to talk about that...that mountain anymore."

"Jenny, that's not true...Those mountains were a big part of your father's life. He loved talking about them. I did this because I thought this might help your—"

"*Help him*, Mom? Help him? Why would he want to talk about something he can't do anymore?"

"Honey, please." Monique tried to reach out to Jenny, but her daughter held her arms up preventing her mother from touching her. Monique stopped cold and quietly listened as her daughter opened another door—a door that no one in their family had yet dared to open and speak about because no one seemed to have the courage to speak about what was inside.

"Why would he want to talk about something that destroyed his life, Mom?"

"Don't say that! His life isn't destroyed, Jen."

"How do you think he feels every time he looks at those photos, Mom? And he sees himself with his legs, doing all those things? Imagine it, what he thinks, looking at all those pictures of himself with his legs, Mom? *Legs!* Would you want to be reminded of what you used to be but aren't anymore? He must...he must absolutely hate it."

Jenny hit the door and shouted, "Just like I hate it! I hate those mountains...I hate you! Every time he'd go to those...those goddamn mountains, he was never with us—Never with us, Mom...Why? Why did Daddy have to go there?"

Jenny sank to her knees, still feebly hitting the door and crying. "Why would he want to talk about it, Mom? He never wants to talk about anything...anymore. But me and Daddy—me and Daddy, we used to talk about everything...and now—now we..."

Jenny slid all the way down to the floor with her head leaning against the bathroom door. She turned to her mother. "Daddy never talks to me anymore."

Monique knelt down beside her daughter and put her hand on Jenny's face to brush away her tears.

"Oh, my darling girl. I'm sorry. I'm so sorry. Daddy doesn't talk to me either. But, Jen, it's...it's...it's my fault, baby. I never talked to him. Not once did I ever ask him to see his legs. Nothing—because...well, because…"

"No, Mom, it's my fault too. You know I never even told him about Kyle because...because I thought maybe he didn't want to hear anything new or anything happy. We don't talk¡—I don't tell him anything. I feel all I do is...all I do is try not to do anything to upset Daddy."

"Me too, baby, me too—"

Kyle's excited voice filled the hallway. "Jenny, it's *your dad!* Jenny, quick! Mrs. Sanchez, come quick—Hurry!"

Jenny sprang to her feet. The moment she bent over to help her mother stand up, the red journal fell out of her purse and onto the floor. Jenny snatched it from the floor as the two of them ran towards Kyle. There was only one entry left to read: Robert's last entry. He wrote it at breakfast time, just hours before he was to be buried under six stories of snow and ice, just two hours before the one moment that would change the course of his life forever.

38. SIX MONTHS AGO – MT. EVEREST

May 19ᵗʰ, 2012, 8 am breakfast, last day at base camp before the journey home!!!

Dearest Love,

Ahhh, the sun has just peeked over Lola—and like someone just turned on the lights—the darkness has just vanished! It's pretty cold this morning. The three amigos—as they called themselves—in last night's webisode—they are truly in full bloom this morning. Phil's been up for hours getting the live-feed all set up and ready. They are really looking forward to seeing the Khumbu Icefall up close. We'll probably just go to the first ladder, I think, and then turn back. I love the feeling these kids give me: seeing everything new through their eyes. Yes, it's going to be fun!

Ang had his old cassette player blaring as we came into the food tent this morning, playing this old song from the eighties...Joe Cocker and someone else, not sure of her name...The three amigos asked him to play it over and over as they tried to learn the words, singing along with it—they thought they might sing it to open today's webisode this morning. The words are something about "mountains being in the way, so we must take it step by step..." Oh, Nancy just looked over my shoulder, and read what I wrote—she tells me the song's called "Up Where We Belong."

It's so weird, that it's that title, because of what I dreamt last night...I've often told you about how my dreams up here are usually so vivid and real that they feel as if I'm actually living them.

Well, last night...whoa, I had the strangest of dreams...

I was climbing and I was right near the top. I was hanging on this cliff. I just had to do one last pull up to reach the summit. And it was so dark and so so damn cold. But my hands, which were holding on to the top of the ledge, well, they were becoming warm. It looked as if the sun was coming up and—oh, I was so cold that I just couldn't wait to pull myself up over that ledge to feel its warmth. But as I tried to force myself up over the ledge, my backpack suddenly got heavier. And then it started to move! Bouncing around on my back—And then it started to get really heavy and it felt as if something inside was trying to yank me down, threatening to pull me off the cliff and throw me off the mountain. The weight of it became so unbearable that I needed to do something before I fell, so I pulled out my knife and was just about to cut it from my shoulders...and that's when I heard this voice come from the top. It kept asking me questions—asking me...why did I pack so much? And so, I yelled, "I didn't," saying that, "the pack, it was almost empty..." Then it asked me, "Don't you know what you're carrying?" I said yes, of course—I always do...and then it asked me, "So why don't you know this time?" I kept yelling, "Yes, I do, I know exactly what's in there!" Anyway, we went on arguing, and then I finally screamed out, "Okay, I'll show you what's in there!"

So, I dropped the knife and with my last ounce of strength, I took the backpack off and threw it up on top. And then, as I pulled myself over the ledge. Well, at first, I couldn't see anything because the sun was so strong in my eyes. But after I rubbed them—then, I saw that I had just pulled myself up onto a subway platform! And you—you were sitting there—sitting on a bench. It looked like that same subway bench we visit every year for our anniversary. But you didn't look at me. You were just sitting there reading a book out loud. It was that book about how if we want something enough, then the universe will help to bring it to us (remember that book?). And then, you looked at me and asked me to open my backpack to show you what I was carrying.

So, I unbutton the top flap and suddenly, all these little kids come running out—they're all different colours and sizes. They just kept coming out of the backpack, tons of them. It didn't stop. They were laughing, singing, doing cartwheels...and then you said that same thing you tell me every year when we visit that subway bench on our anniversary. "That's why I love you, Roberto...because being with you always makes me feel more alive." Then we sat there laughing even louder because now—more things are running out of my back pack...not just kids anymore, but animals and even people out of movies and books...our friends, family...it was the weirdest...yet happiest dream I've ever had!

And so today, as I sit here and listen to the three amigos singing, "Up where we belong," and the sun is coming up, well, my love, I guess I do believe dreams can be lived!

Wow, what a perfect start to our last day!

Okay, I better go...So imagine me, then—up where we belong—you and me, sitting beside each other on that bench and me telling you...I love you too!

39. PRESENT DAY – AT THE HOTEL

This death we live?

He looked up and watched Monique, holding her mouth, run down the steps and push her way through the doors to get out of the Leaning Tower of Pisa. And after Lou had asked Amir to turn up the music, Amir helped Robert down off the stage.

Down on the floor, he had no idea where to go. Should he follow Monique? He rolled three strides and then stopped. 'No,' he thought, 'just to hurt her more?' He looked up into the lively room filled with people, yet Robert felt all alone. He was now truly lost. He turned around completely and passed through the door on the opposite side of the stage. The door that said 'For Staff Only'. Robert wheeled his way into the hallway. There were only three doors. First, he tried to open the door nearest to him, but it was locked. The next door was locked as well. One door was left, twenty feet further down, at the end of the hallway. As he wheeled down the corridor, all he could think about was what Monique had just said to him.

"This death we live?"

A furious anger began to burn deep inside him. *What the hell does she know about what I am living?*

And then telling him how she felt that day when she had heard that he was dead up on Everest and how she and Jenny had to live with that pain...The fire of his anger now really started to rage within him.

Well, that was only one day of pain and suffering she had to go through, but what about me? he thought. *I have to live with this for the rest of my life.* "Does she realize that? Does anyone see that? I have to *be this* for the rest of my life?!"

He reached to open the last door. Locked. And then he heard Monique's voice again saying how it didn't matter anymore because now she knows *he is dead.* He tried the door again, but this time he tugged at it a little more vigorously. He was now pulling at the door with both hands, as if he wanted to rip it from its moorings.

Dead? He was now actually yelling it out loud. "Dead?" He didn't care if anyone heard now. He started banging on the door, finally letting out the flames of anger that raged deep within. "Maybe you'd feel dead too if this had happened to you," he wailed at the door, attacking it with every ounce of energy he had.

"I...I didn't ask for this! Maybe you'd feel dead too if..." He kept banging on the door, yelling with all his might. "*I DON'T DESERVE THIS!* Goddamn it!...Everybody's always 'Oh, Roberto, you can do it. If anyone can, Roberto can.' Well, I can't!!! I just want to be...I just want to be..."

Robert's voice and fiery rage started to hollow out, shifting into something like the cries of a child who has always felt left out. With each word spoken, the child's pain became more pronounced.

"Why doesn't anybody ever mention all the things I can never do again? Why don't you talk about that? Oh, Roberto can do it...he can do it...he can be...Yeah? Be what?!!! *THIS?!!!*"

He reached back and with all his might, he pounded the door one more time. "Who the hell is this anyway?!"

He suddenly stopped.

Slowly, he dropped his hands to the stumps at the end of his knees, delicately touching them as if he had unearthed a rare and precious artifact and didn't want to break it.

"This death we live? How could she say that? How *could* she?" His voice was now barely audible. Robert let out such a deep aching sigh that it caused his whole body to sag onto his thighs. He reached behind and roughly rubbed his hands on his back. When his fingers reached the base of his spine, he grimaced in pain. It had been sore and tender ever since he'd tried on his third set of prostheses and he fell repeatedly. Two nights ago, Monique had seen him trying to rub his back and had offered to do it for him, but he turned away from her, saying he was fine. *Fine?*

His face started to twitch and his mouth began to tremble. Fine? *When the hell did every word out of my mouth become a lie?* He felt that twitch again. Robert was so used to fighting against this beast of emotion. So many times since the accident, it had tried to claw its way to the surface, but he wouldn't let it out. He did what he always had done. He arched his head up, struggled to fill his lungs with enough air to calm himself—calm the beast of tears, and keep it from freeing itself.

But he couldn't shake the sight of Monique's face just moments ago when she spoke those words. "*And now I know you are dead.*" His wife, his love, his soul's partner in life—the woman who always said the reason she loved him was because, "when I'm with you I feel more alive,"—now she spoke of *this death they live!*

The beast was getting stronger than ever. He tried to hang on. He took in another huge lungful of air but it didn't seem to take. There was a breach in his armour. The beast was fiercely fighting back this time and he could feel it climbing ever closer to escape. Robert's chest started to heave. Every vein in his neck was bulging as he struggled for enough air to hold the creature inside. He fought with all his might, again arching his head to fill his lungs. "I can't cry. I can't cry," he said. He knew that this beast would pull him away, like an old rotted stump that needed to be yanked from the earth. But then, that question came again. *When the hell did every word out of my mouth become a lie?* And this time, it was too late. His pride, his stubborn will to not give in to the beast, had finally abandoned him.

The beast violently shook and pulled until the weight of Robert's entire body was ripped from the ground, leaving him with all his roots exposed. Now, lying there unconnected to all he knew, every single part of Robert's anatomy cried.

He wept.

As a climber, Roberto Sanchez's nickname was "The Mighty Oak." On the highest of peaks, he was always the last man standing against any challenge the mountain might present. No matter what the obstacle was, The Mighty Oak was the last one to call it quits and turn back. He was known as one of the strongest and the bravest. And the Mighty Oak never cried about what happened to him.

He had done everything in his power not to cry. He knew the only reason he didn't call Monique the night before his first amputation was the fear that he might cry. Even during that dark cold night, he spent on Everest with his legs smashed and his body pinned against some frozen wall—he didn't cry. Even when he heard no sounds of rescue and knew for certain that he was being left for dead—The Mighty Oak didn't cry. Hanging upside down for hours upon hours, he chipped and scratched at the ice with only a small penknife, trying to free his legs and yet, not once did he give into the absolutely excruciating pain. He never cried because he knew if he gave in to the beast of tears, it would defeat him. The Mighty Oak knew that *not crying* was the only way to survive.

Lying in that hospital in Katmandu, waiting for Monique and Jenny to arrive, Robert had written an unfinished poem in his journal—a poem about tears. He always thought that once he gave in to those tears, they would never stop. He would drown in those tears. In the poem, he described himself as the stump of this great oak tree that had been felled in some horrible freak storm. And now, the stump questioned its identity and its worth. As a stump of a tree, one could no longer be called the tall maple, the sturdy oak or the magnificent redwood. Once the tree became a stump, it no longer had a name. Although it was still deeply rooted and alive, it had lost its worth. The stump knew it would never be that strong, mighty, flourishing tree again. And so, the stump thought the only way to survive was for it to not attract attention; for if it did, then someone might see its uselessness and pluck it from the earth. The stump felt the only way it could survive was to stay firm, deeply rooted and silent.

Robert did exactly that. After the doctor's fatal diagnosis that there was no way to save his legs, he never cried. His survival demanded he quickly pull away from any prolonged hug or sympathetic gesture from his wife, daughter and friends. If he could stay hidden and silent, perhaps no one would recognize the stump was no longer The Mighty Oak. And so, six months ago, halfway up Mount Everest, tangled in a ladder with his legs wedged in a mountain of ice, Roberto Sanchez had begun his struggle to survive in complete silence.

But Monique's words—*"this death we live"*—those were the words that broke through his fortress of solitude. And so The Mighty Oak wept.

The beast roared and ravaged. And he cried. His hands beat hard against his chest. And he cried. Clutching his hair and pulling in every direction, he cried. Slamming his hands on the handles of his wheelchair, he cried. And when there was no energy left to hit or slam and pull, he grabbed what was left of his legs, curled into a ball and cried...

Yet, it stopped! The waves of aching tears ceased and his convulsing body calmed. He had no idea how long he cried. The beast just vanished. Robert slowly uncurled himself and tried to wipe the river of tears from his face with the sleeves of his shirt. Soon his breathing lost all its wild panting and became peaceful. As painful as his crying had been, his roots were still firmly planted. He was alive! He cried and he had survived! It was not the end.

"Are you trying to get into the Taj Mahal?" A voice came from behind him.

Robert turned his head to see it was the doorman he met when they arrived in the morning.

"That door is rarely open," the doorman said as he moved towards Robert. "But today, you're lucky! I have a key!"

Robert again rubbed his face, using both his shirtsleeves to dry his tears. He felt a bit raw and exposed and wondered how much the doorman had seen of what had just happened.

"So if I can just slide you back for a second." The doorman took the back of Robert's wheelchair and rolled him a couple of feet away so he could get in front of him to put the key in the lock. "I'll show you what I was talking about this morning and trust me, wait till you see it! This room is *truly magical!*"

Robert felt an intense embarrassment. He avoided looking at the doorman, to whom he still hadn't said a word. How much had the doorman seen or heard? Here he was, alone in this closed-off hallway, screaming and crying. The doorman was sure to have seen him wiping his face, which must look quite red and flushed at the moment. Did it matter? He wanted to ask if the doorman had heard him banging or seen him crying so he could explain himself, but the doorman's smiling happy voice told him that he was oblivious to the storm that had just swept through this hallway.

So Robert did what he always had done for the past six months, and pretended the emotions he had just gone through had not happened. "Yes, I was interested in seeing the room after you mentioned it this morning, but the door was locked so...um...Great, thank you."

The doorman put the key into the handle and turned to Robert. "My pleasure! Mr. Sanchez, right?"

"Yes, that's right." Robert wiped his face one more time and still didn't look up. He caught himself staring at how shiny and bright the silver key looked in the doorman's dark-skinned hand. He watched him slide the key into the hole and then was shocked at what he saw next.

As the doorman opened the door, Robert saw that the man's other hand was simply not there. Robert closed his eyes and looked again. Where the doorman's left hand should be was just a stump at the end of his wrist. How had he not noticed that this morning? How had he not seen this man was missing a hand? The doorman had helped him from the car and even walked with him all the way to the Leaning Tower of Pisa. How had he done that? And then a crazy thought hit him as well: How could a hotel have a doorman with one hand? How could he do his job?

The doorman then purposely stood directly in front of Robert, blocking the entrance and his view of the room. "Okay, you ready?"

For the first time Robert looked up at the doorman, he noticed how the doorman's smile seemed to fill his whole face, and it was so—the only words Robert could come up with were—it was so absolutely genuine! Robert wondered when was the last time he smiled like that—smiled because he felt it, because he felt a reason to smile.

"All right, Mr. Sanchez, I introduce to you *The Taj Mahal!*" The doorman then walked into the room to give Robert the full view.

The first thing he saw from that doorway was the stage at the front of the room. It was a painted rendering of what the real Taj Mahal must look like at dusk. There were three domed tops, looking as if they were fading into the night. The freestanding white pillars were given more dimension by a huge, white full moon behind them. Gleaming on the stage floor and looking colourfully majestic was the Taj Mahal's reflection. The walls were painted in a pink stone pattern. Two huge red and gold carpets, each with a beautiful flying peacock in the center, hung on two sides of the room. And just like the Leaning Tower of Pisa room, there were fake windows painted on the walls, exposing the beauty of the Indian landscape. Golden, textured arches framed each window. The floor was also a colourful carpet designed to look like stone. Along the outside wall were four tall glass windows and doors that opened up on a beautiful gardened terrace.

"I love coming in this way because you see the stage right away. And you get the full splendour of what it must be like when you first arrive at the Taj Mahal. Hey wait," the doorman interrupted himself. "Did you see me with a coffee?"

Robert shook his head, thinking, *'Okay, you're tossing that key in the only hand you've got and I'm quite sure it's not in your pockets, so...'*

"Ah, I put it down behind you before I opened the door. Hang on." The doorman quickly went back into the hallway and came back with a Starbuck's coffee cup. He held it against his chest with his left stump as he closed the door with his right hand. As the doorman walked passed him, Robert noticed something he hadn't seen before. Robert squinted to get a better look at the side of the man's head. He blinked and rubbed his eyes to see if they were playing tricks on him. He looked again. It was true! The doorman's right ear was missing. How could he have not noticed the man was missing a hand and an ear this morning?

As the doorman closed the door, he spoke in a hushed voice. "I'm not really supposed to be in here. The manager, the one who's on duty today, has these strict rules that when a room is not in use, we are not to use it. Afraid someone might get it dirty or something, I don't know. You see, I don't usually work today, but this morning I got a call to come in to cover three hours for the doorman who—I'm sorry, why am I telling you this?"

Robert tried to hide his surprise at the missing ear and nodded politely. "You're right, it is quite an impressive room."

"Yes, yes it is. Every day that I come to work, I make a promise to myself that I will come in here and...Well, you're lucky the other doorman has just shown up, so I was able to see it now before I left for the day. " The doorman then walked into the middle of the room.

"Come this way," Robert wheeled behind him until they were in the middle of the room. The doorman pulled out a chair, sat down and said, "Now look up."

And as Robert looked up, he saw a stunning ceiling decorated with blue and white glass chandeliers.

The magnificence of it overwhelmed Robert and the words, "It's beautiful" escaped from him without prompting.

"Oh, it's too bad. If the sun was out, all the glass up there would reflect the most incredible tiny rainbows all over the room." The doorman smiled as he took a sip from his coffee but suddenly looked at Robert and said, "Oh my goodness, look at me drinking and you without a drink!"

The doorman then abruptly stood up. "I am so sorry, would you like me to get you something, Mr. Sanchez?"

"No, it's okay."

"Anything. Please, Mr. Sanchez. The coffee shop is just at the end of the hall."

"No, really." Robert leaned towards the doorman to look at his nametag. "Really, thank you, Aaron."

"Are you sure, Mr. Sanchez? It would only take a moment."

"No please, Aaron, I'm really not thirsty."

The doorman nodded. He looked up at the ceiling once more, smiled, and then sat down again. Robert watched the doorman put his coffee cup on the table. After a few seconds, the doorman picked up the coffee cup and instead of taking another sip, he moved it almost into the centre of the table, as if he had finished drinking it and was putting it away.

Robert politely smiled, shook his head slightly and said, "It's okay, you can drink your coffee, Aaron."

The doorman shifted his body and looked directly at Robert. "I like how you say my name."

Robert shifted his eyes in question. "Is there any other way to say it?"

"No, I'm sorry. I'm not saying how you pronounce my name but more that you actually say it."

Robert responded with an obvious shrug. "Well, of course, it's on your name tag."

"Yes, of course, it is. But you choose to use it. You see, Mr. Sanchez, in one day, I meet many, many people—at their car, in the elevator, at their rooms—and...would it surprise you to know that the majority of those people never use my name?" Aaron let out a laugh. "Ha ha...Most of us that work at the front of the hotel have joked that when they create these name tags, they should just print 'hey you' instead of our name, for I think I've been called 'hey you' many more times than 'Aaron.'"

"Well, it's a good name, Aaron Aboga."

"Thank you, but actually it's pronounced I-boga. You see, where I come from, in the Acholi language—my language back home—all A's are pronounced as I."

As he spoke, Robert watched Aaron bring his left arm to his head

310

and scratch his missing ear with the stump of his missing hand. He couldn't believe how he moved as naturally as any person who had hands and ears would, scratching a momentary itch on their head. For the past six months at the rehabilitation centre, Robert found that most of the other patients suffering like him seemed to work so hard to find ways to hide and compensate for the loss of their arms and legs. Rarely had he seen anyone just be—be so natural about their loss like this man.

"Okay, nice to meet you Aaron I-boga." Robert was surprised he was able to engage in this simple conversation, such a short time after being caught in that emotional tsunami.

"And Aboga is actually my first name," the doorman continued. "Where I am from we do not have last names like here. One of our names is a Christian name and the other name comes from the situation we were born into. Aaron is my Christian name and, well, Aboga comes from my situation."

"So what was your situation?"

"Ha ha..." The doorman laughed in that deep resonating tone again. "It has been quite an appropriate name for me so far in my life at least. You see, Aboga means 'took a lot of caring for me to live.' And even at my beginning, I apparently took a lot of caring." He laughed again. "Ha ha...painful caring, so my mother had told me. Because, you see, I did not want to come out of my mother...head first."

"Or maybe you just wanted to have one last look," Robert joked. Robert then smiled to himself. *How could this be?* He still hadn't been able to assess the damage the beast had done and now he was making a joke?

"Ha ha...Yes, Mr. Sanchez, yes, I must have needed one last look. Although I do not think my mother appreciated that! But do you know what I found strange when I came to this country, Mr. Sanchez? I found it strange, and still do, that so many people do not know the meaning of their own names! Back home we can recite the meaning of...well, of many, many names."

"So what does Aaron mean then?" Robert shook his head a little in disbelief. This was maybe the longest conversation he had had with anyone in months.

"Ah, you will like this one! I mean with you being a climber. It means 'mountain of strength.'" And then came that infectious deep laugh. "Haha, can you imagine me a mountain of strength?" As he said it, the doorman flexed his left arm making a muscle, which prominently exposed the stump of his missing hand. Again, it struck Robert how unfazed the doorman seemed about his stump, so fluid and not self-conscious in the least.

"And you, Mr. Sanchez, what does your name mean?"

"Well, Sanchez just means the son of Sancho, which I guess means this Sancho guy had a lot of sons because there are millions of us Sanchez's in the world." *Oh God, this feels great!* Robert thought. *Just talking...I'm talking! And not thinking about my lost legs.*

"And your other name, Mr. Son of Sancho, what is the name given to you?"

"Roberto," he said but then added, "or Robert or Bobby, take your pick."

The doorman's soothing rich laughter again filled the room. "Ha ha...'Roberto.'" The doorman repeated it again. "Roberto, Roberto...ah, I like saying your name. So what does it mean?"

Robert paused and then turned his head to the side with a questioning look. *Aaron was right!* he thought. *Most people don't know the meanings of their names.* For it was only last year that he and Monique had two friends who were having babies and they were caught in one of those familiar discussions about the name. Yet, Robert remembered when these new parents were asked what their own names meant, neither one of them knew.

But Robert knew exactly what his name meant. And he remembered exactly the last time someone had spoken to him about the meaning of his name. It was four years ago. His name was in every local paper and even on some television newscasts. Everyone was talking about his "Climbing to Learn" campaign and how he had led all those people from the school board to the top of Mount Kilimanjaro. That was also the first time Robert had found out that his mother had been keeping a scrapbook of all his climbing adventures.

The scrapbook was given to him on his forty-fourth birthday. His mother sat beside him as he opened the gift. She was bursting with so much excitement that before Robert even attempted to open it, she used her scissors to snip open the blue ribbon that had probably taken her quite a long time to tie. The scrapbook was a thick, blue velvet covered photo album and each page was filled with Robert's achievements throughout the years. Not just his mountaineering experiences but also every single time he was recognized for something: old yellowing news clippings, letters and photos detailing his early adventures in soccer, music, some work at the probation office and his workshops in the schools. Jenny and Monique squeezed onto the couch beside him as he looked through his life. Page by page, Robert's father and most of his brothers and sisters stood around him, laughing and teasing him after each page. Everyone shared some happy/touching/crazy story about Roberto Sanchez.

Robert was overwhelmed with emotion as he closed the book. He turned to thank his mother. Before he could say a word, she quickly spoke.

"Ah, my little Roberto, how proud we all are of you!" He remembered telling Monique that night—the moment she kissed him, his family clapped and Jenny tussled his hair—was the most complete moment of feeling loved he had ever felt.

After the kiss, the applause and hair tussling, Robert's mother had held his face in both her hands and said, "You know, little Roberto, from the moment we saw those big eyes of yours, we knew...we knew of all the names we could have picked for you, 'Roberto' was the right one because 'Roberto' means famous—one that is bright and shining! Exactly what you are my son, bright and shining!"

But just as Robert was about to answer the doorman's question, this memory came, sharp as a stabbing pain in his heart. His smile vanished. He knew the last thing he was right now was bright and shining to anyone, least of all to himself! So, when Robert turned back to the doorman, his response came out flat and dull.

"Famous...One who is bright...and shining."

"Ho ho...that is what it means?" Aaron cheerfully asked. "Well, it seems your parents named you perfectly."

"No, not really."

"But Mr. Roberto Sanchez, look how many people are here today to listen you—to hear you speak about climbing those mountains of yours."

Robert responded defensively, "They are not *my* mountains!"

The doorman ignored Robert's terse reply and smiled. "Of course they are not yours, but something of you touched them, didn't they?"

"Yeah, but..."

"So they're a part of you now, right?"

Robert didn't answer the question so the doorman went on. "And Everest, ah, the amazing Everest! Do you know, Mr. Sanchez, that in my country we have many mountains and most of us cannot name more than a few of them. *Yet,*" he said excitedly, "every child has heard of Mountain Everest. In our eyes—the eyes of my country—you are bright and shining. You, sir, are quite famous for climbing and touching that Everest!"

Hearing the name Everest suddenly caused Robert to feel that old familiar ache in his chest again, that constant festering ache that had been with him ever since his first leg and one of his dearest hopes was amputated.

"And do you know what that's like, Aaron?" he asked. "Being famous for something you can't do anymore?"

"But you *did it*, Mr. Sanchez! You climbed, you touched one of the wonders of the world. Most of us, most of the human beings on this planet, have never done that."

"But *I CAN'T* do it anymore!!!" Robert almost yelled.

Robert's roar didn't seem to faze the doorman. He just laughed.

"Ha ha...my God, there are so many things we all can't do any more, Mr. Sanchez. Look at me!" the doorman said as he held up his stump. "Imagine all the things I can't do now. And of course—we all change, right? We are constantly changing. All of us. Sadly, we become too old to do some of things we used to do. Many of us would love to jump in their mama's arms and have her swing us around, but then we become too big, right? But we still relish in the memory of doing those things we can longer do! And, of course, there are things we can't do because a part of us just can't do it anymore. Like me and this hand. Do you know what I used to love to do?"

Robert silently shook his head. The doorman brought his arms together until his wrists touched.

"Ah...that feeling of clasping my hands together when I was praying to God...and oh, how I loved to clap my hands to the rhythm of the drums...So many things I can't do anymore, Mr. Sanchez. But it does not take away the doing of them! It doesn't stop the feeling that I did them, does it?"

Robert's head jerked up. The doorman's question stung—it stung deep. He felt completely exposed. How did this doorman know this about him? How did this Aaron know how this question ached inside him?

"Aaron, listen. Do you know how people always introduce me? Just like you did now—as someone great because I climbed mountains? Do you know that I've climbed...what...maybe only eighteen different mountains in my life, but I've probably helped hundreds...who knows, maybe thousands of different kids in my life. But every time someone introduces me, they don't talk about that. They always introduce me as that guy who climbed Everest!"

The doorman was now leaning in, then reached out to touch Robert's arm and said, "But people say that because they are proud of you."

Robert started to get a little more agitated. "I know...I know...It's not as if I'm not grateful for that. It's just...that's how I'm known. And it's the first thing everyone wants to talk to me about. Climbing mountains! Is that who I am?"

"But isn't that why you climbed the mountain? So you could be known as the person who was famous for doing it?" the doorman asked with a smile.

"Famous?" Robert almost spit out the word. "You think that's why I climbed a mountain?"

The doorman shrugged. "Why does anyone climb a mountain, if it is not for being known by someone that they did it?"

"But, look at me, Aaron, it's something I can't do any more. Imagine if everyone introduced you as that guy who did this or that but you can't do it anymore...and worse, you will never do it again. So who are you to them now?"

The doorman thought for a second and then responded, "Well, Mr. Sanchez, you will always be the man who did what you did."

"But who am I now? I'm *now* the person who can't do that thing that made him famous! So, what are people going to ask me now? What? Ask me what I'm going to do next? That's like asking that cute kid from those Home Alone movies why he can't do the cute kid movies anymore now that he's grown into this gawky pimple-faced teenager or adult man! Or, a...asking the singer you loved to sing that song that made her famous, but she can't reach those notes anymore. And so now, when people find out I'm that guy who climbed Everest, and then they look at these legs...oh, and when they do—they all get this sorry look in their faces that says, 'oh my God, what's he going to do now?' It's like everyone's asking me, 'who are you now?' It's like...like my whole life has lost all its meaning if I'm not the guy who climbs mountains anymore. "

Robert then grabbed both of his legs and lifted them.

"*Look at me!!!* What on earth can I do now?"

The doorman put his hand on Robert's arm to comfort him. But Robert was now panting hard and taking in deep breaths like a wild horse tied to a fence trying to break away. He was moving his head from side to side, panting furiously, trying to find the words that could set him free.

"I'm sure the hell *NOT* going to be climbing Everest ever again...and why would I? Just look at these!"

The doorman didn't move, he just held on to Robert's arm as he mightily shook back and forth.

"*Look*, look at me! Why would I want to go back there? Why? And why am I here today? Why the hell would I ever want to talk about the goddamn mountain that took my legs?!!!"

Robert jerked his head from side to side, but with each turn of his head, his lips could only mutter and repeat how that mountain took his legs. Soon his mouth was empty of words and only grunts of breath came forth. His head stopped moving. He was still. With one last loud sigh, he closed his eyes. Robert had finally broken free from the fence. Yes, he had finally said it to someone. The truth had been spoken and there was no other pain he needed to unleash into the world.

He had become so accustomed to leaping into the river of self-pitying despair. No matter how many times he attempted to drown himself in the sorrow of losing his legs, it never worked. He would always resurface again—and each time feeling more and more alone. Yet today...this felt...different.

Something had changed. He was not alone.

He felt the firm grip of the doorman's hand clutching his arm. And for the first time in such a long time, he had allowed someone's touch to calm him. Support him. He actually sighed into the warmth and strength of the connection. Robert felt such a welcome relief that, throughout his ranting struggle, this stranger—this doorman, Aaron—had not let go of him, no matter how violent or ugly his thoughts became.

Robert then opened his eyes and looked down to see the doorman's hand, but it was simply not there. The strong warm powerful grip that Robert felt was just Aaron's stump—simply touching him—a stump where the missing hand had once been.

Robert gasped slightly.

How many times had he desperately thrown himself off the bridge into that same raging river of darkness? Yet, this time the river of self-pity had not taken him and swallowed him up. Something had caught him and was holding his head above the painful waters he found he was constantly trying to drown himself in.

And that something was a man without a hand.

Robert looked at the doorman's stump at the end of his arm. It was not a pretty sight—bumpy and uneven. Yet, the dark brown roundness of Aaron's scarred wrist seemed so alive! Even without fingers to clasp, without the tender caress of a hand, this man's stump touching him felt so full of human caring. *But how?* How had he felt such an amazingly strong firm grip from the doorman when he didn't even have a hand to grab him with?

And for the first time since coming out of those painful surgeries of loss, Robert didn't pull away from someone trying to help. He didn't throw the doorman's lifeline off so he could drown alone in his own dark river of pity again.

Robert wanted to look up, to say something. But it felt so incredibly hard because, at this very moment, he had never felt more naked in his life. The truth of his pain was now out in the open—it had been unmistakably spoken. Just like tears, he knew they could never be un-cried. And now he knew the truth of his pain also could not be un-spoken. Robert had never told anyone, not even Monique or Jenny, how he truly felt and what he feared he had become.

The silence of the moment was palpable, but the doorman kept his arm on Robert. But Robert couldn't look at him. He quickly closed his eyes again and questioned himself. *Why is it so difficult to look up? What am I so afraid to see?*

Most climbers called Roberto Sanchez one of the most fearless climbers they knew. He had successfully faced and conquered the most daunting obstacles while scaling some of the most treacherous mountaintops. He challenged impediments that would have had most men turning back. Yet, today, the simple act of opening his eyes and facing this truth was taking more courage than he had ever needed to muster.

But just like tears shed—words spoken—the moment had happened. It was now up to him what he did with it.

He knew there was no turning back and he must forge ahead. He had to see what the damage looked like—to finally face how damaged he looked in someone else's eyes. And so, like a man after a vicious tornado has torn through his home, Robert emerged from his storm shelter to see the extent of the damage. He took a deep laboured breath, lifted his head and opened his eyes. The moment Robert's eyes caught Aaron's, the doorman spoke.

"So then, Mr. Roberto Sanchez, how would *YOU* introduce yourself then? If you're not only the man who climbed Everest, tell me, who else you would be? Or maybe tell me who you'd like to become?"

The questions took Robert by surprise. After the accident, everyone had always asked him how he felt or how he was. Some would dare to ask what he wanted to do now, but no one ever asked who he wanted to be! He thought he was always going to be the man who lost something.

"What...do I want to...become?" Robert repeated the question, slow and precise.

"Ho ho..." The doorman's warm deep laugh was felt again. "I know, I know it seems like a question we just ask little children. But think, Mr. Sanchez, when do ever stop becoming?"

Again, Robert repeated the question back to the doorman. "When do we...stop becoming?"

"Haha, can I show you something, Mr. Sanchez?"

Robert nodded. The doorman released his stump from Robert's arm. Robert's other hand quickly reacted and grabbed onto Aaron's stump. He didn't want the doorman to let go and spoke in a rather panicky tone.

"Where are you going?"

"Ho ho..." The doorman smiled. "Going nowhere, Mr. Sanchez. I just need my hand to open my jacket."

It struck Robert how he still called the stump his hand. He watched as the doorman quickly used his stump to flick open his jacket and with his right hand, he reached inside breast pocket of his jacket.

"Sorry," Robert said, still feeling the warmth of the doorman's invisible hand on his arm. "It's just I...ah...it's just...your hand...Well, thanks for not letting go when I got so upset there. It's just...well, I needed that."

"Good," the doorman simply said. He then pulled out a little pocket-sized paper booklet. The cover was quite worn and dirty and it looked to be maybe ten to fifteen pages thick. He laid it on the table in front of Robert. Robert wheeled himself closer to look at the booklet.

It looked like a child's book. It had a simple white cover with black lettering that read, "The Wonders of the World." There were some black and white etchings of the wonders themselves. Robert could quickly make out some of obvious ones like Stonehenge, the Greek Coliseum, a pyramid, the unmistakable Everest, and the Leaning Tower of Pisa, but some of the other etchings weren't recognizable to him.

Robert picked up the booklet and scanned the pages inside. Each page was dedicated to one of the wonders of the world. There was a coloured picture and maybe ten or so lines describing the picture.

"The last page will explain it," Aaron said.

Robert looked up at the doorman. "Explain what?"

"What we become," the doorman said and then repeated himself. "What we become."

Robert flipped to the back page. It was torn and dirty. About a quarter of a page at the bottom was missing. The heading had bold red letters, "The Taj Mahal—A monument of true love". The photo of the Taj Mahal was striking. The castle-like mansion was glowing in the sunset with the long pools of water in front of it, mirroring its beauty.

Robert looked up from the booklet, looked around the room, and then back at the picture. "You know, it's hard to capture all that beauty, but they did a pretty good job in this room."

"Well, if you think that, you should see this room when the sun shines through those windows. I can't describe it. It just truly becomes a wonder!" said the doorman.

Robert started reading the caption under the photo. "It was built in 1630 by Mughal emperor Shah Jahan in memory of his third wife, Mumtaz Mahal. The Taj Mahal is widely recognized as the jewel of Muslim art in India and one of the universally admired masterpieces of the world's heritage."

He paused and then asked the doorman, "What does this have to do with becoming?"

"At the bottom of the page, read what the Emperor Shah Jahan himself wrote and how he described his monument of love."

Near the bottom was what looked like a four-line poem written in italics. Robert started to read out loud:

"Should guilty seek asylum here,

318

Like one pardoned, he becomes free from sin.
Should a sinner make his way to this mansion,
All his past sins are to be washed away..."

"There's a little more that was ripped out. But what he wrote there, well, that is one of the reasons I come here every day. Because of what I had become and well, now, what I am becoming." Aaron said softly.

Robert looked back down to see what he had just read. The words "guilty," "pardoned" and "sins are to be washed away," stood out to him. He glanced back up at the doorman with a questioning look.

"I have been guilty of many horrific things, Mr. Sanchez. I had become someone who people feared. I was that monster in people's dreams, a monster that came to life."

Robert looked absolutely stunned. How could this gentle man with a laugh that soothed one's soul ever have been anyone's monster?

"Have you ever heard of Joseph Kony?"

Robert sadly nodded his head. "You mean that guy from Africa? That man who runs an army fighting against the government?"

"Yes, Mr. Sanchez, Africa. Uganda, my home, that is where the Lord's Resistance Army is. And yes, that's right, that guy is fighting. But I'm not sure it is the government he is fighting any more. You see, when I was ten that guy came to our village with some of his army. We were out in the fields...my younger brother and I were with our mother. We heard the screams and then people came running towards us. Like a stampede of wild goats, they ran past us. Behind them were the soldiers and it was strange since the soldiers all came with guns, yet there was not one shot fired. I later found out it was because bullets were not to be wasted on running targets. So, we started running. My mother grabbed my younger brother and we turned to run. But that morning we had just dug a small ditch to collect water in and as she turned to run, she and my little brother fell into it. Quickly the soldiers were standing over them. My mother started yelling at them, but when they pointed a rifle at her, she fell and covered my little brother, trying to protect him. He was crying and that was the first shot I heard. I still had the shovel in my hand and I went to hit the soldier who shot the gun, but just as I raised the shovel, I was knocked into the hole with my mother and brother. I pulled my mother close, but her arms just didn't move and neither did my brother's. They were dead. Then the soldier pointed the gun at me and was going to shoot, but then a big voice yelled for him to stop.

"I was thinking it was my father, coming to save me. But then this man looked down into the hole right at me and said to the other soldiers, 'No, God wants this one to fight for Him.' He then grabbed me by my shirt, yanked me out of the hole, and asked me, 'Are you ready to fight for

God and our country?' But I was too...well, stunned to say anything. So he screamed the same question again, 'Are you ready to fight for God and our country?' Still no words came out of me so he nodded his head to this other man who carried this long silver machete. That man came walking towards me and he raised that shiny machete high over my head and just as he came down with the machete, I squeezed my eyes shut and I felt this burning sensation on the side of my head. All I could hear was the man asking me again, 'So are you ready now to fight for God and country?' but this time he asked in a quiet calm voice. I still felt that burning and as I opened my eyes, I saw the man was kneeling right in front of me. He leaned down and picked up something from the ground and then I saw why the side of my head was burning. The man was holding my ear and he brought it right to my nose and he said, 'I'm sorry about this, but you must learn that God really doesn't like having to repeat himself. This is the punishment for those who do not listen. So I ask you for the last time, are you ready to...' But before he could finish his question, I just started crying, 'Yes, yes,' over and over and over again.

"They took me back into our village and along the path, I saw my father. He was lying there, on his back, dead. He had cuts all over. I guess he was slashed and cut up with the same kind of machete they used on my ear. But you know, Mr. Sanchez, when I was looking at my father lying there so bloody and so...so...so lifeless, all I could think was, why did they kill him? Didn't my father show he could fight for God too? Then I watched these soldiers—a lot of them were kids not much older than me. And they were stealing everything they could carry. It all happened so fast. After they rummaged through all the houses, they set them all on fire. It was so hot that day; the fire burned everything so quickly. My home was gone in less than a minute. And then, they all started leaving. No one was holding me or even watching that I didn't escape. I could have just run, Mr. Sanchez. I could have just run right into the forest...but I didn't."

"You were only ten, Aaron," Robert said.

"But I didn't run...Why? And as they all started laughing and singing some soldiers' hymn about God and freedom, well me? Me? I just followed them. It was like I had no choice but to...be...with them now. And so I became one of them."

"But Aaron, you were just a kid and really, what choice did you have?."

"There is always choice. There is always choice in what we become, Mr. Sanchez. You just have to be willing to face the consequences of your choice...and mine was—"

The doorman then held up his stump and touched it as if the hand was still there. "My hand—my beautiful, wonderful hand. Do you know how many things you do in one day with your hands, Mr. Sanchez? So many incredible things—things that we sometimes aren't even aware of. Our hands are capable of so many wonders. We can speak as many words of love as we can, but sometimes just reaching and touching, holding someone's hand in complete silence, can say so much more."

Robert smiled as he looked at his own arm where, just moments before, he had felt exactly what the doorman was saying. He had felt love and care from this man without a word being spoken.

"Do you know, Mr. Sanchez, that my parents never really spoke much to each other and, well, they were never really that affectionate either. Yet, when they held hands...ah, I can see them now, walking to the water hole together, holding hands. Hmmm...when I saw my parents—when they held hands—the world seemed to be at perfect peace. *BUT* these hands...they also can do things that cause so much hurt—terrible, shameful, devastating hurt. And my hands...like me...had become weapons of hurt, Mr. Sanchez. I had become a monster. That's what I had become until that book came into my life."

Robert gave the doorman a look of total disbelief. "But Aaron, I'm sorry, but I just can't believe you could have done any—"

"Have you ever killed a man, Robert?" The doorman looked seriously into Robert's eyes.

"Well, um...no, but—"

"Do you know what it's like to take someone's life—to kill a stranger that has done you no harm? But someone has put a gun in your hands and tells you that this stranger must die...It doesn't matter that the stranger pleads or cries and asks you not to shoot. You shoot because that someone told you, 'You must shoot!' and you don't ask why. You pull the trigger and never ask why. That is who I had become: a mindless monster who never questioned what he was told to do."

Robert wanted to say he refused to believe what Aaron had just told him was true. There was no way that this doorman actually killed another human being. He was probably just saying this to make a point. But before Robert could decide what to say, the doorman, who looked as if he was about to cry had caught himself, cleared his throat, reached for his coffee, took a sip and continued talking.

"I got that book from a girl whose name was Aloyo Grace. Aloyo means victorious, Mr. Sanchez. And just like her name, Aloyo Grace always worked hard to be victorious in whatever she did. She did not want to be defeated in anything, least of all being a prisoner at that camp where I was a soldier.

"I had just turned fourteen and had already been a part of that resistance army for almost three years when we captured Grace. She was only twelve years old when she became our prisoner. The rest of her family had all escaped but she told me that she knew one day she would be free and be with her family again."

The doorman then shook his head with a smile of remembrance.

"Oh...so tiny she was...no taller than this." The doorman held out his stump about four feet from the ground. "And Grace was not a good looking girl either, which was lucky in some ways for her because then she was only used only as a cook and for cleanup duties, not as a sex slave for the older boys and men like most of the other girls. My main job was to keep all these girls from escaping. I think they gave that job to me because I was not a good-looking boy either. And mostly they knew I wouldn't try anything with the girls because of my missing ear. I always stayed my distance when I guarded the girls for I could see how they would laugh and point at my ear behind my back. Yet, they looked at me with that fearful look—afraid of me, like I was an ugly wounded animal that might attack if they came near me."

The doorman took another sip from his cup and cleared his throat once more.

"But Grace, who had been in our camp for maybe one month, well, this little...plain looking girl that most of the boys called a mutt...she would always stop and say hello each and every time she passed me. She'd just say this simple 'hello!' And, although I never said a word back to her, I must tell you...secretly, Mr. Sanchez, I just loved those times! Each time she would simply say hi, ah those moments were...it was like...so...so normal. Like I didn't belong there holding that gun, that I was back in my village and we were just kids passing each other on the way to our chores. The way we smiled and just said hi. You know that simple feeling, Mr. Sanchez? That everyday thing you never question?"

Robert nodded slowly, thinking how he too missed so many of those simple daily feelings.

"'But then one day, she stopped to ask me a question. She spoke with this beautiful confidence and her voice was like...like, oh I know, kind of a princess-like voice. Anyway she stopped, Mr. Sanchez, about eight feet away from me, looked me directly in the eyes and asked, 'Should I stop saying hello to you?'

"Well, to tell you the truth, I was a bit shocked and I must confess, somewhat confused. I didn't know how to respond to her so I just simply asked her, 'Why do you ask me that?'

"And she said, 'Well, every day I see you and I know you are standing there protecting us, but still it doesn't feel nice when I always say hello to you and you never say it back to me.'"

The doorman's voice then became animated and indignant.

"Well, Mr. Sanchez, I still didn't know what to say to her. I think I felt angry at first. I thought to myself, *who is she to talk to me like that...to me? The guy with the gun!* And she was wrong! I wasn't protecting them; my job was to stop them from running away! I mean, didn't she know? Didn't she know I had orders to shoot any one of those girls if had they tried to escape? Didn't she know I was the boss in this situation and it was my right to not say hello to her if I wanted?"

The doorman laughed at himself.

"But then she says right away with this big smile, 'It's okay if that's who you want to be though. If you want to be somebody who doesn't say hello, I guess I can understand.'

"And just her saying that...that she understood started to make me angry. I had been there almost three years and she was only there for a month. What could she understand about me? And so that made me really feel angry but...somehow she confused me at the same time."

"So what did you do?"

"I felt defensive, Mr. Sanchez."

The doorman raised his stump to his head. "And in my head came this burning anger. I thought...*This tiny girl, who does she think she is? She doesn't even know my name. How does she know who I am or who I want to be?* So in my anger, I reacted and lifted up my rifle towards her and then barked at her, 'What the hell do you understand about me?' The doorman lifted his arm and showed Robert how he held the rifle at the little girl.

"And so then she stopped smiling, Mr. Sanchez."

The doorman face grew painfully sad as he spoke. "And then she fell to her knees. And I noticed something I had never seen in this girl before. I realized at that moment—that for the whole month she had been there—that when she looked at me, I never saw fear on her face. And now it changed. I changed her. I saw that same fear, that exact same horrible fear in her face that I saw in all the other girls when they looked at me!"

The doorman slapped his thigh. "Me! I did this. And there she was, Mr. Sanchez, she looked up at me, right at my rifle, and then she started crying and pleading with me, 'I'm sorry, I'm so sorry...Please don't shoot me. I will not say another word, I promise...I will stop saying hello to you...I will do anything you tell me.'"

The doorman then pulled his chair closer to Robert and leaned in. "And do you know what I thought, Mr. Sanchez, right at that moment?"

"What?" Robert whispered.

"I had become the destroyer of the one and only moment I loved. That wonderful normal moment where I thought I was back home again. That brief heavenly moment that made me feel home, I had become the destroyer of it."

Robert waited a moment as the doorman let out a great exhaling sound and rubbed his eyes with his stump. "So, what did you do, Aaron?"

The doorman shook his head and smiled ever so slightly. "First, Mr. Sanchez, I wanted to apologize. I wanted so badly to undo my reaction. I wanted so desperately...I just wanted to clean that fear from her face. I wanted our moment back. I wanted everything to be back to the way it was. Those precious little 'hellos' from her...But you have to understand, Mr. Sanchez, I was barely fourteen and for the past three years I was taught to not have emotions—that emotions can get you killed. So I, well...I...So first I looked around to make sure no other guards were watching and I dropped my gun beside me and I whispered the only thing I thought might get everything back to the way it was. I said..." The doorman shook his head, scornfully snorted to himself and then whispered, "I leaned down to the girl and said, 'Okay, then I order you to keep saying hello.'"

The doorman then lifted his arms high and looked up. "Yes, Mr. Sanchez, that was my way of making it better...I said, 'I order you to keep saying hello.'"

Robert gave him an encouraging smile and put a hand on his knee in support.

"Ah, but it was right then, right at that moment—that is where this little tiny princess showed me what I had become...and more importantly, she showed me that maybe I had a chance...of maybe...maybe changing...becoming something else. After I had ordered her to keep saying hello, she looked up and asked me, 'How?' And I say to her, 'The way you always did before.' And well, her face kind of squeezed into a grimace like that would be too hard for her to do. I could see she was thinking about what I had asked her to do. You could actually see and tell she was thinking it over and over again in her head. After a couple of seconds, she said to me, 'All right, I can say hi to you but you have to tell me how I should say it and I will try to do it the way you tell me.'"

Robert gave him a sympathetic smile.

"Well, now I was getting completely confused! What's so hard about saying hi? I wondered. So I said to her, 'Just say it the way you always did before...' And then she says, 'I will try, I promise you.' So I asked her, 'But why do you have to try? You have been doing it for one month already...Just...say...hello the same way.'

"Then, Mr. Sanchez, she got this really sad look on her face and these huge tears started rolling down her cheeks and then, trying so hard not to cry, she said to me, 'I don't know if I can do it the same way...but I will try to...I promise you I will try.' 'But why?' I asked her. 'Why? You don't need to try, just do it the same way you always did.' 'And what if it's not the same? Will you shoot me then?' she asked me. And I say 'Why can't it be the same? *WHY?* And then she cries out, 'Because I am scared of you now!'"

The doorman stopped. He stared at Robert for a long moment and repeated the girls' words. "Because she's scared of me now! What had I become, Mr. Sanchez? What had I become?" The doorman shook his head to show his disdain in himself.

"And you know, Mr. Sanchez, I had done terrible things as a soldier. They taught me to do these horrific things—things I know I never would have done in my life. And when I held that gun, I always knew why they were afraid. But even though I saw fear in so many people's eyes, no one, not one person had ever told me they were scared of me. Me? Aaron?! Isn't that strange, Mr. Sanchez? The gun I understood they feared, but not me. I never thought I had become scary. I thought it was the gun...or my ugly scarred head that they were afraid of...but not me, Aaron Iboga!" The doorman slammed a fist unto his chest.

"So now, I was all tied in knots. All I'm thinking is how could I get back my moment of home? How could I live that moment again, of her saying hi to me?

"So I said to her, with all my fourteen-year-old wisdom, 'Okay, how about if I order you to do it the same way as before. That I order you to say hello the same way, will that help you?'"

Robert smiled at the doorman's odd solution.

"And she quickly responds to me, 'You can't order someone to feel something,' 'Okay, okay, okay,' I said, and now I was pleading with this little imp of a girl. 'Okay, forget that I ordered you...just please just say hi again. Please let's forget this happened.' Then she said to me, 'But I can't forget; because I'm scared of you now.'

"And then, Mr. Sanchez, I think I said the wisest thing I've ever said in my whole life. And it was like, right at that moment...right at that moment, it all started to help change what I was or even had become. I said to her, 'Okay, let's make a deal. If I will try to do everything I can to help you not feel scared of me, will you please—please try to say hi to me?"

Robert leaned in closer. "So what did she say to that?"

"Just before she could answer, one of the other guards came to me and asked me if she was being trouble. I said no and that she had just fallen down. He then yelled at her to move it and she got up so fast and ran off."

"So what happened next?" Robert asked.

"Well, the next day she did say hi to me and I said hi back. Oh, it wasn't any ground breaking moment, I assure you. It was awkward and forced and she stayed a lot further away from me than she ever had. Also, she didn't even look at me. Whenever I saw her come, I always tried to put my gun behind me to make her feel safe...Anyway, for a few weeks the hi's she shared were pretty quick. You must understand, I had spent the last three years becoming numb to everyone and everything I was doing. But each day with little Grace, I felt something was changing...and you know, Mr. Sanchez, I loved that feeling—that feeling of what I was now trying to become—to become someone who doesn't make other people scared. Becoming someone trying to help. I even started saying hi to the other girls. And even though there was little I could do about what the other guards did, I could at least try to make these girls feel safe around me! And soon, I felt as if I wasn't their guard or jailor anymore. Now I felt like I was actually protecting them! I had become someone they didn't have to fear. As each day passed, my Grace started to walk closer to me and after about three weeks, she started looking right at me. And the hi's became questions— simple questions of 'how are you?' And soon there were answers. We were able to find ways to talk without anyone noticing.

"And one day she had asked me, 'Aaron, what do you want to become?'

"'What can I become here?' I asked her.

"'Well, you've become someone many of us girls feel safe with now.'

"Oh, Mr. Sanchez, I cannot describe to you how those words made me feel! I could not believe what a simple hello could do. It could actually make someone feel safe, safe in that horrendous place, safe with so many mean and cruel people around. Anyway, Grace says to me, 'But that is not what I'm asking you, Aaron. I mean after you are gone from here. What do you want to become?'

"Her question was something I had never thought of. So, I told her, 'I never thought of any other world but here. From the moment I left my village and followed those men into the forest three years ago, I never thought any other world existed.'

"'When I get out of here,' she said to me with this amazing, defiant hope in her eyes, 'when I get out of here...and after I find my family, well, first I want to go to school! And one of the things I want to become is an agriculturist.'

"'What's that?' I asked her.

"'It's someone that helps people figure out ways to grow things where it was impossible before. Or just make things grow better.'

"'Oh,' I said to her. ' And what do you mean one of the things you want to become? How many things can one person become in one life?'

"Grace then laughed. Oh, and she had the greatest laugh, Mr. Sanchez. 'I want to become a wife and a mother, she says. And then she goes on and on. Oh...I want to become a great mother and even a better grandmother. I'd like to become someone people want to listen to. I want to become so many things, Aaron. I want to become like my father.' Then she told me about her father who had gone to a university but decided to go back into his little village to start a school. Many people asked him why he was doing this. Apparently he was so smart that he could have been become anything: an engineer, pilot or maybe even climb a great mountain like you, Mr. Sanchez...or play in a great orchestra...Grace's father, he could have become famous, so people asked him why he chose to be just a teacher. And then Grace told me she questioned her father too and, he told her about a man named Shakespeare who he said had asked the greatest question there ever was. You must know Mr. Shakespeare, don't you, Mr. Sanchez?"

Robert's eyes seemed wet as he laughed and said yes!

"Well, the thing that Mr. Shakespeare asked was..." The doorman stopped, looked up and closed his eyes.

"Okay, the first part is easy...it was *'to be or...not to be!'* And then...it's something like...that is always our question in life: what do we want to BE? And then her father told her, 'You see, my little Grace, your papa is very greedy; he doesn't only want to BE one thing, so that is why I became a teacher. Because, imagine if in my class there is a wee little girl like you and I help her become a scientist and she creates a medicine that cures people all over the world, or a boy who becomes a great leader and frees our country so no one lives with this fear anymore...Imagine, Grace...all the amazing things I could help children become if I am a teacher! And all these things that you think I could do to become famous, well, Grace, look, don't you see? I am doing them, am I not? You see, as a teacher, I have become someone who helps many—even hundreds of children to become so many amazing things—and I can help create so many wonderful beings in this world. Could there be any greater purpose in life? And this helps your papa, Grace. I like constantly becoming what others need me to be to help them become who they want to be. I love being that, Grace...I pray I never stop becoming that until I die.'

"Grace's eyes, Mr. Sanchez, when she spoke of her father, her eyes became like an open field. You know, that kind you feel this sudden urge to run wild in!

"But I had been there so long...so long, Mr. Sanchez. So I said to her, 'Yeah well, I'm not your father. Nor am I in his class and I don't think I can ever become anything good, Grace, because I have done too many bad things to become anything good.'

"'That's not true, Aaron,' she said. 'Look what you have become to so many of us girls.'

"'No...no, Grace,' I said to her. 'Sometimes people do things that are so unforgivable they can never become anything else.'

"Grace then suddenly lifted her hand—it was our sign—the cue we always used if we thought someone saw us talking and we needed to stop. I didn't see anyone but she looked around and saw that no one was watching us and then she reached inside her dress and pulled out that book. She showed me that book, Mr. Sanchez and she quickly opened to this page—the Taj Mahal—and she told me, 'If you want to be forgiven, Aaron, go here, to the Taj Mahal.'

"And then she read out that passage to me:
'Should guilty seek asylum here,
Like one pardoned, he becomes free from sin.
Should a sinner make his way to this mansion,
All his past sins are to be washed away.'

"But I never had a chance to go to India and see the real Taj Mahal, Mr. Sanchez, so that's why I come here each day, hoping to maybe wash some of those sins away and become...well...become someone I want to be."

"And are you?" Robert simply asked.

"Ah...I'm trying, Mr. Sanchez. Life is such a long journey of becoming."

After a moment of silence, Robert looked back in the booklet and the torn page and asked, "So why is this ripped?"

"Grace took it before she left."

"Left?" Robert asked. "Where did she go?"

"Well, there had been talk in the camp that the United Nation soldiers were closing in on us, which meant we had to pack up camp and move. This happened many times. When I told Grace this, she told me she heard that the UN soldiers were helping a lot of us children that had become soldiers to get back to our families and homes. Oh, Mr. Sanchez, seeing the look in her eyes—the excitement of seeing her family again...well...I just knew who I wanted to be then. I wanted to become the one to help her do that! So, that night I came up with a plan to escape. There were six of us—Grace, me and four other girls. You see, whenever we had to move from a camp in a hurry, we had to dig these holes in order to bury anything we could not carry and then we would come back to retrieve it at a later time. Well, there was lots of digging and the girls had to help. And so we dug this extra hole that no one knew about and covered it with some branches and things. The plan was a couple of hours before we were about to leave, the six of us would hide and cover ourselves in that hole. And we knew they wouldn't have time to look for us with the UN soldiers so near and when the UN soldiers got close, we would come out and be saved.

"Each of us guards was given about five girls to watch as everyone

因because

packed up to leave. And I arranged it with another guard that I would take Grace and the four others. But the plan had changed and we were to leave an hour earlier. As soon as I heard this, I ran as quickly as I could to get the girls but when I got there, they had already disappeared. It seemed that another guard told them they were to leave camp with him. This guard had ordered them to gather their things and be ready to leave in ten minutes. But in our plan, Mr. Sanchez, I wasn't coming to get them for another hour but they knew this was their only chance to escape, so in those ten minutes they slipped out and went into our special hole to hide.

"But when this guard could not find the girls, he started yelling and screaming to me about the missing girls. And now, it was too dangerous to join them in our hole—I was scared I might give them away. So, when we were all about to leave, our leader asked where the girls were and that guard who was going to take them blamed me. He said he had seen me always talking to these girls and said I had let them escape. And then the same man who cut my ear came to me and asked me where they were. I shook my head and I told him I didn't know and then he said, 'Do you know what happens when someone loses what I own?' Again, I told him I didn't know. He asked me again where they were. I was so scared, Mr. Sanchez, but at the same time I was so happy...so happy they couldn't find the girls. He then had two of the boys grab my arms and they pushed me to my knees. He kept asking me, 'Do you know what happens when someone loses what is mine?' But for some reason, no matter how scared I felt, I knew I wouldn't tell him where the girls were. Then he lifted up his machete as the two boys held my arms over this bench. First he asked me was I right handed or left. For some reason, I lied and said I was left-handed. And he asked, 'Okay boy, one last time, where are my girls?'"

The doorman stopped and released a peaceful sigh.

"And I just can't explain it to you, Mr. Sanchez. I mean, I knew what they would do to me. I knew if I didn't tell him, he was going to cut off my hands. Yet somehow it was okay because right at that moment, something mattered more to me than my hands."

The doorman held out his arms.

"And do you know what I thought of? All I could think of was what Grace had told me about her father and why he was a teacher, so he could show his students all the things they could become. And I thought that's what I want to do—I wanted to become like him, to give those five girls a chance to become something...anything. So I just said, 'They are long gone, you will never catch them.' And then it came down. My left hand was gone. And just as he raised his machete to cut off my other hand, we all heard a gunshot and everyone started screaming and running...and me, Mr. Sanchez..."

329

The doorman gave one of his deep warm laughs..."Ha ha...well, me...I nobly fainted.

"It was Grace who was there when I woke up. I was in some truck and the UN soldiers were taking us away. All five girls were there and about eight others were rescued. We were all taken to some place they called a rehabilitation centre where they tried to help us erase all the things we had done and become. They helped us just be...just be people again.

"I didn't see Grace a lot at that place because they worked with the boys and girls separately. But one day in one of those sessions, Grace came into our room and asked if she could join our circle. You see, Mr. Sanchez, Grace's parents had come for her and she was leaving the next day. And that's when she gave me that book, Mr. Sanchez. Grace stood up in the circle and showed everyone that book and said, 'This book, in many ways, was my salvation. Whenever I missed my family, I would read about one of these wonders of the world. Whenever I heard the crying of the other children in the camp, I would go to them and tell them about these wonders and imagine we were there. But one boy...' and then she pointed right at me, Mr. Sanchez. 'This boy, Aaron, every day he found ways to make me and some of the other girls feel safe in that mean awful place.' And then, Mr. Sanchez, she handed me the book and said..."

The doorman suddenly had difficulty speaking, so he cleared his throat to quell the emotion behind his words. But the wetness in his eyes betrayed the beauty of what he felt. He brushed his stump across his face to wipe away the tears.

"I'm sorry, but it always makes me cry...Good tears though, Mr. Sanchez, happy ones. Anyway, she handed me that book and said, 'Aaron, I want you to have this book now, not because you need it to be your salvation, but I want to give it to you because I think *YOU* belong in this book. Because you...you have become one of my wonders of the world, Aaron.'

"Then all the other kids clapped. Oh, Mr. Sanchez, I just can't tell you what that meant to me."

Robert wiped away his own tears that now fell freely and openly.

"And do you know, Mr. Sanchez, there's not a day I don't miss my hand? You know maybe forty, fifty times a day I might miss it. Sometimes I reach out to pick up something and it's like, 'Oh my, I can't do it!' I just forget my hand is gone. But you know what I think about when I look at it? Do you know what I think, Mr. Sanchez?"

Robert heard the doorman's question but couldn't help feeling overwhelmed with a question of his own. He looked at the ugly scar where the doorman's ear had once been. Then he stared at Aaron's stump, which only half an hour ago caused him to feel nothing but pity and sorrow for the doorman. Robert thought of all the grief and anger he felt at the rehabilitation centre whenever he caught a glimpse of himself in the mirror or saw the other amputees. All the feelings he never told anyone about having something stolen from him which would never be returned. But now, as he looked down at his own stumps, his own missing legs, he just couldn't hold back a question of his own and so he blurted out to Aaron, "How can I become like you?"

The doorman laughed that precious welcoming laugh of his. "Ho ho. Really? Become like me? Do you want to have no left ear or no hand like me, Mr. Sanchez?"

"No, that is not what I meant, Aaron. I meant—"

"Oh, I'm sorry, Mr. Sanchez, I know what you meant. I'm sorry for my joke. Forgive me. It is just I saw you staring at my hand and ear...so please forgive my joke. I do understand your question. In truth, I do. You see, when I look at myself or when I miss my hand or ear...Well, that's when I ask myself two questions, Mr. Sanchez: do I become a man without an ear and a hand? Or, what kind of man can I become without an ear and a hand?"

"You. Aaron. Do you know how long I've been looking for you?"

"You have been looking for me?"

"Yes...Yes..." Robert laughed then stopped suddenly.

"What is it, Mr. Sanchez? Are you all right?"

"Aaron, what time is it?"

The doorman looked at his watch, "It's five minutes to noon. Why?"

"Oh my God, I have to talk in a few minutes!"

"Well, come, I will take you."

"No, wait...Aaron, I need you to do something for me. If you—"

"Anything, Mr. Sanchez, *anything!*"

"Could you please take me to my car?"

40. SIX MONTHS AGO – MT. EVEREST

Nancy squirmed in her sleeping bag, trying to find the most comfortable position to write and still stay warm. Robert had told them that night at supper that after every climb he ever made, he always wrote a thank you to the mountain. He told them how he would tuck it away under some rock before he left. Troy, Philip and Nancy all vowed that they would do the same.

Nancy had the same book light she used to read each night attached to a small pad of blank paper that her mother had given her from one of her business trips to China. "City of Dreams Macau" was the name of the hotel. Nancy looked at the hotel's logo and smiled to herself, thinking it was the perfect page on which to write her thank you to the mountain. She immediately started to write and then quickly scribbled over what she had written, tore the page off and then tucked it in her backpack.

She started again. *Dear Mount Everest.* She nodded and thought, *Yeah, that's the best way to begin.*

Dear Mount Everest,

Hi, I've never written to a mountain before so I'm not sure where to begin. As a matter of fact, I've never been to a mountain before...well, that's not true, I saw some but I've never really been this close to one before. I guess I'm pretty close since I'm pretty high up on you now. Hope we are not too heavy! LOL...

Okay, before I thank you, I'd like to tell you how beautiful you are. Really, I never thought about it before. I was never much into nature and stuff but it's quite amazing how different you look all the time...I think you're a girl, right? Because Ang and Mingma, they always refer to you as 'she.' Anyway, you're very beautiful!

When we were coming here, we interviewed lots of climbers and when we asked them why they were coming here and climbing you, a lot of them just said it was because you were there. Well, I always thought they were just trying to be funny but now I kind of get it. So, I think the thing I really want to thank you for is for being there. I know that sounds strange 'cause you never move, but you made me move. If it wasn't for you being there—well, here—I probably would never have met Philip and Troy. And if it wasn't for you being here, who knows what would have happened to Satya...He never would have crossed that line.

I think in a way you have helped me cross a line by coming to you. Because I never in my dreams would have thought me...ME! Nancy Olivia Archer would ever-ever-EVER come here to be on you. Not in a kabillion years would anyone have thought of little me on MT. EVEREST. It's just awesome!!!

You know what's strange, Miss Mountain? It's that, as I'm thanking you, I feel like I'm also thanking Mr. Sanchez, too. Without him, my life would never have changed. I wouldn't be here; I'd still be standing on the other side of that line...When I was in the middle of all that cutting and hating who I was, I never thought there would be a place for me to be in this world. And now look where I am!!! I guess maybe that's what all those climbers mean when they say they come here and climb you because you're there...I think you're that other side of the line for many people. You help them face their fear or challenge themselves to be here...and I guess it's always about the choice of crossing that line, isn't it? I'm really happy I was able to cross that line and meet you!

So, not much more to say...Tomorrow we will say goodbye to you but for now, I really want to thank you for being a part of MY life now, Miss Everest!

Love,
Nancy Olivia Archer

41. PRESENT DAY – AT THE HOTEL

"Jenny, come quick, it's your dad," Kyle yelled.

Jenny shot up "Daddy...? Where is he, Kyle? *Where is he?!*"

Kyle was standing in front of the door that led to the Leaning Tower of Pisa.

"Here! Come on, quick!"

Jenny helped her mother up and, with pounding hearts, they ran down the hallway towards Kyle.

"Bobby. Oh, please be okay. Please be..." Monique could not say the last word out loud, yet the word "alive" kept repeating itself over and over again.

When they got about halfway down the hall, Kyle opened the door to the Leaning Tower of Pisa slightly. Suddenly, the hallway filled with a loud, majestic piece of orchestrated music. Monique couldn't stop the thought in her head. *John William's Greatest hits, CD 2, Track 3, Theme from Superman.* She knew this music inside out.

Jenny was moving so fast she crashed into Kyle's arms. The door shut and he fell to his knees.

"I'm sorry, Kyle. Where is he?" Jenny breathlessly said, helping him to his feet.

"Shhh, Jenny, shhh." Kyle reached up and opened the door again just as Monique reached them.

"He's in there, Mrs. Sanchez."

"You saw him? You saw him?" Monique almost begged.

"No, they just said he's about to talk...in here...That's what they told me."

Monique grabbed Kyle's shoulder to move him aside so she could enter the room. She immediately stopped when she got inside, for the room was now almost in total darkness. As her eyes adjusted, she could see a light coming from the stage. The glow lit up the room slightly and she could see everyone's eyes staring forward.

Jenny and Kyle followed close behind Monique. The three of them moved a little further into the room until they could see the screen. The whole back wall flickered with a tidal wave of Roberto Sanchez images. The music was building to a crescendo. The screen was filled with the words "QUEST-I'm-ON" and, with the last crashing beat of sound, the word "QUEST" was left alone and emblazoned on the screen. Slowly the word "QUEST" faded into a picture of Robert celebrating, standing on the highest place on the planet.

The Leaning Tower of Pisa came to life with applause and cheering.

Monique squinted and anxiously surveyed the stage, trying to locate Robert. She could definitely make out the silhouette of Amir sitting at his controls, but where was Robert? Was he up there? *How could they have started the presentation without him?*

A single circular spotlight snapped on, filling the centre of the stage. The applause stayed strong, anticipating Roberto Sanchez's entrance into the light.

Two, three, four seconds, the applause stayed strong. Monique's hands went over her mouth. Five, six, seven seconds. *Where on earth is he?* Eight, nine, ten and there it was: first the gleaming reflection off the metal wheels of his chair and then her husband.

Monique exhaled as if she had just been holding her breath under water for hours. The overall sudden weakness she felt was soothing and peaceful. She tightly wrapped her arms around herself as if attempting to hold that wave of emotion deep inside her. She didn't want this feeling to escape. Oh, how it calmed her aching, aching heart! Robert was not dead behind a door with a wheelchair symbol. *Robert was found!*

"That's my dad!" Monique heard Jenny say to Kyle.

"I know, Jenny, I know," Kyle said as he put his arm around her.

But as Robert rolled to the front of the stage, the applause quickly became stuttered and eventually came to an awkward end.

The distinct contrast of the man standing on the top of the world and the man who rolled into the spotlight was not something most in the audience were expecting to see. Monique, Jenny and Kyle then heard some hushed murmured reactions from the table they were standing beside.

"My god, what happened to him?"

"Does he have no legs?"

"Man, that's sad!"

Monique was about to turn to say something, but then it hit her! The majority of the people in this room had no idea what happened to Robert. Except for the employees of her company who knew of Robert's accident, the rest of the room was applauding to see the same heroic man who graced the pictures on screen. They were anticipating the man scaling impossible heights to come walking into the light with two legs. The impact of seeing Robert now, in a wheelchair, took a lot of people by surprise and the end of the applause reflected that.

Oh no! What have I done? A panic erupted inside of Monique.

42. SIX MONTH AGO – MT. EVEREST

One moment. Such fury. Was it in a heartbeat? The blink of an eye? Didn't matter...however you described it—it happened fast and without warning.

It was as if the mountain just got incredibly angry and screamed with all its might, *"Be quiet! Leave me alone!!!"*

And like scared little children, they all obeyed. It was over in seconds. Only seconds. Yet, the mountain's snowy white temper echoed much longer. Time? Hard to tell. But as the thick white clouds of snow settled, there was only one still figure left standing, encased in snow that went half way up to his chest.

It was Philip. He was still holding the camera on his chest. As everyone else went running, Philip just stood there, incapable of fleeing the tidal wave of snow that descended. Luckily for him, the frozen sheet of white only swallowed him halfway up. On either side of him, the snow was towering over twelve feet high. The dusty clouds of snow had coated him so completely that he resembled a porcelain statute. And with the snow that gathered around the camera just under his chin, he looked like that long-bearded wizard Dumbledore he loved from Harry Potter.

Philip slowly turned his head from side to side. Nothing but white. His snowy beard fell onto the camera as he opened his mouth to speak. "Tro..." His voice was unrecognizable to him. He tried again. "Tro..." but his mouth was shaking so hard that his voice was almost empty of sound. Again, he tried and, although only a meek sound emerged, at least this time the sound made sense.

"Troy?"

Like a lost little child, he spoke, "Troy?" Again. "Troy?"

With the snow up around his chest, he felt like he couldn't get enough air into his body to let himself be heard. It was only when he looked down that he realized he was stuck deep inside the snow. He lunged forward, but his legs would not budge. He tried turning side to side to loosen himself, but nothing happened. He put the camera down on the snow and tried to pull himself up, but again it was useless. He looked again to either side of him, seeing nothing but two walls of snow and suddenly, he started to breathe in quick little pants. The breaths grew quicker and quicker and then suddenly, trying to match the mountain's roar, he screamed with every fiber in his body.

"TROOOOOOOOY!!!"

The sound seemed to echo for so long. But no one answered. Then Philip looked up into the brilliant blue sky and screamed once more with all his might, "TROOOOOOOOOOOOOOOOOY..."

He waited to let his sound drift off, hoping to hear Troy call back. But no sound came.

"Where are they? Where the hell are they?" he cried to himself. Philip's face started to twist as he bit his upper lip, trying to hold back his tears of fear. He struggled for more air. Crying was now hindering him from breathing. He started to gasp and gulp for air as if he was drowning.

He flung his big mitts off and, with his bare hands, clutched at the snow around him, trying to dig himself out. Like a wild creature with its leg caught in a snare, he was moving every part of his body, desperately struggling to get free. The more he flailed his arms, the more he struggled for air.

43. PRESENT DAY – AT THE HOTEL

The applause had died out. They waited. One, two, three, four, five seconds, but Robert still hadn't opened his mouth to speak. "I have to do something," Monique whispered to herself. "I should run onto the stage and explain what happened to Robert." *He looks so small,* she thought, *so small sitting in that wheelchair in front of that huge photograph of him on the screen. I just didn't think we needed to tell people. I...I...I never thought of this. I can't let this happen to him now.*

She briskly stepped around the tables and the people standing near the front of stage to get to the steps. The moment she got there, she stopped dead in her tracks. Robert spoke. "Ah, umm," he cleared his throat, "well, hi."

The spotlight was a bit blinding at first, so he put one hand over his brow to stop the glare and adjust his eyes to the light. He had no idea where to begin. Robert shook his head a little, hoping that might loosen some words from his brain, but it was all blank inside. So, he took in another deep breath and decided to just start talking and hope that the words would fall into the right places and make some sense.

"So ah, well, so...three companies are ah, going to be one now. And ah, that's great. And I...I...ah...well, I guess...I guess—" He looked back to Amir and spoke to him. "I'm sorry—I don't know, I'm not sure how to start." Amir waved his hands for Robert to go on talking. Robert turned back to face the room.

"Okay. Like I said, it's great to...uh—No, I'm sorry."

He looked back at Amir again, who now gave him a thumbs-up. Robert bit down on his lower lip and shook his head slightly. After speaking with Aaron Aboga, he felt inspired—inspired with something he hadn't felt for such a long time: purpose, the simple purpose of being here. The doorman had pried opened a door that, for the last six months, had seemed nailed shut to him. And just minutes ago, he felt that maybe he was ready to do this talk. But to talk, one needed words and no words were coming out of him. It had been so long since his thoughts had formed into any words he wanted to share, so he sat there, biting down on his lip.

Greg took a step, stood beside Monique and whispered, "He's still pretty nervous, I see."

Robert turned back to the crowd and rolled forward a little. "Okay...you know what? I'm sorry. I'm really sorry, I shouldn't be here. I'm...well, I'm..." He stopped again. The Leaning Tower of Pisa was completely still. Greg stepped even closer to Monique. "What? What does he mean he's not supposed to be here? Is this part of his talk?"

Monique didn't answer her boss, she just watched Robert turn his back to the audience again, but now he rolled himself towards Amir.

"Where's he going, Monique?" Greg couldn't hide his concern. The room became restless, everyone murmuring and wondering what was happening. Amir could feel all the eyes in the room turn to him as Robert approached his table. Amir got up and leaned towards Robert.

"What's wrong?" he whispered.

But since Amir had spoken directly into Robert's head mike, his question came out loud and clear through the auditorium speakers. In his embarrassment, Amir turned to the room and blurted out, "I'm sorry, ladies and gentleman, we seem to be having some technical difficulties."

And then he nervously bowed, which caused the audience to laugh. Hearing the laughter only made Amir more nervous, so he bowed again. As Amir was bowing, Robert rolled past the table and closer to back of the stage. Amir then ran towards Robert, which gave the audience the impression of a playful game—one that had Robert trying to get off the stage and Amir attempting to catch him. The audience laughed a little louder, sensing that maybe this was part of the show.

Robert then stopped directly in front of the screen and looked at the photograph of him standing on the highest peak known to man. As Amir reached him, Monique edged closer to the stairs leading to the stage. She knew this was not a game. Just as she was about to take the first step up the stairs, Amir spoke.

First he smiled, then lifted his arm and pointed at the screen, "Speak about that," he said to Robert. "Speak about climbing that mountain." The audience applauded. Yes, hearing him speak about climbing that mountain was exactly what they wanted to hear! Monique froze on the first step, waiting to see if Robert would turn around to speak.

But Robert didn't hear Amir. His head was tilted up, staring at the screen. There it was: he was now face to face with that mountain again—Mount Everest and him. Robert's hands came off of the wheels of his chair. He curled them into tight fists. Monique opened her mouth to call her husband's name, but then Robert slammed his hands back onto the wheels and twirled in one quick motion to face the room.

"I'm sorry." He spoke without any hint of apology. "You're probably wondering, hey, where's the man standing on that mountain? Where the hell is he? Well, let me tell you something. For the past six months, I've been wondering exactly the same thing. Where the hell *is he?*"

The audience didn't react. The moment felt awkward. It was dreadfully silent. Greg pulled Monique down the step with a worried look. Jenny edged closer into Kyle. Even Lou's ever-constant smile sank away.

But Robert surprised everyone when he let out a little chuckle. "Ha ha...isn't that the same question we all ask when something's changed—or is about to change? Why do we have to do it differently? I've been doing it this way for years, why are we changing it now? Or simple little things like, 'Hey, where's my favourite chair? I'm not sitting in that!' Or, 'No way, I don't want to move!' Yeah...well...for me it was, 'Hey, where are my legs?' and, 'What the hell am I going to do now?'"

No one reacted vocally, but there was a distinct interest in Robert's question stirring within the room.

"And your boss, Mr. Wong, he told me something this morning. He said he was worried about the big change all the employees were going to have to go through. He told me a story about a bucket with sand in it. He was saying that sand on its own is like these millions of individual, tiny stones. And they can just blow away if you don't have something to keep them together. And then he explained how all of you are the sand and how the three companies have to become this one bucket—that can hold you all together. I think that's what he was telling me...Anyway, to be honest with you, he just seemed a little scared."

Greg tugged on Monique's arm and whispered, "What's going on, Monique?" She just stared at her husband and shook her head. That, she didn't know.

"Well, I'd be scared too, wouldn't you? The guy's got a lot of responsibility and if he wasn't a little scared that this might not work then he wouldn't be dealing with the challenge realistically, would he? And then, Mr. Wong, he told me that's why he got *me* to talk today. So I could help you...I don't know, maybe stick together better? And tell you about all the challenges I had on those mountains and how I dealt with—"

Robert paused. He took a look over his shoulder. He then lifted his arm and gestured at the smiling image of himself on the screen. He turned back to the crowd. "...How I dealt with all those challenges on the mountain."

Robert chuckled to himself again, and he felt a raw joy bubbling inside of him as the words tumbled out from his mouth, "Ha...but first, you have to admit...it's a pretty gutsy call for your boss to make, don't you think? Having a guy who lost both his legs on that mountain, come here and talk to you about climbing it?"

Kyle hugged Jenny closer at hearing her father speak about losing his legs.

"And you know what? What I said before—it's true, I didn't want to be here today. I fought, kicking and screaming..." Robert paused again and couldn't believe what came out of his mouth next. "Well, I guess it wasn't much of kicking with these," he raised one of his stumps to make a kicking motion. The audience exhaled into a laugh.

"But it's true, I didn't want to be here. Frankly, after what happened to me, I didn't want to be anywhere." Robert raised his arms and, as he asked each of the following questions, he paused slightly, as if he was waiting for an answer to each one: "So what about you? Coming here today—Why are you here? Do you want to be here? Do you need to be here?"

44. SIX MONTHS AGO – MT. EVEREST

"Kong!" A faint voice screamed out somewhere in the distance.

"Kong?"

But Philip was now oblivious to the sound. Every ounce of his energy was being spent desperately attempting to pull himself out of the snow. His body was flailing side to side. The snow was as hard as concrete. No matter how much he struggled, he couldn't move his legs at all.

"Kong! Kong..." The voice was now sounded stronger, closer.

Philip was now in a frenzy, muttering incoherently to himself. He started unzipping his jacket, hoping that would help free him. But the snow was too high up and wouldn't allow him to unzip his coat all the way down. So he ripped at the zipper, trying to tear the coat off him. That didn't work, so he pulled with all his might, trying to get his coat over his head, trying to yank himself free of it.

"Kong...KONG!" The voice was directly in front of him, just as Philip pulled his coat up over his head.

"Kong, holy shit, you're alive..." Troy was standing about fifteen feet in front of Philip and screaming at the top of his lungs to get him to calm down. "Phil? Phil, what the hell you doin'?"

Philip didn't stop; he was still trying to get his coat off his body.

"Mingma, he's here...He's over here!" Troy called out as he furiously threw the snow side to side with his hands, making a path towards Philip.

"It's okay...Phil." But Philip was still going crazy, pulling at his coat. "It's okay, Phil... We're here!" Troy yelled.

Moving the snow with his hands wasn't working, so Troy threw himself on the bank of snow and tried rolling himself towards Philip so he wouldn't sink into the snow. He rolled until he got behind Philip and then wrapped his arms around him to stop Philip's arms from flailing.

"Whoa...easy, Phil... easy..."

Philip tried to throw Troy off him but Troy squeezed tighter to stop Philip from moving.

"It's okay, big guy...you're alright...You are alright," Troy said as he pulled Philip's coat back down, revealing his head.

Philip was now grunting and panting, "Ahhh...haaa...Tra...ahh... "

"Philip!" Troy almost yelled in Philip's ear as he hugged him using all his strength.

"It's okay...It's okay!"

Philip turned his head. Troy's face was an inch from his. Philip's manic energy was slowing down. His body still shook with little minor quakes as the two boys spoke.

"Troy...Troy...why didn't you come when I yelled?"

"I was kind of running from an avalanche. Which you should've done!" Troy smiled and then called out loudly, "Mingma...Mingma...I got Philip, he's okay...He's here...He's here!"

"Where's Nancy, Troy? Where are Nancy and Satya? Where's Mr. Sanchez? Troy, where the hell is everyone?"

45. PRESENT DAY – AT THE HOTEL

"Change? Ah...I have talked about it so many times! How to deal with all the changes you encounter when climbing a mountain. How to plan for change, how to accept change, how to adapt to change. You're all here today because the thing you do every day—your work, your job, maybe even your passion—is about to change, right? The place you go each day and spend a lot of your time, the place where you feel purpose in your life is going to change. And today is the beginning of that change! Maybe it's a big change to some of you and well, maybe for some, it's small. Regardless, you're here because something...something is about to change. And what will that change be? What's it going to look like?"

Robert pointed behind him. "Well, look at that picture of me."

He then turned around and faced the screen. It was an amazing photograph. The top of Mount Everest. One arm jubilantly extended into the air in triumph. With his goggles up on his forehead, you could see the effervescent smile in his eyes. And through his snow-caked beard, Roberto Sanchez's whole face reflected what looked to be a moment of pure, simple joy.

He turned to face the crowd. "Man, I was happy at that moment! It was the absolute toughest climb I had ever had in my whole life. There were so many times I almost quit. I never thought that moment would ever become *that* photograph. We had so many unexpected challenges and change of plans and it was just...just hard to believe it would ever become that reality!"

Robert then rolled his wheelchair to the very front of the stage. "And now...now look at me!"

Jenny let go of Kyle and moved to her mother. "Mom, what's

345

Daddy doing?"

Monique didn't take her eyes off her husband but whispered to Jenny, "I don't know, baby...I just hope..."

Robert then continued speaking.

"You see...something changed." Robert opened his arms again, but this time he lifted his stumps as high off the chair as he possibly could. He waited a moment as he extended each limb as far out as he could, but there was no reaction; the room was deadly quiet. Monique could feel Greg's concern as he turned to her. *Why wasn't Robert speaking about his mountain climbing adventures?* But even as painful as it was to watch Robert struggle, these were new words to her and she desperately needed to hear each and every one of them. So she didn't dare let Greg know she felt his gaze.

As Robert held out his arms and stumps, Jenny let out a little sigh. She suddenly realized that this was the first time since his accident that she had ever seen her father mention or show his legs so prominently. They were always hidden under some blanket or some kind of cover. And now here he was, showing himself off for all the world to see, like some exhibit in a museum.

Robert put his arms and legs down. "You see, this is what my change looks like. I didn't choose this change. And just like you dealing with this change, I have to ask myself: How did I get here? Why am I here? Do I want to be here? Do I need to be here? And how do I deal with this change?"

The audience gave a generous applause, feeling the focus of the talk was now approaching.

"On that screen you saw the words 'QUEST-I'm-ON.' That's the name of my company. And through my company, I've helped a lot of other people deal with change. I thought I knew a lot about that subject but...this—whoa, this is new! This is really unknown territory for me! And yet, look, here I am. That man who climbed Everest. I'm here to talk to you about how all those challenges on the mountain helped me deal with change right?...Can I?...Can everything that I learned on that mountain— can that really help me deal with losing my legs? Well, let me tell you..."

As Robert raised his arm, his finger must have accidentally caught the string on the brown leather bag he had been clutching all day. And as his arm went up, so did the leather bag. It flew up high into the air and landed about five feet beside him.

The loud noise caused some people to let out a little gasp. Amir quickly stood up from behind his table to see what had made that loud bang.

Monique brought her hands to her face. "Oh my God! No!"

"What? Mom, what is it?" Jenny whispered to her mom.

"It's that bag your father has been...he never lets it out of his sight and won't let anyone touch it."

"What's in it, Mom? What's in it?"

Monique turned to her daughter and gravely said, "Really, Jen...I...I think that's where he keeps that...gun."

"I'm sorry," Robert reached out one hand towards the audience, "that wasn't really planned."

He then maneuvered his chair to go pick the bag up. But at exactly the same moment, Lou ran out of his seat to the front of the stage to pick it up for him.

"No, please! Don't touch it," Robert snapped as he reached for the bag. Lou reacted as if he was a robber caught in the act. He quickly shot both his arms high up into the air. The quick gesture of being caught red-handed made the audience roar with laughter.

Robert then sat back up, leaving the leather bag on the floor and looked directly at Lou. "No, I'm sorry about that, Lou. Actually, if you could, would you please pick it up for me?"

Jenny shot a worried look at her mother. "You think there's a gun in there?" Her mother winced as Jenny said the word 'gun.'

Lou turned to face the audience with his hands still in the air and made a humorous questioning face that said, "Should I?" This brought even more laughter. With both arms still in the air, Lou comically inched his way over to the bag. Then he very slowly leaned over, keeping one arm in the air, and snatched the bag off the floor with the other. He held it up high to show the audience he had it. They applauded heartily.

"Whoa, it's heavy. What do you have in here, Mr. Sanchez?" Lou said, looking out to the crowd. "Hope it's not going to explode!" The audience laughed even louder.

"Okay Lou, could you please open the bag?"

Monique moved closer to Jenny and Kyle. Lou then lowered the bag and slowly untied the thick yellow string that held it shut.

As Lou struggled a little trying to open the bag, Robert addressed the crowd. "Here I was, facing this great change and what did I do? Well, like most people, whenever we feel we are about to lose something, we tend to hang on tighter to everything that's connected to it right...? And that's exactly what I did...I hung onto that bag with all my life. Why? Because I thought it was the only thing I had left. So, open the bag, Lou. Tell them what you see."

Lou knew how to play the crowd. He held the bag in front of him like a magician would. He lifted one arm up as if he was about to pull a rabbit out of a hat. He slowly opened the bag and looked inside. His head jerked up in shock.

Jenny squeezed her mother and Kyle so tightly that Kyle actually let out a sound.

Lou looked back into the bag and up to the audience and said loudly, "Rocks?!"

The audience exploded into laughter.

"Yes, Lou, a rock from every mountain I ever climbed! And even yesterday, if you would have asked why I was holding on so tightly to those rocks, I couldn't really have told you."

Lou pulled out a rock and presented to the audience. As the crowd applauded, he handed the leather pouch back to Robert, waved to the crowd and went to sit back down.

"But I get it now. I think, after I lost my legs...I just clung so tightly to the past...hanging onto the time when I had legs because, well, I couldn't accept the change that had happened. And more importantly, I couldn't handle all the change that was now happening around me! And since I couldn't even walk anymore, let alone climb, I looked for something tangible...something concrete to remind me of everything I had done when I had legs. You see, I thought I was...trying to find my way back to who I was! When I should have been...looking for who I am now!"

The crowd cheered warmly. Robert smiled in surprise, for he had no idea that what he said was worthy of cheering.

He put his hands over his eyes to look out into the dark room. He was trying to see where Monique was, but the angle of the light and where he was prevented him from seeing past the edge of the stage. Everyone was mostly in silhouette.

"Change is kind of like—I know you have to look back first in order to move forward but I think my problem was that I got stuck in the looking back. You know, just this morning my wife was driving us here. And she played this song—the same song she always played whenever she would drive me to the airport to drop me off for one of my climbs." He smiled to himself. "We would always get into these funny and sometimes very profound discussions on what the lyrics were trying to say. And this morning, my poor wife, she was trying her best to get me back into one of those conversations about that song. Now, we have played that song so many times I thought I knew it inside out but...as it was playing this morning, suddenly I heard this one question in the song...and I heard it as if was brand new to me, like someone rewrote the song just for me. Do you know that feeling? The question was this: 'Can I handle the seasons of my life?' Pretty simple question, right? Seasons are changes, right?"

"Yes!" a voice was heard behind him on stage. Robert paused, looked behind him and saw Amir's face, stunned that he had actually reacted out loud. Amir whispered that he was sorry and then motioned for him to go on. Robert gave him a thumbs up this time and then turned back. "But for me it wasn't simple. 'Cause I sure the hell couldn't handle *this season* of my life! So I did what any reasonable person does when facing a question they don't like the answer to. I asked my wife to 'turn that damn song off!'"

The crowd laughed. Jenny looked at her mother and wiped away a tear. Greg looked at Lou and accusingly nodded. And Monique? She looked as if she was in a trance. Not a muscle in her face moved; she just stood there with her arms at her sides, staring at Robert.

"Yeah...that's how I handled every question lately...I just tuned them all out. And of course, after my wife did turn it off, well...I just grabbed my little bag of rocks and held them even closer. I thought what was in that bag was the last of my identity—it was the only thing left of me. Rocks...that's right, rocks! It's like I was clinging on to the one thing I couldn't do any more and completely forgetting about everything else I could still do."

46. SIX MONTHS AGO – MT. EVEREST

Mingma ran into the alleyway of snow Philip was caught in.

"Is Satya, my son...was he here with you?" Mingma sounded worried and his breath was terribly laboured.

"No," Philip cried. "And Nancy, where is she?"

"Are you sure they not here under snow?"

"No... Well, maybe, I don't know. I don't know for sure, Mingma, I'm sorry. It all happened so..."

"Baba...Baba!" They heard Satya's voice from around the huge bank of snow.

Mingma turned too quickly and fell face down in the snow after hearing his son's voice. And from his knees he lifted his arms up high and called out, "Satya, Satya...my boy...my boy!"

Slowly, emerging into the alleyway of snow where Philip was stuck came Satya, Nancy and Ang.

"Philip, Troy, thank God...Thank God, you're okay." Nancy looked pale and winced in pain. Satya and Ang were holding her up on their shoulders.

"Nancy, you okay?" Troy asked.

"She just hurt her knee—a twist is all," Satya explained as he let Nancy stay in Ang's arms so he could greet his father.

Mingma jumped to his feet and Satya hugged him with every ounce of energy he possessed. "Baba...baba, I was so worried. "

"Nancy, Nancy, Satya, Ang, Troy, Mingma...Great... great, we're all safe!" Philip joyfully exclaimed. "*BUT* can someone please...*PLEASE* get me outta here?!"

"Here, take this," Ang said, first letting Nancy down to sit on her backpack and then holding out a small folding shovel to Satya. "You dig out Philip. Mingma and me, we go find Mr. Robert." Ang and Mingma quickly ran out of sight.

"Where the hell are your gloves, Phil?" Troy asked Philip.

"I don't know...I...I....kind of threw them off."

"Here, take my extra ones," Nancy said as she pulled out a pair of fleece mitts from her pocket and tossed them to Troy.

As Satya used the shovel, Nancy got up and rolled herself to where Troy was and the two of them began digging with their hands. It took them almost ten minutes to free Philip from his frozen wall.

The moment he was free, Philip checked his camera and a horrible thought came to him. "Oh my God! This thing is still running. All those kids back home who were watching this today might think we're all dead."

Nancy and Troy both said, "See if it's still working...Let's...tell them we're okay."

"No way, we lost the connection. Oh my God, those poor kids...We have to tell them we're okay. We have to call base camp first. Mr. Sanchez...Let's tell him we need to get back in contact with the schools. Tell them everything's okay."

They all moved swiftly out of the hallway of snow into the open space. Twenty yards away, they saw Ang holding out his pickaxe and poking the ground in front of him as he gently walked around. It was where—only fifteen minutes before—a huge crevice and a ladder were. The ladder Roberto Sanchez was crossing. Ang picked at the snow until he uncovered a backpack. Ang picked it up and slung it over his shoulder.

"Where is Mr. Sanchez?" Philip asked. "Where did he run to?"

"Mr. Sanchez...Mr. Sanchez!" Nancy called out. Then Troy and Philip started screaming Robert's name as loud as they could. The three of them then moved around in different directions calling for Robert. Nancy looked behind her and was surprised that the Sherpas were not helping in the search. Ang was shaking his head while walking slowly towards Mingma and his son.

Nancy stopped calling out and watched Ang put his arm on Mingma's shoulder.

"Troy...Phil..." she yelled at the two boys. But they didn't hear her, so she screamed out their names once more. "*TROY! PHIL!*"

The two boys stopped and looked at her. "Do you see him? Do you see him?" They both said excitedly.

Nancy didn't answer them she just held her arm up and pointed at the Sherpas. Philip and Troy looked and saw the three Sherpas. None of them was saying a word.

"What's wrong with Satya?" Philip asked. Troy took Nancy under his shoulder and helped her quickly get back to the silent Sherpas.

When they were about ten yards away, Ang held up his hand, warning them to stop moving.

"Please do not go further. It is too dangerous. The snow might move further into the crevasse."

"But Ang," Troy said, "where did Mr. Sanchez run to?"

Ang's eyes were filled with tears as he spoke. "We must go back to base camp now. I am sorry, but we must go now."

"Wait!" Nancy said sharply. "Wait a minute. We are not leaving until we find Mr. Sanchez."

"Yeah!" Philip added. "Yeah, of course we don't leave without Mr. Sanchez."

Then Satya let out a loud painful cry. "He is gone... I am sorry. He is gone...Mr. Robert is no more."

Nancy, Philip and Troy all quickly looked back and forth at each other with shocked expressions.

"No more? What the hell do you mean, no more?" Troy took a step towards Satya.

Ang then reached out and put his hand on Troy's shoulder. "When the snow came...I tried to unhook Mr. Robert from the ladder, but Mr. Robert, he fall with legs between ladder...and then the ladder turn over and Mr. Robert and ladder go down the hole."

"Then we go down there and get him," Troy said defiantly. "Come on, let's go get him out."

The three started to walk.

"No, stop. Stop now!" Ang ordered. "Listen, that hole was...maybe eighty foot deep. Now look," Ang pointed to where they had all just stood five short minutes ago, "look, the hole all gone. Almost all of hole...all filled with snow. Mr. Robert at bottom."

"Look, it's not all filled in... Over there...look, the whole crevasse is not filled. Come on...let's climb down!" Troy said urgently.

"Mr. Troy, under so much snow, Mr. Robert not breathe."

"Well, he sure won't be if we stand here just talking about it," Nancy said.

"Please," Mingma then said. "Please, we know of these holes and snow. Two years ago, my brother died under only ten feet of snow. We here to protect you. Mr. Robert say if anything happen to him, we must make you safe home."

"But don't you have some avalanche sensors that can tell exactly where he is?" Nancy asked, trying to sound as hopeful as she could.

"Yes," Ang said, "but we know where he is. And we know where the hole is, too...It is just too deep and dangerous for all of us. I am sorry,

Mr. Robert would want me to protect you. We must go now in case more snow come down."

"So he's dead?" Troy asked. "You're sure? Sure he's dead?"

"We have been in the mountains many times...we know when death happens," Ang said softly.

"But what about his walkie talkie? Try calling him." Philip's voice sounded weak.

"Here is his backpack," Ang said, holding out the backpack he had dug out of the snow. "And here is walkie talkie...I am sorry for your teacher...but we must go now."

"He's not our teacher...He's...he's our friend." Nancy started to cry. "He's always been our friend."

Troy opened his arms and Nancy's cry was muffled as she buried herself into his chest.

Philip dropped the camera onto the snow and walked towards Troy. The three held each other tight.

Ang was about to say something, but now it was Mingma's turn to put a hand on his friend's shoulder. He said, "Time, Ang... time...let them cry now. The danger has passed." Ang smiled grimly at Mingma and Satya. They then took a couple of steps away from the three to give them space to weep.

"Oh my God!" Nancy cried. "Oh my God, how can he just die?"

"I don't know. He was the kind of guy you just can't see...you can't see being...being..." Philip couldn't finish his thought so he burrowed deeper into Nancy and Troy's arms.

The three of them stood together and cried. They cried for the man that had helped each of them climb out of the dark sad lives they had been living. They cried for a man—a stranger who cared for them when most, even their families, had given up on them.

After a while, Troy freed himself from the hug just enough that he could face Nancy and Philip. For some reason, in that moment, he needed to see their faces, the faces of two human beings that without Robert, he would not have met in a million years.

"Nancy, Phil?" Troy wiped his face and spoke softly but firmly. "I don't know why I have to tell you this now...maybe 'cause he'd want to hear it...But you know...I never thought I'd have friends like you two, I don't know, I mean...who would have thought...but he did...and now I can't even imagine my life without you two."

"Oh Troy..." Nancy said with tears still in her voice, "me too...me too."

"Yeah, I love you guys," Philip said, sniffling and wiping his nose.

"You hear that?" Troy yelled up into the sky. "You hear that, Mr.

RobertOOooo Sanchez? Look what you've done...you got us fucking misfits thinking we can do things!"

Then Nancy joined in yelling at the blue sky. "Yeah, that's right...that's right...that..." Nancy tried to add more but she was still too choked up to think of anything else.

"That's right!" Philip joined in, raising his fist to the sky.

"We must leave now," Ang said as he slowly walked to the three. Mingma reached down to the ground, picked up Philip's camera and handed it to him. Satya put his arms around Nancy and Troy's backs and started them on the mournful journey towards base camp.

Philip brushed the snow off the camera. With his head bent down over the camera, Philip noticed the little light on his jacket was blinking.

"Troy, Nancy, stop!"

They both turned around. "What's wrong, Phil?"

Philip quickly took a couple of steps towards them and pointed at his jacket. "Is that light blinking?"

Nancy and Troy looked at each other and then with a sad look, back at Philip.

"Is it blinking?" Philip now asked adamantly.

They nodded to Philip. "Yeah, Phil... it's blinking...Now come on, big guy, we have to go."

"It's blinking? It's really blinking? You see it too? You see it too?" Philip asked excitedly.

"It's okay, Philip. Come on, we have to go, it's not safe here," Nancy said, taking Phillips arm.

"No, it's Mr. Sanchez!" Philip said, pointing at the blinking light on his jacket. "It's him...it's got to be him!"

Nancy and Troy walked to either side of Philip and put their arms around him. They tried to move him, but he was rooted to the ground. "It's okay, Phil...we know the light is Mr. Sanchez...we know..." Troy said, trying to move him. Phillip pulled out of their grasp.

"I'm not crazy!!!" Philip yelled. "This is that safety beacon light my parents made me promise I would bring—It's like an emergency light in case I got lost from you guys. I kind of designed and created it so if one of us was lost, the other person would turn it on to notify us that something was up. Mr. Sanchez had one and I have one. I didn't give you guys one 'cause I thought you'd laugh and think I was paranoid."

"How does it work, Phil?" Troy asked

"Well, you have to reach inside your jacket and lift that little switch to notify the other person. My light is green and his light is red. It only blinks when the other person is trying to signal you."

"And you think Mr. Sanchez switched it on, Phil?"

"He had to!"

"Then he's alive?" Nancy questioned. "Then he's alive?"

"He's gotta be...It couldn't have just gone on by itself. Wait. I'll switch mine on."

The red light stopped blinking as Philip switched his on. He let it blink for about ten seconds and then turned it off. They all stared at Philip's coat, hoping the red light would come back on. After five agonizing seconds, the red light started blinking again. They all screamed and cheered.

"Let's go back..." Nancy said.

Ang caught her arm as she turned. "Wait, Mr. Philip, are you sure this thing cannot just turn itself on?"

"No... Ang, no... He's gotta be telling us he's okay!"

Troy put his arms around Philip. "Man, thank god for your parents, you big paranoid...genius!"

Ang looked at Mingma and stroked his chin in serious thought.

"Come on, we have to move now!" Nancy said impatiently.

"Wait, Miss Nancy, Mingma is good with saving but we...we must think how." Mingma smiled at Nancy.

"Come on, let's start digging," Philip pled. "We gotta go now!"

Ang stopped them all with a shout. "No, it is too dangerous." Ang then told them, "If we dig on top on crevasse hole and Mr. Robert underneath snow, we may loosen snow only to fall in with him. First we must plan wisely."

"Look, that crevasse was over one hundred feet long," Satya said. "Look, you can see over half of it is not filled with snow...It's not all filled with snow! Maybe if we go to the end of the crevasse, climb to the bottom. He's probably in some kind of cave where he can breathe."

"Mingma, radio base camp...We will need..." Ang said.

47. PRESENT DAY – AT THE HOTEL

"And this change that is about to happen with your companies...well, most of you probably had no say in it, right? This change is going to happen whether you like it or not. And I'm sure that makes it even harder for you." The audience immediately responded with some clapping and vocal responses, acknowledging the truth of Robert's statement.

"And usually when we confront a change that we have little control over, one of the first things we always ask is, where does that leave me? Am I going to be made redundant? Does anyone really need me now? Will I still have a job? Do I really want to do this? And the whole time you're probably trying to figure out if going through all this change...is it even worth it? Wait...!"

Robert suddenly stopped and looked down at his legs. "Worth? Hmmm...You know...I never thought about this," he said, looking back up. "When this happened to me—this change—losing my legs. I didn't ask for it either—and that word 'worth' seemed to surround everything I thought about. I think that's the thing I kept asking myself: What am I worth?"

He paused to muse over what he had just said.

"Wow, sorry! That's a pretty loaded question, isn't it? But think about it: anytime we go through change, deep down, isn't that one of the first things we ask ourselves: What am I worth? Not just to yourself, but also to everyone else! "

Greg looked at Monique, raised his eyebrow and nodded in appreciation of Robert's question.

"*ME?* I couldn't answer it...but I think the sooner you figure out the answer to that question, the easier you'll be able to accept and adapt to any change you're facing. Ever since my accident that question has been

356

playing in my mind like an irritating song would. You know, that song you absolutely hate but you know all the words to it? And you just want it stop it from playing inside your head, but you can't? Well, that question, I couldn't shut it off. I kept looking at myself and asking...what am I worth now?"

Monique, Jenny and Kyle had edged closer to the front of the stage. Jenny wasn't sure her father even knew she was there, so she lifted her hand slightly to wave, but her father didn't see her. He continued speaking and getting more excited about the question he had found.

"That's it! That's it!" Robert sounded like a man who had been drifting on the ocean for weeks and had just discovered land. "That guy—that guy you saw in all those photos...summiting all those mountains...facing all those challenges...Well, obviously, looking at me now, I can't do those same things anymore, right?"

He paused and then smiled. "Or can I? Is that how we measure worth: by what we used to do with all we had? But when you're facing change, you might not have those things anymore, right? So if you want to move forward, then you have to ask yourself a new question, one that I think I was too afraid to ask. As a matter of fact, I just started asking myself that question only...maybe thirty minutes ago. Who am I now?" He paused and then repeated it.

"Who am I now? Change really makes us face who we are, doesn't it? Change and how we adjust to it helps form our identity, don't you think? Not just how we see ourselves, but how others see us."

Robert looked down to the opposite side of the stage where Monique was. There was the doorman, Aaron Iboga, smiling. Robert bowed slightly and gave Aaron a look that seemed to be full of humility and grace. The doorman then bowed his head slightly, acknowledging him, as Robert went on.

"Look at me! I climbed some of the most difficult mountains on this planet and you know what? You would probably think after doing all that I can handle anything, right? Hanging off all those cliffs, suffering through freezing weather that eats at your bones, sleeping on the edge of some mountain with a wind coming at you so fierce...that you're not sure where you might be waking up...or if you'd be waking up at all!"

The Leaning Tower of Pisa was so, so quiet, yet one could sense never had it been so alive.

"Do you know what my nickname was? Mighty Oak! Yep, I was known as The Mighty Oak. That's what everybody called me. And in many ways, that's how I measured myself. I could face every challenge standing up because, like some massive tree, I was unflappable!...No cold, no snow or wind was ever going to take me down. And I loved being that guy—that big Mighty Oak! Of course, I always laughed it off when anyone called me that, but I loved knowing people saw me as that big strong tree. And, in a lot of ways, I saw my worth through everyone else's eyes. But then I lost my legs...The Mighty Oak got sliced down...and me? Well, what was I now? My identity? I was a...stump! So that question 'what am I worth' was a question I just ran away from. I didn't want anyone to see what happened to The Mighty Oak. What are they going to call me now...The Mighty Stump? Ha ha."

Robert laughed at his own joke. He waited for a reaction from the audience, hoping there was at least a giggle, but none came.

"It's okay to laugh, you know...'cause that's another thing I forgot to do: laugh! Not that losing my legs was funny, but I could still laugh, couldn't I? But I didn't. See, I didn't just lose my legs—no, I let this change *cripple* all the things *I could still do!* I have to tell you something—when this happened, I didn't want anyone to see me. I was so scared of how everyone would see me now—a fallen tree—and we all care how others see us, right?"

The room murmured, acknowledging Robert's thought.

"And I know you have probably all heard this phrase: we all have our own mountains to climb. And me, I used to stand on stages like this and...and I loved to talk about all the challenges of climbing a mountain. I would discuss how you can use those same strategies in your everyday life or at work. I thought I was pretty good at it, too...but you know what? Damn if I could apply any of that knowledge I was selling about mountain climbing to my own situation! It's not that it wasn't still inside of me...I just couldn't find it! I couldn't tap into it! Why? Because I couldn't find me. I let this change stop me from doing all the things I could still do!"

Monique closed her eyes and put her hands over her heart. A delicate voice inside her called out, "Me too...me too."

"It's always about our identity, isn't it? Dealing with—Who am I?" Robert rolled himself closer to the front of the stage. "How many of you are no longer going to be the manager now...or this specialist...have this or that title? Who are you going to be now? It might all change with this new adventure of three becoming one, right? See, who we think we are and how others perceive us, well...we always want it to be the same thing, don't we? And that is almost impossible, isn't it? So...so who am I now? Am I still the Mighty Oak? Because...the Mighty Oak became this stump...and what can a stump do? Or what can Mighty Stumpy do?"

The audience did laugh this time, not loud, but in way that told Robert to go on...they wanted more.

"So what am I worth now as a stump? You see, that was my new mountain to climb: answering that question. So here I am, the Mighty Oak, cut down. Here I was...facing this challenge—my own mountain of change—and what was the first step I took?"

Robert raised his hand and then froze, taking a dramatic pause. "Well, I...*dug a hole!*"

Everyone exploded into laughter. Even Greg was nodding and smiling.

"That's right! The moment I saw the mountain I had to climb, I dug so far down so I wouldn't have to see it!"

Greg now joined in with a quick clap, acknowledging how familiar Robert's choice to hide from change was.

"My first instinct was to deny there was a mountain. And oh, I did something else too. I made sure the hole I dug was only big enough for one! See, I dug it so no one else could see me, get in with me, or pull me out. In other words, me, the guy who climbed all those mountains, telling everyone to face their challenges, rely and work with your team...well, I didn't listen to my own words and of course, you can't blame me. I couldn't hear anyone because I was too busy digging!"

Jenny and Kyle now joined the laughter that filled the room. But Monique didn't laugh; her eyes were still closed and her head raised as if she was feeling each word. She felt every single syllable Robert spoke. It fell upon her like a nourishing, welcomed rain.

"...and it got so deep... it got so dark down there...And since no one could get in the hole with me, what do you think happened? Well, big surprise! I felt completely alone! So all alone and worthless...and who's to blame?"

Robert paused, once again putting his hands over his eyes and scanned the room to find Monique. But everyone still looked like shadows.

"*Me*...I'm to blame! The guy who ran away from every source of support or care I had...I just kept digging! I remember this one physical therapist I had and he was always cheering me on, saying things like, you know, 'Don't give up! Keep going...Never give up!' Well, I listened!!! And that's exactly what I was doing...I was never going to give up on hiding away, so I just kept digging deeper!"

The room erupted into laughter again.

"How many of us do that? You have this situation and you're reacting really badly to it. It's definitely not helping what you're doing. If you were honest with yourself, you would even agree it's actually hurting you. It's making everything worse...it's totally destructive. But you...you still take up that '*Never give up attitude*' and you just keep digging further away from the problem...or the change...and you dig so deep that you lose all perspective! Of course, we know when people say never give up, they are talking about going after the positive things. But when you don't give up on the things that are not helpful... well, I mean, what did I think would happen? The deeper I dug, the more alone I felt. I was trying to get where there was absolutely no light because then I didn't have to see my mountain, did I? Also, then I didn't have face the question of 'what am I worth?' Oh, and there were lots of people up there in the light, trying everything to help me, but the deeper I dug, the less I heard them. It got so bad, I actually—"

Robert cleared his throat. "Okay...well...this is hard to talk about or even admit but...um..."

Robert rolled his chair almost to the lip of the stage. He knew that with what he was about to reveal, he needed to see all the faces that filled the room. Monique opened her eyes and looked at her husband. And finally, for the first time since he had started to speak, he saw his wife. But his new bad habits instantly came back and he quickly looked to the floor and turned away from her. Then, with all the shedding that this day had brought, another deeper instinct took over and suddenly he lifted his hand and reached towards her. It was a slight movement. No one would have noticed. His hand barely came off the chair's handle. But she saw it. She felt his hand reach out to her. And so Monique opened her hand to him, as if to say, "It's okay, I'm here. I'll catch you if you fall."

Robert took in a good strong breath and spoke. "You see, I dug so deep and it got so dark...well...I bought a gun."

Robert could feel everyone in The Leaning Tower of Pisa almost collectively gasp. Amir actually stood up from behind his table. Greg put his hand to his mouth. Jenny bit her lip and pulled both her mother and Kyle even closer.

"Oh, in my deep denial of facing my mountain, I had excuses why I bought it...There had been these break-ins around our neighbourhood. I even convinced myself I got that gun because, well, like I told my wife, I felt I couldn't protect my family without my legs now. But I hate guns. Really, I do! And even when I brought it home, I was scared to death of what I had done. I hid it under my mattress and never looked at it again until, well, there was this one day—a real dark day down there in my hole..." Robert glanced at Monique. He saw her hand open up to him.

"They had been trying these new artificial legs on me that morning—and they didn't work. I put them on and the pain was greater than anything I could imagine. And it was like—this was my last hope of ever standing again—and now it was vanishing. And when I got home that day, I dug a little deeper, further from all reasonable, rational thoughts...and I held that gun, sitting in my wheelchair—with no light on and I know...I know I was filled with some pretty dark thoughts down there in my hole. And I sat there, I was asking this question, and I was hoping the gun had an answer to it... But then, as miracles happen, one I didn't really recognize at the time—my wife came home...she saw me...she saw the gun...but I had dug so far from her, she didn't know what to say to me anymore, But luckily, she found something to save me. She told me our daughter was coming to visit and I should put that thing away."

The audience felt relief and laughed slightly at his wife's odd reaction.

"But it wasn't that she didn't care that I had a gun. It was all my fault. I did the one thing that is guaranteed to destroy the chance for any change to succeed."

Robert looked at his wife for a brief second. She knew that look. She had seen that look so many times before. The one that simply said, "I get it, I understand now."

"I stopped talking! I shut down all communication between us. You can't blame her. She was so afraid. Inside of me I had this...well, I had this sniper hiding in me. And he would just shoot down and kill off all conversations before they could even get started. But here it was—there was no hiding now. I had a gun...I was sitting in my living room without any lights on....I was caught...I could have come clean...I could have shown her, how I felt, who I was now. I could have admitted how lost I was. I mean, how many times in my life had this woman gone through changes with me? She's my best friend, always there...She's always helped me...Why was I not giving her the chance to help me now, to lead me out of this?"

He paused to rub his face and shake his head as if to admonish himself.

"It's amazing! I can't tell you how many times I stood on a stage like this and talked about leadership, telling everyone how the best leaders know when it's time to follow...but I failed. I absolutely, categorically FAILED. I failed to allow anyone to lead me when I was lost. But, when you're lost, isn't that the time to follow someone else?"

Robert then looked over at Monique again, his eyes widening in surprise as now he also saw Jenny. He then spoke the next line directly to his wife and daughter.

"I'm sorry. I couldn't simply ask, 'Help me...talk to me!'" Robert turned back to the crowd.

"You want to face change? You want to lead? Well, don't do what I did! Take every chance you can... open the door to start changing... and do that real difficult thing: *TALK. ABOUT. IT!*"

The crowd clapped loud and hard as Robert repeated and punctuated the words. "Talk about it!" And as those words came rushing out, he couldn't help but think of that window—the window in Seema's office, where the two of them had watched that big yellow kite flying. He smiled to himself. He felt such a happy urge—a real excitement—to talk to her. Tell her that he was wrong; he wasn't the kite. Talk to her about what Aaron had shown him.

"But I didn't talk and I didn't share it because I thought it was my own problem." Robert cocked his head a little as he felt another concept become clear to him. His face was now radiant and he sat so tall and straight in his chair.

"But it wasn't only mine, this problem of losing my legs...This change was no longer just my problem! It was now my family's, my friends' problem. All the people I worked with...every life I touched or that touched mine was affected by it. But I was too busy digging my hole to face the fact that my change affected everyone else too. Just like every change does...like yours will today. The change your companies are going through is also affecting every single person in this room. Look around—you're not alone!"

Greg slapped his hands together and started applauding. There were a couple of others that joined in, but they soon stopped, realizing Robert had not yet made his point. Robert looked at Greg.

"Thanks. I guess Mr. Wong knows what I'm trying to say. That, no matter what we do—we will always—go through a lot in life, and there will always be lots of losses! But my failure was...I didn't let my family share in my loss. If we only share the victories together but suffer the losses alone, then how does anyone really know what you're worth? How can they understand and feel it? You are a company facing a challenge—a great change—so talk to each other, share the losses and gains. Don't go through it alone. Don't dig holes by yourself...climb that mountain together. A company is a team as much as a family is; the strongest teams are the ones that feel and know their own worth—and they will always make sure that everyone on that team knows that they have worth!"

48. SIX MONTHS AGO – MT. EVEREST

I'm writing this as we wait for help to come from base camp...Mr. Sanchez said we should try to write when we don't want to 'cause that's when you will probably write the real stuff. I guess I really don't want to write now...and it's hard writing now, knowing he's down there. We think he's alive...Good thing Phil's such a freak with all that computer stuff...We're all just sitting here, looking at that light on Phil's coat and waiting. Every couple of minutes, we tell him to switch it on and then we wait to see if he responds...and when a light comes on, we all cheer. And suddenly, we all get quiet again....hoping! Man, don't know what we would do without that hope.

I was supposed to write a 'thank you' to this mountain last night but all I can think is angry thoughts now. I guess now's the time, if there's ever a time, to do what he taught me: 'what we think will usually determine how we act'...but I don't want to be angry now. I gotta think positive, but I can't help thinking about how cold he probably is down there...Okay, but he knows we know he's down there, he must know we are going to help him...So, okay then...I'm praying he doesn't give up, like how he never gave up on me...even though I know I was pretty mean to him so many times....And now...a million thoughts come to me...how he tried to talk to me when my brother was shot...and I told him to shut it. Guess that's all I ever did...shut everything up...but he kept my book. He never gave up wondering where I was...Then in prison, when he tried to give me back my book and I ripped it up...and still he never gave up...and then when me and that little baby got shot...and even then, he never gave up on me, not even then...

Phil just switched the light again...and he switched his on...so I hope he knows we ain't giving up on him.

Not sure anyone ever thought I was worth anything but him...Somehow he saw worth in me...and so...I don't know any more words to think...Just don't give up, Roberto Sanchez...'cause we're not giving up on you!

Troy

49. PRESENT DAY – AT THE HOTEL

"Do you know there are two goals in climbing a mountain? One is optional and the other one is not. The optional goal is getting to the top. But the other goal that is not optional, do you know what it is? The goal that is completely non-negotiable? Well, the most important goal when climbing any mountain is this: you have to get back down! And..." Robert then turned to look at Monique and Jenny and said, "You have to get back home!"

He quickly faced the front of the room and questioned, "But who ever really talks about that? Who tells that story? That's only for kids, isn't it? Getting back home? That's just in fairy tales mostly, right? Really, who wants to hear that story? How interesting is that? Oh, today we are going to hear about someone climbing down Everest and getting back home."

The room smiled.

"You know, we live in a world that seems to be so focused on getting to the top—all our success stories are about those people who made it to the top. We constantly celebrate that climb to the top, don't we? Everyone's telling us to listen to them, follow their example and look at what they achieved! And don't get me wrong, we should...*BUT*, whoever talks about getting back down, getting back home? I never did. I never spoke about the most important part! The one thing you absolutely have to do if you are going to climb a mountain! Me, of all people, someone who knows that goal better than anyone...And today I realize why I didn't. Do you know why?"

Robert extended his arm and pointed to the ceiling.

"Because...I never did get back down...*I'm still up there!!!* Yeah, it's true. My moment of change was when I was caught in that avalanche and that mountain snatched away my legs. Ever since that happened, I've done nothing but curse that mountain. A change happened to me but...I haven't changed to live with it! I'm still up there, cursing that mountain with all my being. I'm still stuck up there, bemoaning my fate. So, I didn't complete the ONE non-negotiable goal. Although I was here in this, this half-body, the most important parts of me—my mind, my heart, my spirit—were still up there...I didn't come home. That's right! Ever since this happened to me...ever since this great change happened...I've been stuck on the top of that mountain. So how do I complete my goal? How do I get back down? How do I get home?"

He looked at Jenny and Monique and held out his hand to acknowledge them.

"And oh, don't think I haven't been offered help! Right after that accident, there were so many people trying to help me down, so many trying to guide me home. On the mountain, you never go alone. It's not a good idea. Not safe. When you climb a mountain like Everest, you have these Sherpas. Do you know who they are? Well, they're these amazing guides—they're your lifeline on your way up...and down! And you better listen to them if you want to live...if you want to get back down...if you want to get back home...listen to them!

"And now, me being stuck on the top...with this most difficult change I was facing, did I listen to any of the Sherpas in my life? No, I pushed away every Sherpa trying to guide me back down...I probably couldn't see or hear them with all my cursing and digging!"

Once again, the room enthusiastically applauded Robert's self-effacement.

"Think about it. All those Sherpas in your life: who are they? At home or at work, who are your Sherpas—those people who are guiding you, supporting you; Sherpas, like your family, your friends, co-workers...those people that just stop by each day and ask you—'Hey, how are you doing?' Who are your Sherpas and how much do you listen and thank them? Look around right now. In this room, how many Sherpas do you have? And how often do you show them what they are worth?"

The room started to come alive with the sound of many whispering to each other, trying to acknowledge some of the Sherpas in their daily life at work.

"And for me...I pushed away every single Sherpa who attempted to help guide me through this change. I pushed away my wife...my daughter...I went to a rehabilitation centre where I proceeded to push away every Sherpa that was trying to help me down...the ones that were trying to help me deal with this change...I ignored the very Sherpas that were trying to give me my new legs—a new life! I just pushed them all away! Of course, I didn't know why then, but I see now that I did it...I did it because I thought that getting help—or asking for it—was an admission of my weakness. I was hiding away from my failure in protecting who I thought I was—the Mighty Oak."

A quick hearty applause danced throughout the room.

"But today, something happened. I met a brand new Sherpa—one that I didn't ignore...and he showed me some things. Showed me some things I better start doing if I'm going to achieve that goal. And one of the things I learned is—if I'm going to get down, well,...I better start following my main Sherpa: my wife."

Robert looked down towards Monique and then slowly placed his hand over his heart. The audience cheered as Robert opened his arms for Monique to join him on the stage.

Jenny leaned over and kissed her mother's cheek. "Go, Mom...Come on, Mom, go."

Greg held out his hand to guide her up the steps. Amir stood up behind his table and pounded his hands together. Lou then shot up and was soon joined by all the employees of Elevation. It did not take long for the entire Leaning Tower of Pisa audience to rise up and applaud Monique. So many things had happened in these last forty-five minutes. Robert had touched on so many questions that now echoed inside Monique. She felt dazed. And later that day, she told everyone she could not remember Greg taking her hand and walking her up on the stage. She couldn't recall how Robert and Greg both thanked her for all the work she had done for this event. Jenny would tease her for years to come about how she stood beside Robert as stiff as a mannequin, with one hand up near her chest and the other poised like a runner at the starting line, getting ready to run the hundred yard dash. Jenny would sometimes lovingly imitate how her mother stood, frozen for the whole last part of Robert's speech.

After thanking his wife, Robert turned to Aaron again. Aaron now stood closer to the foot of the stage.

"Yes...yes, of course losing my legs has been the most difficult change I have ever come up against! But when it all happened, I lost something even more vital...and the loss of that was what made it most difficult for me to deal with the change. I lost my perspective! And without any perspective to balance out my loss, I couldn't move forward! Of course, it would be cruel to say to someone in my position, 'Hey, don't get so down—you only lost your legs, look at it in perspective...you're still alive!' That's incredibly difficult to hear. Yet, it's absolutely true...I didn't lose my life, did I? But nothing is as dangerous as losing that—there doesn't seem to be any greater loss—worse than when we lose our perspective."

As the audience cheered, Aaron looked at Robert and pointed at the screen. The picture had now changed. Amir had put a photograph of Robert in one of his workshops at a high school. Robert was standing in the middle of a circle of students who were all connected, shoulder-to-shoulder, listening to him.

Robert looked at the screen and back to Aaron, who smiled and winked. "The one thing I learned today about change is this—that the best way you can ever support anyone through change and guide them to accept it is to first help them with their perspective. You see, for me, I became more and more miserable...I sunk into the loss...but why? I mean, look who I was. I have helped hundreds upon hundreds of people deal with change. You would think all that experience would have helped me...but it didn't! I couldn't rely on all my past experience of helping others. Why? Because I lost all perspective! That's what change can do! If you want to help anyone having difficulty dealing with change, look at their perspective! Then, help change their perspective...or give them some perspective that will help them handle the change."

Kyle was now standing behind Jenny and hugging her closely. He snuggled in next to her ear and whispered, "Are you feeling better now, Jen?" Jenny gently pulled Kyle's head next to hers. Robert looked at Greg, who was standing near the table with Amir. He pointed at his wrist, wanting to know how much time he had left to speak. Greg just waved him on to speak as long as he needed.

"Well, thanks for letting me speak today. I hope this was...well, helpful and gave you some perspective."

The room gave Robert a quick approving cheer.

"I can tell you—this day...it helped me to...ah, to finally stop digging and face that mountain. And mostly, I know I needed to stop being afraid of all those questions I was facing. Because what is any mountain we are about to climb? What is it, really? It's just a bunch of questions that have to be answered, right? Think about it—every challenge, each obstacle we face, presents a question and how far you get up the mountain will depend on how you answer each of those questions."

Robert stopped and smiled at his own thought.

"It really is all about the questions we live, isn't it? The ones that we are willing or brave enough to ask ourselves...and then to be able to live with how we answered it. Like this one: who do I want to become?"

Robert looked directly at Aaron and smiled. And for the very first time since standing on that ladder over the crevasse in the Khumbu Icefall, Robert smiled...and felt it.

"A wise man once told me...well, by once I mean about forty-five minutes ago!"

Light laughter filled the room,

"He told me something I'm not sure I ever knew...I thought I did, but from my behaviour in the last six months, I obviously wasn't living it. He said that when we are little children, everyone always asks us, 'What do you want to become when you grow up?' But as we get older, no one really asks us that question anymore...and so, many of us stop living the answer to that question! In a way, this question—who do I want to become—is more vital the older we get. Because as long as we are *BEING*, we are still becoming, aren't we? So ask yourself today...sitting here, facing this new change in your life, who do you want to become? A content employee—a better friend...happier to work with...less confrontational?" Robert turned to Monique. "A better husband?"

The audience applauded.

Robert then looked at Jenny, "Or maybe a more attentive father."

Jenny raised her hand and gave her father that same wave the little girl hiding in the car from the monsters outside had always given him.

"Or, how about a better listener...or easier to be with? Ask yourself: who in this room, right now—a person you see every day at work—who is that one human being that every day always makes you feel welcomed? Always makes you feel worth something? And then ask yourself: can I become like them? Can I make others feel like they are always welcome? Feel like they belong? Look around the room. Look at all the people you are sitting next to—all of you, three companies—and now all these new faces coming into your life. So how are you going to make that stranger you might be working with next week feel welcomed and feel like they belong? Well, why not start *now*?!"

Robert stopped and waited. At first, nothing happened. But then Lou got up and shook someone's hand, then Kalinda and Dee stood up. Suddenly the room was buzzing and came alive with people saying hi to one another. Greg came to shake Robert's hand. The doorman looked at Robert and gave him a wave.

As soon as it was quiet enough to speak, Robert started again. "And look, three companies now are becoming something new...We are always becoming—and there are definitely going to be those who are going to struggle with this becoming. And maybe they'll act out...Maybe they won't react or behave like you might hope...so, what do you do then? Well, I got another wise person that might help. She is a lady that has to welcome thirty-three eight-year-olds every day! And she has to try to make each of those little people feel welcomed, feel like they belong.

"You see, she teaches grade three and she has this poster on her classroom wall with all the kids' pictures in a big circle around this one equation...It's not a math equation, not a science one either. It's the human equation. A human equation of how to make someone feel welcomed. And it's real simple. It says this: *Believe plus belong equals behave!* You want someone to get along? You want everyone to work at their best, be open and good listeners? You want them to behave in a way that makes your experience at work the best it can be? Well then, help them to believe that they belong...and that's usually how they will behave! Try it, it might work!"

Robert rolled his chair as close to Monique as he could get. He took a long moment to look in her eyes before he turned to the audience. "You see, I can tell you the greatest problem I had dealing with the loss of my legs was...it was when I stopped asking myself any questions that dealt with moving forward. But I only found that out today. That it is all about...asking questions. That's what makes us who we are. It's those questions that create us—our empathy, integrity, our values. You want to find out who someone is? Look at the questions they ask themselves!"

A thunderous applause shook the room.

"And finally, here is one question I have been asked so many times in my life. Almost every climber in the world has this question asked of them: *Why do you climb?* The timeless question, asked of every mountaineer: Why...*Why* do you climb?"

Robert paused and looked at his wife again. Monique had asked Robert this same question numerous times. He always had different answers to it each time, but the way he looked at her now told her that maybe...maybe... he had finally figured it out.

"Why do I climb? I think that question comes from the same thing we ask ourselves every single day, throughout our whole lives. What...can I do? We're always asking that. Yet, every single 'Can I' question we ask will never be answered until we do something about it...right? Nothing happens until we start living that question! I guess that's what we call choice. Simple questions like: Can I wear something like this? So you choose something, right? How can I start this task? You choose where to begin, right? And complex ones, like: Can I feel safe here? Can I belong here? Can I feel worth here? So then you have to choose how to live the answers to those questions. And whether it works...whether it helps you or hurts you...you always have the choice, don't you? Just like any mountain climber, all of us are always constantly asking ourselves: Can I do it? For us climbers we ask: Can I make it up there? Can I endure the cold? Can I take one more step? So the answer the question of why do I climb: it always comes back to 'can I,'...doesn't it?"

Robert waited a beat to let his thought sink in. *This was so simple*, he thought, *so why was this the first time I ever thought this out?* he wondered.

"*Wow*, I never thought of it, but our lives are quite often the sum of how we answer all those 'can I' questions, don't you think? Even simple ones like: Can I pass this test? Can I learn to be patient? Can I get over this loss? Can I deal with this change? Because every question of 'can I' is totally up to you to choose and how to live the answer to it...right?"

Robert stopped and comically hit his forehead. " Oh, I'm so sorry. You see, I've just been piecing this together myself! But, then that would mean that...every time we ask ourselves... 'Can I,' then you're also asking yourself...'Who do I want to become?'"

Monique put a hand on his shoulder and leaned to whisper something. Robert looked at her and mouthed, 'I know'. Then finished his thought.

"It's like one of the first questions we ask ourselves when we are just little babies crawling around: Can I take that first step? If we didn't ask that and answer it, then we'd all still be crawling around!" Lou said something to the effect that sometimes he still felt he hadn't mastered it yet, which brought the room down. And then, Robert laughed—completely and with an abandon that felt so....so brand new.

"We are always asking so many 'can I's', aren't we? It's like this...this great merry go-round with each question—the answer always tells us who we are. *AND* who we are comes from what we do, and what we do comes from answering that question of 'can I?' And the absolutely greatest thing is we always get to choose who we become! We always get to choose the things we believe and stand for!"

Robert got more and more excited as the thoughts came tumbling out of him. "And look at the answer to the question of 'can I?'... if you just turn the words around, what do you have? 'I can!!!' And that's probably what we all want to become...Whether it's climbing to the top of some mountain or taking those first steps into our mother's arms, the answer we all strive for is: 'Yes, I can!...I can!'"

The audience clapped vigorously. Greg came and stood beside Robert and joined in the applause. Robert put up his hand and whispered to Greg, "I'm sorry...I'm so sorry. Please—can I just do this one thing? I have to do this. I really have to do this."

Greg took a step back and nodded graciously. Robert looked at Monique and then down to Jenny. He waited till the room got silent.

"Thank you...Thank you very much. But speaking of can I...well, I spoke of how I'm still on the top of that mountain and it's time I start going home. So after we finish here today, I'd like to start one of the many 'can I's' that I have ahead of me."

Robert opened his arm to Aaron. The audience watched intently as Aaron took a couple of steps to the front of the stage and laid a large green duffel bag in front of Robert. Robert reached out and shook Aaron's hand. The bag made a little sound as it landed.

"Well, folks, don't worry, it's not filled with rocks." Robert reached down and quickly unzipped the bag and pulled out one of the artificial legs that were inside.

"You see, we can't perform our jobs with any efficiency if we are not given the right tools. And like any good mountaineer, I need my tools...and to get down off the top of this mountain, I will need mine. It won't be crampons or any ice picks this time...it will be these."

Robert lifted one of the artificial legs high above his head.

"And when I finish today, I'd like to put these on and start my way down. And that first step," Robert then turned to Monique, "it will be to you, love...to you!"

The crowd jumped to its feet. Robert stretched out his hand towards his wife. Monique's fingers entwined in his. Hands held. The audience cheered.

Jenny leaned into Kyle and whispered, "Daddy's home, Kyle. My daddy's home."

EPILOGUE

ON P.K. PHOENIX'S FACEBOOK WALL

Hi, I'm back!

For all those that I haven't been able to connect with for the last two months, I'm sorry. I was gone climbing to the base camp of Mt. Everest. That's right, Mt. Everest! And I was standing on it—not the top of it, but pretty close to it!

Three of us were chosen to go there for a leadership program. It was somewhere I never in my wildest dreams ever thought I would be. Me on Mt. Everest? And what I learned was that I don't want to live any "if only's" anymore! I don't want to grow up and think, if only I did this or that...Those two words "if only," they are just too sad to live with!

Sometimes I think I was spending too much time living in my own head—with only my own thoughts and my own fears. How boring I must have been! But this journey has helped me see more of who I want to be!

I have to tell you, I was afraid and I really didn't want to go there. I had so many reasons, but then someone told me about what it is like when you live with regrets and I guess that scared me more, so I went! But now I do have this one regret I have to do something about: Our leader had asked us before we left Everest to write a thank you to the mountain and we were supposed to leave it with the mountain. But we were caught in an avalanche (I'll talk about that some other time) and so I didn't have time to write one and leave it there.

Also I guess I was too upset at the time. And since I don't think I'll be going back to Everest anytime soon, I'd like to leave the mountain a virtual message right here. And so that is why I'm posting a picture of Mt. Everest on my wall today and I would like to leave my thank you right here!

Dear Chomolungma or Sagarmatha or Mt. Everest—the mountain with many names!

On my journey to you, my friends and I had met many others that were coming to you as well. And since you're not that easy to get to, that meant the people coming to you must have really had good reasons to be there. What we found was that everyone had so many different reasons why they were coming to you. Some obviously wanted to climb you. But even when we asked them why they climbed, they still all had so many other reasons...so many! And, when I thought about it, I found that I had a lot of reasons to be there as well. So here are all my reasons I'd like to thank you for.

First, thanks for helping us (all the climbers and everyone that comes to you). Thanks for helping us discover those reasons— because without reasons to do anything, we wouldn't have much to live for, would we? So thanks for giving so many of us some purpose in our lives. Thanks for being such a great accomplishment for all of us. Thanks for giving us a reason to believe we are doing something amazing by just coming to you. Thanks for giving us a reason to be courageous and face some fears. And thanks for letting some us live a dream we never even thought we would dream about. Thanks for all the memories created—memories that will stay with me forever. Thanks for the new people I have met and the friends that I hope will stay with me forever.

I must admit, Dear Mountain, it was hard to think of anything positive after what happened on our last day there. That avalanche! Why did you do that? You know, when you let go of all that snow and ice on top of us and almost killed our leader (and me!), I couldn't really understand it at the time. And yet, I do know because of that happening, you helped a young man be a hero and save a life. So thanks for letting Satya scale down that rope to rescue our leader. That was quite incredible because only a short time before, this same Satya was hanging from another rope when he had tried to take his own life and now this time, he hung from a rope to save a life! Thanks a lot for that!

And Mountain, what I'd most like to thank you for is—is for showing me more of who I want to be. Because now I know. I really want to be a lot like you! I want to be able to give people hopes and dreams, purposes and reasons to do things. I really can't think of anything more awesome to do!

And I guess like you, I have also had lots of names that people know me as. But I think from now on, I want to go with only one.

...because my name is Philip Kong and that's who I want to be!

ACKNOWLEDGEMENT

ac•knowl•edg•ment

1. acceptance of the truth or existence of something.
2. the action of expressing or displaying gratitude or appreciation for something.
3. an author's or publisher's statement of indebtedness to others, typically one printed in a book.

Okay, great! Here is where I can make my statement of indebtedness to others. Here is where I will express and display my gratitude and appreciation for something. Here is where I will accept the truth and show the existence of something. And that something is this: without these people in my life this book could not exist.

And I really want to thank them because—Ah, I love that word because: It's a word we use multiple times daily and yet, sometimes I don't think I always see the weight of its meaning. We use because to answer almost everything. Why do I climb a mountain? Why do I write? Why do I love? There's always a 'because', isn't there? Why are you doing something? Because of this or because of that. I guess when we say because, we are really saying: That is my cause to be.

All right, so let me start with my cause to be. I want to thank:

Yvonne and Rich, because you opened the door to show me all the great things I could become. (Good Morning Starshine)

Greg, because you helped me reach somewhere I never thought I could. (We are the Champions)

Elia, because you always showed me inspiration lies in the doing. (The Impossible Dream)

Gabe, because you trusted me enough to take your life's journey as a climber and help you find purpose in telling your story to others. (Born to Run)

Linda, because you teach me so many things—things I sometimes forget and things I would never know if you were not my sister and friend. (I am Woman)

Vera, because you climbed all the mountains first so you could show us how to do it. (Do You Believe in Magic)

Jim, because you held onto my hand and didn't let me fall. (Redemption Song)

Pamela, because you let me into your world and become a part of the care you show and give your students—that world is more awesome beyond any stories ever written. (Imagine)

Linton, because you helped me create, by letting me experiment over and over again without doubt. (Man in the Mirror)

Monica, because you brought me hope that I should continue becoming. (Both Sides Now)

Sandy, because of your care to make a difference. (Beautiful World)

Peter, because you always made me feel I was living the dream. (Still Haven't Found What I'm Looking For)

Brenda, because your perspective and honesty and willingness to learn raise me up. (Bridge over Troubled Waters)

Morgan, because you helped a blank screen look better. (Respect)

Shawn, because your teaching and caring inspire me to believe that teaching is such a noble profession. (How to Save a life)

Celestine, because you always make me feel and see my worth. (In My Life)

Ashley, because you helped this story grow into a healthy tree of words. (Changes)

Willow, because of your inspired thoughts. (Calling All Angels)

Jessica, because your belief in me instils a perseverance that keeps me growing and learning. (Stand By Me)

Michel, because your creative spirit inspires me to always keep creating. (Firework)

Starr, because you helped me take a step when I didn't see the path. (Jump)

Christina, Bridget, Marilyn, Barry and Maureen, because of your openness to read something new and different. (Help)

All the teachers and students who allowed me to be in their life, because without you, I wouldn't have found so much wonderful purpose. (All My Life's a Circle)

And last but not least...

My family, because without the feeling that I belonged to something, many of the wonders that have happened in my life would never have had a chance to exist. (Que Sera, Sera - Whatever Will Be Will Be)

Candace, because watching you become teaches me constantly. (Carry On)

Virginia, because you smile and share everything with me, and because you give me more causes to be than I could ever wish for, and mostly because of you, I love who I'm becoming. (If)

And...

To anyone who listened, because we all really need that. (Raindrops Keep Falling on My Head)

To everyone who made me feel I belonged, because that's where love begins! (Every Song I Love)

ABOUT THE AUTHOR

Jack Langedijk is a passionate storyteller with contagious optimism and original ideas. He has delivered many ground-breaking workshops in leadership and listening to diverse audiences including elementary school children, families and corporations.

Jack founded QUEST-I'm-ON, a not-for-profit organization with a mission to create and foster healthy relationships within schools, workplaces and homes. He received his BFA in Montreal at Concordia University and his MFA at York University in Toronto. Jack has also taught acting and directing at Concordia University and Ryerson University in Toronto.

because is his debut novel which combines lessons learned from his own life with a fictional setting that articulates and instils fresh strategies for social issues such as teen bullying. With powerful anecdotes and vivid metaphors, the novel expresses real life obstacles and the possibilities of achievements for all of us.

Jack lives with his wife and daughter in Toronto, Ontario, Canada.

For more information about Jack and his work, please visit www.because.zone.

CPSIA information can be obtained at www.ICGtesting.com
Printed in the USA
LVOW08s0417070916

503449LV00004B/498/P